I0583469

THE SERPENT QUEEN

A WICKED SOULS NOVEL

TIFFANY ROSEWOOD

ISBN: Ebook: 979-8-9939587-0-5

Paperback: 979-8-9939587-1-2

Hardcover: 979-8-9939587-2-9

Editing by @greenshawbooks and @pages.shredder

Formatting by @greenshawbooks

Book Cover by @viimorte

Map Design by @monsmaps.books

Interior Illustrations by @abookshelfofmagic and @elainem.art

CONTENT WARNINGS

- Violence and blood
- Executions
- References to a negligent parent
- Attempted self-harm
- Suicidal ideation
- Anxiety/panic attacks
- Explicit adult sex scenes: including masochism and choking
- Swearing

THE SERPENT QUEEN IS AN ADULT DARK ROMANTASY INTENDED ONLY FOR AUDIENCES 18+ YEARS OLD.

For all the Sleep Token fans who
relate to the lyrics in Damocles.

Never bury your feelings,
for they are your ultimate superpower.

Wear your emotions with pride.
And above all, know you can get up
and stand tall.

Keep going, even if you think the
diamond days are gone.
You will survive this battle,
even if the empire falls.

You are never alone.
And you will never be forgotten.

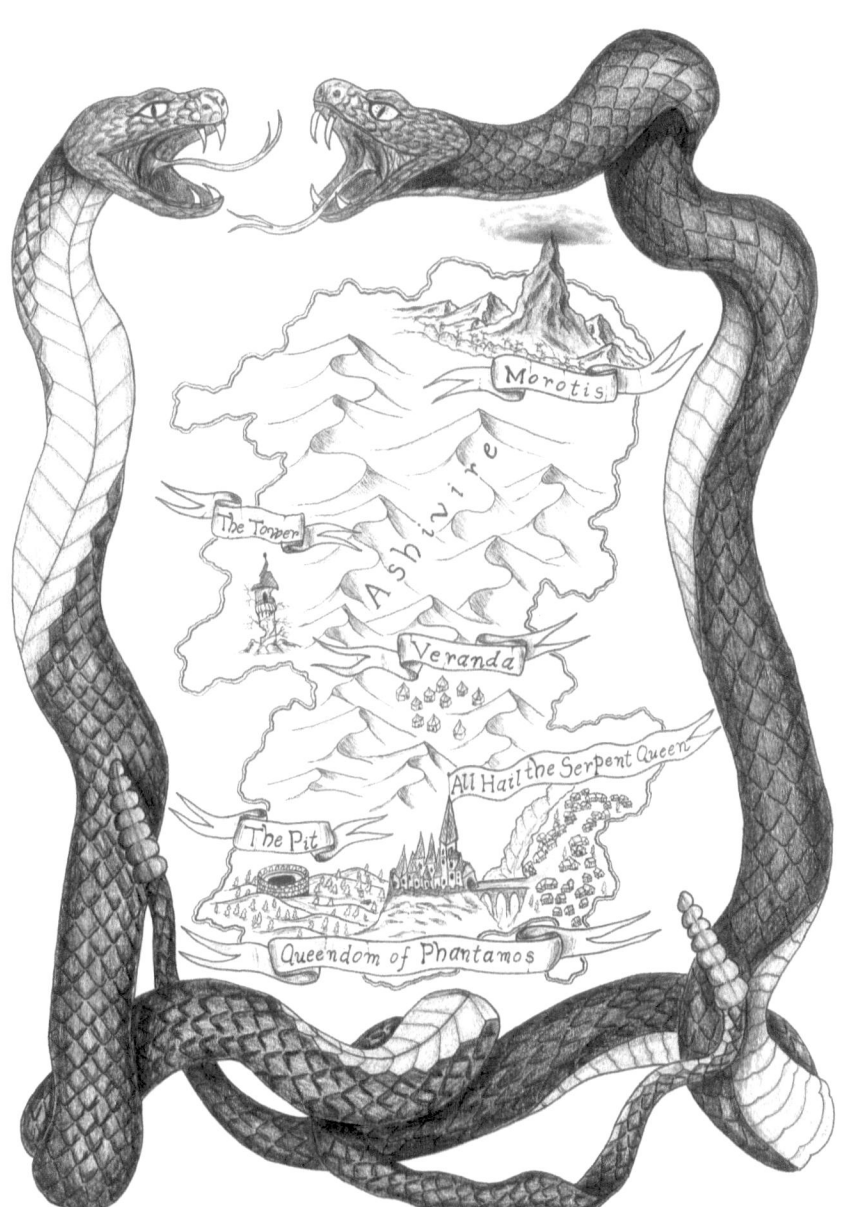

Morotis

Ashivire

The Tower

Veranda

All Hail the Serpent Queen

The Pit

Queendom of Phantamos

The Serpent Queen's Commandments

i. Thou shalt not disrespect thy queen.

ii. Thou shalt not talk back to thy Queen.

iii. Thou shalt not cross thy Queen.

iv. Thou shalt not rebel against thy Queen.

v. Thou shalt not worship or pray to any god besides thy Queen.

vi. Thou shalt not use thy Queen's name in vain.

vii. Thou shalt not steal from thy Queen.

viii. Thou shalt not lie to thy Queen.

ix. Thou shalt not miss an execution if summoned by thy Queen.

x. Thou shalt not kill thy fellow disciples — that is thy Queen's job.

Should any disciple fall out of line and break even one of the Queen's commandments, they will be sent to the pit.

There is no court, no jury, no other opinion that can rule on an execution order. The Queen's word is final.

Simply put, if you break a commandment, you die.

All hail the Serpent Queen.

PART ONE: DARKNESS

CHAPTER I
THE THRONE ROOM

"**B**ring him in."

The hinges groaned as the blood-red wooden doors swung open, the metal chains of tonight's entertainment rattling along the white marble floors as my guards escorted him in.

I inhaled deeply, relishing the bitter smell reeking off the disheveled man as he wearily approached my throne. His movements were sluggish—anyone's would be after staying a week in my dungeons with no food. The scent of his fear caused a shiver to run down my spine, and I took another deep breath, craving more of his delicious scent.

His fear was like my own personal drug, making me feel things I'd long forgotten.

It was intoxicating to be the one who elicited fear, instead of the one who lived in its constant shadows.

My guards tugged on the man's arms, halting him from coming any closer, stopping just short of the six marble steps leading up to my throne.

I looked down my nose at the filthy, pitiful man, my lip

curling into the smile I'd mastered throughout the years of being the Serpent Queen.

"Kneel."

The traitor lifted his pointy chin in defiance, then had the gall to spit on the first step.

Fabulous, it was going to be one of those nights.

One of my guards reacted instantly, using a spiked baton to hit the man in the back of the knees. I offered a nod of approval as a loud crack rang out through the room. My prisoner groaned in agony when his knees crashed into the marble tiles.

What a pleasant sound.

My satisfied hum filled the otherwise silent throne room. "That's better. Now, state your name."

A few audience members coughed, clearing their throats in an effort to dispel the tension rising in the air like a burst of heat.

"Are you deaf? I said. State. Your. Name." Two loud hisses suddenly distracted me from the anger ringing in my ears.

A cool sensation skittered across my skin, and then my snakes were descending my arms, their sights set on the prey before us. As they moved into position, my prisoner finally had the decency to appear frightened, his trembling hands causing his chains to clank irritatingly against the floor.

"T-t-travi-is," the man stuttered, while trying to hide his quivering hands.

I audibly exhaled, raising my left hand and bringing my scarlet serpent, Ember, to eye level. She stared back at me, her eyes as dark as the night sky. Her tongue flicked once at my face.

Speaking in a hushed tone, I conspired with my snake. "You have first dibs if he doesn't cooperate."

A satisfied hiss was her only reply as I rested my arm back on the black wood of my throne. A haughty rattling drew my attention to my right arm, where my black snake furiously gazed at me with his scarlet eyes.

I brought the hissing baby closer to my face. "Don't worry, Dante. There will be plenty of the pathetic man to go around." I raised my voice. "I will make sure you get a piece of our prisoner while he is still alive, just as you like."

Dante let out a small, annoyed hiss, but my words eased him enough to stop his tail from insistently rattling. I straightened, settling my gaze on Travis once more.

His light colored trousers now bore a dark stain right over his crotch, and the smell of urine wafted toward me.

A sinister smile crept along my blood-red lips. "Travis, do you know why you are kneeling before my throne?"

He mumbled in a tone too low to make out, even for an immortal like me who had impeccable hearing.

My guard frowned, disdain further crinkling the fine lines around his eyes. Swiftly, he smacked Travis in the back with his spiked baton. "Speak up when addressing the Queen!"

I nodded at my guard, admiring the brutality behind his strike.

Travis's eyes pinched with pain, but he was smart enough to raise his voice. "I am here because I broke one of your commandments."

I bobbed my head with an air of condescension. "Very good! And do you know what happens when we break a commandment, Travis?"

His clinking chains steadied as his gaze dragged off the floor and met mine, his brown eyes filling with anger. "As queen, you are supposed to protect us, not use us purely for your own selfish entertainment."

Some audience members gasped, while others muttered notions of agreement.

Biting the inside of my cheek, I swallowed my rage at the unrest filtering throughout the room.

Do not let them see any weakness, Seera.

My voice shook the black, stone walls as I stood. "I can do whatever I please as queen. Does anyone else dare to defy me and join this man?" I pointed a sharp nail at Travis, while scanning the audience for more traitors. My snakes hissed at the crowd, daring someone to speak out so their meal would double in size.

All murmuring ceased.

I smirked at my people. "That's what I thought. Remember your place, mortals."

My heels clacked against the marble stairs as I slowly descended them, my sights set on the easy prey below me.

"You broke commandment five: Thou shalt not worship or pray to any god besides thy Queen." My tone was tantalizing, like a mother scolding her child.

A tone I was all too familiar with.

I was close enough to see Travis's nostrils flare. "Maybe your people wouldn't feel the need to pray to the gods if our Queen wasn't such a soulless bitch."

The audience erupted in a chorus of shocked gasps, but, after spearing them with a vicious glare, they snapped their jaws closed.

Rolling my neck side to side, I stopped right in front of my prisoner.

"Oh, Travis." I knelt lower, bringing my face closer to his. "If only you behaved like a good boy while speaking to your Queen, perhaps I would've offered you a kinder death." I tapped my prisoner's nose with a finger, pulling a delicious growl from him while he lurched for me.

My guards anticipated his defiance, swiftly yanking him back by his shoulders and ceasing his pathetic attempt to harm me. I turned on my heel and ascended the marble stairs of the dais, letting the weight of my black dress adorned with a dripping red lace train ground me as I geared up for the climax of tonight's show.

With a grand spin, I fluffed my dress and sat back on my throne. "Ember, he is all yours."

Tantalizingly slow, my serpent slithered off my arm, her black eyes locked onto her next meal. Travis attempted to scramble backward, all previous rage washing off his face as his mouth parted. I inhaled fiercely, savoring the bitter taste of his fear.

"Please! I'm sorry!" My prisoner shouted, trying his best to push against my guards, but their shackle-like grip held him still.

As Travis pathetically tried to break free, Ember descended the dais, prompting him to use what was left of his feeble energy on one final shove backward. One of my guards simply pressed his boot into Travis's back. The kick was forceful enough to make him pitch forward, smacking his face hard against the tiles. A smear of blood shone on the stark white marble, causing a smile to slither across my face.

My throne room was the only room with white floors for this exact reason.

I reveled at the sight of fresh blood spilling at my feet.

Eventually, Travis pulled himself off the floor, only to reveal his nose was jutting sideways at a crooked angle. It was clearly broken, yet he didn't cry out in pain. Instead, it was fear that made him scream as he looked up and saw Ember, now right in front of his face. Her red tongue darted out as she hissed at him, making tears spill down his grimy face.

"Please," he whimpered, foolishly hoping to gain sympathy from my scarlet snake.

I sent a command down our mental bond: *Finish him.*

Without hesitation, Ember lurched forward, quickly coiling herself around Travis's neck. Her long body easily wrapped around him twice, tightening with terrifying strength, making my prisoner sputter for air.

I turned to Dante, who watched his sister with jealous irritation as Travis's lips began to turn blue.

"I promised you a piece of him while he was still alive, didn't I?"

His black head turned toward me. "Go, join your sister, and make sure to give our people a reminder as to why they should never dare to defy us again."

His red eyes flared with excitement, and he dipped his head in agreement. Dante sprung from the throne, rapidly slithering down the steps to happily join Ember in torturing Travis. Ember glanced at Dante as he approached, and I sent her one more command:

Release your grip a little so your brother can have a piece of him while he is still alive.

Her irritated hiss rattled through my mind, but I saw she obeyed since Travis gulped down a desperate lungful of air. The moment he opened his mouth wide for another sweet bit of oxygen, Dante struck.

He dove headfirst into my prisoner's mouth, making Travis's eyes bulge as Dante wiggled further down his throat. A gurgled scream intertwined with the rattling of my serpent's tail, the bottom half of his long body still poking out of Travis's mouth.

While Dante slithered further inside the man's body, a multitude of horrified gasps echoed through the room, one person in the front row even going as far as to retch at the sight of my snakes working together to destroy the traitor.

Ember constricted her body once more around Travis's neck, causing his eyes to roll to the back of his head. His body went limp, and Ember uncoiled herself from around his neck, her job now finished.

She slithered up the dais, joining me once more on the throne. A satisfied hum tumbled from my lips when her heavy body slithered over my shoulders, for my snake's heavy weight always grounded me. Ember finished her ascent, resting her head atop one of the sharp branches twined within my black hair—I hated wearing crowns, so this wooden perch desig-nated for my serpents was the closest I'd ever come to wearing any semblance of one.

As I brushed my finger with the grain of my snake's scales, Ember's small hiss of delight enveloped me. Our moment of celebration was in direct contrast from the sobs that tore through the audience, yet my people fell silent when they saw movement beneath Travis's shirt.

The fools probably thought he was still alive, but a serpen-tine smile spread across my blood-red lips, because I knew what was to come.

Dante shot out of Travis's abdomen, tearing his flesh along with shirt as his razor-sharp fangs came into view. I breathed in hungrily while screams erupted around me.

Little did my people know, their fear didn't upset me—it *fueled* me.

I ravenously gulped down the bitter scent, but I stopped when a twinge of vomit drifted into my nose.

I inwardly groaned at my people's rather weak stomachs. I never understood why they thought violence was so repulsive.

The chaos filtering through the throne room didn't phase Dante. He paid them no mind while he continued to eagerly devour the man's organs.

I pushed off the stone armrest, straightening to tower over my people. I glanced at Dante, who consumed poor Travis as if he hadn't eaten in days.

Considering I had at least two weekly executions, my snake was being a drama queen.

Dante, come. Leave some of him for the others in the Pit.

I tapped my foot while I waited for Dante to finally acknowledge me. His scarlet eyes dragged to mine, blood dripping down his chin and coating his tongue as he flicked it out at me. Regardless of his persistent attitude, he followed my command in the end and ascended the dais. With him assuming his position on the twin branch atop my head, right beside his sister, tonight's show was complete.

"This is what happens when you cross your queen and break a commandment." I pointed at the mutilated body. "Let this serve as a warning to you all."

With a poised and practiced smile, I waved to my disciples.

"I hope you all enjoyed tonight's show. You are dismissed. I shall see some of you *very* soon." My dress grandly fluttered into the air as I threw the train behind me and turned sharply on my heel.

I opted to descend the stairs at the back of my throne, which provided an easy, quick exit. It was essential to have multiple escape routes when ruling as the Serpent Queen, should my people ever get the foolish urge to try to assassinate me again.

A ghost of a smile danced upon my lips as my guards chanted *all hail the Serpent Queen*, and I stole one more greedy breath of air on my way out.

As I left Travis's guts behind for some unfortunate servant to deal with, I let my people's fear soak into the empty spot in my chest—the exact spot where my soul used to be.

CHAPTER 2
THE BODYGUARD

"Your footing is all wrong," Landon said, slamming his sword against mine.

My arms strained from the powerful force my bodyguard possessed, but I quickly spun to the left, deflecting his blow.

I never looked away from my target while I spoke, my words dripping with venom. "That was too close."

"It wouldn't have been if you learned how to use your damn feet and move quicker!" Landon swiped his sword at my ribs, causing me to jolt backward—but not quick enough.

A burning pain licked up my side, making me drop my hand to the gnawing ache settling over me. Carefully, I examined the crimson blood staining my pale fingertips.

"You fucking *cut me?*" I growled, subtly tightening my grip on the hilt of my sword resting at my side. I had opted for a lighter weapon in hopes it would help me move quicker, but so far, it wasn't helping me best my bodyguard one fucking bit.

It was time to change tactics.

Landon's mouth gaped with horror. "Seera, I didn't mean to land that strike. I am so sorry, let me see."

He rushed over to inspect my wound, and I waited until he was close enough to strike. I popped my already clenched fist under his chin, making my bodyguard stumble back in surprise. I wasted no time as I jammed my elbow into his chest and pushed downward at an angle, causing him to fully lose his balance. Then I finished the move by ducking and swiping my arm under his right leg.

Landon let out a grunt as his back slammed against the stone training floor, and I pinned his leg further back, raising my other hand to point the tip of my sword against his throat. He attempted to contain his heavy breathing, an ounce of fear passing through his eyes when the cool metal tip pushed harder into his skin.

"Do you concede?" I asked, a cocky grin on my face. His icy blue eyes flicked to my sword, then back to me.

"I concede, my Queen."

"Good boy." I dropped my weapon, allowing Landon to finally consume precious breaths of crisp air.

Training with my bodyguard was one of the rare moments when I allowed my mask to drop a fraction. Although training was essential to remain strong against any acts of rebellion, it also provided me an excuse to have extra time with Landon.

When I was with my bodyguard, I felt like I could be a sliver of who I was outside of my role as the Serpent Queen, like a snake slowly shedding its skin.

A loud groan tore me from my thoughts, and I looked down to see Landon still laying on the stone floor, rubbing at the spot on his chest where I elbowed him.

I huffed, but extended my hand to help him up. "Stop being dramatic."

His chuckle was rough, as though it was still hard to

breathe after such a brutal fall, but it was necessary we trained on stone—there would be no cushiony mats to break our fall beyond my palace walls, where rebels seeking to topple me from my throne lurked at every turn.

Landon wrapped his warm hand around mine, and I had to tug hard to get my six foot three bodyguard off the ground.

"You sure do love hand-to-hand combat," he said as he rubbed his back, another small groan escaping him.

My victorious smirk only made his scowl intensify. "Don't get cocky. You still suck at wielding a sword."

Landon stretched his back, a crack splitting through the air while he rolled his neck from side to side. "Ready to go again?" he asked, reaching for his weapon.

"As much as I'd love to lay you flat on your ass for the second time today, I have an execution to attend." I shoved the hilt of my sword at Landon.

He frowned but accepted it. "Another execution? Didn't you kill a man in the throne room the other night?"

"How did you hear about that if you only got back from Ashivire this morning?"

Landon gave me a pointed look, his brow arching toward the grey sky.

"Fucking Gustavo . . ." I muttered.

A loose chuckle tumbled from his lips. "Who else spreads gossip as fast as your head butler? Isn't that the reason you hired him in the first place anyways? I believe your exact words were, 'He will create endless chaos, which means endless entertainment for me. The messier, the better.'" Landon tossed me another cheeky grin before moving on to reracking our swords.

He lifted the hem of his shirt to wipe his sweat as he turned to face me, making my mind go blank. I gazed hungrily over the row of muscles rippling across his abdomen, and my tongue darted out to wet my lips as I stared at Landon's exposed light brown skin. But then, his black cotton shirt was dropped and his glorious muscles were hidden once again. My gaze drifted to his strong hands, covered with callouses from hours of training, then wandered over his toned biceps, his wide shoulders, and finally to his lips—which appeared to be moving.

"Seera? *Hello*?!" Landon waved his hands in front of my face.

"Hmm? What?" I cleared my throat, doing my best to stop gawking at my bodyguard.

"Enjoying the view?" His lips twitched with amusement.

I scoffed and rolled my eyes. "Not like it isn't something I haven't seen a million times before." I shot a pointed look at his groin.

My bodyguard followed my gaze, his lips curving into a mischievous smile as he looked at me through ridiculously long, heavy lashes.

"Care to see *it* again?"

I tapped a finger against my lips, humming in thought. After a long moment and a frustrated huff from Landon, I shrugged a shoulder.

"Fine. Come to my room tonight, but not before I have dinner with my guest."

He practically purred with delight. "Fine by me. I don't mind a late night meal." His eyes dipped past my abdomen, lingering on the laces of my black leather training pants.

He bit his bottom lip slowly. "There's only one thing I'm hungry for anyway."

My legs twitched, causing his eyes to flick back to mine. A roguish smile danced upon his lips, and I'd be damned if I let him win this round.

With one stride, I closed the remaining distance between

us and arched my back as I pressed a hand against his torso. My breasts grazed against his chest, making him suck in a sharp breath. Slowly, I tipped my head back and glanced at him through lowered lashes. His heart slammed against my palm as his eyes drifted to my lips—the longing in his gaze tried to scorch me in place, but I stretched onto my toes and brought our lips dangerously close.

As I spoke my next words, I let our mouths lightly graze. "Bring me some useful information tonight from your recent trip to Ashivire, and I *might* feel generous enough to grant you the dinner you so badly crave."

I trailed my fingers down Landon's chest, inching toward his waistband. His eyes darkened as they followed the pathway my fingers scorched along his chest. His hand flexed, as if he was about to grab me and fuck me on the training grounds for all to see, but I quickly stepped back. His frustrated growl chased after me as I backed away, and I chuckled when he dropped his hand to readjust the swiftly growing bulge in his pants. With a spin on my heel, I strutted up the stone stairs leading back to my palace.

Landon's shout reached me as I ascended the final step. "Same time tomorrow, your footwork is trash! You got lucky today!"

I turned to face him as I continued to walk backward, raising two fingers to my brow in a mocking salute. The gesture was considered offensive in my lands, but my bodyguard's laughter boomed throughout the training yard. As I turned back toward my palace, I glanced up at the rolling, dark clouds. Light sprinkles of mist kissed my heated cheeks.

"What a gorgeous day for an execution," I sighed.

My lady-in-waiting scoffed, appearing at my side to offer me a towel to dab my sweaty brows with. I accepted it without stopping, my heels loudly clacking on the black and scarlet marble floors. Reena trailed me, finding it difficult to keep up with my demanding pace.

"Ready to make me look dazzling for tonight's execution?" I tossed a devious smile over my shoulder.

"I've never met anyone who enjoys killing people as much as you do," Reena tsked, shaking her head.

Abruptly, I stopped, making my lady-in-waiting slam into my back. With a quick spin, I towered over her, all the while reveling at the fear saturating her grey eyes. I stared down my nose at her, her throat bobbing. She took a small step away, but I followed her, closing the distance she tried to wedge between us. Reena's hands quaked ever so slightly, but she quickly hid them in her plain grey cotton gown.

I ducked my head so we were eye level and whispered, "That is the best compliment you've ever given me."

Her mouth popped open in surprise, and I smiled, straightening to my full height. Reena's shock melted away to irritation, and she swatted the air as if shooing away a gnat.

"Seera, don't scare me like that!" She clutched a hand against her heart.

My dark chuckle echoed through the black stone halls while I resumed the trek to my quarters. I was going to be late to the show if I dallied any longer to torment my lady-in-waiting, but the fear permeating from her was too sweet not to savor.

"Word of advice, Reena, don't wear your emotions on your face. People could weaponize them for their own selfish intents."

Including myself.

The bitter smell recharged me, making my pace quicken as I anticipated the copious amounts of fear that would fuel me at tonight's execution.

"Is it such a terrible thing to feel, my Queen?"

My lip curled with distaste. "Absolutely."

I braced my hands on the gold knockers adorning my blood-red double doors and pushed. Twin serpents fell from my grip as I strode into my quarters with Reena hot on my trail.

Immediately, she flew over to my wardrobe. "Do you have a preference for which gown you'd like to wear tonight?"

I stopped in the doorway of my bathing chambers, casually shrugging a shoulder.

"A black or red gown will do for tonight's execution. Helps hide the blood better."

Reena's deep exhale was the last thing I heard before slamming the door to ready myself for a fresh round of bloodshed.

CHAPTER 3
THE PIT

The beat of the drums carried a daunting, hypnotic tone through the open air coliseum, and the fear of my people wrapped around me as I entered the tunnel. With a deep inhale, I let their potent emotions wash over me—moments like this were when I felt truly alive.

As much as I loved hosting executions in my throne room, there was something electric about the ones that occurred here. Since the Pit lay on the outskirts of my palace grounds it was a bit of a walk, but I didn't mind as long as I got to see an entertaining show starring a traitor meeting their rightful fate: death by the Serpent Queen's hand.

Torches lined the arena, and a cool breeze licked up my spine, courtesy of my open-back gown that dipped into a scandalously low V-cut. Gold serpent chained straps rattled against my bare back, while a black velvet train trailed behind me. My dress was sensual, alluring—fit for a non-traditional queen like me.

My scalp tingled from my people watching my every move. They were nearly about to break their own necks as I gave them a full view of my exposed back. I flicked my braid over my shoulder, feeling the tips of my hair brushing against my waist. My revealing gown left parts of my tattoo on full display—an unsavory reminder I, too, had to see everyday. The dark ink was to ensure *he* never strayed from my mind, so I would never forget the day *he* permanently marked me.

Fury latched onto me like a beast with thrashing claws as I thought of the serpent tattoo coiling around half of my body, but I refused to wear hideous, modest gowns just to cover it up.

I always loved over-the-top, sultry attire, and I wasn't going to change that because of the king I despised.

Let my people see what I've sacrificed to sit on the throne.

As I approached the steps leading to the royal balcony, a set of frosty, blue eyes greeted me.

"My Queen, you look absolutely ravishing tonight." Landon offered me his hand, helping me up the first step.

The stairs weren't wide enough for the two of us, making our bodies press together. My bodyguard's eyes roamed over my figure, but I proceeded past him. He should know by now that I liked to tease. My bodyguard sharply inhaled as I gave him a grand view of the back of my dress, causing me to cast a devious smile over my shoulder at him. Just as expected, his eyes were glued to my bare skin, slowly trailing over my ample curves. Landon sucked his lip between his teeth, finally bringing his eyes to meet mine as he climbed up a step, closing the distance between us.

"I'm starving . . . are you?" A wicked glint shined in his eyes, causing a thrill to sweep down my spine.

"I am." I leaned in closer, allowing the shadows of the alcove to conceal the subtle brush of my lips against the curve of his ear. "I'm starving . . . for the bitter taste of blood."

When I pulled back, there were no longer any hints of heat blazing in Landon's eyes.

"Well then, I won't keep you from your favorite activity, my Queen." With a quick nod, he turned and descended the remaining steps, assuming his regular position of guarding the entrance to my private balcony.

Without sparing my bodyguard another thought, I spun on my heel, gripping the velvet of my dress between my hands while I ascended the black stone steps. The long train made my pace slow, but my people had nowhere else to be.

Considering their death could be the source of tonight's entertainment, they were beyond lucky to be summoned only as attendees. Besides, my executions were far grander than any measly amusement they'd enjoy in the city.

The Queendom of Phantamos was not a place of revelry and joy.

My queendom was one soaked in rivers of blood and the screams of the tortured.

Finally, I cleared the steps and let the familiar sound of my heels clacking against the stone ready me for tonight's festivities. Glancing out at the crowd, I was pleased to see how packed the coliseum was tonight—not a spare seat in sight.

Looks like my display the other night made a clear statement.

A victorious smirk spread along my lips as the drums concluded their battle cry. On the final sharp crescendo, I assumed my position on the throne. The cool black marble kissed my bare back, and for a moment I was transported to what felt like another life . . .

"You're so fucking beautiful with your hair like this." He dragged his cool fingers down my neck, leaving a pathway of goosebumps to break across my skin.

I dragged a blood-red nail over the serpents carved into the armrests, letting the memories that frequently haunted me fade into the darkest corners of my mind.

The audience's nervous chatter ceased when my twin serpents hissed, alerting they were drawing near from where they perpetually rested—which, on most days, was in my chambers beside a roaring fire.

With just a thought, Ember and Dante appeared at my side. Their bodies spiraled down my arms as their heads hung over the two gnarled branches that made up my crown.

"Welcome to tonight's execution! I hope you all enjoy the show." I raised my arms in a grand gesture. My lips twisted into a sinister smile, while Ember and Dante hissed with excitement at the thought of the bloodshed looming on the horizon.

"Bring in the traitor." I clapped twice, prompting two of my guards to appear with tonight's victim in tow.

Their strong grips tightened around the traitor's biceps as they led her through the dark tunnel and into the cool night air. One could hear a pin drop with how silent it was, leaving only the shuffling of my prisoner's boots to ring throughout the arena. Her hair was long on the top, leaving the sides shorter to reveal a flame carved within the black stubble.

My guards led her straight to the edge of the Pit, where no railing separated her from the vicious snakes lurking in the darkness below. The woman seemed unphased by her imminent death, not even an ounce of fear seeping off her skin. Her stern gaze shot to mine, the vast rectangular pit was the only thing standing between us.

My voice boomed through the stadium. "State your name."

"Meredith." The woman's jaw ticked, and my curiosity rose as the smell of her anger floated toward me.

Not my preferred emotion to consume, but it would do for the time being.

"Meredith, you have broken not one but two of your Queen's commandments, yet you stand before me festering in a cloud of anger. Are you angry with yourself for committing such a horrible act of treason?"

The woman's scoff rang through the arena as her eyes rolled skyward. Fury shot through me, but I gripped the armrests of my throne to hide the only emotion I could feel for the past eight decades. My knuckles turned bone white as I sucked in a small breath, grasping the reigns on my never-ending rage.

There was nothing I hated more than when my people broke any of my commandments, but there was a reason commandment number one was, *'Thou shalt not disrespect thy Queen.'*

I did not tolerate disrespect well.

"Correction, make that three broken commandments." I flaunted three fingers at the crowd.

"I am already sentenced to death. Why should I care to follow your commandments?" She pointed a finger at me, and the audience collectively inhaled a sharp breath. "You are a pathetic excuse for a queen. The only person you protect is yourself—you don't give a damn about the wellbeing of your people. You wrecked our lands decades ago, and you still continue to be a plague to our kingdom." She spit into the Pit, eliciting a multitude of angry hisses from the hungry serpents.

The audience gasped at her brave, yet foolish words. I hid my slight irritation at her blatant disregard for my *queen*dom by glancing at my people and pulling in a deep breath to assess the tone in the coliseum. For the most part, fear remained as the prevalent emotion, yet I smelt a new note that swiftly flourished throughout the audience like a tidal wave. My lip curled at the fresh smell of a floral bouquet . . . it smelled a lot like *hope.*

Well, that just won't do.

With a crack of my neck, I barked at my guard on her left. "Felix, shut her up."

I watched my guard's tied-back black hair swish behind him while he backhanded the traitor. The sound echoed off the stone walls, along with muffled sobs issuing from the front row.

My gaze shot to the woman crying into a gray handkerchief. I glanced between the older woman and Meredith, the latter's cheek stained with an angry red handprint. The resemblance was apparent, and I smiled when I realized the traitor's mother was here to watch her daughter's execution. However, curiosity creeped through me as she continued to weep when Felix slapped Meredith again, making her neck harshly whip to the side.

The smell of fresh rainfall reeked from the woman—her sorrow was overwhelming. It was a rather foreign experience for me to witness a mother care about their daughter with such a ferocious intensity.

Another splitting crack drew my attention back to tonight's entertainment, but my lips swiftly pinched into a pout when I noticed Meredith didn't cry out once in pain.

"That's enough, Felix." I held up my hand, and my guard roughly grabbed the woman by her arm, forcing her to face me.

"Meredith, I hereby sentence you to death, for not only breaking three of my commandments, including conspiring to overthrow your Queen, but also due to your continuous lack of remorse and respect. For these reasons, we will be doing things a bit differently this evening."

The traitor's brows furrowed, and my snakes' delighted hissing wrapped around me as they realized what I was thinking.

"Felix, would you do me a favor and wake up Vesper?" I cooed.

Meredith visibly paled, and I smiled when her fear finally drifted toward me. I savored the bitter, acid scent, letting it soak into the void where my soul used to be.

Felix passed the woman off to my other guard, and the audience grew utterly silent when he cranked the stone lever attached to one of the tunnels leading into the Pit. The metal gears groaned as one of the two iron gates rose to release my feared beast.

Even the traitor's mother ceased her sobbing, her mouth dangling open in horror.

I hummed, immensely satisfied that the only smell wafting from the crowd was fear, all traces of hope demolished.

The ground shook from the vicious hiss ricocheting up from the depths of the Pit. The guard holding Meredith shoved her toward the very edge. Her throat bobbed while she did her best not to peek down at the monster that was about to feast on her flesh and bones.

Getting to my feet, I leaned over the stone balcony. "Oh, Vesper," I sang. "I've brought you a little treat."

The railing I leaned against forcefully quaked as Vesper thrashed his tail in excitement against the walls of the Pit. The rattle was enough to make Meredith lose her balance, one foot slipping over the stone edge. Quickly, she crouched, trying to stabilize herself as she yanked her foot back onto solid ground. Although the shaking ceased, Meredith remained trembling while she finally looked over the edge. Her fear suffocated my lungs, making shivers of pleasure slither down my spine from the bitter scent.

I followed her gaze into the darkness. Vesper's midnight black body blended into the endless shadows, but we all knew what his massive form looked like. When I gained possession of the beast—thanks to my bargain—I presented him to my people before permanently keeping him in the underground tunnels beneath my palace.

Everyone knew Vesper was my most blood-thirsty serpent. After all, he was a beast of nightmares—he particularly enjoyed savoring his victim's eyeballs before moving on to devour the rest of their flesh and bones.

My beast's daunting blood-red eyes and sharp white fangs were the only things illuminated within the dimness.

"Take your time with this one," I drawled to the vicious serpent, and his red tongue darted out in a thrilled hiss.

I leveled one last glare at Meredith, and she must have sensed my gaze because her fearful eyes raised to mine. I was seconds away from commanding my guard to kick her into the pit, but a man yelling from the audience had my jaw snapping closed.

"All hail the Serpent King! He would never allow such cruelty to fall upon us!" The man threw his right fist into the air as he descended the stone stairs leading to the Pit.

A roar of shocked gasps fluttered through the audience, but the only look of surprise I allowed to shine through was the arch of a brow and pinch of my lips. With a sharp inhale, I quickly was able to detect the reek of charred leather permeating off him.

Pure hatred.

The man descended to the base of the rafters, but Felix seized him the moment he tried to shove his way toward the pit and to Meredith. A flash of blood-red caught my attention, dragging my gaze away from the man and to my bodyguard powerfully striding toward the commotion. His jaw was clenched and his eyes were like sharp steel as he assessed the new threat.

I was so distracted by how wonderful my signature color stretched across Landon's glorious muscles I nearly forgot I was in the middle of a show.

Turning my focus back to the spectacle playing out below me, I wickedly smiled at the woman teetering on the edge of death.

"Well, what do we have here? A lover of yours, Meredith?" I purred, causing an anguished growl to tear from the traitor's lips while she thrashed against my guard's iron-clad grip.

Landon helped Felix detain the man who resumed his annoying chatter. "You don't deserve to sit on the mortal's throne, for you are not one of us."

I looked down my nose at the stocky man, who had hatred blazing within his dark eyes. My snakes violently hissed atop my head, ready to defend me at my command.

I've got this, I said down our bond, slowly pacing the balcony. My heels clacking were the only sound filling the tense arena.

"It is rather interesting that you think the Serpent King is less cruel than me." I hummed, giving the man a once-over. "The fact you believe such a statement proves your high level of sheer ignorance . . . and stupidity." I chuckled, making the man roar with fury.

The traitor puffed his chest, trying once again to break free, but, unfortunately for him, I employed the strongest men in all the human lands to be my guards.

I glanced at Landon, and a charged electricity passed between us when our eyes locked.

Correction, I had the strongest guards in all the lands and the most handsome.

I leveled a cold look at the crowd, letting my mask fall back into place. "May this be a reminder to you all. Although I am an immortal, I was once like you. I earned my place as the first woman to rule this queendom, and I bet not one of you could survive the things I've endured in order to be sitting here today."

I sat, taking my rightful place atop the throne, no longer entertained by tonight's execution. I was ready to be done with these ungrateful peasants and soak in my tub till my skin pruned.

"Guards, bring him to join the woman." I barely spared them another glance.

I knew my guards did as I commanded when I heard shoes scuff against stone. It was useless, but the traitor fought my men every step of the way, roaring like a caged animal.

I was cradling my head in my hand, utterly bored, when I smelt something new filling the air around me. I perked up, inhaling his fear like one consumed air to survive.

A crack tore through the brisk coliseum when Landon slammed the man to his knees at the edge of the pit beside Meredith, and I nodded down at him in approval. A vicious hiss rattled below, signaling Vesper was aware his next meal had doubled in size in only a matter of minutes.

This happened from time to time, where two lovers would insist on dying together.

Some considered it romantic, but I found it utterly foolish.

Love made people weak, and this was yet another reminder why I refused to love ever again.

The man gazed into the Pit, then his eyes rose to meet mine, raising his voice for all to hear. "You might excel at making your people live in a constant state of fear, but it won't stop more from rebelling. We refuse to bow at the feet of a monster. You will *never* be as strong as the Serpent King, nor any man for that matter."

My vision blurred, red flooding my sight as I tried to act nonchalant from the slew of hate being tossed my way.

I cocked my head, pouting my lips. It was easier to pretend everything was fine, acting as if his words didn't slice through my gut like a razor-sharp blade.

Instead, a sinful smile slithered across my lips, stretching so wide I felt it kiss the edges of my eyes. "Looks like I am stronger than at least one man."

My remark brought a storm of anger back into the weak, pathetic man's eyes, and I dramatically yawned, patting my hand against my mouth.

"This conversation bores me. Guards, execute them." With a dismissive wave, I looked away from the traitors and set my sights on the audience.

My favorite moment of my weekly entertainment was about to commence.

My guards kicked the two traitors into the Pit, making blood-curdling screams reverberate off the walls and echo throughout the arena. Yet, I did not drop my gaze from the crowd as I assessed their reactions to what the man said moments before. Fear seemed to be etched upon most of their faces, while the sound of crunching bones trickled from the Pit. Yet, a handful of my people appeared angry, some even had their mouths parted in a perpetual state of shock.

My attention snagged on one man with onyx black hair, whose piercing green eyes were shrouded with a gleam of disappointment.

His eyes weren't trained on the Pit, like the rest of the audience—they were fixed on me.

That stare reminded me so much of . . .

I slammed my eyes shut, not able to withstand another torturous moment looking at the man who reminded me so much of my past. I inhaled, zoning in on the overall feeling from the crowd, preparing to delight in the bitter cloud of their fear.

However, my eyes flew open, my mouth tugging into a frown as that awfully sweet scent surrounded me once more . . .

Hope.

CHAPTER 4
THE RITUAL

I couldn't catch my breath.

It felt like I was being stabbed by a thousand knives, and I gasped as I tried to lower myself inch by inch into the freezing water. Counting always helped.

One. Two.

Fuck, my ass was already numb.

Three. Four.

My nipples peaked as they grazed the cold water, making a hiss fly from my lips.

Five, six, seven.

I needed five minutes alone, truly alone. Sadly, the only way to have silence filter through me was by enduring these miserable ice baths.

Eight. Nine.

My mind emptied as I fully dropped into the tub—not even my snakes were able to disturb me during these baths. The big babies couldn't stand the frigid temperature, and it was as if a mental shield was built between us.

Ten, eleven, twelve.

I dunked my head, allowing myself to wash away the mask I wore every day. I let the Serpent Queen's persona freeze off, chipping away piece by piece with each dip beneath the icy water.

All I wanted was one moment to simply exist as Seera.

Thirteen, fourteen, fifteen.

When I dunked beneath the surface for the third time, I opened my lips and *screamed.* The cold water flooded my mouth, eager to race down my lungs and drown me once and for all.

I was tempted to let it.

Sixteen. Seventeen.

Another agonized scream flew out of me as the traitorous man's words floated through my mind—*all hail the Serpent King.*

Eighteen. Nineteen.

Muffled banging made me burst out of the freezing water, and I gasped for air while Reena barreled into the bathing chamber. My lady-in-waiting was too busy fuming to notice I was trying to catch my breath.

"I can't stand Gustavo. He is such a nasty, vile little man. With his thin mustache and his pompous attitude. He is always talking bad about everyone, and today I was the subject of his gossip." A low growl crawled up her throat while she blabbered on about my butler, as if I didn't already know such things.

In fact, it was the exact reason I hired him in the first place.

Reena shook her head, spreading a black towel wide before her. "And don't even get me started on his *ridiculous* getup. Who wears bow ties anymore?"

With my moment of peace completely shattered, I stood from the frigid water. An intense shiver raked down my spine, prompting my lady-in-waiting to wrap the towel tightly around my body. I let out a long breath when the freshly warmed cloth absorbed the frigidness from my bones.

"I have no idea how you stand those baths." She cringed, bending down to unplug the drain at the base of the black-chrome tub.

"Not much bothers you when you are soulless," I said, watching the dim lighting catch onto the tiny specks of grey peppered throughout her chestnut hair. Reena wasn't nearly old enough to have grey in her locks, but she did have a rather demanding role here.

Quite frankly, I was betting she would turn completely grey before the end of this year.

My wet feet slapped against the marble as I made my way to the black-framed floor length mirror in the corner of my bathing chambers. After a few glorious moments savoring the heat from my towel, I let it drop and pool around my ankles.

Let the ritual commence.

As always, I started by examining my eyes, the deep green shade making the inner ring of gold around my pupils even more heightened. Not an ounce of the mortal girl I once was shined through them, tugging a ghost of a smile onto my lips. Yet, my smile faltered when I glanced at the scar situated atop the left side of my lips. Two faded bite marks glared back at me, serving as a permanent reminder of the bargain I made nearly eight decades prior—a deal where I sold my soul in exchange for the power coursing through my veins.

I dragged a hand through my black locks, which trailed past my waist, where beads of water dripped down my pale skin. I pulled my hair to one side, revealing the birthmark that kissed the side of my neck and scoffed. It looked like a drop of blood permanently adorning my skin—rather fitting for the Serpent Queen.

My gaze dipped while I took in the serpent tattoo spiraling

around my abdomen. The head of the snake was nestled right between my breasts, its rattling tail flicking across the top left curve of my ass. Its mouth was stretched wide open, as if it was ready to strike, with its sharp fangs prepared to devour anyone who dared to harm me.

Some days, I wished it would come alive, just to swallow the man who left his mark on me.

This tattoo was the reason I performed such a ritual every night after bathing. It served as a reminder to stay angry, to never let another man close to me for the rest of however many miserable years I had left.

He never told me his symbol would spread across half of my body when we sealed our bargain, and I vowed to bring the Serpent King to his knees one day for marking me in such a permanent way.

"Let's get you dressed before you fall ill," Reena said, shuffling behind me, breaking my trance of hatred.

Her plain grey dress swished while she raced out of the bathing room and into my bedroom chambers.

I slipped on my black silk robe and followed her, but I quickly had to dodge a gown from smacking me square in the face.

"Reena . . ." I growled, making my lady-in-waiting spin to face me, her shoulders caving in when she saw the daggers I shot at her.

"Apologies, my Queen," She turned back to the red and black gown clutched between her small hands. "But you only have two color choices for tonight's dinner, per usual." She muttered the last remark under her breath, but thanks to my impeccable hearing, I still heard it.

I shook my head at the sight of Reena disappearing inside my large ebony wardrobe, her behind wiggling while she searched its depths.

"You won't find what you are looking for. I specifically told the tailor to only make red and black gowns fit for a queen."

My lady-in-waiting's muffled groan had me chuckling as I made my way to my vanity. While I combed my hair, I admired the black and gold serpent wallpaper lining my chambers. The sounds of garments ruffling against the marble floor signaled Reena was having one of her episodes, which always resulted in my quarters being covered in a heaping pile of velvet and silk gowns.

With a heavy sigh, I faced my palm toward the floor, prompting Ember to spiral down my arm. Her scarlet scales gleaming as she slithered across the floor to start cleaning up Reena's ever-growing mess.

"This one will have to do," she muttered, pulling a plain, black gown from one of my many wardrobes.

I glanced at Reena in the reflection of the mirror as she moved toward the bed, laying the dress on the edge of my blood-red duvet.

Her brows scrunched as she stared at the garment. "Would you be open to possibly a color close to black? Maybe grey or silver—" Reena yelped when a discarded gown began to slide across the floor next to her.

Her fear permeated the air, her short legs quickly racing for the corner of the room where a step stool resided for times like this. A satisfied sigh slipped from my lips while I greedily consumed the fear saturating the air, easing the constant numbness in my chest with every bitter gulp.

She continued to squeal, yet Ember barely spared her a once-over glance before continuing to slither up the wardrobe to hook the gown back into its proper spot.

"I hate when you bring them out without warning me!" Reena firmly pressed herself against the wall, almost like she could disappear through it with sheer will.

Her tightly shut eyes had me working hard to stifle a laugh.

I found it rather amusing that the lady-in-waiting to the Serpent Queen was deathly afraid of snakes.

Reena has been in my service for nearly ten years, yet she never overcame her fear of snakes. If I didn't revel in consuming the delicious taste of her fear so much, I'd consider helping her conquer such a silly fear.

But where would the fun be in that?

There were some perks to having no soul, such as not having the ability to feel guilty for such callous thoughts.

I turned to watch Ember as she slithered down the wardrobe with a black gown embellished with a gold serpent spreading throughout the entire dress. One side of the ensemble had a cut out to expose the left side of my midsection.

As much as the mark on my body irked me, I had to admit it looked exquisite in that gown.

Ember dropped the garment at my feet, then slithered her way up my legs and around my arm. I bent down, grasping the fabric while running my fingers over the sharp, gold sequins.

"Excellent choice, Ember." I softly stroked her head, her contempt hiss wrapping around me like a comforting embrace.

For a snake, she truly had magnificent taste.

Rest.

As soon as the command was sent down our bond, Ember disappeared from my arm. An odd feeling raced through me when my snakes no longer graced my limbs . . . I immediately missed their steadying warmth.

"I'll never get used to that." Reena let out a shaky breath as she climbed down from the stool.

I shook my head, clearing the weird sensation spreading within me. As I stood and stepped into the gown, the high neckline brushed against the column of my throat. I turned, allowing my lady-in-waiting to button up the copious amount of buttons trailing the entirety of my spine. Her slender fingers worked quickly, and the room grew silent as I stared at my reflection in the vanity.

"I know that look," I said, watching Reena through the mirror as she gnawed on her bottom lip. Her grey eyes glanced up, meeting mine for a split second.

"What are you dying to say but aren't certain you should?" I arched a curious brow at her.

She sighed before speaking in a hushed tone. "I wasn't the only subject of Gustavo's daily gossip . . ."

I waited for her to share more, but instead she moved to grab the gnarled twin branches hanging on the wall beside my vanity. She nodded at the bench, her grip tightening around my version of a crown.

I rolled my eyes as I sat. "Okay, Reena. I am sitting, so now would be an opportune time to share whatever upsetting news you overheard."

She placed my headdress down, then her fingers laced through a section of my hair with expert precision, braiding my locks for what was probably the millionth time.

She glanced around, dropping her voice to a low whisper. "Gustavo mentioned a rumor spreading across the city—there is talk of a new rebel group forming."

I scoffed. "That is not news. The mortals have tried countless times to overthrow me, yet they never succeed. May I remind you, I am the only one with magic in the human lands. So, there is no reason to fret, unless you know of another queen who can summon and command magical serpents?"

I snatched the tube of lipstick, dismissing this frivolous conversation and moving on to paint a swipe of my signature blood-red color across my lips.

Reena spoke so lightly, an ordinary mortal wouldn't have

heard her. "This group's leaders plan to travel to Ashivire soon."

The lipstick stilled in my hand as my eyes shot to meet hers through the reflection. I clicked my jaw, tension wracking through my body at the mention of my homelands.

"Did Gustavo say what their rumored plans are?" The intensity behind my glare made my lady-in-waiting avert her gaze, swiftly moving on to braid the last section of my hair.

"They want to travel to the border of the moral lands—to hike to Morotis and speak to the Serpent King." She shook her head in disbelief.

All hail the Serpent King.

Instantly, memories of my people's sweet tasting hope seeped down my throat, and I brushed my fingers against my neck as I worked on swallowing my swiftly growing irritation.

Although my disciples have previously attempted coups, they never went as far as to seek out the Serpent King for aid. A nagging feeling speared my gut while I reminisced on the mixture of fear and hope wafting through both of my most recent executions.

Was this why my people felt so hopeful? Did they truly believe this rebel group could be the ones to finally overthrow me?

Such heinous acts called for a grand execution, and the thought of catching these traitors in order to put on a fabulous show began to calm my wild rage.

"The Serpent King will not help them. Surely, they will go insane before they ever make it to meet the king, because of those horrid caves leading to his lair. Mortals can't withstand the whispers filtering throughout his caves." I steeled my mask of indifference into place, relaxing my shoulders as Reena worked on styling the two braids around my black wooden crown.

"You survived them . . ." she whispered, uncertainty quickly scrawling across her features. "Apologies, Your Majesty. I know you don't like to talk about that period of your life."

Raising a hand, I halted my lady-in-waiting's tongue from speaking further of my past life. "I may have survived, but those weak-minded men will not."

Reena's brows rose as if she wanted to say more, but she pursed her lips instead.

While she finished my hair in silence, my gaze roamed over the blood-red jewelry box before me. It was left open for me to select one of the beautiful gleaming jewels to wear to tonight's dinner. I hated myself for allowing my eyes to skim over all of the gems until I found a much smaller piece—an oval ruby ring with a small serpent carved into the golden band.

The stone shone underneath the warm sconces lining the walls, and I felt myself slipping from reality and into a memory I tried to bury long ago . . .

The Serpent King slipped the ring on my finger with a startling gentleness, as if he was afraid to shatter such an intimate moment brewing between us.

"A token, to symbolize how much you mean to me."

My heart skipped as I reveled at the beautiful jewel, but my stomach sank when I glanced up at the king.

I was elated, but the king did not match my awestruck expression. Instead, he looked like someone stepped on his foot, his eyes pinching with pain.

"I'll always be grateful you walked into my realm and changed everything." He cradled my hand, his eyes desperately trying to convey something he left unsaid.

"I'll cherish this forever. Thank you," I whispered.

He smiled, but it didn't reach his eyes. Then, he released our clasped hands and—

I slammed the jewelry box, closing the door on the agonizing memory at the same time.

Reena jumped from the startling noise, but she quickly resumed her work. She untucked a few pieces of my hair, allowing them to fall loosely to frame my face. Such a small act made a startling difference in my appearance, softening the sharp edges of my nose and jaw.

My lady-in-waiting offered me a reassuring smile, but I saw the concern lingering in the fine lines beside her eyes. "You are all ready for dinner, Your Majesty."

"See to it that the grand dining hall is prepared for my guest," I said, formally dismissing her.

With a dip of her chin, she fled from my chambers. The door clicked behind her, leaving nothing behind but the crackling of the fire. Although my rooms were peaceful and quiet, my mind was the complete opposite.

It felt like someone was screaming over and over again as miserable thoughts plagued me.

You are a pathetic excuse of a queen.
You will never be as strong as the Serpent King.
We won't bow before a monster.

Most days, I dreamed of making the voices in my head shut up, of drifting into an eternal oblivion.

Instead of acting on my self-loathing thoughts, I stewed in them as I lined my eyes with kohl, then moved on to dabbing my fingers into a pot of rouge. I patted the deep red shade on the apples of my cheeks, bringing life back into my uncharacteristically pale face.

Over my dead body would the rebels reach the Serpent King.

I'd dealt with a handful of attempted coups, *For Serpent's sake*, I'd even survived a few assassination attempts—I wouldn't allow the mortals to finally succeed in besting me.

I'd do anything to hold on to my throne, to my power.

The day I escaped my mother's tower was the same day I refused to be rendered powerless ever again.

The bench screeched as I slid it back against the stone floors. I paced, contemplating skipping dinner altogether and proceeding straight to allowing Landon to feast on me.

I desperately needed the distraction of his tongue between my thighs.

A sharp slice of light silenced my spiraling thoughts, causing me to turn toward the floor-length mirror. I moved closer, marveling at my reflection and the gold sequins gleaming in my gown from the burning sconces.

As I ran my hands over my dress, smoothing any creases, I noticed my hands were trembling slightly.

How odd.

I usually only shook when I was extremely angry, but I didn't feel the tell-tale sign of the burning kindling in my gut from said emotion right now.

As if they could sense the shift in my mood, Ember and Dante slithered across my shoulders, offering me the best embrace two snakes could. I forced a smile at them through the mirror, then let my eyes drift closed while trying my best to steady the peculiar feeling floating through me.

Their soft hissing comforted me while a plan to stop the rebels wove through my mind. As much as the thought made my blood boil, it might actually work . . .

Slowly, I fluttered my eyes open, my pinched red lips shining as I stared at myself through the mirror.

I didn't express to Reena that there was a small chance one of the rebels could slip through the Serpent King's caves. If they were successful at making contact with that horrid male, I didn't want to find out if he would aid them in their foolish pursuit to overthrow me. I wouldn't put it past the king to help the rebels after how we ended things.

I adjusted my crown, my decision solidifying as I donned the mask of the Serpent Queen for tonight's dinner.

I'd stop the rebels myself.

But in order to do so, I had to go back to the place where I was raised—where I swore never to return to . . .

To Ashivire, the lands that broke me.

CHAPTER 5
DINNER WITH A MONSTER CALLED MOTHER

As I entered the grand dining hall, I admired the way my burgundy heels matched the marble floors. The sconces lining the pitch-black walls made eerie shadows flicker along the vast, blood-red dining table.

It was such a warm and welcoming ambiance for tonight's dinner guest.

Said guest hadn't arrived yet, which was a welcome reprieve. It allowed me to take my proper spot at the head of the table, then quickly down the glass of red wine set before me by one of my servants. I closed my eyes, savouring the bitterness of the wine—it tasted so much like fear.

Plus, I needed all the liquid courage I could get if I was to make it through tonight's dinner without killing anyone.

My moment of relaxation was shattered when I heard the shuffle of all to familiar footsteps, making my eyes shoot open.

"The Queen is ready for you. Dinner will be served shortly, my lady," said a servant, the ruffle of her skirts alerting me that she was fleeing to gather our meal.

Leaving me alone with the monster I called mother.

I fucking *hated* the way she walked, but I loathed myself even more for allowing the cadence of her footsteps to forever be ingrained in my brain, no matter how many times I tried to replace it with the screams of my people as I carved them up in my dungeons.

My mother hadn't uttered a single word, yet she still had the power to make me relive a painful memory from my past.

"This should be enough food to get you through the weekend. I will return at first light in two days." My mother's tone was distant, just like our relationship.

Without another word, she tugged the heavy steel door shut. The only sounds were the clicking of the nine locks as my captor sealed me into my room.

I listened to her footsteps shuffle down the hall, leaving me alone once more, locked away in the tower that was my own personal prison.

My hand quaked as I reached once more for the wine glass before me, taking a hearty gulp to wash away the memory that lurched from the depths of my mind.

The now stranger to me approached my right side, her long black hair an exact replica of mine. She wrung her hands, her brows crinkling together as she looked down the table then back at me.

"Sit down and stop hovering like a damn ghost." I waved a dismissive hand, causing her to finally drift to the chair *three* down from where I sat.

My mother may be heartless, but she was indeed smart.

As she pulled out her chair, the wooden legs screeched against the marble floors, making the odd tightness coiling in my chest heighten. I chugged the rest of my wine, trying to swallow the strange feelings sparking within me. When I slammed my wine glass onto the table, my mother jumped in her seat, stealing a sideways glance at me while a servant flew over to refill my drink.

Actually, the woman sitting before me today didn't deserve the title of mother, not even within the confinement of my mind. So, I'd address her like the stranger she was.

Nedra shifted in her seat while she grabbed the black napkin off her plate, delicately fanning it across her lap. I continued to sip on my wine, staring at her over the brim of the glass.

She hadn't changed much in the past eight decades, which I found very peculiar.

As if she could feel my crucifying stare, her eyes rose to mine. Her deep green eyes mirrored my own, and I hated the constant reminders demonstrating we shared the same blood. Every time I gazed upon my reflection, it was impossible not to imagine Nedra glaring back at me.

She scratched her hand, making my gaze dip to her tear-shaped birthmark. My grip tightened around the stem of my glass at yet another feature we shared.

Nedra cleared her throat, her hands ringing atop her lap.

She glanced away first, taking a small sip of her wine while doing so. "Thank you for agreeing to have dinner with me, Seera. I hope you are well."

I scoffed into my glass, devouring another generous gulp and letting the liquor wash down the slew of insults I wished to spit at my mother—at Nedra.

It didn't go unnoticed how she addressed me by my given name and forwent my formal title. A kernel of anger bloomed inside me, making my grip tighten once more around the stem.

I tossed a sickly-sweet smile at her. "I almost burned your letter before bothering to read it, yet my lady-in-waiting convinced me otherwise. Honestly, I'm surprised you're still alive. Did you, too, make a deal of your own?"

Her pink lips pinched into a tight line, but she lightly bobbed her head. "I am grateful you read my letter."

My hum floated through the room as I noted she avoided my question. Silence stretched between us, but it was thankfully interrupted when one of my servants brought the first course out. The tension shattered with each clatter of the metal trays clinking onto the table before us. A woman servant raised the lid, revealing a leafy salad with an assortment of whatever vegetables could be grown this season.

Although I despised the majority of food spread before me, I had no right to complain.

After all, it was my fault we struggled to grow crops. None of the mortal lands were the same after the bargain was sealed, and I was the only one to blame.

Nedra took a small bite of her salad, and I followed suit, but not before chugging another glass of wine.

I was perfectly fine with getting belligerently drunk tonight and ignoring my mother—*For Serpent's Sake*—ignoring Nedra for the entirety of our meal.

I glanced at the grand clock, at the beautiful depiction of two beautiful intertwining serpents circling one another, their mouths opened and fangs bared at the other. The symbol could be found all throughout my palace, and I often found myself looking for it to comfort me when my snakes were resting.

The ticking of time slowly passing by was the only noise filtering through the dining hall, besides the intermittent crunching from us consuming our salads.

I clenched my jaw on my next bite, suddenly regretting subjecting myself to such a miserable dinner. However, I couldn't help but ponder why my mother reached out to me after seventy-five years—call it morbid curiosity of wondering what my captor had to say for herself after all this time.

Yet now, coming face-to-face with the monster I fled from decades ago felt like a grave mistake. Maybe I could leave early . . . I glanced at the clock once more, deciding to give Nedra another fifteen more minutes before feigning ill and escaping to my late night meeting with my bodyguard.

"So, how is it living in the Kingdom of Phantamos?" she inquired between bites.

"Queendom."

"Pardon?" Nedra's fork stilled in her hands.

"It's the Queendom of Phantamos now, and I like it much better than being trapped alone in a tower." I instantly regretted the truth that spilt from my lips, but it begged to be released after being swallowed for decades.

I didn't balk, not even when Nedra's lips slightly parted and started to quiver. Instead, I ignored her, going back to consuming my meal while discreetly watching her out of the corner of my eye as she took a small sip of wine.

"You don't miss Ashivire at all?" Her quiet words tore through the air like an arrow aimed straight for my heart.

I wanted to scream at such a ridiculous question, but I scoffed as I worked to grip the slippery reins controlling my never-ending anger.

"What's there to miss? Those lands have been in ruins and ash since the day I came into power." I looked her dead in the eye. "But they never were a place full of happy memories before that day, were they?"

Her eyes brightened as they grew watery, prompting her to quickly look away and stare into the crimson liquor inside her glass instead.

"You don't miss the safety of those lands? I've heard about

the attempted coups, Seera." Her gaze lifted toward mine. "I worry about you."

With a dramatic groan, I rested my elbows on the table.

I never gave a shit about royal manners anyway.

"Spare me your sympathy, Nedra."

She flinched as if I physically slapped her by using her given name, causing the scent of fresh rainfall to flood the dining hall.

How dare she act all timid and concerned now? Where was this version of her when I begged for it? When she locked me away from the world, depriving me of a normal existence?

She deserved to feel every drop of sorrow dripping off her slender figure.

I gestured at the extravagant room. "As you can see, I am much better off here. I'd take attempted coups and a lack of safety any day if it meant never living within the confinement of four cramped walls."

My venomous words hit their mark, making tears drip down Nedra's face.

"I did what I thought was right. You don't understand how much my actions pain me. I wish I could reverse time and do it all differently." Her voice broke as she dabbed her crocodile tears with her napkin.

"Well, you can't. I have to live with the decisions I've made as queen, and so do you." I tipped my glass to my lips, the fury inside me growing with each sip.

Her glassy eyes flew to mine, the skin beneath them growing puffy from all her fraudulent crying. "I never wanted this life for you. If I knew my actions would push you to make such a dangerous decision, I would take it all back in a heartbeat. You can hate me all you want, for I deserve your animosity, but please do not forget who you really are—who you are pretending to be today is nothing like the sweet girl you once were."

I slammed my glass onto the table, making the metal trays rattle. "No one is pretending here besides you. I might have made a bargain rendering me soulless, but you left me with no other choice." I rose, shoving my seat with such an intensity it toppled over. "I am exactly who I was always meant to be."

Nedra dropped her gaze, her shoulders shaking as she fell into another fit of sobs. She looked so small curled in on herself, and that image nearly stole my breath, bringing back such awful memories . . . back in the tower, there wasn't a night that passed where I didn't cry myself to sleep, curled up in a ball, wishing for someone to save me.

Isolation drove me to madness—it made me seek out the Serpent King and bargain away my soul.

I glanced at the clock.

Her fifteen minutes were up.

"I have a meeting to get to. Feel free to stay and finish your meal." I threw my napkin onto the table, glaring at my mother —at Nedra—for what I hoped was the last time.

She lifted her gaze, her lips pouting with disappointment. Her weak nod was the last thing I saw before spinning on my heel and heading for the exit. I was almost out of the dining hall, but her parting words made my feet stick to the floor.

"Happy Birthday, Seera."

I stiffened before striding out of the dining hall.

My birthday . . . I had completely forgotten it was today.

Shortly after turning immortal, I stopped celebrating, for I looked the same with each passing year. The only thing that changed as time withered away was the festering numbness sinking its fangs into my chest like a venomous serpent.

I dragged a finger against the void inside me as memories of my past threatened to drag me under.

I was only twenty-five when I escaped from my mother's tower and fled to Morotis, to the caves of doom and death—to the home of the Serpent King. After my bargain was complete, my birthday ceased to exist. Instead, it shifted into the anniversary of something I always dreamed of: being the most powerful being in all of the human lands.

I braced a hand against my sternum at the mere thought of the man I despised, finding it harder than normal to catch my breath. My legs grew heavy as I rounded the corner to my chambers, the taste of my mother's sorrow still coating my tongue.

The scent was suffocating me, and I clawed at the high neckline of my gown while gasping for air. I quickened my pace, nearly running now as I grew more desperate to get out of this dress and underneath my bodyguard. I needed to feel something beyond Nedra's sorrow, beyond the numbness festering inside me like an oozing sore.

So, I ran down the halls and coped with my struggles the only way I knew how to.

I ran from my problems, from my past, from the memory of the girl who died at the young age of twenty-five.

CHAPTER 6
THE ATTACK

Reena was waiting outside my room, her mouth parting when she saw me running straight at her. She quickly threw the doors open, allowing me to storm into my chambers.

I clawed at my neck, gasping for air. "Reena, get this damn dress off me right *now!*"

I barely registered her clicking the door shut and rushing after me.

My heart was beating so damn fast.

I gripped my chest as that old familiar tightness coiled within it like a venomous serpent. The feeling overpowered me, and my knees cracked against the marble floors.

"My Queen!" Reena yelled, dropping behind me.

"Get it off. Get it off!" I roared, barely registered my lady-in-waiting's trembling fingers against my back.

She worked to undo the many buttons lining the back of my dress, but she wasn't moving fast enough.

The tightness in my chest constricted harder.

I couldn't breathe.

I could't *breathe.*

Just like that, I was no longer kneeling on the floor of my palace rooms—I was trapped within four tan walls.

The sound of chalk grating against stone made me shiver, but this was my only way of keeping track of time—of how many days I've been locked away in this godforsaken tower.
As I finished dragging the charcoal down the wall, I shuffled back and counted the tallies.
I stood there for what felt like an eternity, but I had nowhere else to be.
As I approached the final row of markings, tears blurred my vision.
2,191.

The pain racing through me wasn't only physical, but mental.

I groaned loudly as my past slammed down on my chest like a thousand bricks.

"What happened to her?" Landon's stern voice tore through the room as the doors burst open.

It sounded like he drew near, but I couldn't see anything besides the black spots flooding my vision. My panic was so severe, so consuming—I knew I was a moment away from passing out.

"I don't know! She sounds like she can't breathe properly. I'm trying to get this dress off her as fast as I can." Reena's fingers brushed a bare part of my skin, yet she still had so many buttons to unfasten . . . too many.

Right as I was about to succumb to the darkness, her fingers flew from my back and the sound of tearing fabric split through the room. A chill licked up my back, causing me to glance over my shoulder.

Kneeling on the floor behind me was my bodyguard, a wild

look shining in his bright eyes. I glanced down at my exposed back, at one of my favorite gowns now torn straight down the center. Golden buttons still rolled along the black marble floor.

I inhaled deeply, letting my head droop with relief. A shudder coursed down my spine, and I remained kneeling, for my bones felt far too heavy to stand. I was greedily sucking down air and doing my best to calm the panic nestled inside me when a warm hand fell against my bare back. I jolted at the unexpected touch, swiftly glaring over my shoulder.

"It's only me, Seera." Landon's eyes pinched with concern from where he knelt behind me.

He never left my side.

My bodyguard tenderly extended his hand toward me. "Let's get you off this cold floor, and Reena can help you change. I'll be right outside to rejoin you whenever you are ready."

A small nod was the only reply I could force out as I placed my hand in his. Another shiver ran through me when our hands locked, and the warmth radiating off Landon chased away the chill settling deep within me.

He brushed a stray piece of hair from my face, dipping his head so we were at eye level. "I don't need to come back in if you don't want me to."

My gaze speared into his. "I want you to."

He smiled softly. "Then I will return when you are ready. Call me, and I will always come to your aid, my Queen."

He looked me over once more before assuming his position right outside my door.

"May I, Your Majesty?" Reena pattered toward me cautiously.

She gestured to the scrapes of fabric hanging off me, and I nodded, reaching out to hold onto her arm as she helped me climb out of what remained of my ruined dress. She moved quickly, discarding the gown and replacing it with one of my satin black robes. I barely had any energy left to tie the sash at my waist while she helped me remove my heels.

"I will draw you a warm bath," she said, disappearing into my bathing chambers, but I couldn't stop staring at the floor, at the buttons, at my quaking hands.

What just happened?

Tucking my hands into the pockets of my robe, I tried to rid myself of the heavy chill lingering in my bones, but I failed as shivers continued to rake down my body. I was still shaking when heat slowly trickled along my arms. My snakes slithered up them, their sharp gazes examining my face. Dante's scarlet eyes flickered with concern—an emotion he never felt toward me before. Ember curled around my neck, and the weight of her body settling against my chest had me closing my eyes.

Their comforting embrace soothed any lingering panic creeping through me, but nothing could rid me of the memories that tormented me mere moments ago.

My mother.

The tower.

The isolation.

The loneliness.

My eyes flew open as I felt warm liquid splash across my face. I swiped it away, marveling at the water coating my fingertips. More liquid ran down my cheeks, and my gaze shot to the ceiling in search of any leaks from the storm that tore through the queendom today. Yet, the wooden black ceiling was perfectly intact, the golden serpent design untouched.

My bare feet slapped against the floor as I ran to my vanity mirror.

Glassy eyes stared back at me, perfect teardrops of water leaking from them.

Impossible.

I gathered the liquid from my skin, staring down at it like it was a monster.

Brushing my wet hand against my robe, I squeezed my eyes shut as my mind raced at how this was feasible.

The bargain I made with the Serpent King stripped me of various emotions, such as happiness, joy, and love, but I also made him agree to take away the feelings which frequently cursed me as a mortal: anxiety, panic, fear, and even the ability to cry.

I stared back at my reflection, horror slicing through my veins like a sharp knife.

"Your bath is prepared, Your Majesty." Reena appeared in the reflection of the mirror, but she stilled upon seeing my disheveled appearance. "Seera, is everything okay?"

She sounded genuinely worried about me, but I didn't deserve such concern from my lady-in-waiting—especially since I was a monster who reveled in the bitter scent of her fear.

I swiped the last of my tears away, looking down at the water once more as it soaked into the pads of my fingertips.

My eyes locked back onto Reena's through the reflection, her mouth parting as it dawned on her that I was crying.

Reena hadn't seen me cry once in the ten years of her being in my service.

In fact, no one had—not since before the bargain.

"You may not speak a word about what you witnessed tonight to *anyone*. Do you understand?" My tone was as menacing as the beasts lurking in the Pit, making my lady-in-waiting promptly nod at me.

"I will not breathe a word about it to another soul, you have my word."

"Then you are dismissed for the night. Tell Landon he can

re-enter in half an hour's time." I waved my hand toward the door.

Reena nodded, and I watched as she fled from my chambers.

The moment the door shut behind her, I collapsed onto the ebony bench.

Gripping the sides of my vanity, I stared into the mirror, my stomach sinking as I realized I couldn't avoid the inevitable any longer.

As much as I dreaded returning to my homelands, I'd rather visit Ashivire a million times over than ever set foot in Morotis again.

But if anyone knew why my forbidden emotions broke free this evening, it would be the man I bargained them away to in the first place . . .

After nearly eighty years, it was time to pay the Serpent King a visit.

CHAPTER 7
A MUTUAL AGREEMENT

There was only one thing that brought me absolute solace when the darkness looming in my mind threatened to devour me whole: the fresh spill of blood.

Although my bath helped ease my nerves a bit, there was still a perpetual chill gnawing at my bones. So, since I had no executions lined up for at least another twenty-four hours, I oiled my favorite dagger instead. After dragging an oil-soaked cloth along the blade, I wiped it clean, gripping the handle as I twisted and examined it. The golden hilt gleamed from the flames flickering beside me, making me admire the twin serpents intertwining up it. Their mouths were stretched open around the base of the blade, and I resheathed the weapon, satisfied with my work.

This dagger would come in handy with my impending visit to the Serpent King.

My jaw ticked as I drifted toward the bar cart beside the roaring hearth. I desperately needed liquor to course down my throat and burn away these horrid nerves.

After so many years, the thought of seeing the menace who owned my soul made me want to rage. Quite frankly, I'd rather stick a dagger through my own chest than ever see that wretched man again.

I shook the image of piercing emerald eyes from my head, reaching for the black crystal decanter and not even bothering with a glass. The bottle was cool in my hands, providing a stark contrast to the liquid fire blazing down my throat as I shot back the amber liquor.

Gentle hissing pulled my attention toward the two velvet black chairs beside the fire, where Ember and Dante laid curled up together on one chair. A ghost of a smile tugged on my lips at the sight of my two vicious snakes practically purring in their sleep next to the cozy fire. They loved being anywhere warm, and I was convinced this was exactly how they looked when they disappeared from my side.

Two content, hissing babies.

However, my smile quickly dissolved when I realized I took them to the one place notorious for never seeing sunshine; instead, my lands were drenched in an eternal cloud of rainy nightmares.

A clicking sound made me glancing over my shoulder, my gaze roaming over Landon as he leaned against the door. His stare was a mixture of confusion and concentration, almost like I was a riddle he couldn't solve.

"Stop gawking at your queen and instead come have a drink with her." I gestured to the vacant chair next to me. "Sit."

Landon strode toward the chair, settling into the plush fabric as I poured him a glass of whiskey. I loved how he listened to my commands, how he always obeyed his queen.

He was such a good boy, and my excitement to play with him tonight reignited within me like the blazing flames warming my cheeks.

My bodyguard stretched out, crossing his ankles and making his black knee-high boots gleam against the firelight. Our eyes locked as I handed him the glass of amber liquor. Silence stretched between us, prompting me to arch a brow in a silent command to speak.

With a shake of his head, he finally replied. "Apologies, my Queen. Are you—" His lips pinched together, shaking his head as he took a sharp sip of his drink and tried again. "Are you okay?"

There was a note of hesitation laced in his question, and he bowed his head as if I was a lioness readying to snap his head between her jaws for asking such a thing.

"I'm fine." The lie easily slipped from my lips, one I'd told for decades.

Sometimes, lying was a necessity to make it through such a horrid existence.

I needed to lie to myself in hopes that I, too, would believe my false statements one day, because the numbness where my soul used to be grew achingly stronger with each passing day.

And if I was being honest for once in my life, I wasn't sure how much more of this miserable life I could take.

While I shot back another gulp of liquor, I silently cursed myself for not making the Serpent King take away my self-awareness during our bargain. I may not feel most emotions nor have a soul, but the consciousness of my actions would be my downfall.

Landon hummed thoughtfully, as if he could see behind the shield I raised high enough to keep everyone at an arm's length. My bodyguard always searched for the good in people, and I had a sneaking suspicion that was exactly what his icy blue eyes were doing in this moment as I glared down at him.

He knocked back the last of his drink, setting the glass onto the black crystal bar cart. As always, his attention drew back to his queen, and I met the intensity raging within his stare.

Slowly, I sauntered toward him, and his eyes darkened as they dipped to my hips. His breath hitched as I lifted one leg, then the other, and settled onto his lap. Since I was only wearing a silk robe after my bath, I felt every glorious inch of him harden beneath me.

His eyes dropped to where my robe fell open, exposing an ample amount of cleavage for his eyes to devour. He ran his fingers down my hair, ever so slightly brushing the back of them against the curve of my exposed breasts. My hips involuntarily moved, my legs tightening around his powerful thighs. The motion had Landon's eyes dipping between my legs, where my robe had fully parted, leaving me on display for him like his own personal feast.

"Fuck, you're beautiful." His eyes lingered over my center. When he dragged them slowly back to mine, they were darkened with desire.

With a coy smile, I leaned closer, the motion making my nipples harden from brushing against the roughness of his coat. I glanced down at the uniform I so carefully crafted for my bodyguard, at the gorgeous blood-red coat with my royal crest—marking him *mine* for all to see.

Fuck, I loved a man in a uniform.

My core tightened as I whispered against his lips. "Shall we get to our meeting?"

I jolted from Landon's feather-light touch as he dragged a finger right between my breasts, making me bite my lip to stifle the moan clawing up my throat.

He leaned closer, his lips brushing against my ear and the warmth of his breath caused a small shiver to ripple down my spine.

"Which matter of business should we attend to first, my

Queen? The part where I tell you about my trip to Ashivire and all the intel I gained for you, or . . ." His fingers trailed further down my body, until they were dipping into the wetness between my thighs. "The part where I get the honor of dropping to my knees to pleasure you until you can't bite back your moans for another second?"

Fuck, this might be the best decision I've made as queen.

From the moment I appointed Landon as my bodyguard, there had been an undeniable spark between us. What started as lingering stares from across the courtyard turned into being pulled tightly against his chest while he had me in a chokehold during our training sessions. The next day, we practiced escaping a regular choke, and I knew I was in trouble when he had his hands wrapped around my neck, and I enjoyed it. I craved him doing it again later that night in my chambers. Thus, one year ago, our mutual agreement commenced.

Considering I received intel *and* multiple orgasms out of our deal, I'd say it was a win-win situation.

"Hm, we could do both parts of our agreement at the same time," I said, beginning to loosen the buttons on his shirt.

Landon's laugh was deep and delicious, making my legs involuntarily clench together around him. He responded by grinding his hips, pulling a groan from me at how his hardness pressed against my center.

"How will I be able to give you my report if my mouth is wrapped around your clit?" he whispered into my ear.

My breath hitched as I imagined his lips sucking onto mine, right between my thighs where heat sparked to life like a wildfire. An annoyed hiss rattled through the air, signaling my snakes had taken the hint and finally left us alone to play with one another.

My bodyguard nipped at my ear, then slowly dragged his teeth down my neck, making it *very* clear what matter of business we were attending to first in tonight's meeting. I dipped my fingers between my legs, working myself as he peppered kisses along my neck and collarbone, but a low growl made me pause.

"Bad girl. That is my job, my Queen." He swatted my hand away, but I didn't have the chance to miss my fingers since his quickly replaced mine.

He worked my clit in circles, then dragged his fingers down my center. I moaned as he circled his thumb around my clit, then slipped another inside me. Simultaneously, he kneaded my breast with his other hand, leaning down to suck it into his mouth. I cried out in pleasure when he clamped his teeth around my nipple, causing a rush of pain to course through my body.

As if he was starved, he moved onto devouring my other nipple, his tongue languidly licking, then sucking hard enough to make an agonized hiss fly from my lips.

Landon knew how much I enjoyed pain, especially inside the bedroom.

The mix of pain and pleasure brought me the closest to feeling truly alive.

I craved the pain, if only to simply feel something— *anything.*

I nearly climaxed as his fingers and tongue worked in perfect unison to coax my pleasure from me, but I forced myself not to.

Not yet.

I didn't want to grant him the satisfaction of knowing he could get me off so easily, so I took a steadying breath, preparing to continue playing our little game.

"Is this the part where you fall to your knees for me?" My voice came out breathier than I'd intended, my control slipping with each caress of his tongue against my skin.

Instead of answering with words, Landon picked me up. His calloused hands dug into my ass as he spun us, lowering me onto the chair. I leaned into his lingering warmth as the most beautiful sight happened before me.

My bodyguard's knees crashed into the black fur rug, his eyes glued to mine as his lips crept closer to my center. He lingered there, dragging a finger along my wetness even though he knew his tongue was what I craved.

"Are you going to make your Queen beg?" Annoyance laced my words.

He tilted his head at me, his eyes gleaming with an animal-istic hunger, then lifted one of my legs over his shoulder, scooting even closer to my center so I could feel his breath against me.

His eyes speared into mine. "A queen never has to beg."

Then, he pressed his tongue against me with a brutal intensity, licking me with punishing strokes that had me tipping my head back in ecstasy. I cried out as I felt his mouth wrap around my clit, sucking *hard*.

My moans intertwined with the crackle of the flames, and I was sure nearly everyone in my palace knew of our mutual agreement from how I cried out when we were together in my quarters.

Fuck it.

They were going to gossip about their queen anyway, best to give them something good to talk about.

"*Gods,*" I moaned loudly as Landon slipped a finger in me, all the while sucking my clit.

However, my moan turned into a growl when his lips pulled away from mine, but he simply smiled at me with glis-tening lips.

"Careful, Your Majesty. Isn't it a crime to speak of any god besides the goddess before me?" He dragged his tongue across his bottom lip, enjoying my pleasure like it was the finest meal he'd ever consumed.

A small laugh escaped me at Landon's fearlessness to point out my mistake, and I couldn't help the thrill skittering across my skin at the way he defied me.

"You have two seconds to find a better use for that mouth besides challenging your Queen, or you may find yourself as the Pit's next victim."

His eyes widened, but not with fear. Not only did the games we play together stimulate me, but they excited Landon as well. His eyes shone with delight as he lifted my ass and wrapped his hands underneath me. His grip on me was punishing while he moved closer to my center.

"You're such a bad girl for threatening the one who is on his knees, ready to offer you a mind-shattering release." I shook with anticipation when he lightly pressed his lips against me, but the moment I tried to grind against his lips, he reared back.

"Landon," I growled.

He had the audacity to drop my leg from around his shoulder and stand. Although he was slowly backing away from me, his eyes never left mine. Anger buzzed through my veins at the prospect of being left high and dry until I saw his hands drop to his belt buckle. I settled into the chair, arching my back to sit up straight. My breasts bounced as I moved, and Landon bit his lip while he feverishly watched their hypnotic dance.

Slowly, my bodyguard unzipped his trousers, lowering them inch by inch in a tantalizing private show meant only for his queen. His pants fell around his ankles, then he worked his undergarments down his hips and legs, along with shucking off his boots.

Greeted with the sight of his beautiful hardness, my mouth

watered.

Landon was gorgeous, and my tongue darted out to wet my lips as need coursed through my every fiber.

My fingers dug into the velvet armrests—when I was with Landon, I constantly was struggling to keep a solid grip on my leash of control.

A serpentine smile spread across my lips when my bodyguard took off his coat and shirt. Once he was fully naked standing before me, I proceeded with the next command for my bodyguard.

Time to take back control.

"Crawl." I raised my chin, looking every bit like the queen I was, my spine straight, legs crossed, and arms resting on the plush armrests.

Landon's lips slightly quirked as he dropped to his knees and started to crawl toward my makeshift throne.

I couldn't contain the victorious smile sprawling across my red-painted lips.

Bringing men to their knees was intoxicating, but seeing them crawl sent a sickening pleasure through me.

Before I knew it, Landon was right before me. His large hands gripped my crossed knees, forcefully yanking them apart to put me fully on display for him.

"Who said you could close these gorgeous legs? Should I punish you for such defiance, my Queen?" He licked his lips as his gaze stayed latched onto my slick center.

"I'd have it no other way." I worked my sharp nails through his curly brown hair, twisting his locks as I brought his face to my lips.

This time, Landon's tongue was much more brutal, punishing, and completely relentless. He feasted on me like he was a prisoner in my dungeons, and I was his last supper. My grip on his hair tightened as my head lulled back, and I screamed out while I finally allowed myself to go over the edge. My body-guard didn't come up for air when my climax shattered every inch of my resolve, instead, he continued to punish me with his tongue.

Although I was already gasping for air, I craved *more*.

"Fuck me, Landon."

After another moment devouring, he pulled back and planted a kiss against my inner thigh. "With pleasure, my Queen." He whispered against my skin, swiftly moving to stand.

Landon leaned down, offering me a punishing kiss to taste my pleasure before yanking me up to spin me around. My knees dug into the soft fabric as my hands latched onto the top edges of the chair. Landon nudged my legs open wider with his knee, and I felt the tip of him push against my entrance. I cried out when he thrust into me with one brutal movement. The stretch his cock provided made me groan, and the room filled with the sound of my ass slapping against him as he pounded into me again and again. Right when I was close to falling over the edge, Landon purposely slowed down. I slammed my ass back against him, not allowing him to play one more game with me.

I was a queen on a mission, and that mission was to forget about the worrying events of tonight with one final mind shat-tering orgasm.

Finally, Landon caved like the good boy he was, slamming into me with a renewed intensity. When he wrapped my hair around his hand, intensely tugging on it while spanking me with his other hand, I lost it. The jolt of pain intertwined with his brutal thrusts, making me scream out as my climax tore through me.

My bodyguard called out my name as he found his own release, quickly pulling out of me as I never allowed him to finish inside me. Which is why I kept extra clothes stocked on the bar cart for this exact occasion—this was not the first time we found our mutual release in one another, nor would it be the last.

Our heavy breathing was the only sound filling the air besides the crackling of the fire, and I looked over my shoulder as I felt a light touch against the base of my spine. I watched Landon plant a soft kiss against my back, my gaze locking onto the way his cock slightly gleamed with our shared pleasure. It took what remained of my self-control not to grab and suck him into my mouth. I stood as quick as I could and grabbed my discarded robe, tying the sash around my waist while I gazed after Landon as he strolled across the room to tug on his pants.

He remained shirtless as he flopped onto the blood-red duvet, and I admired the view of my bodyguard in my bed while I poured us another round of drinks.

"I suppose we should get to the not-so-fun part of our mutual agreement." I sighed, moving to sit at the edge of the bed. I handed him the amber liquor as I crossed my legs and scooted closer toward him.

Landon leaned onto his elbows, happily accepting the liquor and taking a large swig of it before dropping onto his back again. He ran a hand through his hair, further messing up his curls from when I had my fingers tugging through them.

"I'm afraid I bring you bad news from my recent trip to Ashivire." He didn't meet my eye, instead continued to gaze at the canopy above my bed.

My grip tightened around the glass as I tried to hide my nerves, my gaze also roaming up to the sheer black canopy with golden serpents stitched throughout it.

The silence was deafening, leaving me to wonder if Landon would prove his loyalty and share the news Reena told me earlier about a new rebel group.

A flash of brown skin stole my attention away from the canopy, making me shift to look at my bodyguard as he stretched an arm behind his head for support. My gaze flickered over the way his muscles rippled from the movement, sparking another wave of desire between my thighs.

"There is another rebel group forming, with plans of a coup in the works." He glanced at me out of the corner of his eye. "They are gaining popularity with the residents of Ashivire, and their numbers grow every day."

I swallowed a breath of relief at my bodyguard's honesty, instead opting for my signature eye roll as I brought my glass to my lips and muttered into it. "Surprise, surprise, another coup." I shot back my liquor, shaking my head as the amber liquid burned my throat. "My people bore me."

I wished more than anything the alcohol soaking into my veins was the smell of the rebels while they begged for their pathetic lives.

Although this wasn't the first time my people attempted a coup during my reign, it irked me nonetheless.

I'd slit their throats for such a betrayal.

"While I don't doubt your abilities—" Landon hesitated when my eyes speared into his.

I arched a brow, silently warning him to tread carefully.

"It would be wise not to underestimate the people of Ashivire." He turned onto his side to face me, cradling his head in his hand. "Their lands were impacted the most by"—he glanced toward the door as he whispered—"your bargain."

I planted my empty glass on the duvet, stifling my growing irritation by picking at nails.

"I'm aware of what Ashivire used to look like, considering we both hail from those horrid lands." I glanced at Landon just in time to see the shadows of his past flicker in his eyes, temporarily dimming their brightness. "I know how the sands used to be tan, but now are pitch black as if the rolling dunes are filled with ash. I know how there used to be ample food growing at the base of the mountain leading to Morotis, yet there is now nothing but rodents and ashroot for them to feast on. I am aware, Landon, of what my bargain did to my homelands, but I had no idea such damaging effects would plague the mortal lands upon sealing my bargain with the Serpent King."

My bodyguard's eyes hardened at my mention of the king, but they softened when he looked at me. He shifted, moving closer to gently trail his fingers against my thigh.

"I don't blame you for what happened to our lands, my Queen. I am simply relaying what I heard from the residents of Ashivire during my trip."

I forced myself to take a deep breath, willing the anger rising within me to settle.

"Is there anything else you learned from your visit?"

His fingers stilled against my skin, his lips tightening into a white line as his gaze dropped.

For Serpent's Sake, what more could there be beyond an attempted coup?

"The rebel leaders plan to cross the border into Morotis in hopes to speak to the Serpent King face to face." His gaze roamed up to mine, and I smelt the notes of rain—of his sorrow—at the same time I saw it in his eyes.

It wasn't unusual for Landon to smell of rainfall; he constantly lived in a cloud of sorrow since the day I saved him in Ashivire. However, I caught the way it heightened in this moment as he looked at me.

"They want to gain the king's favor and use his aid to dethrone you, once and for all," he whispered, his words nearly swallowed by the roaring fire.

Rattling filled my ears as Ember and Dante descended my

arms, awoken by my growing anger. Dante glanced at me, a hint of irritation shining in his scarlet eyes at the fact I had accidentally awoken him from his slumber.

My people are attempting a coup, be nice.

I shot the command down our bond, and I swore Dante rolled his eyes. Without sparing me another glance, he slithered off the bed and to the chair closest to the fire, curling upon the top once more. An exasperated huff flew out of me at his attitude, but Ember's soft hissing drew my attention away from my sassy snake and toward my affectionate one. She nudged my cheek with her head, the gesture quickly steadying me.

I fixed my attention back on the problem presented to me.

"They won't make it to the Serpent King's lair without losing their minds first."

Landon rolled onto his back, drawing his hands together and steepling his fingers beneath his chin as he stared up at the canopy.

"While that may be true, it is too great a risk to take."

Ember hissed her agreement as she turned to meet my gaze. Her black eyes gleamed, and I closed my eyes tightly, knowing what that look meant.

Since Ember and I had a mental bond, she always knew what I was thinking. Thankfully, Landon couldn't read my mind. I was happy to keep him in the dark about my plans to continue onward to Morotis to see the Serpent King after I was done slaying the rebels. I considered telling him, but I didn't want to argue right now. My nerves were already fried from the constant panic clawing at my gut from the mere thought of visiting my homelands.

My stomach turned to knots, my mind swiftly fading into the haunting memories of my past.

My room was so dark, because my mother didn't deem me worthy enough of having a window.

The door rattled as its nine locks clicked into place.

Then, my mother's footsteps trailed down the hall, leaving me alone with nothing but my books to keep me company.

"Seera?" Landon's voice tore me from my grim thoughts. "What are you thinking about?" He reached for my hand, but I quickly scooted off the bed, working to swallow the knot of emotion gathering at the back of my throat.

"Nothing," I replied, avoiding his gaze and instead focusing on Ember as I lightly brushed a finger down her head.

Her gentle hisses and the crackling of the fire helped ease my nerves, but I faintly heard Landon's exasperated sigh as I approached the flames.

I knew what had to be done, but that didn't make me hate my plan any less.

"Tomorrow, we leave for Ashivire at first light."

CHAPTER 8
ASHIVIRE

"Do you miss me, my Queen?" Piercing emerald eyes gleamed with wicked delight, his full lips tugging into a delighted smile.

Against my better judgment, I reached for him.

Even after he broke my heart, I craved his touch.

But like every time I dreamed, he slipped between my fingers, disappearing into a plume of smoke. His eyes brightened as his body dissipated into the shadows.

The Serpent King vanished from sight, just like he did after our bargain was completed . . .

I woke with a gasp from the same vision that plagued me for the last seventy-five years. Wiping the sweat gathered atop my brow, I flopped back onto my pillows. The constant ticking of the clock pulled my focus, but I already knew what time it was before I glanced at it.

3 A.M.

He visited my dreams like clockwork every night at this hour.

Glancing at the silk pillows, I could almost see his looming figure lying beside me. I could nearly smell the intoxicating blend of scents that constantly clung to him—amber and musk, mixed with the most alluring hint of smoke.

Wetness spilled down my cheeks as I felt myself cry again for the second time in decades.

I cried for the life I dreamed of and never got the chance to experience.

I cried because I hated the man who broke my heart, leaving me to pick up the pieces all on my own.

I fell back asleep with tears spilling down my cheeks and thoughts of those emerald eyes that still haunted me after all these years.

Fine grains of black sand whipped against the window pane, encircling my carriage in darkness. A scoff escaped me at the irony that this was the way Ashivire greeted me after all this time, yet it was only fitting that darkness surrounded me while we crossed the border into my homelands—darkness and I had become great friends in these lands, after all.

A warm touch against my leg anchored me back to the carriage and away from the past. Just as I had decreed, we left for Ashivire at first light. My bodyguard and I shared one carriage, while my guards led the way ahead in another. Reena and a few servants followed behind us in a separate carriage.

Landon leaned toward me, and I could tell by the glint in his eyes what he was about to suggest.

"As much as this sandstorm sucks, we could pass the time in a more pleasurable way if you please, my Queen." His finger trailed up the slit in my gown, creeping closer to what he desired.

I swatted his hand away, looking down my nose at him.

"Unless you have more intel to share, keep your hands to yourself."

Landon's lips twitched with amusement, but he raised his hands in surrender. Other men would burn with humiliation at such a rejection, but my bodyguard thrived on the chase.

We both glanced out the window, the grains of sand flicking against the glass, the only sound filling the growing silence between us. It was still hard to believe the black sand once used to be a smooth, tan shade, marveled at by many who came from far and wide to see the dunes and creeks lining the mountainside.

What was once a hidden oasis was now a desolate desert of destruction and ash.

I dug my fingers into the plush, blood-red seat of the carriage as I tried my best to keep my mind from wandering to the past. Yet, my attempts were futile, for I was pelted by the memories like the sand pelting against my carriage.

The tower.

A metal door.

Nine locks.

My mother's footsteps walking away.

I was never once allowed to feel the sun kiss my cheeks or dance in the creek beds flowing at the base of the mountain.

No, I spent my mortal life in Ashivire surrounded by darkness, so it wasn't the sandstorm rattling the carriage that scared me, but the memories that came rushing back.

My eyes burned as I worked to swallow emotion begging for release.

I'd slit my own throat before crying two days in a row.

I let the memories of the past fade as I tore my gaze from the window. Much to my surprise, Landon wasn't staring at the sandstorm. Instead, he was watching me with that look he gave me the other night, as if I were a puzzle he desperately wanted to solve.

I narrowed my eyes at him. "What?"

He narrowed his eyes right back. "What happened in your room the other night?"

"Which part? The part where you were on your knees for me or the part where I made you crawl?" My lips tipped into a wicked smile as I adjusted my dress and crossed my legs.

Landon crossed his arms over his chest, and the way his muscles strained beneath his cotton midnight-blue shirt stole my focus . . . apparently, for long enough that my bodyguard felt the need to clear his throat to capture my attention once again.

"Seera, you know what I am talking about. Tell me what happened when you were writhing on your bedroom floor, unable to breathe." No amusement shone in his eyes. Instead, a heavy wrinkle dipped between his brows.

"Talking about our feelings was not a part of our agreement." I picked at my nails, surveying him through lowered lashes.

"It is when it is imperative for me to be aware of. Shall I remind you, I am your bodyguard. If something is going on with your overall well-being, I need to know so I can prepare on how to better protect you."

Landon's overprotectiveness was insufferable at times, causing me to groan and shift my gaze back to the sand still drumming against the window.

"I can protect myself."

"Why am I here then?" His tone was sharper than usual, making me turn back to him.

There was something peculiar shining in his eyes, so I sniffed the air to better detect what emotion my bodyguard was feeling—the overwhelming smell of night-blooming jasmine made my nose itchy.

Landon was *hurt* over my crass comment.

Silence stretched between us while I struggled to find the right words to correct my mishap.

Making people feel better was not my specialty, and my bodyguard's eyes burning straight into me and through the darkness shrouding the carriage was not helping.

I lifted my eyes to the black steel ceiling of the enclosed space, in an effort to buy myself time on what to say to appease Landon. Since the assassination attempt, I upgraded my carriages from a simple canvas material to military-grade steel. The traitor who tried to kill me with a flaming arrow got what was coming to him for striving to assassinate the queen: three weeks in my dungeons. I enjoyed taking my time carving up every piece of the hateful man before feeding what was left of him to the beasts in the Pit.

The creaking of the carriage bench pierced the silence, breaking my thoughts of bloodshed to see Landon fitfully shifting back and forth across from me.

Just to gather a moment of peace from his restlessness, I forced myself to attempt to say something nice.

"Landon, you are here for an extra level of protection. Although my people can't kill me with ordinary weapons, it is annoying nonetheless to be speared by a flaming arrow." Landon rolled his eyes, but began to relax a little as I leaned closer. "And your intel as my secret spymaster has proven to be invaluable."

His tense shoulders dropped an inch with the small bits of reassurance, but there were still remnants of hurt lingering in his eyes. Something in my chest cracked at the fact I was the one who dimmed his usually beautiful, bright eyes.

"I may not be able to show you my appreciation as one

normally would, but I notice your efforts and all you do for me." I forced a coy smile to my lips. "And I don't let just anyone between my legs . . . I think that says enough of how I feel about you."

Landon's lips parted, his eyes widening at the prospect of me aimed to make him feel better. My lips pulled into a frown as the realization hit me at the same time.

I've never cared about the feelings of those I hurt before, so why did I now?

"All clear!" one of my guards yelled, and a moment later, our carriage lurched forward, causing me to jolt off the seat.

Strong arms gripped mine, stopping me from smashing my face into the bench.

I glanced up and was met with eyes as beautiful as a clear desert sky.

"And apparently you are here to save me from breaking my nose on my carriage bench." We were close enough that I could feel his breath slip against my lips.

"I'll always save you, my Queen." His lips brushed mine as he spoke, and heat flared within me when his eyes dipped to my lips.

How odd, for I felt this spark low in my gut . . . I usually felt my desire for Landon solely right between my legs.

Very odd indeed.

Before I could do something I'd later regret, Landon pulled away first, helping me back onto my side of the carriage. I sighed at the instant loss of his warm breath against my lips, and at my body's strange reaction to the moment that just transpired between us.

With a shake of my head, I looked out the window in hopes of concealing my frustration.

Stolen kisses were not a part of our agreement, and it would do us no good to get distracted right now.

I was not in Ashivire for a romantic getaway—I was here to slaughter some rebels.

Two happy hisses filled the air, and I felt like I could breathe a little easier as Ember and Dante spiraled down my arms. They must have woken from the sliver of sunlight piercing through the window, and the sight of them extending their heads towards the warmth made the corners of my lips twitch into a small smile. I swore it looked like Ember was smiling up at the sun, the sight was so enduring I felt *something* spread inside that empty void in my chest—right where my soul used to be.

My hand flew to my sternum, my breath coming in short pants at the foreign feeling.

"Seera, are you alright?" Landon braced a hand against my knee.

I squeezed my eyes tightly shut. "Fine—I'm fine." I forced the words out between sharp rasps as I forced myself to breathe through the pain now piercing through me.

It was as if the bargain recognized I shouldn't have the ability to feel anything beyond anger, and I was being punished for doing so.

This was *not* the type of pain I found pleasure in.

An involuntary groan slipped past my lips, and I hinged at the waist, dropping my head between my legs as I tried to breathe through the agony curling inside me.

"You do not look fine. Tell me what is happening." Landon's voice pitched higher in concern as he rubbed my back with soothing circles.

Typically, I'd shove him off for offering such a comforting gesture, but it felt too good to consider doing so right now. I found my breathing evening out from his soft touch, enough that I could sit straight and lean my head against the padded wall.

"I don't know what is going on with me." I inhaled deeply, letting my eyes shut.

I felt braver expanding on my thoughts when I didn't have to stare into my bodyguard's worried eyes.

"Ever since dinner with my mother"—*For Serpent's Sake*—"with Nedra, I've felt . . . different."

"Different how?" Landon asked, his voice starting to even out into its normal comforting timber.

I gently rubbed my pounding temples while deciding how much I wanted to reveal about my past. Landon wasn't alive when I made my bargain, so he only knows of the rumors my people spread through my lands, or what I choose to share with him—which wasn't much.

So, I decided to offer him part of my truth.

"My emotions changed when I made the bargain with the Serpent King. I lost the ability to feel certain emotions, but the other night I felt things I haven't since before my bargain."

I cracked an eye open, only to see Landon rubbing his jaw.

"These emotions you lost . . . do you think they will *all* return to you?" He glanced at me with an odd expression I couldn't decipher.

With a discreet inhale, I identified the floral scent with ease, my lip curling at the putrid scent.

Hope.

I forced my disgust down, donning my mask of indifference as I met Landon's hopeful stare.

I stared at him without an ounce of remorse. "No, I don't think my emotions will come back, and I don't wish for them to return even if they could."

His face drooped with disappointment, but he quickly shook the emotions away, turning his gaze to the rolling black dunes.

After Landon didn't say anything else, I followed his lead

and watched my homelands pass by. The vast dunes began to fade into the distance as the capital city of Ashivire came into view, if one could even call Veranda a city—it looked more like a small town full of canvas tents and wooden carts, with not even one solid building still standing.

Only rubble remained of the once glorious city that stood here before my bargain.

The carriage came to a startling halt, and I was quickly blinded by a burst of light. With a hand shielding my eyes, my vision slowly swam back to me to see that one of my imbecile guards yanked open the carriage door without any warning.

I most definitely would be firing him the moment we got back to the Queendom of Phantamos.

The metal of the carriage creaked, signaling Landon was exiting first, as was customary. Smoothing the bodice of my gown and fluffing my hair, I prepared myself as best as I could for what I would face beyond this door.

I've only returned to Ashivire once since escaping seventy-five years prior, and I swore never to return again.

Unfortunately, I was a notorious liar.

My hand slightly trembled as I placed it in my bodyguard's and stepped into the bright light.

Landon and Reena think I came back to Ashivire simply to stop the rebel group, but there was more to my plans than I had shared.

As the carriage rolled away, I glanced over my shoulder, toward the sole mountain towering high into the sky on the horizon. It was carved out of pure obsidian stone, dark clouds rumbling around the peak, creating a stark contrast to the clear blue skies gathered along the base of the mountain. My sharp eyesight lingered at the very tip of the peak, where I knew the opening of the caves was—Morotis, the caves of doom and death.

A chill raced down my spine at the thought of the Serpent King's realm, but I forced myself to look away from my past and toward the city awaiting me.

The people staring back at me had weathered and wrinkled skin, proof the brutal sun in these lands was unforgiving. They wore linen cloths tied around the bottom half of their faces to aid against the frequent sandstorms, and my lips pursed at how dirty they all looked while gawking at their queen's arrival.

I threw a sharp smile at the residents of Veranda, and my snakes hissed ferociously as they assessed the peasants. One man with a cane nearly jumped out of his skin as my snakes hissed, quickly hobbling behind a cart to seek refuge. The crowd dispersed when they, too, realized their deadly mistake at blatantly staring at me.

"This way, my Queen." Landon led me through the small town and toward the largest tent lying at the edge of the ruins.

He held the cream linen open for me, but another chill licked up my spine, prompting me to stop on the threshold. It was almost as if there was a magnet between me and the place beckoning to me as I turned toward the mountain I could never forget. My eyes cut back to the daunting summit looming in the distance.

By tomorrow, the rebel group would die by my hand, and I would walk through those caves once again. My jaw tightened at the thought, but I forced myself to remember how far I've come.

I was no longer the powerless, broken, mortal girl I was when I first stumbled through those caves on my twenty-fifth birthday.

I was a monster.

I was the Serpent Queen.

CHAPTER 9
MEMORY LANE

Ashroot soup was disgusting.

How the hell did the people of Ashivire eat such a ghastly dish?

The soup soured in my stomach as I remembered I was the reason they had to dine on this dreadful meal. I pushed away my bowl, rising from the plain wooden table to make my way toward the amber liquor calling my name from across the room. The glass bottle was warm, courtesy of the brazier blazing with charcoal. Yet another reason not to visit this sorrowful place—I couldn't have a proper fire lit inside my tent.

My lip curled with disdain as I swigged the liquor straight out of the bottle. After the whiskey burned any remaining hints of ashroot soup from my tastebuds, I dragged the decanter away from my lips.

A burst of cool desert air slapped against my back, making my spine stiffen at the possibility of someone entering my tent uninvited. I spun around, but the tension eased from my body when only Landon entered, ducking his head as the canvas fluttered in the wind.

I scoffed when I saw he, too, was holding a bottle of whiskey. The linen flapped as it closed, leaving Landon and I staring at each other, each with a full bottle of liquor in tow.

"Ashroot soup is terrible." My bodyguard dramatically shivered at the mention of Ashivire's signature dish.

I nearly laughed, but I stopped myself by quickly bringing the bottle to my lips and muttering around it, "Tell me about it."

After another delightful gulp, I set the bottle back on the table and moved to the makeshift bed to fetch my blood-red cloak.

"Going somewhere?" Out of the corner of my eye, I saw Landon subconsciously move his free hand to the hilt of the sword hanging against his hip.

"For a walk." I worked to clasp the golden broach of my royal crest around my neck.

"It is not safe, my Queen."

A scoff tumbled out of me. "Ashivire is a wasteland. Who is going to harm me when they don't even have enough sustenance in their bodies to walk a few feet without fainting? I can handle myself against the scarce residents remaining in these ruins."

He pursed his lips, and I *knew* that look.

He was going to put up a fight, and I didn't want to deal with arguing.

"Come walk with me if you'd like," I shrugged.

His lips parted, shock spreading across his features from my offer.

I rolled my eyes and breezed past my bodyguard, yet, when our shoulders brushed, I lingered next to him. We glanced sideways at each other, standing so close together I could smell the whiskey wafting off his breath and the trickle of rain seeping off his skin.

His eyes darted to my blood-red lips, his hand flexing at his side as if he wanted to wrap it around my waist and tug me against him. I leaned in, waiting for the moment when his eyes fluttered closed and his lips. Then, I snatched the bottle of liquor straight from his hands and made off like a bandit.

I was parting the flap of the tent open when I heard his inviting chuckle and the scoff of his boots trailing behind me.

Wearing a satisfied smirk, I slipped out of the tent and into the darkness.

I didn't make it very far up the dune before shucking off my stilettos.

The feeling of cool grains of sand between my toes was actually rather nice, grounding me to the lands I once fled from.

How different I am from the girl I was when I lived here.

"What are you thinking about?" Landon climbed beside me, his breathing steady, as if we weren't scaling a massive hill.

"I'm thinking about how I need to partake in more cardio when we return home," I panted between steps.

He rolled his eyes toward the stars twinkling high above. "I've been trying to get you to join me on my morning runs for years now."

I frowned at such an absurd thought. "It is not ideal to run in heels."

"Crazy idea here, but have you considered running in literally any other footwear?"

I halted, and my bodyguard followed suit.

"Landon, I don't even remove my heels when we fuck. Why would you think I'd do so for running?" I scoffed, resuming my trek while doing my best to hide my labored breathing.

His deep chuckle chased after me like the wind whipping our hair into a wild frenzy. "You really are unlike anyone I've ever met."

I was so out of breath that all I could do was grunt in reply as we finally crested the top of the dune. As Landon spread out a blood-red blanket atop the soft black sand, I took a few moments to steady my breathing.

"I didn't know you brought that." I tilted my chin at the fabric, and he tossed me a charming smile over his shoulder as he finished straightening the wool cloth.

"I'm always prepared for anything you throw at me."

I bit my lip, stopping myself from smiling at how well my bodyguard knew me.

He was one of the few people I'd allowed, in my terms, relatively close to me, yet I still kept him at an arm's distance. But that was for both of our best interests.

I was incapable of feeling, of experiencing, emotions like love.

I was doing him a favor by building a stone wall between us, for no one wanted to fall for a monster like me.

After some final adjustments, Landon sprang to his feet and gestured for me to sit. He offered me a hand, and I reveled in the warmth that kissed my palm as our hands braced. Our eyes locked for a split second before I lowered myself onto the blanket, tossing my heels to the side. Landon gently sat beside me while I ran my hands through the black sand over and over.

I did this.

I caused these lands to forever be changed.

"I know that look, Seera." Landon pulled the glass bottle of liquor from the breast pocket of his coat, nudging it at me with a playful smile spreading across his lips. "Perhaps, this will help?"

I couldn't help the small twitch of my lips, but it dissolved as soon as my fingers latched around the bottle, washing away all hints of joy from my face with each burning swig.

"Easy now, save some for me." Landon reached for the liquor, and I begrudgingly handed it over.

The silent desert air stretched between us while we took turns sharing the beverage. Our gazes were trained on the horizon—on the sparse lights shining down where Veranda laid. As my eyes roamed past the ruined city, I was greeted with complete darkness. What once was a land filled with thousands now consisted of maybe a measly hundred people, if that.

My immortal abilities were both a blessing and a curse in this moment, for I couldn't stop myself from gazing toward that damn onyx stone mountain jutting into the sky.

"You're quiet, for once." Landon said, nudging my shoulder.

Maybe it was the liquor, but I laughed at his remark. My bodyguard arched a brow at me and smiled, clearly satisfied by my reaction.

"Tell me what you're thinking about, Seera. And please do me a favor and spare me the bullshit this time. I want to know what *really* is racing through that beautifully wicked mind of yours." He stared at me with a mixture of wonder and that same quizzical look he reserved only for me.

My lips curved into a rather soft smile, and I reveled at how I actually enjoyed the way Landon spoke to me bluntly.

"You want to know what I'm thinking about?"

He leaned in, close enough for me to see the stars reflecting within his glassy eyes.

"Spare no detail, my Queen." He snatched the bottle of

liquor from my grip, and I slapped his shoulder as he chuckled against the bottle and passionately drank.

This man was something else, pulling the exact move I did to him earlier, and I hated how it felt strangely *pleasant* to be playful with my bodyguard. The void in my chest warmed a little, making me rub a finger against my cloak, wishing the simple motion could cease the warmness spreading through me.

"I'm waiting," Landon sang, and I waved at him to shush.

For the second time today, I decided to offer a piece of truth to the man who stood by my side during my reign as the Serpent Queen.

"I'm thinking about how I haven't returned to these lands since the day I met you."

My words instantly washed the smile off Landon's face, and I nearly regretted them when a deep wrinkle knitted between his brows. He tore his gaze from my eyes, glancing off into the blackness.

I chewed on my lip as only the whistle of a light wind responded to my dark statement.

If it wasn't for my impeccable hearing, I would have missed when Landon spoke next, in a tone so soft it was nearly swallowed by the wind.

"The day we met was both the worst and best day of my life." He glanced at me, and I was greeted with the fresh smell of rainfall dripping off his skin.

"Landon . . ." My tone was unusually gentle, but he cut me off by raising his hand.

"I've wanted to say this to you since the day we met." He glanced sideways at me again, uncertainty shining in his eyes. "May I speak freely?"

Every part of me knew I should say no, but my curiosity burned as brightly as the stars. So, I offered him a small nod.

His raised brows were the only signs of shock he displayed before continuing on.

"You've seen me at my worst, Seera. I was on death's door the day you stumbled along the ruins that were my family home. I'll never forget when I saw you through the window —you looked like a goddess with the way your hair whipped around you from trudging along on horseback with your guards . . . I still don't understand why you stopped that day."

I glanced at my nails, the familiar color sparking another truth to spill from my lips. "I saw the trail of blood and was intrigued."

He groaned at my morbid words but carried on. "You could have left me strung up in the middle of my house, bleeding to death from the whips those men cracked against my skin over and *over* again."

My shoulders tensed as my gaze drifted to his neck, to the white scars peeking out from beneath his cloak. Fury spread through my veins but, as I glanced at his gorgeous face, I was yet again left to wonder why they never scarred his face.

"However, there is one thing I still can't figure out." He scanned my eyes, searching for the answer to a question that was about to change everything. "Why didn't you leave me to die like my family did?"

I sucked in a sharp breath.

I always knew my bodyguard would ask me this question one day, but I never wanted to face the reality of why I actually saved him.

Perhaps, it was all the liquor sloshing around in my stomach or the newfound emotions plaguing my mind, but I decided to answer him truthfully for the fourth time today.

"When I saw you in that small, dilapidated home, tied up, with rivers of blood streaming down your chest, your back, your arms . . ." I shook the memory from my mind, trying to steady my rapid breathing from the anger brewing in my core.

Staring deep into Landon's eyes, I allowed myself to share a part of me I locked away from the rest of the world. "When I saw you all alone, I thought of how I prayed every night as a mortal for someone to save me from the hell that was my life."

He moved closer, bracing his hand against my thigh. His warmth seeped into my skin, and I glanced down to see my body trembling.

When did I start shaking?

Softly, I dragged a finger over my bodyguard's hand. "Seeing you like that . . . I killed hundreds of people before meeting you and was never affected by their battered bodies, but when I saw yours—" Slowly, I dragged my eyes to meet Landon's gaze. Silver lined his eyes, and, a moment later, a tear broke free to stream down his face.

As I continued, I swiped it away. "Maybe I saved you because I wished someone did the same for me all those years ago. I know I should regret it, but I don't. Saving you is one of the only good things I've done since becoming the Serpent Queen."

His eyes crinkled as his lips tugged into a pained smile, tears freely flowing out of my bodyguard. I didn't think it was possible for his eyes to burn an even more vibrant blue, but between the tears pooling in them and the stars reflecting off the glassy surface, I marveled at how gorgeous Landon was.

Not only was he beautiful to look at, but he had one of the purest souls I'd ever come across. He could be strong when I needed him, but he also felt so deeply.

He reminded me of who I once was.

The girl I hated to think about today.

Warmth flooded across my cheeks, prompting Landon to caress my face. When he pulled his hand away, he stared at the tears coating his fingertips in awe. He glanced between the tears and myself with a stricken expression. I touched my face, my suspicions confirmed as wetness kissed my fingers.

For Serpent's Sake, I was crying again.

With a groan, I flopped onto my back, covering my face with my hands.

"What is happening to me?" I muffled while straining to swallow my emotions.

Ever so tenderly, Landon grasped my hands, tearing them off my face. He leaned over me, dropping his face so close I was sure he was going to kiss me. But instead of his lips crashing into mine, they gently pressed against my tears, savoring each one as if they were the only water left in the desert around us.

I let out a shaky breath at the extremely intimate gesture, but somehow, with each feather soft press of his lips against my flushed skin, I relaxed into the sand.

I should push him away. I should stop him from scaling the wall I'd built between us for all these years, but my resolve crumbled each time he savored my tears like they were something to not be ashamed of.

Like it was okay to *feel*.

Slowly, his lips trailed lower, hovering over mine, but he hesitated.

We didn't share moments like this. If we kissed right now, *truly* kissed, we would be crossing a line that would be nearly impossible to come back from.

I was about to shove him away when the smell of a fresh rainstorm poured down my throat. Although Landon always had a cloud of sadness lingering around him, this felt different. It was like a wild storm—destructive and deadly.

I convinced myself what I did next was because I couldn't stand to choke on his misery for another moment, not because I needed it as badly as he did.

My lips wrapped around his as I tugged him against me, fusing our bodies into one. I dug my fingers into the soft velvet of his coat while his lips moved against mine. Our kisses were soft at first, until they turned wild, almost like my lips were the only antidote to his perpetual sorrow.

I rolled him onto his back, never letting our lips stray as I straddled my bodyguard. His fingers dug into my thighs while we devoured each other for what felt like hours.

Our bodies worked in harmony, moving as one in an endless dance of despair.

I loosened his belt, allowing Landon to free himself as I raised my gown and slipped onto his hardness. My head lolled back with pleasure, allowing me to marvel at the beauty of the desert, at the stars shining above as I grinded against him.

However, my brows tugged together when I saw a golden glimmer in the sky blaze brighter.

It was as if the star was winking down at us, at the queen without a soul and the man with a fractured one.

CHAPTER 10
DRESSED TO KILL

A gentle hiss had my eyes peeling open, but the brightness that greeted me had me swiftly slamming them shut once more. I smothered a pillow over my face, my head pounding from all the liquor I consumed last night. Sadly, I couldn't ignore the hissing that became as violent as my rule as queen.

"I'm up, stop your whining," I groaned, throwing the pillow over my face in the direction of the annoying noise.

I propped myself up onto my elbows, watching the pillow land rather close to where Dante laid coiled up at the end of the bed. His crimson eyes flared as he glared at me.

Sometimes he stared at me like a disappointed father witnessing their unruly daughter coming home drunk for the first time. At least that's what I imagined what a father's reaction would be, since I grew up without one.

I didn't even know his name. My mother didn't deem that information important enough to share with me.

"Where is your sister?" I glanced around the tent with only one eye cracked open in search of Ember.

Dante didn't respond, instead opting to ignore me as he slithered out of the tent. With a rather dramatic flick of his tail, he kept the flap open a moment longer, causing a blinding stream of sunlight to spear directly into my eyes. A hiss burst from me as I shielded my face with a hand.

Rude ass snake.

Once the linen sealed shut and black spots were no longer clouding my vision, I forced myself to crawl out of bed, gulping the water left on the makeshift bar cart.

"Well, would you look at that, the Queen has risen!" Reena's chipper voice pierced my ears.

I made sure to let her know how I felt about her cheery tone by tossing a sharp glare at her over my shoulder.

My lady-in-waiting simply laughed as she straightened up my bed, but she paused upon hearing my gasp.

I was horrified when I caught my reflection in the floor-length mirror on the opposite side of the tent. I moved closer, closely examining the kohl smudged beneath my eyes, and the red lipstick smeared around my lips.

I looked like I was a part of the fucking traveling circus that passed through my queendom every year.

"*For Serpent's Sake,*" I muttered, dragging a hand down my face as if it could fix my disheveled reflection.

If there was one thing I hated more than feelings, it was looking a mess.

My appearance was my mask, my persona—it anchored me to who I was as the Serpent Queen and helped push me further away from the broken, mortal girl I once was.

Reena tutted as she came behind me. "Let's get you cleaned up."

She motioned to the wooden partition, and I went behind the screen to clean myself with the warm washcloth she handed over to me.

"What would you like to wear today, Your Majesty?" Her voice floated over the partition as I considered her request.

"Did you bring my black leathers?"

Something slapped against the wooden partition, prompting me to glance behind myself to see my favorite fighting outfit now hanging over the divider.

"I brought two, considering what you came here to do . . . I figured you might need a backup, should the first ones get ruined."

"You know me so well." I clutched my hand against my chest, even though I knew Reena couldn't see me.

She snorted, and the sounds of her skirts whipping around rustled as she no doubt hurried to straighten up the rest of my tent as I dressed. The promise of today's bloodshed had me swiftly hopping into my leather pants and shimmying into my matching top.

I had to admit, I was slightly impressed. Reena must have had the tailor work overtime to create this garment in time for our trip. Instead of my normal long-sleeve leathers, this version was sleeveless and better suited for Ashivire's desert climate. I held the top in place as I moved out from behind the partition and back in front of the floor-length mirror so my lady-in-waiting could lace up the corset.

As Reena took her place behind me and worked to tighten the strings, I admired how the leather hugged each and every one of my curves.

I loved executing traitors, and I *especially* loved looking ravishing while doing so.

Oh, yes. Today was going to be a marvelous day indeed.

I was swiping my preferred shade of lipstick across my lips when Reena's arm shot up in the reflection, some horrid brown boots dangling from her hands.

"What the fuck are those?" The lipstick stilled mid swipe, a frown quickly flowing onto my face.

Her hands started to sway with uncertainty. "I thought you were going to the mountain today?"

"I am, but I refuse to wear whatever the fuck those monstrosities are." I scrunched my nose at the abominable boots my lady-in-waiting cradled in her arms.

"You couldn't have the tailor make some custom heeled fighting boots? Or at the very least, pretty leather ones? Honestly, Reena, what in all the lands were you thinking, presenting those *things* to me?" I resumed applying my lipstick, then moved on to swiping some fresh kohl along my eyes.

"They are pretty hideous . . ." she mused, making me sneak a sideways glance at her through the mirror. Her lips were curled with disgust. "Apologies, my Queen. I shall have a custom pair made for you when we return to the Queendom of Phantamos."

With that, she dropped the sad excuse for footwear onto the floor.

"As long as they have a heel, I may consider forgiving you for suggesting I wear *those*." I glared one more time at the brown, chunky boots, a shiver coursing down my spine at how revolting they truly were.

Reena brought my attention back to gaze at my reflection as she latched my custom holster around my hips. The golden hilts of my daggers sparkled from the fresh polishing I did right before our trip, a ritual I always performed before entering battle.

She positioned twin blades to hang from my hips, along with a slightly shorter dagger that was safely secured at the back of my waistband. She handed me additional holsters, and I swiftly attached them around each of my thighs, then placed a sharp dagger into each one.

After my weapons were secure, I straightened, my gaze catching onto the head of my serpent tattoo, which peeked out from between my breasts thanks to the sharp V-cut of my top.

Reena presented a pair of stilettos before me, and a vicious smirk spread across my face at the pair she picked out. Wickedly sharp, gold spikes gleamed along each skinny heel, brightening as a stream of light flashed against them from someone entering the tent.

While I stepped into my heels, my bodyguard's reflection came into view as he, too, assumed his position behind me.

My blood-red lips curved into a sinful smile as I looked at him through the mirror.

"Shall we get to today's festivities?"

CHAPTER II
A TASTE OF BLOOD

I barely registered the carriage rolling away as it creaked back down the dirt path and back toward Veranda. I only had eyes for the looming mountain towering before me.

The sun blinded me as my gaze rose toward the onyx peak, but two happy hisses anchored me back to the task at hand.

My snakes' weight against my arms and shoulders reminded me of why I was here, while they enjoyed basking in Ashivire's stifling heat. Even though I was eager to slay some rebels, I allowed Ember and Dante to enjoy the sun for a few more moments.

Considering they were going to help me kill some traitors, it was the least I could reward them with.

"You are certain the rebels will make their ascent to Morotis today?" I glanced sideways at Landon while stroking a finger along Ember's scales.

He gave me an irritated look, the one he reserved for whenever I doubted him.

For Serpent's Sake, what was wrong with me?

My bodyguard's voice brought me back to scanning the

trails instead of reveling in his minute quirks. "That is what I gathered from my trip—they are around here somewhere."

There were only two pathways leading to Morotis: one was an easier trek, but it took double the amount of time to ascend its winding curves. Although the other pathway was faster, the climb was extremely steep and much more difficult. My gaze drew toward the fresh coat of dirt lingering along that trail. I moved closer, and knelt down, examining it. It made sense that the rebels would take the harder route, for they wanted to speak to the Serpent King as soon as possible.

"They went this way," I said, showing my bodyguard what I'd found.

Landon nodded his clear agreement. "Your tracking skills are impressive."

I smirked at him. "Of course they are. Now, let's go."

I took off down the path, the dirt trail swiftly turning to stone with each grueling step up the mountain. My bodyguard quickly caught up with me, moving to flank my right side. Our footsteps were light and in sync as we ascended the path, bracing ourselves for the battle ahead.

This was not the first time Landon and I would fight together, just the two of us, nor would it be the last.

Up and up we went, blisters forming as the steep climb carried us further away from the clear blue skies and into a sheet of grey. Although my immortal healing quickly stitched my torn skin back together, the vicious cycle repeated itself with every daunting step.

I silently cursed myself for my unwavering love to kill in heels.

Landon's voice broke the silence, offering a distraction from my bothersome feet.

"Did you enjoy last night?" He glanced out of the corner of his eye at me.

"Hm?"

He gave me that *look* again. "Last night, under the stars? You truly have nothing to say about it?"

"What is there to say? I drank a ton of liquor. Quite frankly, I don't even remember how I got back to my tent."

There was a heavy pause before Landon let out a strained whisper.

"I carried you."

My steps nearly faltered, but I caught myself and continued onward.

"You fell asleep in my arms after . . ." His eyes shot to the gloomy sky. "After you rode me." Letting out an exasperated sigh, he fully turned to face me. "You honestly don't remember?"

I hummed while I searched through the drunken fog clouding my brain from remembering the events of last night.

Glimpses of stars and soft kisses that turned wild.

Soft lips upon my cheeks . . .

Did Landon really kiss away my tears?

I swallowed the discomfort knotting in my throat at how vulnerable I allowed myself to be around my bodyguard in my drunken stupor.

However, one night of vulnerability couldn't undo the years of brutality I presided over as the Serpent Queen.

There was no way I would admit my feelings in the light of the day, let alone sober, so I stopped and stared at him with a bored look of indifference.

"No, I don't remember," I offered, but my lie didn't roll off my tongue as easily as all others did. Instead, it left a rather sour taste in my mouth.

His brows knitted as his eyes fell, never returning to meet mine for the rest of our trek. We shared no more words either. Instead, I was forced to inhale Landon's annoyance the entire time, and something else, something I couldn't easily decipher . . .

It was better this way, to keep a divide between us.

I was not meant to live a life of stolen kisses underneath the stars.

I was meant to live a life of bloodshed and destruction.

Boots crunching against gravel sounded ahead, and I slammed my hand against Landon's chest, halting him. My bodyguard may have years of training in combat, but my immortal senses would always surpass his abilities.

Landon eyed me as I closed my eyes to zone in on the footsteps—one, two, three, four, five. I raised a hand at Landon, and he nodded in understanding. The final thing to do was send a command through the bond to my snakes, who were still clinging to my arms like a second skin.

Five around the bend. Ready to have some fun?

Excited hisses rang through my head, making me smirk at my snakes. Before we rounded the last bend separating us from the rebels, Dante lunged off my arm and slithered along the onyx stone mountain. His dark body blended in seamlessly with the landscape, and I steadied my hand onto the hilts of my daggers, allowing a sense of calm to wash over me.

We had the upper hand, for I was most likely the only one to ever ascend this mountain.

With Landon and my serpents beside me, I was unstoppable.

I smelt the rebels' sweat a moment before I saw them, their exhausted bodies trudging slowly as they panted for air.

For Serpent's Sake, was it too hard to wish for somewhat of a challenge?

Landon's hand drifted to the hilt of his sword, his tell he was ready for the fight to come.

It was showtime.

"What do we have here?" I purred, making the group jump.

The men quickly whirled toward us, simultaneously drawing their weapons. Only a few feet separated my bodyguard and I from the traitors permeating in a cloud of hate. The shortest of the group lifted his battle axe, pointing it directly at me.

I tsked while wagging a finger at him like a bad dog. "Is that any way to greet your Queen?"

The man spat on the ground, then zoned in on me with his beady eyes. "You are not my Queen."

I pouted as I looked down at the spitball on the ground, then back at him. "Well, that was rude."

He puffed his chest, clearly satisfied with his foul actions, and his pathetic companions raised their weapons in solidarity. Ember's hiss filled the tense silence crackling between us, but I continued to assess the rebels who stared at us like the villains we were.

I smelt each one, quickly noting the smoke and ash radiating off them—their pure hatred suffocating my lungs while they glared at me like I was a monster with two heads.

Well, then. I suppose it was time to show them how much of a monster I truly was.

I did not hide my deep inhale, allowing their hatred to seep into the void in my chest. Their potent emotions rejuvenated me for the bloody dance that was about to commence.

"Since I am a fair queen, I will ask the rest of you if you, too, share the same sentiment as this dunce." I pointed a sharp nail at the short man, making him growl in response to my insult.

The men scoffed at the fact I even had to ask, but they all muttered their agreement.

"What a pity. Looks like I will have to execute every last one of you then for breaking commandments one and three." I glanced between the traitors. "Who wants to die first?"

A man with greasy hair standing in the middle of the bunch began to quake, his sword quivering in the air. At last, I caught a whiff of fear drifting from the pathetic group.

I devoured the scent, savoring the bitter taste dancing across my tastebuds. However, my feasting on their emotions was halted when the tallest of the men looked down his nose at me with disgust.

"We didn't break your commandments, for those two lines state do not disrespect nor cross your Queen. Yet, you forgot that we do not consider *you* to be our Queen." He spat on the stone, and I felt a bit of his putrid bodily liquid spray against my ankle.

I swallowed my anger, instead covering it up with an insidious laugh that echoed off the mountain. "If you are born in the mortal lands, I am your Queen." I pouted my lip, giving him a once over glance. "Or are you too dense to understand such simple concepts?"

The man's jaw slackened briefly before he snapped it closed, lifting his sword as a fresh wave of anger speared into my chest.

Looks like we were done talking then.

A wicked smile plastered upon my lips, and I had no need to reach for my daggers because I had a far more deadly weapon.

I watched with delight as Dante leapt off the sharp rock right beside the traitor, landing atop his shoulders. The man's surprised yelp was short-lived as my snake tightly wrapped himself around the peasant's neck. Once I saw that his face turned purple from lack of oxygen, I moved my attention to his fellow companions.

Finally, the entire group reeked of fear, and I breathed in their emotions like a starving prisoner, letting each gulp fuel me as I grabbed the dagger attached to my right hip. With a swift flick of my wrist, it whipped through the air, landing directly in the neck of the rebel who was reaching to tear my snake off his friend. The traitor's knees crashed into the stone as he clutched his throat, gasping for breath.

"Who's next?" I raised my hands in a grand gesture, adrenaline pounding through my veins.

Another man ran toward me with unnerving speed, but Landon moved quicker. My bodyguard flew in front of me, blocking the rebel's killing blow. Their swords tangled together like two lovers. I let the sounds of battle float through me, the melody beautiful and enchanting.

My fingers inched toward the hilt of the dagger sheathed to my left hip, and I glanced at Ember who intensely watched her brother finish up with his first victim. Dante swiftly moved on, slithering toward the barely alive man who still had my dagger in his throat.

A vicious smile spread across my face as my black snake prepared to feast on the man's insides before finishing him off for good.

I purred a command down the bond while glancing at Ember. *Let's show these men how it's done.*

My snake's black eyes raised to mine, her hiss the only response I needed to advance on the two remaining men. One of them had blazing red hair, his green eyes locked onto my approaching figure.

"I guess we found who will die next." My voice was like ice, spearing right at the man full of hate.

His scowl deepened as he raised his battle axe and raced for us. However, he was too short and weak to carry such a weapon, so it was easy to dodge his sloppy strike. His balance quickly flew off center, and Ember took the opportunity to lunge from my arm. She tightened her body around the man's thick neck.

Before he could even attempt to raise his hand to swipe his axe at my snake, I tossed the dagger I was rolling between my hands, letting it slice straight through the air and toward the traitor.

A blood-curdling scream reverberated off the mountainside as the man dropped his axe to clutch his bloody wrist. I could tell my dagger sunk into the bone by the way he cried out. And since I liked to have a bit of fun with my prey before finishing them off, I grabbed a dagger from my thigh holster, throwing it into the air as I did a grand spin.

After all, putting on a show was what the Serpent Queen did best.

The hilt was cool as I caught and whipped it straight at the man's non-injuried wrist. For the second time, I hit my intended mark. The glorious sounds of cracking bones fluttered toward me. Then, the rebel with hair that reminded me of a warm fire groaned in agony before passing out from the combination of Ember strangling him and my twin daggers piercing into his wrists.

I rolled my shoulders back, an air of confidence gracing my stride as my eyes locked onto the final traitor standing before me. His brown eyes were brimming with hate.

I crept closer, like a hunter about to pounce on its pathetic prey. The rebel's fingers tightened around the hilt of his dagger, making a sinister smile tug at the corners of my lips.

"That's my favorite weapon, you know? It will be an honor to slice your throat with the same blade you clutch onto."

As intended, my words baited him into a fit of rage. I greedily sucked down his anger, the emotion lighting a fire within me. The man charged, making it apparent once again that this group lacked technique.

If these buffoons were the rebel's leaders, they didn't stand a chance at defeating me.

He thrust his dagger at my heart, but I quickly blocked his attack with an open palm at the same time I sidestepped left. Without hesitation, I slammed my other palm against his hand that still gripped the dagger, pushing the blade further away from me. I didn't hesitate as I completed the technique Landon taught me years ago—I kicked the side of his knee, pulling a beautiful agonized gasp from the man as I dug my spiked stiletto further into the soft spot right behind his leg, forcing him to bow beside me.

If my subjects wouldn't voluntarily bow at the feet of their Queen, I was more than happy to force them to do so.

The scream that tumbled from his traitorous lips was delicious, and I let the melody flow through me as I launched myself behind him, pinning his arm in the process. He weakly tried to grip onto the dagger, but I yanked it from his hand. Then, I wrapped my arm around his throat and pressed his very own weapon against the base of his throat.

"You can kill us all, but I promise you this—more will take our place. We will never bow to you, Serpent Queen." A wave of heat speared through my chest as the man's hate burned through me. He tried to escape my punishing grip, but I simply reacted by pushing my dagger further into his skin while bending closer to his ear.

"I, too, hold true to my promises." Then, without an ounce of remorse, I flicked my wrist and slit his throat.

Blood splattered against my cheeks, and the traitor gurgled as he choked on his own blood. I kicked his back, making his body crash forward. His head cracked against the stone, and I smiled while I licked his blood clean from my dagger. The bitter taste trickled down my throat, renewing my energy to press onward and claim even more lives.

Yet when I spun around, I was greeted with battered bodies scattered all around the pathway.

I pouted while my bodyguard finished pulling his sword from the chest of a clearly dead man.

"*For Serpent's Sake*, Landon. I only executed two of them." I threw my hands up in exasperation, my gaze roaming over the bodies for any faint twitch or groan. Any sign I could carve them up for a little while longer, but all their eyes were wide open, mouths gaping in a perpetual scream.

Landon glanced over his shoulder at me with an incredulous expression. "I'm your bodyguard, Seera. It is precisely my job to defend and protect you. Are you truly mad at me for fulfilling my duties?"

I rolled my eyes, dismissing him with a wave of my hand. Ember and Dante slithered up my legs, greeting their queen with satisfied hisses after a victorious battle. I blew a loose strand of dark hair from my face as I mentally spoke to my snakes.

You couldn't leave one slightly alive for me to have fun with?

If a snake could roll their eyes, I knew Dante would do so at this moment, but Ember let out a soft hiss as if to apologize. I softly trailed a finger along the top of her head while offering a sharp nod to Dante for a job well done. He rattled his tail, a slight acknowledgment of my praise, but he was clearly perturbed and expected more gratitude next time he strangled enemies on my behalf.

Movement caught our attention, making our eyes lock onto my bodyguard who advanced our way.

He raked his gaze over my body. "Are you hurt, my Queen?"

Landon reached for the crimson splattered against my ribs, but I waved him off.

"The blood is not mine—it most likely belongs to that one." I pointed the dagger still lingering in my hand at the rebel I claimed it from, the pathetic man lying face down in a puddle of his own blood.

Glancing at the dagger, I sheathed it into my thigh holster.

It was a fun hobby of mine, collecting treasures from each of my victims to commemorate their successful executions.

My lips curved into a delighted smile as I replayed the memory of slitting his throat and licking the blade clean—at least I had one bloody death under my belt from today's mission.

Landon nodded to himself as he sheathed his sword into the holster slung around his hips. "Well, that's a relief."

I admired his broad back as he turned to begin the descent toward Ashivire.

"Now, let's get out of these horrible lands and go home."

"I will not be joining you," I said, picking at my nails.

My bodyguard stilled mid-step, slowly turning to face me once again. His brows were pinched with confusion, so I tipped my head to the sky, nodding at the peak of the mountain to make it clear why I wouldn't be returning with him.

Landon followed my gaze to the swirling black clouds thundering above.

His jaw went slack with horror as his eyes slowly crept back to mine. "Absolutely not."

"I have to go see him," I shot back.

"Over my dead body." His jaw ticked while he took a powerful step in my direction.

"We can arrange that if you'd like." I arched a brow, practically hearing his teeth grind from over here.

His hand flexed at his side, almost like it was taking all of his self control not to yank me over his shoulder and carry me all the way back to my queendom.

"Seera, please. We stopped a rebel group, can't that be enough? Let's go home." Landon's eyes softened as he crept closer, close enough I could see his concern shining brightly within his eyes.

I took a step back, watching as concern rapidly faded to hurt.

"No, it's not enough, Landon. I won't be able to rest until I know what is going on with my emotions. Aren't you the one who said you needed to know how to better protect me?"

His lips tightened into a thin line, but I saw his resolve start to crumble.

"If you honestly care about keeping me safe, then you must understand why I have to continue to Morotis. The Serpent King is the only one who might have the answers I seek." A sudden crack of thunder split the tension stirring between us.

I only revealed what my bodyguard needed to know, while still keeping a piece of my plan a secret.

Not only did I want to see the Serpent King to speak about my newfound emotions, but he might be able to aid *me* in crushing this ever-growing rebellion. This group wasn't the first to try to usurp me, and they wouldn't be the last. As much as the thought made my jaw clench with anger, I might be able to entice him into another bargain in order to gain more power.

Dominance was always the answer to crushing an enemy rallying against you.

Besides, I would no sooner see the land of the wicked before I let my queendom fall into a man's hands, let alone anyone else's.

A question still nagged at me, though. *What more could I offer him?*

He already owned the best part of me: my soul.

Landon's voice pulled me from my scheming thoughts. "Then I'm coming with you."

I merely raised my brows at him.

Another crack of thunder boomed through the air, the air noticeably chillier here, and dropping a few degrees each hour as the day slipped away from us. Pitch-black darkness would descend upon the mountain in mere hours.

If we were going to finish our ascent to Morotis, we needed to leave right now—which left me no time to debate the man glaring at me.

So, I smiled and said, "I'd expect nothing less from my ever loyal bodyguard."

CHAPTER 12
THE CLIMB

lood trailed behind me like a shadow with every step toward the Serpent King's lands. I discarded my spiked stilettos hours ago, leaving my bare feet vulnerable to the elements. If I was mortal, I'd have bled out an hour ago from all the cuts and scraps peppering the soles of my feet.

Pebbles of loose stone crunched beneath my feet, and I was lucky I couldn't feel pain during times like this.

At least that part of our bargain seemed unchanged.

I didn't ever want to feel the discomfort of pain again, not after everything that happened seventy-five years ago . . .

At least I didn't have to carry my shoes, for Landon immediately seized them from my hands the moment I stepped out of them. He nearly picked me up to carry me the rest of the way, but I refused. I had every inkling to believe he would sprint in the opposite direction of the place I swore never to return to, just in a futile attempt to keep me safe.

We walked in silence, too exhausted to attempt menial

conversation. An involuntary shiver passed through me as the wind picked up, signaling we were starting to approach the summit of the mountain.

"You're cold." The metal clasp of Landon's cloak clicked as he unhooked it from around his neck, quickly wrapping it around me.

"I'm fine." I tried to shrug him off, but he merely hugged me tighter, moving in front of me to latch the scarlet cloak securely into place around me.

My bodyguard lingered before me, his mouth parting, but it quickly snapped shut. A war of emotions raced through his eyes, which were dim in the growing shadows of the caves. Thunder boomed in the distance, and a soft mist began to sprinkle against my flushed cheeks.

Landon brushed his thumb over the water gathering along my skin. "We'd better pick up our pace, unless we want to get caught in that." He glanced toward the sky.

Following his gaze, I marveled at the way the climate differed so drastically from my homelands. No stars shone this high up into the sheet of darkness, and an odd feeling raced through me as I craved one more night beneath the desert stars of Ashivire—one more night with Landon, before coming face to face with the man who claimed my soul while simultaneously crushing my heart.

"Stop right there." An unfamiliar voice had my gaze drifting from the clouds and to the two men standing only a few feet away.

How did I allow myself to get distracted this close to the entrance of the caves?

I really wished I had put my heels back on before being confronted by the Serpent King's guards, if only to have the ability to look down on the shorter one who glared at me with disgust.

The fools unsheathed their swords upon seeing me motion to Landon for my shoes, and I dramatically rolled my eyes as I slipped into my stilettos.

"Calm down, boys," I muttered, making the man with the blazing mohawk growl.

Out of the corner of my eye, I saw my bodyguard's hand drift to the hilt of his blade.

Why did men always feel the need to wave their swords at each other to compare whose was bigger?

"No need for weapons." I held my hands up, clearly demonstrating I meant no harm . . . at least not yet.

"Do not come any further," the other guard said, his light brown eyes cold and calculating as they glanced between us.

The wind was so feverous it made the guard's hair whip into a wild frenzy. The gale at the peak of the mountain felt different, almost like a bad omen. It was so strong I had no choice but to take another step toward the men in an effort to speak to them.

The sound of hissing metal rang through the air as the guards unsheathed a second set of swords from behind their backs, aiming them straight at our hearts.

For Serpent's Sake.

"As much as I love to play games, I've grown tired of speaking to you two," I shouted. "Now, be good guard doggies and alert your master that the Serpent Queen has come to pay him a visit."

The first guard's green eyes widened, but then he scoffed and shook his head, causing beads of water to flick off his spiked hair.

The gesture, in my mind, solidified that the Serpent King's guards were indeed just like dogs.

"Yeah, right. No way *you* are the Serpent Queen." His slimy eyes trailed down my body, his nose pinching with disgust.

I glanced at the guard with the wild hair, who narrowed his eyes at me as if he could decipher my true intentions by simply glaring at me.

Doubt inked through my veins as I forced myself not to squirm beneath his stare.

I never learned the entirety of what the king's people could do—their magical abilities were still very much a mystery to me, and the way this male was looking at me unsettled me.

"Who's he?" The guard nodded his chin at Landon.

"It wouldn't be proper for a queen to travel without her bodyguard, now would it? If we are done with the greetings, we will be on our way." I started for the entrance of the caves once more, but the guards stepped together to barricade the path.

"Either you get out of my way," A crack of thunder split through the air as I summoned my snakes. "Or, I can make you move. What's it going to be, boys?"

Ember and Dante descended my arms, their eyes locked on the threat directly before their queen.

That all too familiar bitter taste coated my tongue, signaling at least one of the males had the decency to be fearful.

Took them long enough.

I zoned in on the emotion, quickly detecting it was permeating from the male with the spiked hair. My tongue darted to wet my lips as I closed my eyes and tipped my head to the sky, the taste of my drug of choice drenching my veins.

When I opened my eyes to set my sights on the two guards before me, there was a beautiful gap between them.

My lips curved into a victorious smile as I strode toward the yawning cave's entrance.

I brushed past the shorter guard, patting him on the head. "Good doggie."

His nostrils flared while he stepped toward me, but Dante extended off my arm, hissing viciously at the buffoon. He jumped back with a gasp, the idiot so startled he hit his head against the rock wall behind him. My laugh echoed throughout the cavernous chamber as Landon and I finally stepped into Morotis, but my jovial mood quickly died when the darkness wrapped around us.

It didn't take long for the whispers to smell fresh blood.

A low growl reverberated up my throat at the taunting voices that circulated through these lands, courtesy of the Serpent King's horrid magic.

I swallowed my anger, trying to focus on anything besides the insidious voices begging to penetrate my mind.

I counted my steps, letting the sound of my heels clacking against the stone calm me.

I listened to the distant dripping of water and Landon's heavy breathing.

Oh, fuck. I forgot to tell him.

I whispered through gritted teeth. "Don't listen to the voices. Do whatever you can to block them out, and, above all, do not talk back to them."

All my bodyguard could offer in response was a small nod, making the void inside me crack at the agony flickering across his face. The voices must be tormenting him with memories of his past, and a strange emotion filtered through me.

What was that smell radiating from me? It emanated the earthy smell of soil.

It couldn't be sympathy—could it?

Maybe it was my emotions faltering, or maybe it was because of sheer exhaustion, but I couldn't stand the pain racing across Landon's face.

Thus, for the first time in my rule as the Serpent Queen, I broke one of my commandments.

I didn't believe in the gods, but, just in case, I cast a prayer into the darkness . . .

Please let us make it out of Morotis alive.

CHAPTER 13
HIS MARK

What do we have here?

The Serpent Queen has returned.

My jaw hurt from how tightly I clenched it, doing everything in my power to ignore the taunting voices.

These caves were like a living thing, a small glimpse of the power that lay beneath the Serpent King's pasty skin. Try as I might, I failed to keep the voices at bay as flashes of the past pelted my mind.

His cruel smile.
The electric shock of coldness that speared through me as his arm snaked around my back, tugging me snugly against him.
His lips enveloping mine to seal the bargain.
The ground quaking beneath our feet.

Landon's groans drew me from my trance, and I reached for my bodyguard. He was so warm, so unlike the king. I wrapped my hand around his bicep, trying to anchor him back to the caves and not the darkness flooding his mind.

Yet, my touch wasn't having the effect I intended. Instead of him coming back to me, another agonized moan tumbled from his lips while he clutched his head with his hands.

A moment later, my bodyguard dropped to his knees. A strange feeling raced through me, something akin to shock as I watched him seize up in pain.

Usually, I loved the view of him on his knees before me, but not like this. Not with his brows pinched together in agony, as sweat beaded along his hairline, causing his curls to stick to his forehead. At this moment, I was grateful I could feel rage, for I burned full of it like a wild inferno.

The void in my chest sparked to life like a wildfire of vengeance, and my sights trailed further down the dark cave— all the way to where I knew a jet-black stone door stood.

I was going to kill *him* for hurting Landon like this.

But first, I had to do something for him.

Turning back to Landon, I noted his eyes were still tightly closed.

"Landon, the voices are not real." I towered over him, giving his shoulders a rough shake.

He merely groaned louder, his body quivering beneath my grip.

"Landon, snap out of it!" I dug my nails into his biceps, drawing a bit of blood in the process, but it didn't work.

He didn't come back to me.

Rather, his eyes rolled toward the ceiling.

I was no stranger to anger, having experienced it nearly every day of my godforsaken life, but the energy coursing through my veins right now was unlike anything I'd experienced.

Imaging the Serpent King's face in front of me, I backhanded my bodyguard so hard that he went crashing into the ground. His head smacked hard against a rather sharp bit of stone, and he remained face down for far too long, making my fury dissipate into panic.

Fuck, what have I done?

I moved quickly, my heels slapping against the stone as I knelt down, checking him for consciousness.

I carefully rolled him onto his back. Although his eyes were closed, he was no longer quaking.

That had to be a good sign, right?

However, that was the same moment I noticed his chest not rising and falling in its normal rhythm.

Oh gods, did I . . . but how?

My chest constricted as the darkness pressed in around me.

This couldn't be happening.

I refused to lose Landon all because of my selfish need to see the Serpent King.

This was all my fault.

My cheeks grew hot and wet, and all I could do was watch my tears fall onto Landon's lifeless face.

When did I move so close to him? Better yet, when did I start straddling my bodyguard?

Landon was the one good thing in my life, the one bright spot in the all-consuming darkness that was the Serpent Queen's reign.

I couldn't lose him.

I *vowed* not to lose him.

Softly, I gripped his face, cradling his cheeks between my hands.

"Please, come back to me," I whispered, sealing my lips to his.

I was greeted with stiffness, so I tried to deepen the kiss as best as I could with such an inactive participant.

I put as many good intentions behind my actions—well, as

many as a person without a soul could. I nearly gave up, but then, ever so slowly, Landon kissed me back.

His lips seemed uncertain at first, confused.

Then, it was like the flip of a switch.

Landon's hands were in my hair, pulling me against him and devouring me like I was the air he needed to survive. He leaned forward, finally sitting upright, but never letting his lips slip from mine.

I'm not sure why I didn't break the kiss, since he was clearly conscious.

All I knew in that moment was it felt good to be kissed like this.

The kiss softened, signaling its impending end. A pang of something like sadness strained through my chest as he finally pulled away. Yet, he didn't unlace his fingers from my hair. Instead, he trailed them down the base of my head, curling a finger around the edge of one of my black locks.

"Seera," he whispered, and I could feel the heat from his breath dance against my lips.

Relief pounded through me at the sound of his voice. There were a slew of thoughts I wanted to share with him as I felt the weight of our kiss lingering upon my lips.

I wanted to tell him I was here for him.

That I was so scared I lost him.

That I was going to kill the Serpent King for having his voices torture him.

I didn't say any of that though. Instead, I said, "Can you walk?"

Fucking idiot, Seera.

He pulled back, every inch of space quickly feeling like a roaring crevice dividing between us.

"What? You—I—that kiss . . ." Landon sucked in a deep breath, his shoulders dropping a few inches. "Yes, I can walk."

I nodded, bracing my feet against the ground to stand. Instantly, I missed my bodyguard's warmth against me as I stepped back, allowing him a moment to gather his bearings before continuing on.

My gaze roamed over the walls around us, along the faint flicker of light emitting from the handful of torches lining the obsidian stone. Flashes of ancient symbols were etched into the caves' walls, and I felt a pull toward them.

Landon's footsteps trailed close behind as I approached the markings. I dragged a blood-red nail along the symbols as they wove together the more we traversed down the pathway. My fingers danced along the rattling tail while my eyes soared to the ceiling to the snake's massive body curving all throughout the tunnel.

The exact mark that marred these tunnels was imprinted onto my very own skin: the Serpent King's mark.

A pit formed in my stomach the closer we got to the serpent's head, signaling we were nearly there. I considered turning around to flee in the opposite direction when I glimpsed the onyx door. Right above it was the head of the snake, its mouth stretched open, fangs bared and pointing at the entrance.

Welcome home, my Queen.

The voice slithered into my mind, pulling a sharp inhale from me at the deep timbre the cave imitated.

A voice I once craved but grew to despise.

I shoved my panic deep down as we approached the door. My bodyguard's hand drifted to the hilt of his sword, again, and I let out a sigh. Landon's eyes shot to mine, confusion tugging his brows down.

"Do not make that motion around the Serpent King." I pointed my chin at his hand that now tightly gripped the base of his weapon. "Unless I command you to be on guard, stand down. We are here for answers, not a fight."

"This man is dangerous." Landon's eyes flashed with fury, and I took a step closer.

"So am I."

A deep, sensual chuckle wrapped around me, causing my head to whip toward the familiar sound. The onyx door was cracked open—an invitation to enter.

Even though I swore never to come back here, I pushed the door wide open and entered the Serpent King's lair.

CHAPTER 14
THE LAIR

"To what do I owe the pleasure of my Queen finally visiting me after all these years?"

The oily voice that haunted my dreams laughed, but he remained hidden from sight.

I wasn't sure if it was Landon's growl or my own that answered the King's greeting. Darkness surrounded us, the stone room completely barren. The Serpent King's lair was a place where only *he* could deem who was worthy to enter.

There was no furniture, no artwork, nothing to hide behind as you awaited your judgment.

Although the dimness made it impossible for a normal person to see clearly, I was far from normal. My eyes quickly adjusted, searching through the thick sheet of black.

There he was.

In the corner of the room, there was a faint glow. It was as if golden flakes danced in the air—the telltale sign of the Serpent King's power.

It never made sense to me why his magic appeared golden and not black like his soul.

"Stop hiding in the shadows and greet me as a queen should be." I straightened, thankful my heels added a few glorious inches to my already abnormal height for a woman. Yet, my height was nothing compared to the behemoth that was lurking nearby.

The darkness began to lighten as shimmering particles vibrated closer, practically buzzing with excitement.

Then *he* was right before me.

A cold finger snaked underneath my chin, forcing me to tilt my head up and meet those piercing green eyes I could never forget.

The man who haunted my dreams.

Darkness fled from us, as we were enshrouded in our own bubble of faint, golden light. Landon's voice barely pierced through the shield the King placed around us, but I heard him cry out . . . it sounded like he was asking if I was okay.

Typical Landon.

I sighed, watching the Serpent King greedily claim the air I blew from my lips.

My lip curled in disgust, while his twisted into a cruel smile.

"I knew you wouldn't be able to resist coming back to me, my Queen."

"I am not *your* Queen." I attempted to rear my head back and out of his grip, but he simply snaked his other hand around my lower back. My breasts pressed against his chest, prompting his gaze to dip and drink in the sight of our bodies colliding.

I planted my hand against his chest, trying to create space between us, but his grip was too strong against my back.

"Do you know what happens to men who touch me unsolicited?" I seethed.

"Enlighten me," he purred, his eyes finding mine through the darkness.

It was my turn to offer him a chilling smile.

"First, I cut their hands off, ensuring they never have the ability to touch anything ever again. Then, they stay in my dungeon for a week or so, until I grow tired of carving up every piece of their body." I dragged my hand up the king's chest, wrapping it around the back of his thick neck, tugging him nearly an inch from my face. "Finally, I allow my snakes the pleasure of slowly choking the life from them, but not before Dante eats their insides while they're still breathing. Whatever is left of them is fed to the beasts in the pit." I sunk my nails into his skin, reveling in the way his body tightened around my hand. "So, you have two seconds to get your filthy fucking hands off me, or I will grant you the same royal treatment I give mortal men."

"Lucky bastards." He chuckled, but his fingers disappeared a moment later from beneath my chin and from cradling against my back. Warmth instantly flooded my veins, now that our bodies were no longer touching.

"Who is Dante?" Curiosity seeped into his deep voice.

As if the sound of his name summoned my snake, Dante appeared, spiraling up my arm. A moment later, Ember joined him, matching his movements on my other arm.

Dante slithered along my shoulder and atop my head, bringing himself face to face with the Serpent King.

Although I may be who my snakes answer to, they know this male was their maker. It was only natural he was curious about the menace standing before us.

"Ah, you must be Dante." He lifted his hand toward my snake, as if he was a pet he could simply stroke. Dante's tail rattled against me as his vicious hiss tore through the bubble of magic encapsulating us.

"The same rule of no touching unless permitted extends to my snakes." I stroked Dante's body, grateful that his insufferable attitude was pointed at someone else for once.

Much to my surprise, the Serpent King lifted his hands as if to surrender.

"Lesson learned." His eyes shined with delight as he observed Ember and Dante protectively coiling their bodies around my arms and shoulders.

"I can feel it, you know." His eyes dipped, meeting mine.

"Feel what?"

"Your bond with your snakes. It is strong—stronger than most animal bonds."

I shrugged. "Maybe that is what decades of killing together will do to a relationship."

He shook his head, causing a piece of his perfectly swooped back black hair to fall into his eyes. I tensed when he dipped his head, bringing us eye level.

"I also feel you," he drawled, looking at me through his stupidly thick lashes.

Why did a slight thrill shoot through me from those four words?

Clearing my throat, I feigned ignorance. "Wouldn't you have to be touching me to feel me?"

His lips curled into a feline smile. "On the contrary, my Queen, I can feel your magic—my magic. It *sings* to me." He dared to brush his thumb over my parted lips, and I couldn't hide the sharp breath I inhaled from his cold touch. He leaned closer, bringing us nearly one wrong move away from having our lips crash together.

"Careful, Serpent King. Have you forgotten what happened last time we kissed?" I arched a brow, doing my best to calm my traitorous heart.

"How could I forget the kiss that shook the world?" He bit his lip. "As much as I'd love nothing more than to kiss you again, I doubt you came here only for another taste of my perfect lips."

"You're disgusting," I groaned, but he laughed like I just called him the most charming man in all the lands.

"Are you going to tell me why you are here, or"—his emerald eyes twinkled with mischievous glint—"I can always have my voices float into your mind? Perhaps, they can conjure some old memories to fill our time together?"

Panic lurched through me at the mention of the cave's whispers, prompting me to gnaw on my lip in an effort to hide my heightened emotions from the king.

His eyes shot to my lips, not missing a beat. He breathed deeply, and I knew my efforts to calm my emotions were futile when a deep wrinkle formed between his black brows.

"Care to tell me why you reek of panic?" His eyes pierced into mine with a sudden ferocity, and I swore he could see straight through my soul—well, if he didn't already own it.

"Seera," he breathed.

Again, there was that strange feeling akin to surprise rattling through me at the intimate way he said my given name.

He hadn't called me by my name since before the bargain . . . since the day he broke my heart into a million pieces.

Luckily, I wasn't able to feel the true weight of my heart break, for the king stole my soul in the same breath he shattered it. I always wrestled with whether I should hate him for ridding me of such terrible feelings or if I should thank him.

The cool sensation of his fingers grazing against my wrist brought me back to his question.

I took a moment, for I suddenly felt a knot of complicated emotions gather at the back of my throat. "My emotions—they are changing."

"What do you mean?" His fingers stilled against my skin.

"A few days ago . . . I had a panic attack for the first time since you rid me of such an emotion." I pursed my lips as I waited for him to offer me an answer, but he only rubbed his chin and stared at me.

Landon's voice pierced through the shield louder this time, causing the Serpent King to dramatically roll his eyes.

"Gods, does he ever shut the fuck up?" With a snap of his fingers, the golden bubble burst, expanding to illuminate the rest of the room in glowing light.

My bodyguard was on the other side of the room, but his head snapped toward me the moment he could see better. He raced over, inserting himself between me and the king.

"Back away from my Queen."

The Serpent King's laugh boomed, grating across the stone walls like nails on a chalkboard.

"Your Queen? She was mine far before you ever existed, mortal." He looked down his nose at Landon, as he had at least half a foot on my bodyguard.

However, that did not deter Landon from holding his ground, staring right back at the king. I sniffed the air, not catching a whiff of fear wafting off his muscular frame.

I taught Landon well.

As he continued to glare at the ferocious immortal, he proved how far he had come in the years since being in my service. He was a far call from the broken man I found in Ashivire.

If I could feel a sense of pride, this would be the perfect moment to do so.

Yet, I quickly grew tired of their standoff, so I stepped to the side and out from behind my bodyguard's human shield. He glanced at me, his eyes glinting with displeasure, but I held my hand up, silently commanding him to stand down. His chest rose while he took a steadying breath, fighting against every urge in his body to protect me from the man who intensely tracked our encounter.

I didn't need my bodyguard to fight my battles, and it was time to make my point to the Serpent King *crystal clear*.

My stilettos clacked against the stone as I swayed toward the menace, and when I was within reaching distance, I poked a sharp nail into his chest—right where his skin was exposed, courtesy of the many buttons he left undone on his silk black long-sleeve.

"You may own my soul, but you will never own me. I will never be *yours*." I twisted my nail further into his skin, pulling a precious bead of blood from the Serpent King. His gaze dropped to watch the fresh line of crimson trickle down his chest, only to disappear beneath his shirt. When he looked up at me through his lashes, delight was the last thing I expected to see.

"Don't tease me with a good time, my Queen." He wrapped his large hand around mine, forcing my nail deeper into his skin, making more blood trickle from the fresh wound. "Pleasure and pain are a beautiful combination, wouldn't you agree?" His wicked smile made something long dead inside me flare just as I felt my cheeks warm.

Damn this man.

I refused to give him the satisfaction of seeing me blush. I desperately needed to regain control.

I leaned closer, tipping my head up to whisper, "You are nothing more than a monster."

Somehow, his smile widened, revealing his elongated canines. Flashes of them digging into my flesh, right above my lips, pierced through my mind.

He leaned in, his breath brushing against my ear. "You know you can call me Alaric."

My heart lurched at the name I forced myself to forget every day, only to be haunted by each night as I slept.

"Enough!" Landon's growl caused me to take a step back so I could glance over my shoulder. His eyes burned into me, no doubt noticing the newfound color sprouting across my cheeks. Then, his eyes shifted to where the Serpent King held onto my hand—where my nail dug deep into his chest. I inhaled, quickly being greeted by an overly sweet and fruity smell.

My bodyguard was *jealous.*

His eyes continued to scorch into the spot where the king held me, but, when I tugged my hand back, his grip tightened. I peered up at the king, only to find his attention elsewhere.

He was smiling at my bodyguard, as if he were winning in the pointless battle over me. His gaze dropped to mine as he raised his free hand to stroke my cheek. The action was not soft and romantic, instead it was a clear display of possession.

His next words were loud enough for both of us to hear. "You are mine, whether you accept that fact or not." His fingers trailed down my cheek, all the way down to wrap around my hand wound tightly at my side. He lifted my tense hand and brought it toward his lips.

Was he about to do what I thought he was going to do?

No, he wouldn't be that foolish. We didn't know what caused the ground to shake beneath our feet on the night of our bargain, but we guessed as much that it had something to do with when our lips touched. For shortly after we kissed, the world as I knew it changed forever.

Would the Serpent King truly dare to kiss me in any sort of capacity just to get under my bodyguard's skin?

My heart nearly stilled when he pressed his lips against my hand, his eyes trained on Landon all the while. My bodyguard's growl filled the quiet space, the only sound besides my thundering heart—which I hoped no one else could hear.

I held my breath, waiting for the ground to quake, for the world to end . . .

But nothing happened.

Interesting.

When the Serpent King's gaze shifted to me, his lips spread into a bloodthirsty smile against my skin, and I knew at that moment he indeed heard the effect his actions had on me.

Stupid, fucking traitorous heart.

If I could live without the organ, I'd have carved it from my own chest ages ago.

As the king dropped my hand and straightened to his full height, I hated how I missed the way his cool lips soothed my flushed skin. I made a show of wiping away his kiss on my pants, wishing the motion could also make me forget about the hunger that flashed in the king's eyes the moment his lips met my skin.

"I shall help you investigate more about this lapse in your emotions, but I will only speak with you." The king gave Landon a pointed look, his lips twitching with amusement upon seeing my bodyguard tense.

Landon stepped toward the king, but I twisted and planted my hand firmly against his chest to halt him. He was so foolish thinking *he* could challenge the Serpent King. My bodyguard's nostrils flared as he slowly glanced at where I touched him.

I internally groaned at the fact that I, of all people, was stuck playing mediator.

Typically, I'd revel at being between two gorgeous men. However, being between my bodyguard, who I casually slept with, and the immortal man who owned my soul, was a *bit* too complicated for my liking.

The Serpent King's dark laugh made me have to suppress a shiver. "Oh, what fun I'm going to have with you two."

Before Landon could mutter something stupid, I raised my chin at the king. "I agree to speak with you alone."

"Seera," Landon said through gritted teeth, the reek of panic intertwining with anger floating toward me.

His chest started to rise beneath my hand, so I gently rubbed my thumb across his shirt in an effort to calm him from making this situation even harder for me. It must have worked, for his breathing evened out, and I could finally drop my hand now that I wasn't worried he'd leap at the king and strangle him . . . or at least attempt to.

A small sigh escaped me as I turned to face the tall menace, but he didn't meet my gaze. Instead, his eyes were glued to my hand resting at my side—the one I just caressed Landon with.

His hands were curled into fists at his side, his knuckles turning white from how hard he clenched them. When he raised his gaze to my face, his usually bright green eyes were darker, as if an inky storm was brewing within him.

"Have dinner with me tonight." His tone wasn't sharp enough to strictly be a command, yet it wasn't soft enough to entirely be a question.

I frowned, glancing at my blood-soaked fighting leathers.

"I still have some gowns in your old chambers." The king's words made my head snap up to look at him. "You can freshen up and wear one of those."

I couldn't stop myself from gaping at him at his casual mention that I still had a room here, let alone clothing, but I quickly snapped my mouth shut.

As the memories of our past threatened to drown me in a fresh current of despair, I barely could force out a small nod in response.

The king stared at me for a moment longer, then turned on

his heel as he began to work his hands into a spiraling motion. Gold dust shimmered between his palms, reminding me of all the times I saw him do this motion in the time I lived in Morotis.

He was conjuring a portal.

"After you, my Queen." The Serpent King said my title mockingly while looking at my bodyguard.

Eventually, his focus returned to me as he gestured toward the glowing portal. It looked like a wall of golden sparkling dust dancing in front of me, but before I could even take one step forward, quick footsteps sounded.

Landon blocked my way. "I will go first, to ensure it is safe."

I sighed at the same time the Serpent King chuckled at Landon's bravado, but he didn't fight his request. Instead, he extended his hand with a grand flourish for my bodyguard to enter first. Landon didn't hesitate as he stepped through the golden portal.

As much as he annoyed me at times, his lack of hesitation to do anything for me also made me want to reward him later —in the currency of bending over to allow him to fuck me senseless.

My relationship with my bodyguard was complicated, to say the least.

I jumped as the king's voice pulled me from my dirty thoughts. "Now that your guard dog is gone, let's try this again." He nodded at the portal, clearly irked at how long this whole ordeal was taking. "After you, my Queen."

I bit the inside of my cheek to hide any signs of hesitation. The last time I traveled through a portal was seventy-five years ago, and it ended in me viciously throwing up the moment the horrid contraption spit me out. The fact I heaved right on the Serpent King's shoes was humiliating back then, but I honestly wouldn't mind fucking up his overly shiny dress shoes right about now, especially after his possessive claims over me.

That thought steadied me as I marched up to the shimmering portal and stepped through into the golden light. The Serpent King's magic enveloped me, working to transport me deeper into his lands.

Secretly, I enjoyed the way his magic embraced me, almost like a paramour.

The king mentioned prior how my magic sang to him, and I would never admit this aloud but . . .

His magic also sang to me.

CHAPTER 15
A FATAL MISTAKE

I t felt like being tossed into a pit of glass as the Serpent King's portal spit me out onto the floors of my old chambers. My knees collided with sharp stone, making me bite back a groan as I nearly heaved up what little food lingered in my stomach. I took a few deep breaths, clutching my pounding head while working to ground myself.

I fucking hated the after effects of portal magic.

"At least you didn't throw up this time. I do love these shoes." The Serpent King's shiny black shoes appeared in view of where I crouched on the floor.

Slowly, I dragged my eyes up his long, powerful legs. His trousers were a green so deep it almost looked black, fashioned with a dark belt, the golden buckle of which portrayed a snake eating its own tail. The king's arms were crossed over his chest highlighting his muscles, though his silk shirt hung loosely over his broad shoulders.

Finally, I raised my gaze higher to meet those mesmerizing eyes. Somewhere between his lair and here he'd fixed his black hair, because it was perfectly swept back now, not a single strand out of place. He cocked his head as he looked down at me, and the firelight from the roaring hearth made his hair burn to a deep shade of green in the blink of an eye. The first time I met the king, I thought it was a trick, but, sure enough, his hair color shifted depending on the lighting.

"What a pretty picture, you on your knees before me." His lips curled into a wicked smile.

My nose twitched with disgust, taking his crass comment as my cue to push off the floor and back onto my feet. Unfortunately, I moved too quickly, stumbling once more as the room spun.

Before I could collapse again, strong arms snaked around my waist. His smooth laugh made my skin pebble, and, being this close to the Serpent King, I was able to see the sparse flecks of gold gleaming within his green eyes.

"Falling for me already, my Queen?" he drawled.

I firmly planted my hands against his chest. "You lost any chance of that happening the day you kicked me out of Morotis," I spat, and I swore I saw something akin to hurt flicker through his eyes, right before I shoved out of his arms.

For the second time, I tripped, but this time over my heels snagging on the jagged floors. Cursing underneath my breath, I managed to right myself.

I never stumbled, so why was I swiftly unravelling before the man I swore never to show weakness to?

The lack of my bodyguard's angry growls and threats at the Serpent King's crude remarks drew my attention. Quickly, I scanned the room for a glimpse of his curly locks or those gentle eyes, but it was only the Serpent King and I in my old chambers.

I narrowed my eyes at the king, who shrugged his hulking shoulders nonchalantly. "Where is Landon?"

"I may or may not have made his portal . . . delayed." A smug smile twitched along those infuriating lips.

"If you hurt him again, I swear—" My words were cut off by a loud *whoosh*, then a deep grunt sounded as my bodyguard was spit from the golden portal.

Surprisingly, Landon landed flat on his feet, yet he grimaced, folding over while clutching his stomach. He had rather quick reflexes for a mortal . . . maybe I should start joining him on his morning runs.

My bodyguard swiftly gathered his composure, lifting his head to where the Serpent King and I still stood *very* close to one another. His gaze shifted past us, and I glanced over my shoulder to see we were nearly pressed against the large four-poster bed. Landon's eyes narrowed as he assessed us once again, his eyes roaming over me entirely before casting a scorching glare at the king.

"You," Landon growled with such ferocity, even I was taken aback.

A quick glance sideways at the king revealed similar surprise, his eyebrows shooting up as a dazzling smile spread across his face.

"The guard dog can bark, but can he bite?" He gnashed his teeth at Landon.

The fucking fool was about to take his bait, charging toward the king and ready to finally shut that cocky mouth of his.

I couldn't blame my bodyguard for wanting to fight this intolerable immortal, I'd wanted to pummel the king myself *many* times. Yet, I didn't have the answers I sought, so whatever was brewing between my bodyguard and the Serpent King needed to stop right this instant.

I stepped in front of the king, holding a hand up to my bodyguard. "That's enough."

Landon's murderous gaze switched from the king and over to me, his rage quickly dissolving into complete and utter disbelief. "You're taking his side over mine? Truly?"

My heels slapped against the stone as I slowly stepped closer to my bodyguard. "I take no man's side. You *both* are acting like a couple of fools."

Landon's jaw slackened further before I whipped my furious gaze at the Serpent King.

The king scoffed, rearing back while clutching a hand to his heart.

"My point, exactly." I glared as I looked him up and down, then nodded at the door across the vast room. "Now, get out so I can get ready for dinner."

His grin was absolutely feral as his eyes dipped, hungrily roaming over my body, but he said nothing else, only bothering to point a finger at the deep green chrome tub in the corner. The sound of water drifted toward me while the Serpent King sauntered for the door.

On his way out, he lingered beside Landon, muttering something so low even I couldn't hear, yet I knew it was nothing good when I saw Landon's face. There was a fresh wave of anger sparking in his eyes. Then, the door clicked behind the king, leaving us alone.

Fuck the Serpent King, for now I had to deal with Landon's moodiness.

"You cannot be serious about having dinner alone with that despicable man."

I groaned as I moved to sit at the edge of the bed, bracing a hand around the black wooden poster for support as I removed my stilettos.

"I did not come this far just to give up when I am this close to finally gaining the answers I seek." After discarding my shoes, I trailed my fingers over the black duvet, softly tracing the outline of one of the golden snakes within its pattern.

Since there were so many memories scattered throughout this room, it was nearly impossible not to slip into the past . . .

"You're so fucking beautiful with your hair like this," His cool fingers dragged down my neck, leaving a pathway of goosebumps in their wake.

"Stay with me tonight?" My voice was barely a whisper, quiet enough it was smothered by the crackling of the fire.

The king's hand stilled atop the curve of my breasts, his enchanting eyes flickering from my chest and up to my face.

"If I stay the night, there is no going back, Seera. Whatever we are doing right now becomes much more real. Are you certain?"

I didn't hesitate as I said, "I am."

He laced his fingers behind my back, tugging me closer. "Then, I'll stay."

Pushing off the bed, I let the memory that frequently haunted me dissipate into the steam drifting into the room.

In the end, our time together meant nothing.

The Serpent King made that crystal clear after our bargain was completed . . . so why couldn't I still get him out of my head after all these years?

As I neared the tub, I dipped a finger into the water. It was boiling hot—exactly what I needed to let the memories of my past melt away once and for all.

"I don't like it, Seera. I don't like this whole thing." Landon's exasperated tone made me glance over my shoulder while leaning over the bath.

I needed silence, and, in order for that to happen, I needed Landon to shut the fuck up.

I knew one guaranteed way to make men be quiet.

With my back turned, I worked my fingers against the buttons of my fighting leathers. Then, I slowly shimmied my ass back and forth, stripping out of my pants. I glanced behind me, satisfied to see the anger extinguished from my bodyguard's eyes. Now, they flared with desire as he took in the glorious sight of me half-naked, bending over the tub.

I kicked my pants away, making a show to shake my assets as I purposely struggled while reaching behind me for the corset laces covering the entirety of my back.

After a few futile attempts, I pouted my bottom lip and glanced at Landon.

"Could you lend me a hand?" My voice dipped to a low and sensual timber.

Landon moved toward me like a moth drawn to a flame, his eyes glued to my bare ass the entire time. I straightened, allowing him to undo the laces of my top, but I did take a step back to close the sliver of space between us.

The evidence of how much my small striptease affected him greeted me as I pushed my ass against him, tugging a beautiful groan from his lips. His fingers moved quicker, as if he needed to dig them into my bare flesh right this instant or he might perish.

Finally, he got the strings undone, and I shrugged out of my top with my back facing him. The sound of leather slapping against stone split through the air as he chucked the garment across the room, his eyes never straying from my skin. He brushed his fingers down my back, but his brow crinkled as he stilled when touching the serpent tattoo wrapping around my torso—a constant reminder of my bargain with the Serpent King. Within the depths of his eyes, Landon's fury rekindled once more.

I spun around, hoping my ample assets were the handfuls of distractions he needed to stop thinking of the king. Sure enough, his gaze dipped to my chest, hungrily devouring the way my breasts bounced.

His eyes softened while he bit his bottom lip.

"You know," I said, wrapping a finger around his belt loops and pressing myself against him, making my nipples lightly graze his chest.

He sucked in a sharp inhale, all while devouring me with his eyes.

"I can't stop thinking about how assertive you were earlier." I looked at him through heavy lashes.

He reluctantly tore his gaze from my chest for only a moment. "Oh?"

I hummed. "The way you were ready to defend me, to fight for me. Do you know what it makes me want to do to you right now?"

His throat bobbed, his eyes lingered on my lips. "Please, do tell."

"First, I want to strip you out of these." His belt buckle clicked as I undid it and loosened the buttons on his trousers.

I yanked them down, along with his undergarments, quickly greeted with how excited my words made my bodyguard. His clothes pooled around his ankles, and my gaze dipped to consume every inch of him. We stood so close I could feel his hard cock pressing against the bottom of my stomach.

"What comes next?" His voice was a low whisper, almost like if he spoke too loudly it would shatter my rare moment of generosity.

I brought Landon's hands to my chest, allowing him to grope me. He bit on his lip *hard* as he kneaded my breasts. A bead of blood pooled along his bottom lip, making me brush a finger against it to collect his blood.

I sucked the crimson drop into my mouth, and my bodyguard's eyes swiftly turned into an inferno of desire while watching me suck on my finger.

A loud pop sounded as I released my finger from my lips, now dragging it down his chest and toward my next surprise. "Next, I'm going to touch you."

"But, you've never touched me—" He started, but he stilled upon me glancing at him with an arched brow.

I ceased my downward pursuit. "Should I stop?"

"No." The word rushed out of Landon, and he shook his head as if the motion could erase his foolishness.

My delighted hum wrapped around us as I began to pump him in my hand. My bodyguard moaned, looking the most relaxed I'd ever seen him. His lips slightly moved, almost like he was praying this moment could last forever.

I couldn't allow him to get used to such generosity—I was only doing this to shut him up.

At least that's what I told myself.

I picked up the tempo of my strokes, making his relaxed face swiftly shift to pinch with pleasure. Faster than lighting, Landon gripped my waist, shoving me backward. My legs slammed against the edge of the tub as he kneaded my ass in his hand. I inched onto my toes, prompting him to wrap his other hand around the bottom of my thigh, yanking and wrapping it around his waist. I used the heel of my other foot to stabilize myself against the bath, but I didn't even need to, Landon held me so firmly in place.

My breath hitched as I moved the tip of him toward my entrance, making an animalistic sound claw out of his throat.

"Fuck, Seera," he groaned, dropped his lips to my neck to graze softly against the column of my throat.

"That's exactly what I was thinking would come next." My chuckle was breathy, very unlike the cruel one most heard.

He pulled back, his eyes scanning mine. "But I don't have any intel for you."

I arched against him, the motion making his cock drag along my center.

"Consider this my way of showing you my gratitude for your loyal service, Landon."

His fingers laced through my hair, pulling me closer. Yet, he hesitated an inch from my sinful lips.

"Are you going to fuck your Queen or do I need to take matters into my own hands?" I whispered.

When his lips curved into a smirk, our lips brushed.

My bodyguard tried to make it a slow kiss, one with passion and meaning, but I ramped it up by biting his bottom lip. He moaned, nipping my lip back and forcing a shock of pain to spear through me. The metallic, bitter taste of his blood coated my tongue, and I gasped into his mouth at the same time he shoved himself deep inside of me.

Landon definitely understood what I needed in this moment, for he fucked me hard and fast.

I broke our kiss and gasped for air, tipping my head back. He dropped my leg wrapped around his waist, wasting no time as he flipped me around. My hands flew out to grip the edge of the tub, which offered no reprieve from his ruthless thrusts, but I delighted in the brutality of our fucking.

And we were *finally* not talking about the Serpent King.

About the infuriating man with those electrifying, piercing green eyes.

I arched my back in frustration, but my bodyguard took it as a sign of my enjoyment.

He reached a hand around, pinching my nipples hard enough to tug a gasp from my lips. Pain and pleasure flooded through my veins while he continued moving in me.

Pain and pleasure are a beautiful combination, wouldn't you agree?

The Serpent King's deep baritone drifted through my mind, and I felt myself creeping closer to tipping over the edge as *his* fingers brushed against my clit, working me while he moved deeper inside me.

I screamed out as I climaxed, choking on the name I nearly yelled while my release tore through me.

A roar tore through the air, making me glance over my shoulder to see a different man than the one's fingers I just imagined were inappropriately touching me.

Slowly, I turned back toward the water. It was rippling from our feverous fucking, and my hands tightened around the cool chrome edge of the bathtub.

I glared at my reflection in the water, a mixture of surprise and horror flashing across my face as I mulled over the fact that I had almost called out the name of the man I swore to hate forever as my bodyguard was deep inside me.

I thought I would be fine coming back to Morotis after all this time, yet *he* had already infiltrated my mind during the most intimate times—during the moments I found a bit of reprieve from acting as the vicious Serpent Queen.

My lip curled while I watched the water calm, a chilling thought making my flesh prickle.

It was a fatal mistake coming to see the Serpent King.

CHAPTER 16

DINNER WITH THE SNAKE

E ven after seventy-five years, the Serpent King's formal dining hall took my breath away.

An oval pond was situated directly in the center of the large cavernous space, with a gold serpent fountain in the middle of the body of the water. The ambiance was warm and enchanting, providing a false calm which washed over the room where the king hosted his *dinners*.

As I neared the edge of the pond, I stared into the golden water. This pond always had a magnetic pull on me . . .

"Everyone, this is Seera." The Serpent King waved toward me, and I felt so small as hundreds of eyes glared in my direction.
Their eyes trailed along my torn, dirty gown, a look of disgust quickly spreading across their beautiful faces.
A terrible, gut-wrenching feeling slammed into me as I realized I may have escaped one beautiful prison just to enter another.

I was snapped out of my trance by the clanging of metal trays dropping out of mid-air, clinking against the nearby table. Wrapped around the entire pond was a rosewood dining table, each seat offering a stunning view of the shimmering golden waters.

The configuration felt more appropriate for a meeting space than a dining hall.

Oh, what a great idea.

I would simply consider this a meeting rather than a private dinner with the male I most definitely was not just thinking about while being fucked by another man.

I refused to let my feelings from the past haunt me, especially when I had a new rebel movement on the rise, ready to tear me down at the first sign of weakness.

My position of power was more important than whatever I felt in the past for the Serpent King, so I'd treat this exactly like any other dinner to discuss business . . . maybe without the part where it ends with someone dead by my command, but the night was still young.

My stomach growled, distracting me, and I focused on the smell of the steaming food laid out before me.

When was the last time I had eaten? Surely, it couldn't be the ashroot soup before my night under the stars with Landon?

After another loud groan, I sat down, digging into a steaming turkey leg, not even bothering to wait for my lovely host to arrive.

After all, he was the one late to the dinner *he* invited *me* to.

I had no patience to deal with a fork, so I used my teeth to shred directly into the meat. It melted off the bone and straight down my throat. I forgot how exquisite the food tasted in Morotis. The human lands had nothing remotely as savory and delightful as whatever coated the meat I hungrily devoured.

After sucking every last bit off the bone, I reached for another and moaned again from the incredible flavor exploding in my mouth.

"My gods, where are your manners?" a deep voice rumbled, causing me to look up as I continued to chomp on a mouthful of meat.

The Serpent King loomed over me, his gold diamond buttons gleaming as I roamed my gaze over his forest green button-up. When I glanced at his face, I was pleased to see his brows furrowed and lips curled into a frown.

I didn't break our eye contact as I lifted the turkey leg to my lips, ripping another piece of meat between my teeth. His brows shot up at my barbaric manners, but frankly, I couldn't care less.

Wait, maybe my poor manners could work in my favor . . . if he viewed me as an unattractive, wild animal, maybe he would stop staking his claim over me around my bodyguard, and we could solely focus on the problem with my emotions.

The corners of my lips twitched around the turkey leg at the mere thought of my devious plan.

Suddenly, I looked forward to putting on a new type of show this evening.

I chomped vigorously, not even bothering closing my mouth between bites as I continued to stare directly at the Serpent King. His green eyes flicked to the chewed food left on full display, making him brace a hand against his stomach, as if it could stop him from gagging at my repulsive behavior.

After what felt like ages of gnawing on the turkey leg like an animal, I threw the bone back onto the silver platter. He tracked the movement, his mouth gaping in horror as the bone bounced off another steaming turkey leg, only to land at the king's feet.

Slowly, his gaze rose to mine, right in time to see me swiping my greasy lips with the back of my hand. Nonchalantly, I reached for my bubbling champagne as the king lingered.

"Dear gods, what has come over you, woman?"

I opened my mouth to respond with something undoubtedly witty, but a burp flew out instead. On instinct, I nearly raised my hand to cover my mouth, but I forced myself to act casual as I took a small sip of my champagne and glanced up, batting my lashes at the insufferable man still hovering beside me.

His jaw was practically on the floor, his eyes carefully observing me as if I was a wild beast that was also about to consume him for dinner.

He wished.

"Are you going to stand for the entirety of our dinner, or would you like to take a seat?" I grandly waved toward the chair across the pond—the one furthest from me.

The king gave me a look that warred between disbelief and wonder that I dismissed him in his own lands. His scoff filled the silence, and I went back to ravenously eating another turkey leg. Finally, he took my lack of regard for his presence and sauntered over to his seat. Yet, I swore I heard him mutter something under his breath while he walked away.

Something along the lines of "beastly woman."

I smiled around the piece of meat while watching him take the seat I gestured to. Now, there was a whole body of dazzling golden water separating us.

Hopefully, it would be enough of a divide to keep my anger in check.

That notion was quickly thwarted when the Serpent King fiddled with his deep green cloth napkin. He fanned it out with an air of drama before placing it neatly on his lap. I suppressed the urge to roll my eyes at his pompous show—he clearly had manners, unlike the *beastly woman* he was dining with tonight.

Since I still required a favor from the menace by the end of the evening, I opted to control the strong urge to scoff at the king, who was now straightening the gold cutlery placed before him.

I broke the silence, glancing around the space. "This room hasn't changed, I see."

The sconces lining the stone walls, provided a warm, yet dim glow. The main source of light in the dining hall came from shimmering gold magic stewing in the pond beneath the table.

The king took a small sip of his champagne, wiping the corner of his lips with his napkin before delicately setting it atop his lap once more. This time, it was impossible to stop myself from rolling my eyes at his over-the-top manners, but he mercifully missed the gesture looking about the room.

"Were you ever even in this room?" His brows pinched in thought.

I pursed my lips as anger swirled inside me like a flurry, along with another emotion—one that I most definitely should not have access to feel.

It almost felt like . . . *hurt.*

No, I refused to ever allow him to hurt me again.

I swallowed the foreign emotion trying to bubble up to the surface from his lack of regard for our time spent together.

"We had multiple dinners here," was the only response I could force out as I focused on my rage, instead of the other lingering and more vulnerable feelings.

The Serpent King's glass hovered before his lips, his eyes squinting while he gazed into the pond.

"Doesn't ring a bell." He shook his head, taking another dainty sip of liquor.

An ounce of my anger released as I dug my nails into the wooden armrests.

"Of course it doesn't. Why would the Serpent King

remember the insignificant presence of a mere mortal?" I spat the last word in disgust, pulling a smile from him.

"I'm so glad you understand." He raised his glass at me, as if I had said the most beautiful toast, then downed the remainder of the fizzing bubbles.

Red flooded my vision, and as my hands curled into fists, I stabbed my sharp nails into the flesh of my palms in hopes to relieve more of my ever-growing fury. Warmth swiftly licked my fingertips, the familiar feeling of sticky residue pooling beneath my nails. It calmed me for a mere moment, and I closed my eyes while pretending my blood was actually the imbecile's sitting across from me.

When I first became queen, I struggled to manage my anger, like a ticking bomb ready to explode from one wrong look. Over the years, I learned how to negate the fury gnawing at my bones with three simple options.

Option one: Go on a killing spree.

Option two: Fuck my bodyguard until red no longer flooded my vision.

Or, option three: Distract myself by breathing through my rage.

Considering options one and two were not feasible at the moment, I focused on my breathing.

Inhale, exhale.

The Serpent King dragged his knife across his turkey leg, cutting it into bite-sized pieces, which only sparked another wave of anger to wash over me.

Inhale, exhale.

I nearly had my anger in check, even though the king was still eating like a royal priss, but then his previous comment rang through my head . . .

Doesn't ring a bell.

It was rather comical how he staked a claim on me in front

of Landon, yet now he acted as if our past together was truly forgettable.

A mere blip of time in his endless, immortal life.

Soft hissing broke me from my bottomless pit of anger, and I easily recognized the calm cadence. Closing my eyes, I let Ember's hissing ease my heightened emotions. Slowly, my hatred for the menace sitting across from me dissolved, and I sent two words down our mental bond.

Thank you.

Ember's scarlet head snapped toward me, her black eyes temporarily flashing with awe.

My head lurched back at those two simple, yet horrifying words I'd just uttered to my snake.

I never once said thank you in all my decades ruling as the Serpent Queen, the positive emotion of gratitude completely foreign to me. It was another feeling that was erased in my bargain with the Serpent King . . . I stared at the blood staining my hands. Then slowly, I lifted my gaze, only to see piercing green eyes already locked onto me.

The king's nostrils flared, his nose pinching with disgust. "Why do you smell like chocolate and oranges? Such an uncommon scent, I haven't smelt it since . . ." he trailed off, his gaze dropping to the golden pond. He stared at the trickling water falling straight from the stone serpent's stretched mouth.

For once in my life, I opted to stay silent, allowing him to work through whatever was troubling him. My champagne flute sizzled as fresh liquor poured into the glass, and my gasp tore the Serpent King's gaze from the waters and back to me.

"Did you do that?" I gave a pointed look to my once-empty glass that was now brimming with champagne.

"The magic that just filled your glass is essentially an extension of me, so I suppose I did." His lips tightened, almost like he was upset he revealed that tidbit of information to me, but he swiftly changed the subject.

"I see what you mean about your emotions faltering." He tapped a pale finger against his annoyingly full lips as he assessed me with narrowed eyes.

"Do you have any idea why emotions I shouldn't have access to are returning?" My question hung in the air while the king drummed his fingers against the wooden table.

I swiped my champagne flute into my greedy grasp, tipping it against my lips and swallowing my growing impatience along with the bubbling liquid.

"I have an inkling of what is happening to you." The serpentine smile he cast at me made my skin crawl.

"Are you going to share said inkling with me, or are you going to proceed to smile at me like a scoundrel for the rest of the evening?" I tossed my own sickly sweet smile back, trying to act calm instead of like the raging bitch I was about to turn into if he continued to play games with me.

The Serpent King's smile widened as he inhaled, revealing his elongated canines. They gleamed against the golden water, making him look every bit like the snake he was.

"Such an angry serpent." His eyes danced with amusement, the legs of his chair making a horrible screech against the stone floors as he pushed it back to stand.

I, too, shoved to my feet, my chair making a matching screech.

It seemed even our chairs were bickering with each other.

"Are you seriously not going to share what is happening to me?" I snarled, slamming my hands on the table.

The king's delighted smile nearly had me launching myself across the water to smack it off his perfect face. He made a show of rubbing his jaw as he contemplated my request again, but ultimately shook his head.

A growl worked up my throat.

"What's in it for me?" He picked at his nails.

"What's in it for you?" I parroted back through gritted teeth.

He casually strolled around the table with his hands tucked in his pockets. "You want information from me, but what do *I* get in return?"

As he prowled closer, I envisioned commanding my snakes to wrap around his thick neck, if only to squeeze that smug smile straight off his lips.

Inhale, exhale.

First, gather information.

Then, we can kill him.

I rolled my shoulders back, letting the anger sweep off my back with the movement.

"What do you want?" I asked.

A delighted hum curled around me as the king stopped right in front of me, close enough that his cologne suffocated my lungs. The familiar scent of smoky amber threatened to pull me straight back into the memories of our past—the memories I worked so hard to lock away.

I swallowed my discomfort, not giving him a chance to detect any of my bothersome emotions.

The king leaned closer, bringing his face level with mine.

"Isn't it obvious what I want?" His eyes gleamed with hunger.

Upon my silence, he said three words that nearly brought me to my knees.

"I want you."

CHAPTER 17

THE DEAL

I wasn't breathing.

The Serpent King wanted *me?*

Three simple, yet utterly devastating words.

I want you.

Three words I once dreamed of hearing.

Subconsciously, I took a step away from the king, as though putting distance between us could protect me from the man who made me lock away my heart in the first place.

My attempt was futile since he matched my step, his eyes never straying from mine. A wicked gleam shone in them, like a hunter ready to pounce on its prey.

"You already own my soul." My voice came out far weaker than I wished.

"Now, I want more. I want all of you. I want you to rule beside me, as my Queen."

Dread sliced through my veins, making me take another step backward. "You can't be serious. Did you forget you were the one who kicked me out of Morotis after our bargain?"

Something flashed in his eyes, but it disappeared too

quickly for me to decipher. Whatever emotion he felt rapidly shifted back into a wicked hunger.

"I have to admit, I like this fiery side of you. You are nothing like you were when you were a mortal." His eyes dipped to my lips, the desire in his gaze growing.

Despite the cruel intent behind his words, they felt like a compliment, for I wanted nothing more than to distance myself from the pathetic, quiet, scared mortal girl I once was.

The Serpent Queen was not the same person.

I made sure of that.

Although I liked being admired for my strength, I would never show gratitude to the menace before me, who wanted to own me like a shiny trophy.

So, I defaulted to hiding my true feelings behind my sharp tongue. "How does a simple piece of information I require equate to an immortal sentence of servitude as your personal harlot?"

He wagged his finger before my face. "I never said you'd be my harlot, unless you're interested?" He arched a thick brow, but swiftly continued on when he heard the low growl creeping up my throat. "I want you to be my Queen, nothing else. Are you not the Serpent Queen, after all? It only makes sense that you finally sit beside your king." He raised his hand as if to cradle my face, but I blocked his unwanted advance with my forearm.

"You are not *my* king. I answer to no one but myself." Venom coated my words as I bared my teeth at him, yet he only chuckled down at me.

The Serpent King was a fool for playing with fire, because I was ready to ignite.

I wanted to become an endless wildfire that would tear through his lands until there was only a wake of ash left behind.

If he wanted to see the monster he made me become, so be it.

"Since you've failed to listen previously, I shall remind you for one last time. I will *never* be yours. I refuse your offer. I refuse to be *your* queen." I shoved my sharp nail into his chest, right where I sliced his skin mere hours ago.

For the first time tonight, uncertainty flickered in the king's eyes.

"I will figure out my unwanted emotions on my own. Coming here was a mistake, one I will never make again. Goodbye, Serpent King. I hope our paths never cross for the rest of my days." I spat, already spinning on my heel for the exit.

I wouldn't allow him another opportunity to toy with me.

I was ready to grab Landon and forever flee from this wicked man.

"Wait," he said, finding the audacity to grab my arm, even after countless times I told him not to touch me unsolicited.

In this moment, one of the mortal sayings floated through my head . . .

She was asking for it.

Such a stupid way to fault women for men not being able to control themselves; a crass excuse to touch us however they pleased, without a lick of our consent.

Well, two could play this game.

Instead of fighting him, I let him spin me around, only so I could use the momentum I gained against him. My already curled fist collided with his perfectly straight nose, producing a satisfying crunch. He reared back in surprise, releasing me from his tight grip, cradling his now crooked nose.

"You asked for it." I smiled at him.

When he pulled his hands away, he gaped at the blood coating his fingers.

"You . . . you broke my fucking nose." He glared at me, and I expected to see vengeance burning brightly in his magnetic eyes.

The last thing I expected to see was delight.

I smothered my surprise with a shrug of the shoulder. "What did I say about touching me unsolicited, Serpent King? A broken nose is the least of your problems when it comes to dealing with the wrath of the Serpent Queen."

A sickening crack split through the air, and I watched with violent dissatisfaction as his nose healed itself within seconds, almost like the punch I dealt never happened.

Damn immortal healing.

Although his nose was straight yet again, I was pleased he no longer sported the amused smile he wore for the entirety of our dinner. Instead, his brows were crinkled with concern as his eyes flickered to my still curled fists. If he intended to keep me here against my will as his queen, I was ready to fight my way out of Morotis.

The Serpent King was in for a rude awakening, because there was nothing more dangerous than a trained woman itching for revenge.

Almost like they could sense a battle brewing, Ember and Dante appeared, their hisses ringing through the cavernous space. As they descended my arms, their eyes were trained on the Serpent King.

A small kernel of warmth fluttered through my chest at the fact I wasn't alone.

My snakes were here with me, and they were ready to defend their Queen, regardless of whether their opponent was also their maker.

The king raked a hand through his hair, blowing out a frustrated breath. A black lock loosely fell over his forehead, drifting into his eyes when he turned to gaze at the pond. The golden, shimmering water reflected against his hair, shifting the color from black to dark green, then swiftly back to black as his eyes returned to me.

Something curious flickered in them, and I rapidly sniffed the air to catch the newfound emotion. A thick cloud of smoke threatened to pull a cough out of me as the king's regret suffocated my lungs.

"I will tell you what you want to know. No strings attached." He held his hands up, his shoulders sagging in surrender.

My snakes and I glanced at each other, then narrowed our eyes at the Serpent King.

"Why the sudden change of heart?"

"I was simply having fun with you. After you've been alive as long as I have, things get boring. It was my source of entertainment for the night to rile you up." He shrugged, as if he didn't just say something wildly offensive.

His words were like a match falling against a mountain of dead brush, and I allowed the fire I caged within me to finally blaze wild and free.

I launched myself at him as fast as lightning, throwing a punch directly between the lower part of his pecs—right where Landon taught me if I hit hard enough, it would steal the air from my opponent.

The Serpent King may be immortal, but he could still have the breath knocked out of his arrogant ass.

He stumbled backward, hinging at the waist and bracing his hands against his knees. Though he tried to act nonchalant, I heard a slight wheeze escape his throat. Dante readied himself to join in on the fight, his red eyes glowing as he locked them onto the king's neck, ready to cut off his air supply.

I shot a silent command down our bond: *Don't you dare. He's mine.*

Dante's irritated hiss filled my head as both of my snakes disappeared from my arms, leaving the Serpent King and Serpent Queen to duel it out.

While the king was busy catching his breath, I made my next move. I rammed my knee, with the entirety of my force, straight into his nose. His howl intermingled with the sound of bones breaking as he stumbled backward. I smirked while I watched blood trickle down his, once again, crooked nose.

Before the night was over, I'd make sure he knew never to touch me unwarranted again.

Plus, the Serpent King broke my heart, so it was only fair I broke a piece of him a few times.

I channeled my rage, finally allowing myself to remember the moments I tried so hard to forget.

His lips smashed against mine, our tongues intertwining.
I could physically feel him sucking my soul out of my body, and I nearly fought back. It felt wrong to let such an integral part of me go, but I had to.
I never wanted to feel so deeply again.
I wanted power.
I wanted to be someone my mother would fear.
I wanted to be someone the world would never think to cage again.
So, I let the Serpent King take my soul.
When I felt completely hollow, he broke our kiss, only to sink his teeth into the flesh above my lip. I should feel pain from a bite like this, but, as I let the king infuse his magic into my veins, I felt nothing.

I stopped myself from recalling the next bit of that memory, for what happened next was something I never wanted to relive. Instead, I let all the fury I carried throughout the decades fuel my next kick. I slammed my stiletto into the king's chest while he still cradled his nose, an animalistic snarl tearing from my lips when he reared back.

I moved with him, never letting him out of my grip.

This immortal once thought I was easy prey for him to sink his sharp teeth into.

But now, the prey was the hunter.

I unsheathed the dagger strapped around my thigh, the golden hilt of the intertwining serpents gleaming brightly from the glare casting off the pond. Bending down, I yanked on the collar of his shirt, bringing him back to his feet.

"Apologize." I pressed my dagger slightly into the Serpent King's pale throat.

His throat bobbed but quickly stilled, almost like he was holding his breath. Maybe he was in shock, or maybe he was smart enough to know I'd truly slit his throat, even if it wouldn't kill him.

From what I understood, immortals couldn't die easily. That was all I gathered from the few weeks I lived in Morotis, yet I'd happily spill more of his blood tonight just for the fun of it if he didn't cooperate.

His throat worked again, as if he wanted to say something but didn't want the blade to nick his flawless skin. Rolling my eyes, I eased my grip and pulled the blade slightly off his skin.

"I apologize." He croaked.

"For?" I mockingly cocked my head, causing him to purse his lips.

"I apologize for putting my hands on you."

"And?" I cooed, the dagger hovering mere inches from his throat.

The king looked like he wanted to protest, but his eyes dipped to my blade, then back to me.

"And for treating you like a possession I could own." His jaw ticked.

It was apparent the Serpent King most definitely never apologized for anything in his life, and he was not happy to be doing so right now—and to me of all people.

The Seera he once knew would never demand an apology, but the girl he knew died long ago.

The corners of my lips twitched into a smug smile, and I nodded at him in a silent command to proceed. He scoffed—well, at least tried to—but the motion was halted when I pressed my blade against his throat.

"What else do you want to apologize for?" I pulled the blade back, allowing him a chance to speak.

He grumbled his next words, but my heightened senses heard every beautiful word spilling from the Serpent King's vile lips.

"I'm sorry for trying to take advantage of your predicament," He muttered.

I sniffed the air to see if his apology was sincere, and not said simply because I had a dagger against his throat. However, the spicy pepper scent associated with lies did not hang in the air. Instead, it smelt like smoke for the second time tonight.

The Serpent King reeked of *regret*.

I lowered my dagger, slowly sheathing it into the holster around my thigh. Now that my blade no longer threatened to nick his perfect skin, the king sucked in a greedy breath.

"I don't recall you knowing how to fight at such a high caliber." He arched a brow while rubbing his chest, right where I kicked him seconds ago.

"My bodyguard taught me," I said, looking down my nose at him.

He let out a distasteful huff at the mention of Landon, his hand drifting down to his nose. Even though it was perfectly aligned once more, he winced upon touching it. The pain of having his nose broken not once but twice, must be lingering within his bones, though he had no scars to show for it.

I smiled victoriously at the sight of the Serpent King in agony from my own actions.

It was about time he had a taste of his own medicine.

He shook his head in disbelief, making his hair shift between black and dark green.

"Your fighting reminded me of . . ." A pained look flashed across his face, but he quickly shook it off. "Never mind. It doesn't matter."

I arched a brow, a seed of curiosity firmly rooting itself inside my chest.

He shook his head again, as if to erase the thought. "I have a theory of why your emotions are returning, but it would be easier if I showed you something first."

I narrowed my eyes, but, before I could ask what he meant, he turned and approached the black stone wall closest to us. When he lightly pressed his hand against it, I staggered forward in awe as the wall stretched open, almost like it was yawning and awakening from a deep slumber.

Now, a tall archway stood above the king, revealing a secret passageway.

"How did you do that?" I marveled at the opening while peering into the tunnel.

He backed away from the entrance, his smug smile quickly returning. "These caves answer to me, remember? My magic built these lands, so I can shape them into whatever I please."

I knew the Serpent King was powerful, but this was beyond what I could imagine. I only had an inkling of his power. If he could shape an entire mountain of stone into a vast network of ever-changing tunnels, that meant he had more power to share with me.

Perhaps, I could kill the rebel movement for good if I made another deal with the menace.

The king cleared his throat, tearing my power-hungry thoughts back to the green eyes staring at me. "Do you still want those answers?"

I glanced at the daunting archway, then gave him a pointed look as I waved my hand to the passage and tossed back his words from earlier."After you."

He rolled his eyes but casually strolled through the entrance and into whatever laid on the other side. Hesitantly, I crept forward, stopping at the threshold. An endless darkness stared back at me, making me pause before following a man I didn't trust into what looked like the entrance to the land of the wicked.

Then again, this is what I came here for.

If I had to follow the menace I loathed into the darkness in order to gain the answers I sought, I'd do it.

I was ready to rid myself of these horrid feelings, once and for all.

I wanted to *never* feel again.

So, I stepped into the passage and followed the Serpent King, letting the darkness embrace me like an old friend.

PART TWO: SECRETS

CHAPTER 18

LUMINOSO

P anic surged through me like a raging storm the deeper we went in the tunnel. Even though I could see because of my sharp immortal eyesight and the dim flicker of a few sparse torches, my palms grew slick at the thought of getting trapped down here.

It was so dark.

Too dark.

It reminded me of the tower, of the perpetual darkness I had lived in.

"Just a little further." The king's voice echoed through the cave, distracting me from the panic attack readying to consume me.

I forced myself to breathe through the tightness pressing on my chest. "Where are you taking me?"

He chuckled darkly. "Still impatient as ever, I see."

I grumbled a slew of curses to myself but kept following after the behemoth. The pathway forked into three routes, and he confidently walked down one. After a few more moments, he abruptly stopped, moving to face one of the walls surrounding us. With a simple touch against the stone, it creaked open to reveal a secret door.

Morotis was full of hidden passageways—a reminder at how dangerous this place truly was. This deep into the caves, it would be a wonder if Landon could find me. I swallowed the worry and forced myself onward as the king disappeared into the hidden room.

At least I knew how to fight, and I held on to that thought as I continued to focus on steadying my breathing.

If this was a trap, I would not hesitate to break the Serpent King's nose for a third time.

My anxiety dissipated like a plume of smoke as I took in what laid beyond the door. Warm light twinkled above, portraying a sea of stars drifting across the onyx ceiling. They drifted across the space, as if there was a phantom wind blowing them, yet it wasn't one I could feel. The only reasonable answer to how this was possible this far into the caves was magic.

Sure enough, I caught a glimpse of the subtle glow of golden particles dancing between the stars. I felt a tug toward those shimmering flecks, my hand subconsciously reaching for the stars overhead. As pieces of the sparkling magic wrapped around my fingertips, I had the same hypnotic trance come over me, just like when I gazed at the golden pond.

Your magic sings to me.

I quickly snapped my hand down, shaking off the warmth spreading within the void in my chest. My skin prickled as the sensation of being watched crept over me. I turned, catching those piercing green eyes curiously peering at me through the darkness. The Serpent King's lips twitched upward, as if he saw how his magic affected me, how it intertwined around me with ease, how it *sang to me.*

"What is so amusing?" I challenged.

"Well, you, of course."

I scoffed. "You may be the only person who's ever found me amusing."

His brows pinched and silence filled the air as he waited to see if I'd elaborate.

His stare was so intense, taking me right back to the moment he first laid those haunting eyes on me . . .

His gaze was calculating. I felt like I was stripped for all to see simply by the way his eyes roamed over my body. My bare feet shuffled in place against the cool stone as I awaited his judgment. After what felt like an eternity, his tantalizing lips spread into a smile that made me want to run, yet also fall to my knees.

"Seera." The king rolled my name off his tongue, almost like he was tasting if I was worthy to enter his lands. "You and I are about to know each other very well. Welcome to Morotis."

The wicked man from my memory cleared his throat, rooting me back to the present, where I couldn't be further from the mortal girl who balked before the immortal Serpent King. A lot changed over the last seventy-five years—except those damn eyes. Those were the same, especially in the way they assessed me like I was the most fascinating creature to ever exist.

Wait, what were we talking about again?

Think, Seera.

Oh, he thought me amusing.

"I don't think my people would agree, considering they constantly rebel against me."

The king's brows rose toward the stars, curiosity racing through those probing eyes of his.

This was the opening I needed.

I came here not only for answers about my emotions, but to crush this newest rebel movement for good.

"The rebels think you will aid them in their pursuit to overthrow me. In fact, a group was on their way to see you earlier today, but their journey ended . . . abruptly." A serpentine smile spread across my face as I remembered the sweet taste of the traitor's blood I licked straight off the blade, the same one I slit his throat with.

What a bunch of boneheads for thinking they could best the Serpent Queen, but I had to admit they came closer to visiting the Serpent King than I'd like.

The king's husky laugh rumbled through the cave, bringing my gaze to his.

"Why in all the realms would I help the mortals dethrone my Queen?"

I scowled, my lips tightening into a thin line at his casual use of my title. His eyes trailed down to my sides, where my hands started to curl into tight fists.

"Apologies, bad habit." He rubbed his neck, looking slightly uncomfortable as his gaze floated up to the stars still drifting above us.

I followed his gaze, letting my anger float away with the stars. As I watched them drift by, my thoughts drew back to Landon—to the other night underneath a similar view. From the way he softly kissed my tears, to how I rode him with the stars winking down at us, to how he apparently carried me all the way down the dune and safely settled me into bed.

In all my rule as the Serpent Queen, I've never let anyone that close to me. It was a foreign feeling to have someone care, worry, or even want to protect me. Warmth flooded my chest as I thought of my kind bodyguard, who I most definitely didn't deserve.

I squeezed my eyes shut, wishing away my increasingly confusing feelings for Landon.

After all, the Serpent Queen did not feel, and I preferred to keep it that way.

That was one thing I appreciated about the Serpent King: he never pressed me about my feelings for him while I lived in Morotis . . . I used to hate that fact, but I was grateful for it now. It also spared me from sounding like a complete and utter dunce when he didn't return my fond feelings for him.

Slamming my emotions deep down into a steel box, I opened my eyes to find the king not staring at the stars anymore.

He was staring at *me*.

I had to say something to distract him from looking at me like—like he could see straight through the mask I wore everyday.

"Is this the part where you tell me what is wrong with me, or should we settle this with another fight?" I held up one finger. "I suggest option one, since you didn't fare well earlier against my wrath."

His laugh was deep and rich, and the bright stars above illuminated the twinkle of amusement dancing in his eyes.

"You can unleash your wrath on me any time, any place, Serpent Queen," he purred, his gravelly voice nearly making me shiver. "By the way, I meant to tell you earlier"—a ghost of a smile still graced the Serpent King's lips—"but you were too busy pressing your dagger to my throat."

I rolled my eyes, but curiosity crept through me at what he would reveal next.

"This gown . . ." He dragged a finger along the golden trim detail wrapping around my flared sleeves. "This one was always my personal favorite. The trim brings out the gold in your eyes."

His fingers skimmed over the serpent embroidery, lingering when they brushed an exposed sliver of my skin. But then, as if he hadn't just given me a surprisingly kind compliment, the king turned on his heel, leaving me only a moment to release a discreet breath.

He *still* had an effect on me, even after all these years.

The infuriating menace moved to the center of the room, and my breath hitched as he dropped to his knees.

I hated myself for immediately thinking what a beautiful sight it was to see the Serpent King kneeling before me.

Get yourself together, Seera.

He slammed his hands against the stone ground, closing his eyes as he started to chant in a foreign language—whatever language it was, it was beautiful. After another moment, the king rose, stepping back as the floor split open. White light blinded me as it speared from the crack in the ground, causing me to quickly shield my burning eyes. I blinked rapidly, willing away the spots swimming in my vision.

"Ah, yes. I should have warned you about the light." The Serpent King said over his shoulder in a nonchalant tone.

Asshole.

When I glanced toward the newly formed crevice, I blinked a few more times to make sure I was seeing things correctly.

A giant crystal orb floated in the center of the cave, my mouth parting as I slowly approached it. I'd never seen anything of this sort, and I jumped back when light illuminated from the ball. Moving images flashed by, of what looked like lands I'd only read about in books. Foreign creatures prowled across the orb, some sporting horns while others had tentacles instead of legs. The most stunning woman flashed across the device, but my gaze snagged on the side of the crystal, where it was projecting a black stone castle shooting high into a sheet of grey clouds.

My castle.

"What the fuck is this?" I glanced at the king, my face draining of blood.

He looked at the orb, the colors flashing across it making his hair appear dark green.

"This is a Luminoso, which basically is a fancy name for an all-seeing crystal ball." He pinched the smooth surface showcasing my queendom, making it larger.

My servants came into view as they walked across the bridge, which connected my castle to the city and overlooked a daunting gorge of dark mist. I glanced at my training grounds, even spotting the coliseum off in the distance.

"You've been spying on me?" Rage flickered in my gut at the violation of privacy.

"Believe it or not, I have much better things to do with my time than watch you execute your people in that Pit of yours." Yet he couldn't meet my probing eyes.

"So you have been keeping tabs on me?" I arched a brow, and I grinned as his cheeks grew rosy.

"No, I—I've heard some things about you over the years." He glanced sideways at me, ruffling a hand through his hair. "I don't spy on you."

It was a rare day to see the Serpent King flustered, and the smug smile I cast at him only made him blow out another frustrated breath.

"I simply showed you your kingdom so you would understand how this device worked. That is all."

"Queendom."

"Excuse me?" His lips curled down.

"You called my home a kingdom. Yet, there hasn't been a king ruling over Phantamos in nearly eight decades. So, you shall address my lands correctly—it is a *queendom*." I stared down my nose at the king, whose brows were rising toward the stars.

"Apologies, Your Majesty. I will not make that mistake again out of fear of being your little Pit's next victim . . . "

I could tell the menace was trying to rile me up by the way the corner of his lips twitched upward, but I would not give him the satisfaction of knowing he indeed spiked my blood pressure.

"Mhmmm," I hummed, as my gaze danced over the beaming images.

My curiosity rose as I studied the fantasy lands and creatures.

"What exactly am I looking at here?"

He spread his arms wide as he stared at the Luminoso. "These are the realms of the gods."

Time stilled as my mind refused to accept his words, but the flashing images of my queendom proved this crystal ball did indeed show real places.

Yet, it was impossible, for the gods weren't real.

I must have spoken my last thought aloud, because the Serpent King whispered something back that made my cold heart nearly stop.

"Oh, the gods are very real, and one of them is messing with your emotions."

CHAPTER 19
A DEADLY PROMISE

If the gods were real, why did they allow me to suffer for so long?

The thought rang through my head as I stared at the beaming images radiating off the Luminoso.

When I was mortal, I was ignorant enough to pray to the gods—I prayed for them to free me from my mother, from my life in total isolation. I begged for a normal life, to experience friendship, adventure, and maybe even love.

Yet, the gods never answered my prayers, so I stopped believing in them the day I broke free and fought to forge my own destiny. The day I climbed the mountain and entered Morotis was the same day the gods ceased to exist in my mind.

Yet now, the Serpent King expected me to accept they were real? How could I accept the fact the gods truly existed, meaning they deliberately left my prayers unanswered?

The rage simmering beneath my skin was like boiling water, begging to explode.

Anger was an emotion I had no problem dealing with—I'd

just tear the life from a traitor in my lands to dispel the beast gnashing within me.

I reveled in bloodshed, in the one act that made me feel alive.

Maybe, if the gods answered my prayers all those years ago, I wouldn't have been desperate enough to escape the claws of one monster just to slip into the grip of another.

"Why did they abandon the mortals?" My voice shifted to the cold tone I used in my dungeons, the one I reserved for when I carved up my people.

"What made you think the gods cared about the mortals in the first place?" He frowned, crossing his arms while turning to fully face me.

My vision blurred as my rage seeped into every inch of my body.

These were the gods my people prayed to?

The ones they thought would save them from the likes of me?

My subjects were bigger fools than I thought.

Glaring at the gods, I made a silent vow, or more so, a deadly promise . . .

I'd kill them all for abandoning us.

A sinister plan wove through my head. If my people witnessed me defeating the gods they worshipped, they would have no other choice but to bow to me.

I tugged my lip between my teeth as the idea took root deep inside me, making me realize I didn't have to make another bargain with the Serpent King after all.

Squaring my shoulders, I worked on replacing my anger with determination. Even though my anger still lingered in the shadows, I placed it to the side for later.

For the day the gods met their reckoning by my hand.

"Show me the gods' faces."

"I don't see how that is relevant—" The king started, but I cut him off by pointing a sharp, blood-red nail at the orb.

"Show. Me. Them." I suddenly wanted to learn everything about the gods I had long ago abandoned, so I could figure out the best way to destroy them.

His lips pursed as his brows bunched together at the violence creeping into my voice. However, he didn't push any further, instead swiping a finger across the crystal orb. A moment later, it illuminated with five beautiful faces—each one unique enough that I could commit every detail to memory.

I imagined such fine features twisted in agony. I'd make them beg for mercy, just like I did all those years ago.

"Tell me who they are."

The Serpent King gave me one more sideways glance before pointing a pale finger at the furthest screen of the orb. A fair-skinned woman with blazing red hair flashed across the screen.

"Hestia, goddess of the fire realm, also known as Ignitus."

The god smiled at someone off-screen, giving me time to memorize her every feature, down to the splatter of light freckles dusted across her nose and cheeks.

Once I digested every detail of the fire goddess's visage, my gaze drifted to the section beneath her. A woman with light brown skin swam through a body of water, an iridescent purple tail whipping gracefully behind her.

"Who is that?" I pointed at the stunning creature.

"That is Vasara, goddess of the sirens. She rules the realm Echandria."

The goddess held a cruel beauty to her, with her lips painted a deep shade of purple, nearly appearing black, as they perpetually sat in a sinister smile. She swam through the murky waters, her black hair streaming behind her, carrying a magenta shine to it as sparse sun rays streamed across her face.

She reminded me a lot of myself, but that fact would not spare me from unleashing hell on her the day we met.

Before I could ask who the woman with deep brown skin and the most gorgeous brunette hair featuring honeyed high-lights was, the king spoke.

"That is Aradia, the goddess of witches. She rules the realm Caraway."

"She doesn't look like a witch," I said as I stared at her friendly face, appearing nothing like the old hags with moles I read about in fairytale novels.

"Don't let her sweet face deceive you. She is not to be trifled with. I avoid the witch realm at all costs." He looked at Aradia once more, but then quickly glanced away—as if she would look through the orb and cast a wicked spell on him.

Besting the goddess of witches seemed like it would be challenging, considering the bitter scent wafting from the Serpent King . . . but nothing worth having came easy.

"Wait." Curiosity crawled through me. "Can you travel between realms?"

The king's smile was dripping with cockiness as he puffed his chest. "Of course I can." His eyes trailed down my figure. "Would you like a private demonstration of how powerful I am?"

It felt like someone sparked me with a live wire, right between my thighs. I squeezed them together, annoyed that the Serpent King's words affected me in such a way. His eyes dipped between my legs, not missing a single thing I did. He chewed on his lip as he inhaled the sparse bit of air between us, and I silently cursed myself for letting my mask slip around him once more.

For Serpent's Sake, I needed him to stop looking at me like he wanted to consume every glorious inch of me.

Flicking my hair over my shoulder, I turned my gaze back to the Luminoso, pointing at the bottom of the orb. "And who is she?"

A stunning, sun-kissed woman with blonde waves loosely flowing around her heart-shaped face flashed across it. Her hair whipped around, almost as if she was caught in the eye of a windstorm. Even with her hair a mess, she radiated pure beauty.

Her emerald green eyes shone at whoever she was looking at, then she tipped her head back as if she was laughing. There was no sound emitting from the Luminoso, but I knew without hearing her laugh it was probably perfect, just like her.

She was sunshine personified.

The Serpent King chuckled, prompting me to glare at him. He met my stare, his lips twitching as if he was holding himself from completely bursting into laughter.

"What is so funny?"

"Oh, I'm simply thinking about how you will react to the next piece of information I share." He tapped his fingers against his mouth, making my anger rear its ugly head.

I clenched my jaw, giving the king a scowl that promised death if he made me wait in anticipation for a moment longer.

His dark laugh echoed through the cave while he rubbed his jaw. "Are you sure you are ready for the truth of who that woman is?" He pointed a finger at the goddess who rivaled the sun.

"Tell me who she is, before I pummel the answer out of you." My hand tightened into a fist, and his eyes flickered down, noting my movement.

He grinned, then breathed five words that changed everything.

"That is the Serpent Queen."

CHAPTER 20
GOD IS A WOMAN

Blood pooled underneath my nails as I pinched my thigh to wake me from this ever lasting nightmare.

This menace of a man did not just tell me there was a god who was also called the Serpent Queen.

No, I refused to believe this was reality, for if anyone dared to assume my title, I'd cut them into a million pieces while savoring every single scream they shed.

"You might want to wipe that murderous look off your face, considering that woman is the reason you have any powers," the king said, confirming I was sadly awake.

My head snapped to meet his gaze, only to find an arrogant smile dancing upon his lips.

I had an intense urge to summon Dante right about now, just to wring the king's fucking neck.

Instead, I opted for a safer option—threatening him.

"You have two seconds to explain everything before I stick my spiked stiletto far up your dark abyss."

The king gaped, clearly never before having such an intimate threat uttered at him.

I would be more than happy to finally shove my heel up his ass after all he put me through. He tousled his hair, making his black locks messier than I'd ever seen them. I was getting under his skin, and a thrill shot through me at the power I held over the king.

"The Serpent Queen is the goddess of the Emerald Glades." The menace gave me a sideways glance, gauging my reaction before continuing. "But she also happens to be my mother."

My jaw nearly dropped in disbelief, but I ground my teeth together to stop myself. There was a heavy pause before I asked something I was always curious about.

"So, does that make you a god by default?"

The Serpent King huffed, looking very offended by my remark.

"Nothing about me is by default." His lip curled with disgust. "But, yes, technically I could be a god one day."

He was being rather cryptic, and I could tell he was withholding information from me.

"What are you then?" I narrowed my eyes at the snake.

He defensively crossed his arms over his chest, clearly not liking being in the firing line of my questions.

"I'm powerful enough you should fear me and quit using such an irksome tone."

Inhale. Exhale.

Don't kill this motherfucker . . . at least not yet.

The only thing preventing me from sicking my snakes on his pompous ass was the fact my powers were tied to this godforsaken man.

I took a menacing step closer. "Maybe I wouldn't use such an *irksome* tone if you were more straightforward when answering my questions."

"Now, where would the fun be in doing that?" He gave me

a charming smile, making that silent ticking bomb of anger that resided inside me fuse to life.

Inhale. Exhale.

I wouldn't allow him the satisfaction of getting underneath my skin.

"Is there literally anyone else who can tell me about the gods besides you? Maybe a library, perhaps? Frankly, I've had just about enough of you to last me a lifetime."

He clutched his chest, as if my words wounded his cold, black heart.

Gods, spare me.

Well, that was new.

It was rather nice—using the gods' names in vain. I had no qualms with doing so, considering they were indeed real, and very much selfish bastards.

It might actually become my new favorite pastime to curse their names at any given moment.

"There is a place I could take you to, but aren't you forgetting to ask me a vital question, Serpent Queen?" A cocky smile graced his lips, causing me to cross my arms over my chest so I didn't do something I'd later regret—like slap that stupid smirk straight off his lips.

The king's eyes dipped to my chest, and I followed his gaze to the way my breasts now perked up from my new position.

Apparently, it didn't matter if you were an immortal or mortal man, since they all were the same in the end—fools easily distracted by a woman's curves.

I groaned in disgust, rolling my eyes. "For someone who prides himself on having perfect manners, you sure are acting like a pig. You ought to look me in my eyes when you're in the presence of royalty."

He gawked at me, a mixture of disbelief and amusement fueling the chuckle that burst out of him.

"You are something else," he muttered.

I was quickly losing any remaining shred of my already thin patience. "Out with whatever else you need to tell me, Serpent King."

He arched a dark brow. "You never asked me which god was toying with your emotions."

Oh.

How could I be so foolish?

The moment I found out the gods were real, my rage blinded me from thinking rationally.

"Tell me then, who dares to mess with the Serpent Queen?" I took another step toward him, making my chest brush against his.

His gaze roamed over my face, pausing on my lips before latching onto my eyes. "I'm starting to understand why your people fear you."

"I'd think the fact I broke your nose twice earlier solidified why my people fear me, but I am happy to remind you what happens when I don't get my way," I cooed with a false innocence.

"As much as I'd love to feel your hands on me, in any capacity, we will save that for another night." He tossed me a wink before turning his attention back to the Luminoso.

His fingers swiped across the crystal orb, then what looked like a map blinked onto its surface.

"This is an overview of all the realms." He pointed to a dark mountain near the bottom of the orb. "We are here, in Morotis." His finger trailed lower. "Below, is your lands, or the mortal realm as we refer to it." He dragged his finger above our realms, gesturing to the majority of the map. "Then, the gods' realms rest above Morotis."

I digested the map as best as I could, but my head was

starting to pound. Everything I thought I knew was fictitious, and I prided myself on always being right.

Fucking gods, this was a lot to handle in one night.

Right when I was about to glance away from the map, my eyes snagged on a black speck as big as my fist.

"What is that?"

The Serpent King sucked in a sharp breath. "That is Rime, the realm of frost and crystals. And I believe the Ice Goddess is the one you have to thank for your unwanted emotions."

I shot an accusatory look at the king. "Why didn't you show me her earlier when I asked about all of the gods?"

"Because I can't see her, hence the dark spot." His jaw ticked, prompting me to sniff the air. The pleasant scent of rotten fruit drifted down my throat, signaling the king's irritation.

Planting my hands on my hips, I tapped my fingers against the smooth velvet of my dress as I contemplated his words.

If this Ice Goddess could avoid being seen by the Luminoso, then she must be extremely powerful. My plans to destroy the gods just got a tad more complicated, especially if I had no idea what one of them looked like.

"You truly have no images of her?" I searched the crystal orb for a glimpse of this mysterious entity.

He released a heavy sigh. "No, I don't. However, I can tell you her name."

I perked up, eager for any clue that could help aid my new plan.

"Her name is Isolde."

"Isolde," I repeated, mentally adding it to my hit list.

"Wait, the gods are all women?" I asked incredulously.

"Indeed, they are." The Serpent King didn't seem as perturbed by this fact as I thought he would be. Instead, there was a glint of what looked like pride flickering in his eyes, as he, too, stared at the gods.

I nearly marveled at his reaction, but I also had an intense desire to scream.

The gods were all women, yet I was born in a world ruled by men.

Life was so unfair.

If only my story turned out differently, if only I wasn't born in the human lands.

My mind spiraled with what ifs, anger coursing through my veins over the fact I'd never gain insights to these hypothetical scenarios.

Because they weren't my reality.

To distract myself from getting further lost in my rage, I forced myself to focus on the images of the gods.

"Why do you think Isolde is messing with my emotions? Shouldn't that not be feasible considering our bargain was made based on you taking my emotions—thus, gaining my soul—in exchange for some of your powers?"

"This may shock you, but I don't think this has anything to do with you." The king's lips turned down, and I chose to ignore his slight jab as I was more curious in what he would say next.

I almost thought he wouldn't divulge more, but then he spoke in a softer tone.

"Isolde and I had a falling out decades ago."

I batted my eyelashes, feigning surprise. "The all-powerful Serpent King has a mortal enemy, but how could that be? He is *so* charming." I softly fluttered my hand against my chest, my voice simulating what I imagined a fairytale princess to sound like.

His frown deepened, swiftly shifting into a full-on pout.

Something sparked in my chest at how much I enjoyed

bantering with the Serpent King, making it feel as if no time had passed between us.

No, stop it, Seera.

For once, I was grateful the king spoke, since it halted me from going any further down such a perilous path.

"I'll have you know plenty of people find me charming." He popped the collar of his shirt, like a bird ruffling its feathers.

I chuckled, reaching up and patted his shoulder condescendingly. "I'm sure they do."

He scowled down at me, his hand flexing at his side.

I looked at him through my lashes, portraying total innocence as I smiled sweetly up at him. "Now, if we are done discussing how amazing you are, can we get to the part where your feud with the Ice Goddess affects me?"

"You are becoming a thorn in my side," he said through clenched teeth.

I simply smiled at the compliment.

He groaned, swiping a hand over his face. When he finally looked at me, it was with a menacing glare. But I'd take that look any day over the other option—his piercing stare that made me feel things I'd long since buried.

"I've felt a shift in my power," he confessed.

"A shift, as in . . . ?"

"As in I can't access all of my magic as easily as I once could."

I chewed on my lip. "Do you remember when this change began?"

I glanced up when the Serpent King remained silent, noticing his eyes lingering on my bottom lip. I stopped biting it, hoping it would help him focus on my question.

He shook his head, as if to clear the image from his mind, then peered at the stars still drifting above.

"I noticed a change about three days ago."

Three days ago . . . what happened three days ago?

I let my gaze wander over the stars as I scoured my mind for an inkling of what could have happened to cause such a monumental change.

Holy fucking gods.

My dinner with my mother.

My birthday—the same night I had my first panic attack in almost eight decades.

"Have you experienced any inconsistencies with your powers over the last few days?" The Serpent King's question tore my attention from the stars.

When I glanced down, our eyes instantly locked.

"Not that I remember—only the unwanted emotions . . . are Isolde's powers truly strong enough to mess with your magic?"

"As much as I hate to admit it, it is possible. On top of her being a god, she is an incredibly powerful sorceress. After all, she used to be the ruler of the witch realm." He looked like he was trying to suppress a shiver.

"The witch realm? I thought you said she was the Ice Goddess?"

"It's complicated . . ." the king winced.

While I waited for him to elaborate, I took in a discreet inhale.

I was curious what emotion was racing through the king, the one that made his shoulders inch up with tension. A foul, bitter taste coated my mouth, and I easily recognized my favorite emotion to consume.

The Serpent King *feared* the Ice Goddess.

I tucked away that rather interesting and useful piece of knowledge.

"I believe Isolde is syphoning bits of my magic to get back at me, which in turn is weakening my power and indirectly affecting you. With my magic depleted, I could become unable to uphold my end of our bargain."

All my remaining questions about the gods disintegrated, my curiosity swiftly replaced by the panic lurching through my chest at what the Serpent King was implying.

"Our bargain is weakening," he said, staring into my eyes with such a severe intensity, my knees nearly buckled.

"Your soul has started to gradually return to you, Seera, and the only way to prevent it from completely coming back is by working together."

CHAPTER 21
THE PLAN

Although the walk back to the formal dining hall was quiet, my mind was loud with thoughts clamoring for my attention.

It raced a mile a minute, trying to unpack everything I had learned tonight.

The gods were real, and they had abandoned the mortals.

There was a goddess who also called herself the Serpent Queen.

And to top it all off, the man who broke my heart proposed we come together to kill a god?

I needed a fucking drink.

Defeating a god was not the part of the Serpent King's plan that worried me; it was the thought of working with him that shook me to my core.

I could barely stand to be around him for one evening—how was I supposed to journey through the realms with him? A scoff slipped from my lips at the mere thought of us as allies again.

"What are you thinking about?" the king's voice rumbled through the caves, breaking my reverie.

I threw a glance over my shoulder. "I'm wondering how you expect us to work together when I detest you."

His steps faltered, but he quickly resumed his casual pace.

"I expect you to suck it up and do what is best for you, as you always do."

I halted, slamming my palm against the behemoth's chest. "What do you mean by that?"

He glanced at my hand like it was a bothersome gnat, then flicked his eyes to mine. "The Serpent Queen has a tendency to only look out for herself, does she not?"

Instead of doing what I wanted to do—which was ram my knee straight into his groin, making him keel over in pain—I smiled and leaned closer.

"That's rich coming from the king who collects souls."

The menace dipped his chin, bringing his face mere inches from mine.

Those damn eyes burned through the darkness and straight into where my soul used to be.

"I've collected only one soul in my lifetime, and it is my most prized possession."

His tongue darted out to wet his lips, making me curl my nails into the flesh of my palm as I worked to restrain myself from smacking away the smile that crept across his face.

"You are a monster."

He dipped his head, brushing his lips against my ear. "You can pretend all you'd like, Serpent Queen, but you and I are more similar than you care to admit."

I growled, turning on my heel and continuing my pursuit to get far away from these lands and the man who had just indirectly called me a monster.

Yet, he wasn't wrong, which made a fresh wave of anger

wash over me. No one else knew how I truly felt about myself, and I intended to keep it that way.

Let my people presume I loved the life I was dealt if it kept me safe, in a position of power.

I'd gladly be the villain, if it meant I'd never be the failed hero.

The Serpent King was just as much of a fool as my people if he thought I'd willingly be his ally.

After what felt like an eternity, the dark caves brightened as the golden pond greeted us. I strode straight past the shimmering waters for the exit, turning to face the king one last time.

"I won't be your ally. You will have to go on this journey alone to defeat the so-called Ice Goddess. As it is, I have my hands full with my weekly executions. Best of luck, Serpent King."

The last thing I saw before turning away was the way he crossed his arms, studying me like I was a book he was dying to read.

I had nearly disappeared from view down the passageway when his voice halted me in place.

"And how exactly do you expect to keep the rebels at bay if your power disappears?"

My jaw tightened at the possibility of a powerless life.

"I'll figure something out," I muttered. It was easier to lie, when I really had no other plan.

"This is one problem, Seera, that you cannot run away from." His voice was softer than usual, and the way he said my name . . .

"Seera," he whispered into my hair, tugging me against his body. "You've ruined me."

No. I couldn't entertain such a dangerous idea of conspiring with the Serpent King.

I'd worked too hard to rebuild myself just to go crawling back to the man that discarded me like vile trash.

But his words affected me, just as intended.

I always ran from my problems.

I fled from the tower, from my mother, from my complicated feelings for Landon.

From *everything*.

It just was . . . easier.

However, if my powers disappeared, there would be no running away from the mess I created while ruling as the Serpent Queen. I'd have to rely on my fighting capabilities alone to hold onto my throne. While Landon would fight with me, I didn't know if the same would be true for the rest of my guards. They had proven to be loyal thus far, but they could reconsider joining the rebels if they saw my magical abilities waning.

My snakes, and the fear they caused, made them stay in line.

I hated that *he* cast this newfound doubt in my head, but I loathed myself even more for considering the prospect of working with the Serpent King.

But . . . *it was time to come face to face with the ghosts of my past.*

"*If* I decide to ally with you to defeat Isolde, how would I keep the rebels in line? I can't abandon my throne during such hostile times." I glanced over my shoulder, catching a small wince flicker across the king's face.

"I have a plan, but I know you won't like it."

My lips tightened while I braced myself—how could tonight possibly get worse?

He looked away, not able to meet my eyes as I fully turned and faced him.

"I plan to have someone else sit on your throne."

The growl that clawed up my throat was as natural as breathing, an instinct to protect the one thing I fought so hard for when I returned to the mortal realm as an immortal.

My throne meant everything to me.

"No one sits on my throne besides *me*." I dug my thumb into my chest.

The king simply rolled his eyes, as if I were a child throwing a tantrum.

"Good thing you won't have to abandon your pedestal then." He picked at his nails, donning his usual mask of arrogance.

My brows knitted in confusion. "What?"

With a clap of his hands, a shadowy figure emerged from a secret passageway. As it crept closer, the golden light radiating from the pond illuminated the person.

My hand flew to cover my mouth as fresh panic lurched through my gut.

The spitting image of myself strolled toward me, her blood-red lips curved into a devious smile.

CHAPTER 22
THE IMPOSTER

I was staring at myself, yet there was not a mirror in sight.

"What sorcery is this?"

The imposter tossed a cruel smile in my direction. "Pretty neat, eh?"

I threw the Serpent King a sharp glare, not amused by whatever was unfolding. He clapped his hands together again, and the woman began to morph into something else . . . no, *someone* else.

Her green eyes faded to a rich hazel color, and the imitation of my sharp nose went crooked. Her black waves flowing past her curvy hips disappeared into a shaggy mess of blonde waves. The red lipstick painted on her lips floated away on a phantom breeze to reveal thinner pink ones, and the imposter's jaw lost its heart shape, becoming chiseled and lined in a thin layer of stubble.

"Did you miss me?" The man flashed a dazzling smile in my direction.

"Evander?" My voice was a mere whisper as I gaped at my old friend, glancing between him and the Serpent King.

"Someone better start explaining what is going on right this instant."

The king gestured at the roguishly handsome male. "My second-in-command is a shapeshifter. He will sit on your throne while we are away, meaning your people won't realize you were ever gone in the first place. He is one of the most talented, if not the best, shapeshifter of his kind."

I stared at Evander in awe, all the while he puffed his chest from the king's compliment and tossed me a prideful grin. His smile was so innocent, making the void in my chest warm a little. The man standing a mere few feet away was the only person I remotely came close to calling a friend in all my years.

I bit the inside of my cheek, starting to feel a torrent of emotions swirling inside me from simply gazing at Evander.

Curse these blasted feelings.

What was I thinking—that I could walk out of here and deal with all of this on my own?

I swallowed the ball of emotions gathering at the back of my throat, then met the king's second-in-command's captivating eyes.

"I see you never healed your crooked nose from when I broke it decades ago."

He tipped his head back, an enchanting laugh overtaking him. The sound wrapped around me like a warm blanket on a stormy night, making it easy to remember why I grew so fond of this man. He had one of those laughs that was contagious, so much so I had to gnaw on my lip to stop myself from smiling as well.

"I kept it crooked so I'd never forget the day you brought me to my knees, even if it was because of agony and not for pleasure." He tossed a wink at me, and this time I couldn't stop my lips from twitching into a small smile.

Someone obnoxiously cleared their throat, stealing my

attention away from the shapeshifter. My gaze snapped to the king, whose jaw was clenched as he glared at us.

I was about to sniff the air to see what emotion was spiraling off him, but a warm hand gently touched my arm, breaking me from my thoughts.

"Seera, I promise to guard your throne with my life. It is the least I can do after—after everything." Evander rubbed the back of his neck, his eyes searching mine, almost like he was silently pleading for my forgiveness.

This time, I smelt the air to detect what Evander was feeling, and smoke quickly suffocated my lungs.

There was so much regret permeating around me since stepping back into Morotis . . .

"You better." They were the only words I could choke out with Evander's regret still lingering in my mouth.

My simple statement had his eyes softening as he nodded. Emotion threatened to crawl up my throat as I stared back at Evander. He was the only person that easily welcomed me into these lands nearly eighty years ago. With him standing before me, I was more reminded once more of all I lost the night of the bargain—of the friendship I dreamed of, only to have it stolen away from me. Another wave of emotions swarmed my chest like a hive of bees.

This was insufferable.

This was my own personal form of torture.

Monsters don't deserve to feel.

I knew what I had to do, because there was only one choice if I wanted to never feel again.

Turning to the Serpent King, his intense eyes were already pinned on me.

Typical.

I looked down my nose at him. "I agree to work with you, but I must bring two people along on our journey."

Subtle movement at the king's side caught my attention, my gaze dipping to find his hand flexing against his leg. When I brought my eyes back to his face, the wicked smile he usually cast my way seemed a tad forced.

"Let me guess, you want to bring that boy you call your bodyguard?"

"His name is Landon, and I can assure you he is *not* a boy." I shot a pointed glance at the Serpent King's groin while smirking. The gesture awarded me the pleasure of seeing his cocky smile falter.

I made the menace flustered, which made me merely smile brighter. For a man that prided himself on always being put together, it was intoxicating to watch the Serpent King unravel before me.

A tense silence stirred through the air, the only sound was the king sucking his tongue between his teeth while he closed his eyes. When he opened them again, they were clear of all previous traces of irritation.

"And pray tell, who is this other person you'd like to bring on our deadly mission?"

"My lady-in-waiting," I said, gesturing to my gown. "Unless you want to be the one to undress me every evening?" My smile took on a life of its own, reveling at the sight of the Serpent King's eyes darkening.

He inhaled sharply, dropping his gaze to my gown, but then swiftly forcing his eyes away from my chest to fiddle with his diamond cufflinks.

It was in that moment I realized getting under the Serpent King's skin was my new favorite form of torture.

"Well, I really must get back to my queendom, but I refuse to walk back down that beast of a mountain." I tilted my head at the king in challenge. "Do you have enough magic left to port me back to Phantamos?"

He scoffed. "Easily."

"Then do it."

He tugged on the collar of his shirt, shaking his head. "Barking commands already, are we?"

A muffled cough interrupted our showdown, causing both of us to glare at the shifter, who had a hand against his mouth, like he was trying to smother a laugh.

"Do you have something to say, Evander?" the king said through gritted teeth.

Evander's eyes darted between us with his lips pursed. He blew out a long breath, the hints of a smile still dancing upon his lips.

"You two will be lucky if you don't destroy one another before even getting the chance to defeat the Ice Goddess."

"I'll play nice if you do," the Serpent King shot back.

He prowled toward me, offering me his hand to shake on it. *He couldn't be serious, could he?*

As his hand dangled in the air, he looked me straight in the eyes.

Well, I guess we were doing this.

I took a deep breath. I could easily pretend—I've done it every day ruling as the Serpent Queen.

Two could play this game.

I arched a brow, smiling all the while as I shook his hand. He gave me a chilling smirk, squeezing my hand harder. I didn't balk. Instead, I squeezed right back, giving the king my most cruel smile I reserved solely for executions.

We might both be pretending to play nice, but I had no intentions of upholding this fraudulent agreement. And based on the way the king was grinning at me, I doubted his words held any truth either.

As I stared into his cold eyes, I was already scheming how to make his life a living hell for the entirety of our journey.

Maybe this trip would be fun after all.

CHAPTER 23

THE CHALLENGE

The Serpent King's portal spat Landon and I out fast, giving me barely enough time to bend my knees as I hit familiar stone floors.

We landed in my personal chambers in the Queendom of Phantamos, with not a minute to spare. After a frosty goodbye to the king, I gave them one day's time to meet me in my palace.

"Reena!" I shouted for my lady-in-waiting, already striding for the door.

"Where in the gods—" Reena started, but she quickly bit her tongue upon realizing her mistake. "Where did you two come from?"

I turned, catching her head peeking out of my bathing chambers with one of my plush black robes already between her hands.

I ignored her question, moving quickly to remove my earrings. "Send orders to the servants to clean the entire castle. I want everything sparkling to perfection."

"*Everything?* Shined in one day—" She paused when my

eyes cut to hers through the vanity mirror.

"And do pass along the message to Gustavo and his side of the staff," I said as I sat and kicked off my heels.

Reena grumbled something under her breath in a tone even too low for me to hear. Yet, I caught hints of my butler's name rolling off her tongue, along with what sounded like a slew of curses. A ghost of a smile tugged on my lips as I rose and strolled toward the bathing chambers.

I desperately needed to scrub every bit of Morotis off my skin, along with every unsolicited touch from *him*.

"This all seems a bit extreme." Landon's words made me pause at the threshold.

I nearly forgot he was in the room with us.

Planting one of my hands on the stone doorframe, I glanced over my shoulder.

"I've been away for multiple days, between Ashivire and Morotis. Knowing my servants, they've been slacking off while I was gone. Is it so *extreme* for a queen to not live in filth?" I arched a dark brow at him.

My bodyguard opened his mouth, but snapped it closed just as quickly.

"Why did you agree to go on a journey with that horrid man in the first place?"

Reena let out a startled noise, but she quickly covered it with a cough.

"I'll run you a bath, so you two can speak in private." She whisked past me, ignoring my displeased glare the entire way to the bathing room.

Damn you, Reena.

I groaned, turning back to re-enter the sitting room.

I knew Landon, so I knew there was no chance I'd get to bathe in peace without first providing him a few answers.

"Have you forgotten my emotions are coming back to me?"

I asked, striding to my vanity and taking a seat upon the ebony bench to face the mirror.

I was just beginning to tie back my hair when Landon came into the reflection, standing close enough that the smell of rain filled my lungs. His icy blue eyes speared into mine through the golden framed mirror.

"No, I didn't forget, but if I were in your shoes, I'd rather have my emotions back than travel anywhere with that snake." His lip curled back in disgust. "And who cares if he loses his powers anyway?"

"I care."

My two words split through the air like a bolt of lightning, and I watched as Landon's brows shot as high as the vaulted ceilings.

I never divulged these specific bits of my bargain to my bodyguard, but, if it got him off my back, then so be it.

"The Serpent King and I are—our magic is linked. If he loses his magic, I lose mine. We are, for a lack of a better word, bonded."

"You are *what*?" he seethed.

The clasp of my necklace coming undone was the only sound filling the tense air brewing in my chambers. I dropped the blood-red rubies into the velvet tray atop my vanity before spinning toward my bodyguard. As I stood, my breasts grazed against his chest as I lowered my voice to a lethal whisper.

"He owns my soul, Landon. Don't you understand that by now? Of course, we are bonded."

"Well, just another grand reason not to go on this journey. Let the bargain break, so you no longer are bonded to that monster!" The roaring fire nearby brightened his blue eyes, illuminating the fury blazing within them.

"You expect me to sacrifice my powers just to rid myself of

the Serpent King?" I scoffed, the words sounding absolutely ridiculous rolling off my tongue.

"It's not only to rid yourself of him," he said while his hands softly grabbed mine and brought them to rest against his chest. "Do you ever wonder what life would be like if you still had a soul?"

His eyes no longer burned with fury, instead they took on an entirely different emotion, one I had to steal a small sniff of air to detect.

My nose crinkled when I was greeted with a rosy bouquet of flowers.

Hope.

Landon looked down at me with wide eyes, the words he left unspoken hanging in the sliver of space between us.

Do you ever wonder what we could be if you had a soul?

I knew it was a mistake being vulnerable with him that night under the stars, exactly because of the way he was looking at me right now.

It was unacceptable.

He stared at me like I deserved to be saved, but he was sorely mistaken.

"You confuse me with someone you wish I was, Landon." I yanked my hands free from his, watching those beautiful eyes flood with devastation. "I am happy remaining as I am, with no soul. This is the life I want."

More like, this is the life I *deserved.*

There was no salvation for the wicked.

There was no redemption for a monster like me.

"As my bodyguard, I expect you to accompany me on this quest. Are you up for the challenge, or do I need to find someone else to fill your role?"

Landon stumbled backward, as if my words were a sharp

dagger plunging deep into his heart. But I held my ground, not daring to show an ounce of weakness.

My bodyguard needed to remember his place within my service, and how I could easily replace him. There were plenty of mortal men who would trip over themselves to create a *mutual agreement* with the Serpent Queen, and, based on the way Landon's mouth gaped as he shook his head, I think he, too, realized my hidden implications.

After another moment, his gaze found mine, revealing a coldness I've never seen from my bodyguard before. "That won't be necessary, my Queen. I am up for the challenge."

"Then go make preparations to leave tomorrow." I pointed a blood-red nail toward the door.

Landon's jaw worked, clearly not happy with either my tone or the clear dismissal, for he stormed off, loudly slamming the door closed.

The moment I was alone, I hissed out a long breath, my knees failing to hold me a second longer. Collapsing onto the vanity bench, I slowly dragged a thumb over the ache spreading within the void in my chest.

How could I be so daft to allow Landon to think we were ever going to be more than what we currently were? He was my bodyguard and secret spymaster, who I occasionally fucked.

We were nothing more.

I should've never cried that night underneath the stars, nor offered any sort of comfort to him. I cursed the Ice Goddess for making my soul slowly return, simultaneously causing everything to fall to ruin.

"Your bath is ready, Seera." Reena's voice was barely above a whisper as she hesitantly popped her head from the bathing chambers.

She most definitely heard our entire argument.

"I'll be right there," I called out.

My lady-in-waiting disappeared back into the bathing room, giving me one final moment to sit with my thoughts. I turned on the bench to face my vanity mirror, despising the sight I was met with. Tears pooled in my eyes, making the gold in them blaze to life.

This was exactly why I didn't want my soul back.

I refused to be plagued with emotions that would only weigh me down, that would try to consume me. When I was mortal, I felt too much, too often, making it unbearable. Many times, I thought I'd drown in a river of my own tears as I cried myself to sleep every night trapped in the tower.

As I watched the tears streak down my face, smudging the kohl lining my eyes, I made a vow to myself.

Never again.

Never again would I allow my emotions to make me fragile, to drag me into the depths of despair.

That was not the life I wanted for the Serpent Queen.

Those emotions would only make me weak, which was the last thing a queen could afford to become. On the contrary, I needed to be stronger than ever to cut down the rebels who dared to rival me.

Resolve shuddered through me as I swiped away my tears like the annoying pests they were.

My bodyguard would never understand what it was like to live with the decisions I made while having no soul. He was too good, too pure, and I never believed in that ridiculous mortal saying that opposites attract.

No, Landon and I were not right for one another, and he was an utter fool if he ever thought I'd allow my soul to come back to me.

The weight of my actions as the Serpent Queen would crush me—I wouldn't survive if I reclaimed my soul.

My back stiffened, cold determination settling deep in my bones.

If the price to never feel again was in the currency of killing a god, then I'd happily pay it.

In fact, what was one more life in comparison to the thousands I'd already stolen?

CHAPTER 24
LET THE GAMES BEGIN

The clock chimed six times, emitting an eerie ambiance over the formal dining hall. Between my fight with Landon and the weight of what was at stake with this impending mission, my nerves were getting the best of me. I'd forgotten what a nuisance anxiety was, but these feelings provided me another reason to ensure the bargain never broke.

We would defeat the Ice Goddess.

All would be well.

At least that's what I tried telling myself, but the insistent tapping of my fingers against my thigh said otherwise.

A day had passed since returning to my queendom, and Landon, Reena, and I now stood in the grand dining hall. Instead of speaking, we let the ticking of the clock fill the tense silence. It seemed I wasn't the only one experiencing jitters as Reena moved to straighten the place settings for what felt like the millionth time.

However, my gaze kept finding its way back to my bodyguard, noting the way his jaw ticked, though he kept a casual stance.

Since our argument last night, I'd barely seen Landon, only in passing as he fled to the outdoor training grounds this morning, not even bothering to invite me to train together as we usually did. So, I did my best to not let Landon's childish behavior get under my skin by spending the day packing for the upcoming journey.

Well, Reena packed while my snakes and I recharged by the fire.

I was still contemplating how to tell my lady-in-waiting and Landon about what I'd learned of the gods' existence, when a familiar nasally voice sounded behind me.

"Your Majesty, everything is set for tonight's guests," my head butler said, his dress shoes tapping against the blood-red and black marble floors.

Reena's shoulders visibly inched up as she kept her back to Gustavo, her grip tightening on the gold fork in her hand. Ever since I hired Gustavo a few years ago, Reena despised the man, but I tolerated his annoying habits purely for all the gossip and havoc he wreaked.

There was never a dull moment when Gustavo was around.

"Marvelous. You gave the servants the night off, as I commanded?"

He stopped a few feet away, straightening his bowtie as he stood stiffly and side-eyed Reena. His black hair was slicked back, and his thin mustache appeared freshly trimmed. It was such a hideous shape, and maybe without it he might actually be handsome—if it also wasn't for his pompous attitude and grating voice.

"I did, Your Majesty." He braced his right arm across his midsection, offering me a bow. "Yet, it seems one lingers." Gustavo glanced sideways at my lady-in-waiting once more, causing her to finally spin toward him while holding a golden butter knife.

"I am the queen's lady-in-waiting, may I remind you, not some servant." She pointed the knife at my butler.

My brows rose at Reena's outburst. She was never one to display acts of violence.

As if remembering herself, her mouth parted and her eyes found mine.

"Apologies, my Queen." She set the knife on the dining table, then wrung her hands in her plain grey cotton dress.

"Don't stop on my account. I do love a good show." My lips curved into a satisfied smile, causing Reena's cheeks to turn pink from my approval.

I was all for putting a man in his place, especially when he talked down to me. So, I was pleased to see my lady-in-waiting finally taking after her queen.

Gustavo, on the other hand, looked furious at her behavior, puffing his chest while restlessly adjusting his bowtie. Reena rolled her eyes, making me bite the inside of my cheek in order to stifle a laugh.

Gods, the two of them were so entertaining—I should have made them put on a show over dinner years ago.

The clock chimed again, pulling me from my thoughts and reminding me I had guests arriving any moment. Gustavo most definitely couldn't be here when the Serpent King arrived, and he absolutely couldn't witness Evander shapeshifting into a direct reflection of his queen. Knowing my butler, he would spread that bit of gossip like no tomorrow, and our whole plan to fool my people into believing Evander was truly the Serpent Queen would crumble before it even began.

"That is all. You are dismissed for the evening, Gustavo."

He offered me a nod and one more deep bow, backing

toward the exit but not before throwing Reena one last disapproving glare. The daggers she shot back made his lips purse as he turned on his heel and shuffled off.

Someone tapping their foot drew my focus, and I glanced around to quickly discover it was Landon creating such an irksome sound. I glared at him, willing him to stop, yet he avoided my eye, making a point to look everywhere but at me. He glanced down at his blood-red cloak, making a show of smoothing a nonexistent wrinkle, all the while looking like the perfect picture of boredom. Then, his gaze rose to the ticking clock, the buckles on his knee-high boots rattling from his insistent tapping.

"Stop that," I commanded.

My bodyguard pursed his lips, the only indication he heard me as he continued to fidget his foot.

"Landon, you're being ridiculous."

He whistled to himself, glancing at his shoes instead of responding. My teeth ached from how hard I clenched them to stop myself from saying something that would undoubtedly make the situation worse. So, I bit my tongue while we waited for the Serpent King, but this disrespect from my bodyguard would be addressed at a more appropriate time—like when I wasn't waiting for an immortal male who apparently didn't understand what it meant to arrive on time.

Looking at the clock once more, I noted he was creeping close to being ten minutes late.

Bastard.

How dare he make the Serpent Queen wait?

I let out a loud exhale through my nose, because what choice did I have but to bide my time when I lacked portal magic? Even if I did have such abilities, I wouldn't know how to navigate through the gods' realms to the library the king discreetly mentioned. As much as it irked me, I needed the

Serpent King's assistance to successfully take down the Ice Goddess.

It was when I was blowing a piece of loose hair falling in my eyes that I noticed small, golden particles sparkling before me. The shimmering dust began doubling in size as they glowed brighter, practically vibrating the air. Then, there was a bright burst of golden light, causing me to quickly shield my eyes. Landon cursed, blinded by the sudden luminescence.

I smirked at that fact as I shielded my eyes. When I could see again, I dropped my hand and smelt the haunting notes of smoke and amber, right as my eyes locked onto the Serpent King's hypnotizing eyes.

A beautifully wicked smirk was upon his lips, and his green eyes popped against the dark green button-up he wore. Ever so slowly, his gaze trailed down my body, snagging far too long on the high slit of my burgundy velvet skirt fanning onto the marble floors.

I did my best to not fidget under the weight of his stare. Instead, I looked down my nose at him, though the behemoth was at least half a foot taller than me—even in my beloved heels.

"For someone who preaches about manners, yours are truly lacking. First, you're late. Now, you forget how rude it is to stare."

My words pulled the king from his trance, his eyes dragging up my figure to finally meet my gaze.

"It's not rude to stare at a gorgeous piece of art, now is it?"

An irritated scoff rang through the tense air, and I knew without seeing that it belonged to my bodyguard.

Behind the menace lurking before me, I caught sight of Evander glancing at the black ceiling, his brows raising as he stared at the golden serpents carved into the crown molding.

"This place is so—" he started, but I cut him off.

"Sensational, isn't it?" I puffed my chest with pride as I, too, glanced around the room and towards where he stared at my scarlet, rectangular dining table.

"I was going to say something more along the lines of over the top, but sure, sensational works too." Evander gave me a small smile, finally turning his attention to me.

I clicked my tongue as a scoff trickled from my lips. "You literally live in a damp cave. Thus, your opinion on my decor is irrelevant."

Now, it was the king's second-in-command's turn to wear a shocked expression, his jaw hanging open as I strode past him.

"Everyone, sit. My cook prepared supper before I dismissed him for the evening, along with the rest of my servants. No one will bother us."

Taking my seat at the head of the table, Reena promptly fell into action. She served me a scoop of rosemary potatoes, since I had no servants to do it for me tonight. However, my gaze flew past my lady-in-waiting and to the man who was taking a seat at the other head of the table. The Serpent King smirked at me as he picked up the black napkin atop his plate, fanning it out onto his lap once again like a pompous asshole.

I clenched onto my armrests as he acted like he was my equal by assuming the seat across from me. He was doing exactly what I did to him in his realm.

Fucking. Menace.

The sound of irritated hissing filtered through the room. The king arched a quizzical brow as he speared a large piece of steak onto his plate, his eyes flicking to the irritated serpents now spiraling protectively around my arms. My budding anger must have awoken them.

"Do your snakes typically dine with you?"

"They make better company than certain guests," I

quipped, giving him a cursory once over as I popped a potato in my mouth. I bit down hard, hoping to release a smidge of the tension coiling within me.

However, there was no curbing my irritation as the Serpent King languidly started to cut his steak into small, bite-sized pieces.

"It's rather unusual behavior for a queen. Typically, the snakes in my realm stick to the deepest and darkest parts of the caves, never daring to venture into the *formal* dining hall, of all places." He gave my snakes a pointed look, earning him a hiss from Ember as she stuck her tongue out at the king.

I lightly dragged a finger along the top of her head while narrowing my eyes at the king. "My snakes don't need to stick to the darkness, for it resides in every inch of my castle."

All noises ceased to exist following my grim words.

I glanced at the king, noting a hint of sadness lining his eyes.

I had to do something to break the awkwardness, to kill off the pitiful glances I was receiving from Reena and Evander.

Leaning forward slightly, I snatched a champagne bottle off the table, pushing hard to release the cork. A loud pop rattled through my ears as the cork shot up and ricocheted off the golden, crystal chandelier, making Reena squeal. Then, as if the gods finally took pity on me, the wooden cork shot straight toward the Serpent King.

Unfortunately, it didn't smash into his perfect face. Instead, it landed on top of his plate, right on the piece of steak he was about to spear next.

When I saw his lips turn down into a sharp scowl, I lost it.

My laughter was so strong that it shook my snakes, who were still wrapped around my shoulders and arms. Warm laughter intertwined with mine, and I saw through the tears pooling in my eyes that Evander was laughing along with me.

The king threw him a withering glare, which only made his second-in-command's shoulder shake harder.

After pouring myself a hearty glass of champagne, I passed the bottle to my lady-in-waiting on my left. "Drink up, we will need all the help we can get if we should survive this journey through the realms with the likes of him." I winked at Reena before leveling my gaze at the snake across the table, sipping on my champagne with a cruel smile.

It was clear by the way the king's jaw ticked that he was restraining himself from exploding at my clear display of disrespect. He wiped the corners of his mouth with his napkin, before setting it on the table.

"*Someone* would really benefit from learning a bit of manners before we travel to our first destination." He smiled down the table, looking directly at me.

"And when will *someone* learn I despise being told what I should or shouldn't do?" I smiled sweetly at him over the rim of my glass, before raising it in a mock cheers and downing the whole glass in one go.

He raked a hand through his perfectly slicked back hair, causing a long, dark lock to curl down his forehead, brushing into his eyes. Cracking his neck, he, too, helped himself to a glass of champagne.

Oh, it was too much fun getting underneath the Serpent King's skin, and I was just getting started. After all, we had a whole journey together for me to irk him at any given chance.

"Where are we headed to anyways?" Landon's sharp voice cut through the palpable tension between the king and me, causing us both to glance at my bodyguard.

Frankly, I forgot he was in the room with us, with how silent he'd been throughout the course of dinner. The Serpent King assessed Landon, a devious smile twisting on his lips.

"She didn't tell you about the gods, did she?" The king glanced at me, amusement gleaming in his eyes.

"The gods?" Landon asked incredulously, looking between the king and I, then settling his gaze, regrettably, on me. "Seera, what is he talking about?"

"It's so interesting you call her by her given name. Rather informal for a bodyguard if you ask me," the king muttered into his glass, earning him a vicious scowl before I turned to face my bodyguard's line of fire.

"The Serpent King informed me yesterday that the gods are, indeed, real, and one is messing with our bargain. We are going to work together to stop her." I shrugged a shoulder, taking another gulp of my liquor as if I didn't just drop a bomb.

"What?!" Landon and Reena simultaneously exclaimed.

"*For Serpent's Sake*," I muttered into my glass.

Surprisingly, the king distracted their glares from boring solely into me when he spoke up.

"We are headed to the Emerald Glades. It houses one of the largest libraries in all the realms. If there is anywhere to search for information on how to defeat a god, it would be found there." He took a small sip of champagne, moving to wipe the corners of his lips with his napkin once again.

I glanced sideways at Landon, only to find him gripping his fork for dear life. He looked about two seconds away from flying across the dining table and either stabbing me or the king for our deceit.

Technically, I didn't lie to Landon . . . I merely withheld some *minor* details.

My bodyguard continued asking questions, but I didn't hear if anyone deigned to answer his insistent nagging. The onset of a headache blurred my senses, yet I did happen to overhear one of his questions, making one of my own bubble to the surface like the champagne sizzling in my flute.

"How exactly are we going to gain access to a god's personal library?" My attention snapped to the king, whose serpentine smile was answer enough.

"It's easy when your mother is the ruler of said realm." He pushed his chair back, the wooden legs screeching from such a harsh motion. "Well, this was a lovely dinner. Thank you, Seera, for your unwavering hospitality. Now, who is ready to meet the real Serpent Queen?" He rubbed his hands together, his eyes flaring with a wicked delight.

Reena's gasp rang through the hall right as Evander rose and leaned toward the king, muttering something underneath his breath. I couldn't hear what they said, as the pounding in my skull grew. The way the king informally addressed me would've had me seeing red if I weren't so distracted.

On top of it all, he had the audacity to call his *mother* the real Serpent Queen in front of my closest staff.

My grip tightened on the armrests of my chair, my nails digging hard enough into the wood I left behind claw marks. The Serpent King whispered to Evander, all the while throwing a smug smile down the table at me, as if to tell me he won this battle.

I let my own forced smile grace my lips, sending a cruel and silent message back to him. His grin faltered, as he was smart enough to finally look a bit unnerved.

Let the Serpent King think he won tonight's battle, for ultimately it would be I who'd win the war brewing between us.

CHAPTER 25

A WARM EMBRACE

"Fret not, for no one will know you are even gone, Serpent Queen." Evander winked at me, already wearing my face as if it were his own. It was unnerving how his voice contained the hint of sweet malice I had perfected over the years.

"Don't forget you must make a show out of at least two executions per week, or my people will grow suspicious. I've maintained this schedule since the day I became queen, and you will have to answer to me should you break my seventy-five year streak." I quirked a brow in challenge, but Evander simply cast a coy smile at me.

This had to work.

"Yes, Your Majesty. I will be as ruthless as the queen currently gracing me with her presence. Don't worry your pretty little nose." He tapped said pretty nose, and it took everything in me not to snap my teeth at his finger.

Why was it that men could not wrap their small minds around the fact it was rude to touch a woman without her consent?

TIFFANY ROSEWOOD

Evander was lucky I had a soft spot for him, since I've executed men for less.

I narrowed my eyes at him before turning to my lady-in-waiting. "Is everything packed and ready to go?"

Reena didn't hear my question, because she was too busy gawking at the shapeshifter who wore my beautiful face surprisingly well. I sighed, readying myself to snap her back to attention, but a troubling thought stopped me in my tracks.

"Wait, this plan won't work if my people notice Reena and Landon are missing for too long."

The Serpent King's exasperated sigh made my shoulders tense, causing me to turn and glare at the menace, who was examining his nails as if I didn't just present a major flaw in his plan.

"I already thought of that and took care of it."

My eyes burned into him, the ball of my burgundy heel tapping with impatience. The king's gaze flicked to my shoe, then dragged up to my face, annoyance spreading across his symmetrical features.

"While Evander is my most talented shapeshifter, he does have a sister who possesses the same ability. She will stand in for Reena."

My brows bunched while I scoured my memories from my time spent in Morotis. I couldn't put a face to the woman he mentioned, but I had a vague recollection of Evander speaking highly of a female relative he was very protective over. I glanced at my body-double, who was looking down at his—I mean, *my*—breasts in awe. He ran his hands over his chest, his mouth gaping at the sheer size of my chest.

"Gods, help us," I muttered.

Evander's gaze rose to meet mine, and color danced across his cheeks as he realized I caught him groping himself—well, technically me.

"I—I actually have no good reason to explain what I was just doing, beyond these are fucking incredible." He turned side-to-side while glancing at his chest once more, earning a very displeased glare from the Serpent King.

"Evander, knock it the fuck off." The king pinched the bridge of his nose. "The queen asked you a question." His jaw worked as he continued to glare at the shapeshifter.

Evander cleared his throat, shaking his head as if he finally was remembering to act like the Serpent King's second-in-command and not some schoolboy excited to have his own pair of breasts.

"Uhm—my gracious Queen, could you please repeat the question?" He batted my dark lashes at me.

I pinned him with an annoyed look before having to do one of the things I hated: repeating myself.

"Where is your sister?"

"Ah, yes—my sister." He snapped his fingers. "She is on her way and will be here by the time your servants are set to return. She is tied up at the moment while trying to convince the other piece of our plan to get in line."

I stared, silently demanding him to elaborate.

"My father will stand in as Landon's body-double, but he is taking a bit more convincing than anticipated. He isn't super keen on the fact he would technically be serving *mwah*." He placed a hand against his chest, and my lips curved down when he snuck in a subtle squeeze of my breasts.

For Serpent's Sake.

"And if he doesn't show?" I challenged.

"He will." The Serpent King answered for Evander, and I turned to find him watching me with that intense stare of his.

"Evander's father is respected throughout my realm, hence why we gave him this false sense he had a choice in the matter. When in reality, he answers to me. Come first light tomorrow morning, if he isn't in this castle wearing your bodyguard's face, I will personally drag him here myself. You have my word."

The king's eyes simmered with something I recognized plenty of times while looking in the mirror. He was delighted at the prospect of dragging someone here by brutal force, and I was starting to realize I may be more like the menace standing before me than I cared to admit.

I nodded, for I had no choice but to place my trust in the king at this moment. The thought of leaving my throne to anyone else made me want to rage—to spill blood—but the reminder of what would happen if I didn't go on this mission, if we didn't kill the Ice Goddess, was what forced me to leave my queendom behind.

I glanced one last time around my castle, memorizing all its magnificent details. The dark marble below my heels shined, looking like a river of crimson blood. My lips tugged into a small smile, because it appeared Reena got my servants to polish every surface of my palace, just like I demanded.

However, I had a nagging feeling I was forgetting something. My gaze roamed around the room, and, when I saw a head of full, luscious brown curls, I knew what I was missing.

Landon.

He was so silent for the entirety of the night I kept forgetting he was even present. My bodyguard's posture was rigid—he was likely less than pleased at the idea of some immortal acting as himself while he was gone. After asking countless questions I missed at dinner, Landon kept to himself, not muttering another word—a trait I hated about him. He could be so damn stubborn when his ego was bruised.

"Now, can we get on with this mission, or do you have another round of questions, Your Majesty?" The Serpent King's voice was sharp, earning him one of my infamous eye rolls.

The king mistook my silence for complacency, while in reality, I was breathing through my anger and the desperate need to sic my snakes on him.

His hands began to spin before him, producing sparks of golden particles which began to swirl into a growing cyclone. After another minute, he dropped his hands, discretely masking the deep breath he released. I, however, noticed it, along with the small beads of sweat gathering along his hairline. If conjuring a portal exerted the king this much, then we were running short on time. It seemed Isolde was working tirelessly to weaken him, in turn weakening our bargain.

Fury spread through my veins at the cruel goddess who thought she could toy with our lives for fun. Another reminder that life was utterly unfair, because I somehow got dragged into an ancient feud between the Ice Goddess and the Serpent King.

Hadn't I suffered enough?

A warm touch brushed against my tightly curled fist, which was shaking from my burst of anger. Landon must have drifted to my side, for he was close enough that his hand grazed mine in an attempt to break me from the spell of fury preparing to consume me whole. I glanced at him, a deep wrinkle between his brows as he looked at me.

Even though Landon was clearly angry with me from our fight, he still attempted to comfort me. This was not the first time he'd saved me from spiraling. I'd gone on benders throughout the decades—the worst one consisting of two straight months of me carving up traitors in my dungeons just as an outlet for my unrelenting anger.

The only thing that broke me from that episode was my bodyguard.

So, yes, Landon knew me better than most and had learned the early signs of when my fury was threatening to break free.

Ever so slightly, I brushed my hand against his. Landon's eyes widened from returning his gesture in public, as this was the first time I'd ever dared show an ounce of affection outside the bedroom.

A foreign emotion rattled through my chest, almost like I was experiencing what I could only assume was . . . *regret.*

Well, that was new.

Another wave of the emotion coursed through me, making me feel like a fucking monster for the other night, and for all the nights that made Landon now act surprised at the smallest gesture of affection from me.

A sharp stab of pain continued to spear into my chest, causing me to brace a hand against my heart. I hissed through the uncomfortable feelings as they pelted the void in me like an unrelenting hail storm.

My feelings for my bodyguard were growing far more complicated than I ever intended. Maybe if I was still a mortal girl, I could entertain the thought of being loved by someone as pure as Landon. But that girl died the day I made my bargain with the Serpent King, the same day I relinquished my soul and locked away my heart for good.

Monsters don't deserve to be loved.

Someone loudly cleared their throat, pulling me from my dark thoughts. My attention snapped to mesmerizing green eyes, which were currently burning a hole between the small sliver of space between my bodyguard and I.

How long had he been watching us?

Based on the intensity of his stare, I'd say it was safe to assume he saw our whole little moment.

As his eyes lifted to mine, a storm raged within them. I scoffed loudly, utterly sick and tired of the Serpent King acting possessive over me.

I was never his to begin with. He made that crystal clear

the moment our bargain was sealed with a world-shattering kiss.

A kiss that still haunted my dreams.

"After you, my Queen." The king offered me a mocking bow while gesturing to the shimmering portal swirling before us.

I moved toward the wall of iridescent gold light but paused in front of Evander. "Take care of my queendom."

He placed his hand over his heart—no longer groping his new body. "I meant it when I said I'd guard your throne with my life."

There was no joking grin dancing along his lips. Instead, his hazel eyes shone with sincerity.

His reaction appeased me enough to sharply nod before continuing toward the portal.

"Seera?" Landon's voice made me halt.

I glanced over my shoulder and met my bodyguard's worried eyes.

"Would you like me to go first? To ensure it is safe." He looked at the portal, concern tugging on his brows.

Even after I was terrible to him yesterday, after I crushed his hopes of us ever being more than what we were, he still worried about me. Emotion knotted in my throat, preventing me from speaking for a long moment.

Once I felt like my voice wouldn't crack and betray my true feelings, I shook my head.

"I will go first, but thank you, Landon."

His pupils widened at the same moment I flinched, realizing my mistake.

I never once said thank you to Landon, and now I did so for the first time in a public setting. I wanted to crawl out of my skin—I didn't recognize myself anymore.

This was all Isolde's fault, and I was so ready to end her for trying to turn me into a soft and thankful queen.

I wasn't *that* girl anymore. I worked too hard to make something new of myself—someone who didn't cower, who didn't hide, who withstood misery, wearing it like a badge of honor.

I stepped into the portal, ready to rid myself of my soul once and for all.

The Serpent King's magic wrapped around me, and as I was transported through time and space, a handful of golden shimmers softly caressed my cheek, as if to offer me a warm embrace.

CHAPTER 26
WHAT IF

A rainbow of colors swirled by while the Serpent King's portal carried me through the realms. It was unlike anything I'd ever experienced, and it was quite glorious never to take a single step, yet be transported through space.

Portaling would make heels far more comfortable to wear as often as I did.

However, this portal felt different than the others I'd been in. Perhaps, it was because I'd never seen such landscapes, but it felt special . . . magical, almost like the fairytales I read about when I was younger.

Worlds flashed by, yet the shield of the king's golden magic prevented me from hearing any outside noise. So, I simply watched the realms pass, noting all the various creatures living within them.

A man appeared, and he looked human until my gaze dipped to two hairy legs ending in hoofs. He bathed in a river beside a woman who made a fire spark between her pale hands. Sharp, black mountains could be seen in the background. Some of them had smoke billowing out from the peaks, along with a red liquid spurting into the blue sky.

Before I could marvel at the foreign picture any further, a new realm came into view. This one took me into the depths of a vibrant aquamarine ocean. A woman with turquoise hair swam past the shield, and I jumped back upon seeing the eight tentacles floating behind her, propelling her through the clear blue waters. I dared a step closer to the shimmering wall of magic, marveling at the look on her face while she swam.

She looked so *free*. As if she was truly happy and at peace with her life.

A spark flared to life inside my chest.

No, please, no—anything but another horrid emotion.

I wasn't entirely sure what was passing through the void within me, but it felt like I was missing out on something fantastic as I watched her swim without a care in the world.

Was this . . . longing? Yearning for something I never could have?

Before I could drown in my self-pity, the siren's realm zoomed by, leaving me in a pitch-black night sky. It nearly reminded me of what Ashivire looked like in the evenings, with how bright and glorious the stars shone. However, besides the stars shining silver instead of gold, there was another major difference . . .

Hundreds of women floated in the dark sky.

But that was impossible.

I squinted, trying to see what I was missing.

Then, the dim sky lit up in a variety of colors as the women burned into—wisps of air?

Shaking my head, I tried to make sense of what I was seeing as I watched the once tangible woman take on the form of a spirit of the air. Their auras shone brightly in various hues: neon pink, sea-foam green, ruby red, and so on. Some of the spirits tipped their heads back as if they were cackling, while others had their lips parted in conversation or song. The one thing they all had in common was how fucking stunning they were.

A feeling crept into that endless void in my chest as I watched the band of women drift through the night sky.

For Serpent's Sake, not again.

Longing festered inside me like a caged beast. Deep down, I always dreamed of having a group of people I could be myself with—my real self, not the version I became when I donned the mask of the Serpent Queen.

Just me, Seera.

In moments like this, it was hard not to let my mind wander and think about how life could have panned out differently if I'd never made a bargain with the Serpent King. There was always a kernel of curiosity buried deep in my core that wondered about who I'd become if I had the chance to be free of my mother, if I had been raised by someone who demonstrated what it felt like to be loved . . .

Would I be kind?

Would I meet people who understood me?

Would one day, someone see all of me—all of the horrible darkness slowly consuming every inch of me—and would they choose to stay?

Would they love every sick and twisted part of me?

Water splashed across my cheeks, making me glance above as worry crashed into me that the portal was cracking. Did it malfunction and take me back into the siren realm?

When I looked up, I saw no leak in the golden shield. Glancing around, I confirmed I was indeed still moving forward. A new realm appeared, painting the scenery with thick, dark green trees that jutted high into a slightly golden sky. Animals swung lazily between the branches, and there was not one rain cloud in sight.

I swatted the water droplets off my cheeks, as I realized I must be crying again.

Curse these damn emotions.

I had to get a grip on myself, for the vibrant emerald color splashed across this forest gave me a sneaking suspicion this was my final destination.

My hopes and dreams were not what they once were. If I could lock away my feelings forever, I'd do so in a heartbeat. The bad emotions often outweighed any good ones I used to experience. I once despised being so lonely, so broken—like I was never enough. So, the day after my bargain, I was actually relieved I couldn't feel anything beyond a vortex of anger.

Cold determination grounded me as a bright golden light flashed to my right. A circular passage opened up, signaling the exit was fast approaching, so much so I barely had time to bend my knees and brace for the undoubtedly brutal impact.

The lush environment around me could only mean one thing.

I made it to the *imposter* Serpent Queen's realm.

It was time to see what this fraud's lands had to offer.

CHAPTER 27
THE TUMBLE

I was not anticipating the extreme velocity at which the portal spit me into the Emerald Glades. It was possible this exit felt different from my other experiences because I traveled a much greater distance. Yet, I cursed the king for not warning me about such a change as I tucked my knees to my chest and barreled into this strange, new realm.

Covering my head, my skirts swirling around me as I tumbled, whipping harshly against my face. My skin burned as twigs and leaves whipped around me, scattering across the forest floor. After what felt like a century, I came to a crashing halt, and my body slammed into something solid, making a loud crack ring through the otherwise quiet glade.

Slowly, I lowered my hands from shielding my head, blinking slowly as I tried to comprehend the vast world around me. Towering high above, there was a tree unlike anything I'd ever seen before. Its trunk was so large it would be unthinkable to wrap my arms fully around it. I blinked harder, willing my head to stop spinning.

Since I was far too dizzy to stand without collapsing, I

remained lying on the ground, all the while watching an animal drift between the branches high above in the canopy of the jungle. My mind raced as I tried to figure out what animal it was . . .

A monkey! That's what it was.

Back when I spent my days reading in my tower, there was one story I loved about a princess and a thief. The thief had a monkey as a friend and accomplice. He was my favorite character in the book—such a sassy, scrappy, yet clever little thing.

Gods, why did I ever stop reading?

Staring at the creature, I felt something swirl through my chest, but a nearby rustling had my head swiveling to see what was lurking nearby. Relief flooded through my veins when I realized it wasn't a massive predator trying to eat me alive. Instead, I was greeted by a gorgeous orange snake slithering along a low-hanging tree branch. Its cerulean blue eyes found mine, and it let out a soft hiss—almost like it was saying hello to me. My rapidly beating heart calmed upon hearing the familiar sound, my eyes drifting closed to savor the snake's steady cooing.

Something about this place felt oddly comforting, as if I was carried off to a land I once dreamed of.

Warmth flooded my cheeks, and I cracked an eye open. I was met with a stream of sunlight peeking through the thick canopy of trees. As it danced across my skin, a harmony of happy hisses flooded my mind.

I nearly thanked the gods that my snakes were still with me. Which meant my powers extended across realms. I tucked that very useful bit of knowledge away for later.

A crunching noise, like someone eating, stole my attention back to the lush jungle.

Was that—?

Indeed, a sloth ever so slowly crept along a branch, stopping along the way to munch on leaves. The furry creature's claws were exceedingly long, so much so I thought I should feel a twinge of nervousness with it hanging nearby . . . but how could I fear an animal with such an adorable face? Its lips were tugged into a lazy, content smile, and a strange urge crashed into me to scoop the fuzzy animal into my arms to cuddle it.

Where the fuck did that come from?

There was that odd sensation from earlier rattling through my chest . . . what was it? Wonder? Awe?

A delirious cackle bubbled from my lips at how insane I must look in this moment, with my limbs tangled around the base of a ginormous tree, my skirts all torn and ruffled, as I contemplated cuddling an animal for the first time in my life. I was certain I looked nothing like the Serpent Queen, but, in the safety of the solitude of the forest with only the critters as witnesses, I didn't care.

It was the first time I felt free to just *be*.

Yet, my jovial mood was short lived when a loud crack split through the air, and I saw the leaves high above furiously shaking. That's when I saw a thick tree branch thrice as long as I was crashing through the canopy . . . and headed straight for me.

I tried to leap to my feet, but something tugged me backward, making me slam back into the dirt floor. Quickly glancing over my shoulder, I saw what prevented me from escaping—my skirts were tangled within the roots of the tree I crashed into. Panic speared through my gut when I glanced up and saw the branch had rotated—a point as sharp as an arrow was now facing down while gaining speed.

I yanked my skirts with all my might, but my hands were vehemently shaking from the panic sinking its claws into me. Every time I pulled on my garments, it was as if they further tangled into the roots, almost like the tree was somehow growing in real time. The hair on the back of my neck prickled as nausea passed through my gut—it looked like the tree wanted to devour my skirts, like it wanted to consume me.

"What the fuck," I breathed in disbelief as I saw the roots move, my insane theory becoming reality before my eyes.

I glanced once more above, seeing I was seconds away from finding out if an immortal could survive being speared to death.

I doubted the odds would be on my side, since they rarely were.

For the first time in seventy-five years, I was truly *scared*.

But maybe, it was time for me to give up on a fight I was never going to win—not only the fight with these stupid tree roots, but the one with my people. Maybe, this wasn't such a bad thing, for it was what I deserved after all I had destroyed. Maybe it was time to retire from my reign as the Serpent Queen and meet whatever lies beyond in the Land of the Wicked.

All my fight left me as I let the darkness I fought to keep at bay everyday invaded my thoughts. My eyes fluttered closed, because I didn't want to see when the spear-like branch would pierce through my black heart.

Deep down, I knew an immortal couldn't survive such a fatal wound, so I whispered a prayer.

A final, desperate plea to atone for my sinful life as the Serpent Queen, in hopes there would be one kind god listening. If they were, I hoped they would let whatever shreds of my soul that remained rest when I perished.

I didn't deserve what I prayed for, but I did so anyway. It provided a false sense of comfort, one thing even a monster craved during their final moments.

As I muttered the last words of my plea and stole a final breath of warm forest air, the sensation of floating came over me. An unforeseeable strength snaked underneath my arms, yanking me backward with a brutal force—it all happened too fast for me to comprehend.

Then, my back was crashing into the hard ground at the same moment an ear-splitting sound shook the forest. The tree branch that was on track to end my life must have reached its final destination.

Slowly, I fluttered my eyes open, still not convinced I survived. Perhaps, I was about to be greeted with the lands where wicked souls went after winking out from existence.

My vision was hazy at first, but then a familiar, lush green canopy of trees blinked into view. The monkeys remained swinging from branch to branch, and birds sang while they flitted between the trees.

I was *alive*.

Maybe the gods were listening . . .

A groan sounded beneath me, making my breath catch.

Wasn't I lying on the forest floor, so why did the ground sound like it was moaning?

Slowly, I glanced over my shoulder, preparing myself to be greeted with a magical forest floor that might swallow me whole.

Instead, I was met with piercing green eyes glinting with mischief.

Much to my horror, I was lying directly on top of the Serpent King.

CHAPTER 28
THE EMERALD GLADES

"**W**hat the fuck!" I screamed all the while I hurried to scramble out of the king's arms, but it only made him clutch tighter around my chest.

"Is that any way to thank the man who just saved your life?" His warm breath caressed the tip of my ear.

I growled, wiggling harder against him while making sure to emphasize pressing my ass against his groin. The king's breath caught at the same moment his grip loosened, giving me the opening I needed.

Gods, men were so predictable.

Snaking my foot underneath his knee, I propelled us to flip to the left. His surprised grunt rang through the forest as our positions reversed. Now, I was facing the ground with his chest still pressing against my back, but I quickly ducked to the right, shrugging out from beneath him. The moment I was no longer bent in front of the Serpent King, he fell forward.

Sadly, instead of breaking his nose for a third time, the

imbecile had quick reflexes as he threw his hands in front of himself.

I sprang to my feet while smirking at the king down before me on all fours, feeling proud of myself for escaping such a compromising position. However, my joyful mood drifted away with the soft breeze when he glanced over his shoulder toward me—amusement brightly shimmering in his eyes.

Then, the fucker had the gall to tip his head back and *laugh.*

"What is so comical about getting your ass handed to you?" I glared down my nose at the menace.

He didn't reply, instead his dark chuckle tapered off as his eyes dipped lower to rake over my body. My brows bunched while I followed his line of sight, and a squeak burst from my lips as I saw what made the bastard chuckle in sick delight.

My legs were completely bare, my skirts nowhere to be seen. A cool breeze licked up my skin, making it pebble.

I was standing in only my black, strapless corset, along with a matching pair of lacy undergarments, in front of the Serpent King of all people.

He didn't even try to hide how he dragged his eyes up to mine, the hunger blazing within them making the green dissipate into a cloud of black.

Most people would be humiliated in such a situation, but this was one of those moments when being soulless paid off. I squared my shoulders, not daring to cover myself nor hide from his scorching gaze, which merely made him raise a brow, as if he was impressed.

"Take a good look, for you will never see me this naked again." I grandly gestured to my curvy figure.

"We will see about that, my Queen." The king slowly dragged his tongue over his bottom lip all the while his gaze roamed once again over every bare inch of my skin.

My stupid legs twitched, squeezing together from the way

he was so intensely staring at me. He looked like he wanted to devour me, especially when his gaze continuously roamed over the apex of my thighs and across my lacy undergarments. He must have noted the way my body responded to his stare, for a cocky smile spread across that stupidly perfect face of his.

How could you be such a fool, Seera?

I rolled my eyes, trying to cover up my body's traitorous response. To top off the act, I was about to call him a vile, disgusting pig, but a shout boomed through the forest and made me bite my tongue.

"Seera!" Landon rushed from behind a tree, heading straight for me.

The moment he saw my bare legs, a furious scowl etched across his features. He wasted no time snapping off his cloak while he ran.

Reena trailed behind, carefully moving down the small dirt hill that separated us. My lady-in-waiting gasped, quickly covering her mouth with a hand as she took in the view of her queen, standing half-naked before the Serpent King.

I lost sight of Reena when Landon stormed in front of me. Swiftly, he dropped his velvet cloak around my shoulders, making sure to secure the clasp around my neck and pull it tightly around my figure. After triple checking I was no longer exposed, he turned his fierce attention to my face, lightly brushing my tangled hair back to tuck it behind my ear. The way he was doting on me should make me sick . . . but, for the first time in many years, I felt *self-conscious*.

I ducked my head, my shoulders slightly caving in as I realized I must look like a royal mess.

When I appeared put together, I felt confident, like I could bring anyone to their knees. But when I looked like a wreck, it made me feel weak, vulnerable—like that pathetic, helpless, mortal girl I ran away from.

"Look at me," Landon whispered.

My bodyguard hooked a finger underneath my chin, gently raising my gaze. His eyes flickered over every inch of my disheveled face, his fingers softly brushing against my cheek. Pain seized through me, tugging a sharp hiss to slip past my lips when he grazed over a few lingering cuts. Yet, after another moment, the pain eased when my immortal healing finally kicked in, stitching closed the cuts peppering my skin.

"Did he hurt you?" Landon's voice was as lethal as a blade when he glanced at the Serpent King.

As my bodyguard glared at the perpetual thorn in my side, the king smirked and let his gaze dip back to my legs. Landon's jaw tightened, and I knew he was about to start something he most definitely could not finish.

For Serpent's Sake, why was I always playing mediator between these two fools?

"Oh, stop your fussing. I am fine, just a minor miscalculation when exiting the portal."

"A minor miscalculation?" he challenged, glancing back at me and plucking a twig from my hair.

"Okay, perhaps I tumbled a bit across the dirt and into a tree."

His brows arched toward the golden sky. "That still doesn't explain why you were halfway naked when I found you."

I groaned. "It's possible a large tree branch was about to pierce me to death because my skirts were tangled around some roots." His eyes widened at my casual recounting, but I quickly sped through the rest of the incident. "But it didn't impale me because the Serpent King saved me. He yanked me rather aggressively, so much so that my skirts completely tore off my body."

"He *what?*" Landon's jaw dropped, searching for the male in question.

Our gazes flicked to the king, who laid propped up on his elbows, one of his legs casually draped over the other. The fucking prick was twirling a flower between the pads of his fingertips, as if we were all having a lovely outing and he didn't just save me from nearly dying.

Landon grasped my shoulders, pulling my attention back to him.

"I should have been the one to save you." His lips pinched into a thin line, his brows furrowing.

I knew that expression—he was beating himself up for failing to protect me. "I would have been here sooner, but *he* cut me off when I tried to enter the portal after you." He angrily huffed, his jaw tightening in sync with the way his hands gripped harder onto me.

Glancing above, I noted there wasn't a cloud in sight, yet the fresh smell of rain pelted my senses.

My bodyguard reeked of sorrow—which was nothing new —but today it bothered me more than ever. Something rattled in the void in my chest, and I had a startling urge to comfort Landon. Hesitantly, I raised my hand and gripped his, brushing a finger against his rough skin. The smell of his sorrow wafted away as his eyes locked onto where I held onto him.

"I am fine, Landon. With how many enemies I have, I'm sure there will be plenty of future opportunities for you to save me." I tried to crack a teasing smile at him, but his frown only deepened.

"Your safety is not a joke to me, Seera."

Another wave of sorrow wafted at me, along with something more—was that cherries?

I wasn't familiar with that scent . . .

Clearing my throat of the strangely intoxicating smell, I gave one final attempt to clear Landon of his guilt.

"If it wasn't for you and your cloak, I'd still be standing here in my undergarments."

His eyes flicked down to my legs, his dark garment long enough to cover the entirety of my thighs. If Landon's pinched lips were any indication of his mood, I'd say I was miserably failing at comforting him. Considering it was my first time ever trying to do so as the Serpent Queen, it wasn't surprising I fucking sucked at it.

I stepped around him and approached the king, who now stood and was dusting off his deep green trousers. My gaze lingered on the way his pants clung to his body in a sophisticated way—not too tight, yet not ill-fitting. If I was forced to admit one nice quality about the Serpent King, it would be that he sure knew how to dress.

"Who was it that said it was rude to stare?" His cheerful voice broke me from my trance.

I looked up to find an amused smile painted across his face, all the while he brushed dirt from his black button-up. Again, I was delighted in the way his shirt hung slightly off his massive frame. He worked to re-roll one of the long sleeves midway up his forearm, and curiosity trickled through me as wisps of dark markings were revealed to me.

They licked up his arms, so his sleeves hid the rest of the ink, but that didn't stop my eyes from roaming upward and over the bare skin peeking out, courtesy of the few diamond buttons he left undone along his pale chest. Small glimpses of black swirls could be spotted there as well, but not enough to see what the full design looked like.

"My eyes are up here, Seera," the king cooed, pointing two fingers at me and raising them, indicating for me to raise my eyes to his.

My cheeks burned."I—I must have hit my head harder

than I thought." I cleared my throat, doing my best to act confident in the lie I was woefully spinning.

The Serpent King tilted his head, his eyes lighting with delight. *For Serpent's Sake,* I knew he didn't believe a word I said, so I desperately needed to change the subject.

"Since your homelands nearly took my life, you can repay me by now escorting us to this vast library." I gestured toward the path for him to lead the way.

He chuckled, swiping one last patch of dirt off his shoulder. "Such an impatient creature."

With that, he turned on the heel of his black dress shoes and strutted down the pathway, softly whistling along with the birds cheerily chirping around us. I grumbled a few not-so-nice things about the king as I took off after him.

Two sets of footsteps trailed me, and I threw a quick glance over my shoulder. Reena was scurrying directly behind her queen, her grey eyes brimming with fear while they scanned the forest. For her sake, I hoped she couldn't spot any snakes slithering nearby.

Trailing at the rear of our lineup was Landon—he, too, was assessing the forest with one hand rested atop the hilt of the sword slung across his hips.

"Watch your step," the king called out from the front, bringing my attention back to his broad shoulders.

He barely turned his head to ensure we were following along as he shouted his next words. "It is a crime to injure a snake in this realm, so do make sure to tread lightly so you don't step on one of our precious serpents. Unless," he drawled while tossing a smirk at my bodyguard. "You fancy spending some time in the Emerald Glades' prison."

A whimper pierced my ears, and I knew it was Reena as she panicked upon hearing there were snakes in these lands. What did she expect? After all, we were in the faux Serpent Queen's lands, so it only made sense such a creature resided here in some capacity.

As I remembered a god had the same title I killed to make my own, I clenched my jaw. While I stewed in my hate for said god, a plan began to spin in my head like a spiderweb.

I made a mental note to check the library for an answer I now desperately sought.

If there were a way to ensure the Serpent King's magic was not directly linked to his mother's, then perhaps I could take care of the title dilemma I faced . . .

My lips tugged up into a sinister smile at my new ploy.

I may have only agreed to killing one god on this mission, but I'd happily remove another if it meant I'd earn the sole title of the Serpent Queen.

CHAPTER 29
AN UNEXPECTED STOP

Besides that beautiful saffron-colored snake that was slithering in the jungle, I hadn't encountered another serpent during the long trek to the Emerald Palace. I glanced behind me at my lady-in-waiting, who still looked like she was about to jump out of her skin at the mere snap of a tree branch. I had half a mind to join in on her nervous antics after what happened earlier.

It was so odd, how the roots physically *moved*.

My curious gaze swept across the darkening forest, wondering what magic lurked within its cool shadows. You'd think the Serpent King would have briefed his *queen* on what dangers to prepare for in The Emerald Glades, but, of course, everything he did was for show.

It didn't matter that he'd saved me only hours ago, he didn't truly care about me. He needed me to save his own powers—nothing more.

The king abruptly stopped, raising a hand to signal for us to also halt.

"Why are we stopping?" I asked, glancing side to side.

I found nothing out of the ordinary, just the soft chirping of birds fluttering past. I folded my arms across my chest, huffing with irritation. I was exhausted, filthy, and had nearly died today. The last thing I wanted to deal with was any more of the Serpent King's games.

I stole a furious glance at the menace next to me, feeling a fresh wave of irritation at the sight of his immaculately straight nose. How many times did I need to strike him for it to stay crooked? If only he didn't possess the gift of immortal healing, then I'd be able to stare at the damage I'd inflicted on him with pride. Instead, I was left to stare at his perfect face . . .

He might have said he was not a god yet, but he sure looked like one.

The king didn't deign to respond to my question, beyond raising his hand and pointing to a yellow sign that was nailed to a nearby tree that read: *Snake Crossing*.

My brows tugged inward, my gaze dropping to the ground in search of any snakes, yet none slithered along the dirt pathway.

"I've had enough of your games. We haven't seen a single serpent in the hours we have traversed through this realm." I huffed again, prompting the king to finally tilt his head to glance at me.

His eyebrow arched at the tone I used with him, but I could give a serpent's tail if he was bothered by me. The feeling was mutual.

I glared back at him, prepared to continue onward regardless of what the menace instructed.

However, my foot stilled mid-step when I felt the ground beneath me start to tremble. Panic pinched my gut as my eyes shot skyward, looking for any broken branches hoping to strike me down for good—but there was nothing beyond swaying monkeys drifting high above.

A rustling sound pulled my attention to the tops of the trees, but this time to my left.

The leaves atop the canopy shook with such a strong intensity I worried the entire forest was about to topple and crush us all. The crack of a whip split through the air, making me jump back just in nick of time as the largest snake I'd ever seen darted before us.

It must have been at least fifty feet tall and just as wide, its gorgeous golden body gleaming with emerald scales as the sunlight streamed down upon it. I couldn't tear my gaze from the magnificent creature as it continued to slither past us. I glanced to the very top of the beast, catching a flash of something on its back . . . no, not some*thing*.

Some*one*.

Rather, it was a group of people straddling the snake as if they were casually riding a horse on a nice summer day. The men wore no shirts, leaving the dark ink swirling across their deep brown skin clear for any onlooker to see. The women were barely clothed as well, only small bits of emerald leather scraps clung to cover their most intimate parts. Gold weathered bands were tied around all of their foreheads, each person holding a variety of weapons that ranged from spears, to swords, and even some crossbows.

One of the men glanced down at the king, bowing his head deeply as their eyes met. Out of the corner of my eye, I caught the king offering him a kind smile in return as he nodded back at the man.

How peculiar.

It seemed these people respected the Serpent King—and vice versa.

What a bizarre notion.

Lost in my thoughts, I only caught the last glimpses of the serpent before its tail flicked at us with one final splitting sound. Then, we were left with only the faraway sounds of the birds chattering once more.

"Now, we may proceed onward." The Serpent King started down the dirt road, acting as if this realm was as familiar to any of us as it was to him.

My feet remained planted to the ground, shock and . . . what was that other emotion? It felt like what I experienced earlier, when I saw the sloth gliding in the trees.

Was I truly feeling a sense of wonder and awe?

The bargain must be weakening further for so many uncanny emotions to return to me . . .

Could that be why the Serpent King's portal shot us out hours away from our intended destination?

It made sense, for why else would he force himself to trek through the jungle with people he could barely tolerate. Stealing a glance at the king, I noticed how his normally pale complexion was ashier, like how one appeared after falling ill.

As if sensing my scrutinizing stare, he stopped walking, turning to look at me with his arms crossed over his chest. He stared with such an intensity, it felt like he was looking straight into my mind to read my racing thoughts.

I cleared every doubt I had of him losing his magic from my head—just in case. Instead, I replaced my critical stare with a look of shock, letting my mouth slightly part as if to pretend I was still reeling from the gigantic serpent we saw.

He relaxed a little upon seeing my dumbfounded expression, then muttered, *"For Serpent's Sake."* He spoke up as he said, "Are you all going to stand there with your mouths wide open for the poisonous bugs within these forests to fly straight into? Or can we continue to my mother's palace now?" He looked at us like we were sorrowful peasants, shaking his head in disgust before turning on his heel to resume his leisurely trek.

I quickly closed my mouth, turning in time to see Landon and Reena following suit.

I tried to collect all I learned of this new realm as I composed myself once again . . .

First, there were magical growing tree roots that latched onto me, nearly causing me to die.

Then, there was a ginormous snake that could swallow all of us whole.

Lastly, the king informed us of poisonous bugs casually flying about?

The Emerald Glades was very deceiving with its beautiful landscape, considering all the deadly dangers it was home to.

A rattling sound made me gaze toward the forest in search of its source, but it was only my lady-in-waiting's hands shaking. Her face was white as a sheet, making a pang of what felt like worry crash into me.

Another new feeling . . .

I had no time to dissect the wave of empathy racing through my veins, for Reena seemed moments away from passing out from shock.

Moving quickly, I came beside her to brace a supportive hand on her lower back and help steady her quaking legs. She jumped as I touched her, swiveling her head to see what monstrous beast was latching its claws around her. I sniffed the air, smelling her fear before I saw her eyes glaze over with said emotion. She furiously trembled beneath my hand, and that cursed emotion speared through the void in my chest again.

"Reena, breathe. The snake is gone," I commanded, knowing the sense of normalcy of me ordering around my lady-in-waiting would help ground her.

She inhaled shallowly, her lips quivering as she blew out a

shaky breath. My attention swung to my bodyguard, whose pupils were also blown wide with surprise.

"Landon," I whispered, making his blue eyes swiftly shoot to mine. "A little help." I nodded toward Reena, gesturing for him to grab her from her other side.

His eyes cleared upon hearing my command, and he quickly moved to Reena's right, offering his arm to steady her. She glanced at his extended arm with wide eyes, but accepted it with her trembling hands.

With my hand supporting Reena from fainting backwards and Landon preventing her from falling forwards, we all continued onward at a far slower pace. Reena shuffled her feet in the dirt, constantly looking around for any danger lurking in the forest. For my lady-in-waiting's sake, I hoped she could remain upright and make it the rest of the way to the palace. Considering she most definitely knew the alternative would be to summon that beastly serpent to carry her the rest of the way, I knew she would push through.

Reena was stronger than most people I knew. She had to be in order to succeed at being the Serpent Queen's lady-in-waiting.

As I glanced at her, I caught my bodyguard's eye, who was also checking on Reena. There were no lingering traces of anger in his eyes from our previous argument. My lips curved into a small smile, the best I could offer to let him know I appreciated all he did for me today. He cast a sad smile back at me, all too used to my lack of appreciation.

I wished he realized I was trying, in my own way.

For me, a smile was not something I willingly dished out to many people—if any.

In fact, I couldn't remember the last time I smiled and meant it . . .

My gaze dropped from his as I sank into a new fit of pity,

this time aimed at myself and not my lady-in-waiting. I kicked a small rock to expel some of the emotions gathering at the back of my throat.

It felt like I was tirelessly working to swallow my newfound emotions, along with any thoughts about how my life might've turned out under different circumstances. Yet, this life of torture and misery—of ruling and leading by fear—was the life I chose, and I had to stand by my decision.

After being devoid of a moral compass for decades, I've completely lost myself within the darkness, and there was no turning back.

I reveled in inflicting pain on others.

I craved the smell of their fear as I carved my dagger deep into their skin.

I preferred their tortured screams over the sound of laughter.

I was who I was always meant to be.

CHAPTER 30
THE SERPENT QUEEN

"Welcome to the Emerald Palace," the Serpent King said, grandly gesturing to the castle shooting into the vibrant golden sky behind him.

Slowly, my eyes trailed upward, taking in the sheer size of his mother's palace. It was large enough to hold three of my castles within it. The sun was beginning to descend over the rolling green hills surrounding us, casting a brilliant warm glow upon the stained glass windows lining the entire front of the structure.

I couldn't tear my gaze away from the windows as I continued to marvel at all the colorful snakes hidden within the stained glass. The only reason my attention drifted from the intricate design was because a voice as soft as silk caressed my ears.

"Welcome home, Alaric." Her voice wasn't the only thing that was beautiful about the female approaching us.

With her arms wide open, the king drifted forward, bending down to wrap the woman into a tight hug. My eyebrows flew up at the surprisingly affectionate gesture coming from the man who reveled in the fact he owned my soul.

"I've missed you, son," his mother whispered into his ear while they warmly embraced.

I felt like I was intruding on a rather intimate moment, but I couldn't look away from the goddess.

She was more stunning in person than the Luminoso portrayed. Her blonde hair flowed in wild waves around her heart shaped face, stirred by a warm breeze. Curiosity passed through me as I wondered what the Serpent King's father looked like . . .

Was he the one to thank for the king's midnight black hair that shifted to green with rays of light?

The wicked man most definitely inherited his porcelain complexion from his father, because his mother sported golden, sun-kissed skin. She looked like the type of person who relished being outdoors, and the golden leather band adoring the crown of her head suggested she might even ride alongside the warriors, who straddled that enormous snake.

However, the goddess had a more detailed band, and I studied the serpents etched within the leather that wrapped around the entire scrap. An emerald jewel dangled from the middle, bobbing across her forehead as she finally retreated from her son's crushing embrace.

The moment her eyes locked onto mine, I knew where the Serpent King got his piercing green gaze from. She assessed me with a severe intensity, just like her son had many times before, and I forced myself to stand taller—I refused to squirm underneath a god's glare.

But then, as if it was a mere trick of the light, warmth flooded through her eyes, replacing the coldness that was there mere moments ago. She moved toward me, her smile radiating as bright as the sun. Before I could introduce myself, she wrapped her strong arms around my figure, pulling me into a tight hug. I bit back my surprise and buried my initial urge to grasp for the dagger strapped around my thigh, ready to eliminate the threat who now wrapped her entire body around me.

No, I told myself, *now was not the time.*

The gods would all meet their reckoning by my hand, but, first, I needed to learn their weaknesses in order to defeat them.

"Welcome to my home," his mother softly whispered, still squeezing into me.

It was then that I realized I did not hug her back.

When was the last time I hugged someone, if ever?

"I've got you," he said, tugging me into his solid chest.

I shook off the flashes of the last time I was hugged seventy-five years ago, drifting back to the moment where I was presently feeling unbearably awkward. But since I didn't want the god to recognize my contempt, I lightly patted her back, all the while praying she would finally break our too-long embrace.

After what felt like a tortuous century, his mother pulled away, but she quickly grabbed ahold of one of my hands.

"Please feel free to call me Adalina. I loathe formal titles." She continued to flash her brilliantly bright smile straight at me.

I could barely force myself to nod, but she seemed satisfied enough since she released my hand.

For Serpent's Sake, this goddess's kindness deeply unsettled me. On top of her otherworldly beauty and kindness, she even had a stunning name.

Although Adalina and I both claimed the title of the Serpent Queen, we were complete opposites. All the way down to the fact I realized I was frowning at the goddess who still cast a warm smile in my direction.

Oh fuck, was she waiting for me to say something back to her?

I plastered the fake smile I wore everyday as the Serpent Queen onto my painted lips. Thankfully, she pushed the conversation forward, ignoring my awkward pause.

"Seera, it is so nice to finally meet you."

"You know my name?" My brow quivered with surprise.

"Of course I do! Alaric told me all about you." She slapped her son's shoulder playfully, dragging my gaze to the king.

His lips were pulled into a paper thin line as he shot a withering glare at his mother.

"Is that so?" I smiled coyly at the king, who started to shift uncomfortably on his feet.

Well, well, today truly was full of a bunch of first times.

The Serpent King's pale cheeks brightened with pink splotches, as if he was embarrassed by what his mother just revealed.

She continued on, completely oblivious at how uncomfortable she was making her son. "Oh, yes. He's told me all about how infuriating of a woman you are. He even went as far as to say—"

The king's low growl cut her off. "Mother, shouldn't you greet your other guests as well?" He gave a pointed glance toward Landon and Reena, who waited a few paces behind us.

"Oh, of course. My apologies, bad habit of mine. I tend to overshare when I'm excited." She covered her mouth with a hand, but I saw the sliver of a small smile peeking out from behind it.

Now *that* was music to my ears.

I gave her a sweet smile. "No need to apologize. I'd love to know more about the Serpent King's mother, the female who also calls herself the Serpent Queen." I tossed my fakest smile yet at the god. It took every scrap of my control to remain calm from my own words, even though I wanted to spit at Adalina's feet.

"Ah, that's right. My son told me something about you taking on that title in the Mortal Realm. How are things going for you as queen?"

I suppressed my scoff at her niceties and feigned ignorance.

All the gods surely had their own Luminoso devices to spy on us with.

"Wonderful, couldn't be better." The lie slipped through my teeth.

Like hell would I reveal the truth of the disarray my lands were currently in to this fraud. She may love to overshare, but I certainly did not trust Adalina one bit.

The Serpent King cocked his head at me, his lips slightly twitching into a knowing smile.

He could tell I was lying, yet he didn't tattle to his mother. He only stared at me with narrowed eyes, curiosity replacing his amusement as he worked on figuring out what game I was playing at.

Little did he know, the king was the biggest wild card in the game I was mapping out on how exactly to defeat the gods. Although we were allies in this moment—merely to defeat the Ice Goddess—I would never reveal all my nefarious ploys to him.

He broke my trust the night of our bargain, and it would not be something easily won back.

Besides, I didn't think he would take my plan to kill his mother and all the rest of the gods very well.

"So, who did you bring with you to my home?" Adalina's cheery voice pulled me from my scheming thoughts.

"Allow me to introduce my lady-in-waiting, Reena, and my bodyguard, Landon." I motioned for them to step forward.

Reena bowed into a deep curtsy. "Pleased to meet you, Your Majesty."

I bristled at her overly polite greeting, not liking how it felt to have *my* lady-in-waiting bowing to someone else, let alone calling them 'Your Majesty.'

As if she could sense my irritation, Reena glanced sideways at me. Her eyes widened, as if to say sorry, but I only narrowed my eyes at my lady-in-waiting's shriveling figure to let her know we would speak about this when we were alone.

"The pleasure is all mine, Reena." Adalina grabbed her hand, causing a bloom of color to spread across Reena's pale cheeks.

Then, the god set her sights on Landon, gently dropping Reena's hand as her eyes gleamed with curiosity.

"And that must mean you're Landon."

He offered Adalina a stiff bow, not as deep as Reena's, but still very unpleasant to witness.

"Thank you for welcoming us to your lands," Landon said, not making eye contact with her.

"As I said, the pleasure is all mine." She practically purred the words at my bodyguard, her gaze soaking in every glorious inch of him.

My blood heated from the way she was looking at *my* bodyguard.

The feeling of possessiveness sparked through my chest, and it rattled me—I never felt such a strong urge to keep Landon solely to myself, as if he were my own personal belonging. Maybe, like the Serpent King, I too had a bad tendency to be possessive over people.

I loudly cleared my throat and stepped in front of my body-guard, cutting off the god's roaming eyes to focus back on me.

"Adalina, would you be so kind as to show us your home and allow us to get settled? The journey to your palace was quite exhausting." I internally cringed at how proper and regal I was acting. But if I had to play by the royal handbook to have her not grow wary of my true intentions, I'd grin and bear it.

Adalina softly patted her hand against her forehead. "Of course, where are my manners?! Right this way." She linked her arm through mine, leading me straight through the arched entry doors.

They, too, were completely made of emerald stained glass, and the serpent designs shimmered a blinding gold as the sunset streamed through the window panes.

"How does a warm bath and a home cooked meal sound? I was about to whip up my famous tomato soup and a side of fresh cheesy bread, but, if that isn't to your liking, I can make something else for you?"

My nose scrunched in distaste. "You make your own food?"

"Who else would?" She laughed, making my irritation coil within me like a venomous serpent because even her laugh was beautiful.

I hid my growing temper, opting for an incredulous tone as I replied, "Perhaps, your servants?"

Her lips turned down into a frown. "Oh, Seera. We don't use that term in my realm. My people are my equals, and those who serve me in my palace do so out of their own free will. I handle creating most of the meals for my staff—I've always loved cooking." She squeezed my arm, and I forced my lips to tilt up instead of the scowl it wanted to fall into.

Gods, this female was far too nice for my liking. I'd rather lead her to one of my infamous executions than take a tour of her gaudy palace, but I had a role to play in the game we entered the moment I set foot in her realm—well, *tumbled* into.

"Tomato soup sounds wonderful." My words tasted sugary rolling off my tongue, and the craving to taste something bitter raced through me.

I desperately needed to sort out how I was going to get my daily fix of fear while in the Emerald Glades, for it seemed like no one had any reason to live in such a state of emotion here. I'd have to resort to bringing Ember and Dante out while Reena was around if I couldn't come up with a better plan, since there was no way I'd survive multiple days without consuming a lick of fear.

Adalina led me further into her home, all the while pointing out small details within the stained glass windows. I prompted her to answer casual questions about the history of the Emerald Glades, along with her interests. She easily indulged me in anything I wanted to know the entire way to my new chambers, and I greedily soaked up every piece of knowledge she divulged, hoping it would aid in my plan to defeat her one day.

I smiled sweetly at the goddess who spilled her secrets to a complete stranger, at the so-called Serpent Queen who failed to notice the deadly serpent she had just willingly welcomed into her home.

CHAPTER 31
THE DOLL

"Y ou are drooling," a deep voice drawled, pulling me from my sleep.

The same piercing green eyes I was dreaming about stared at me, familiar notes of amber and smoke floating in the air.

"Why are you in my room?" I swiped at the corner of my mouth as I lifted my smushed face off the emerald silk pillow.

I was, indeed, drooling, considering the back of my hand was now wet. The Serpent King smiled down at me, as if to say I told you so.

He bent at the waist, bringing his face closer to mine. "You may be a guest in my family home, but I can go wherever I please, whenever I want."

"I don't give a serpent's tail if you were the very ruler of this realm, you have two seconds to get the fuck out for disturbing my slumber, or I can force you. We all remember the other night, hm? The one where I broke your nose not once, but twice? Ringing any bells for you, Serpent King?" The last thing I saw before flopping onto my back and rolling away from the menace was his furious scowl.

I snatched the cashmere green blanket and pulled it up to my chin, preparing to sleep for a while longer. Yet, as I was snuggling into the soft bed, cold air splashed over my bare legs. A grimace settled onto my face as I planted my hands behind me onto the golden silk sheets, lifting myself to face the king. The snake was wrapping my blanket around his neck, wearing it like a scarf.

He finished draping it across his neck with a smug smile. "Mhm, this blanket is rather cozy. I can see why you looked so comfortable just a moment ago with it wrapped around you." His eyes flickered over my bare legs, before he lifted the longer part of the blanket dangling along his chest to his nose, inhaling the cashmere deeply.

"It smells like you . . . " He sniffed the garment again. "Cinnamon, jasmine, and—ah, of course." He gave me a sickly sweet smile. "Dead roses."

"Something is deeply wrong with you." My lip curled at the menace who was grossly detailing my scent.

The smell of something I only dreamed of tasting after nearly eighty decades cooled my annoyance like a lovely breeze. I inhaled like an animal on the hunt, my eyes scanning the room for the glorious scent. On the table before the hearth was a tray with one mug, with steam rippling from its surface.

The king's gaze followed mine. "There is cream and sugar, just as you like."

My gaze shifted to him, noting how his spine stiffened after uttering his last words.

"You brought me coffee?"

Slowly, he turned to look at me. "I remember how much you enjoyed it, when you—" He cleared his throat. "When you resided in my realm." He started to shift on his feet, all hints of his previous charm gone.

The Serpent King brought *me* coffee.

I peeled myself from the cozy sheets, drifting toward the delicious aroma beckoning me. My mouth watered as I neared the beverage, but I didn't reach for either the cream or sugar. Instead, I took the black cup of coffee and turned to face the king. With my lips against the rim, I looked up at him through my lashes as I blew on the piping liquid.

"I don't like sweet things anymore, and I'm not the girl you once knew. It'd do you some good to remember that." His eyes dipped to my lips as they wrapped around the forest green mug.

For Serpent's Sake, how did I live without coffee for all these years?

A moan slipped past my lips, and the king's eyes darkened upon hearing the sound.

Fuck, he was looking at me like—like he wished to be the cup of coffee my lips were snuggly wrapped around.

I quickly strode to the bathing chambers to escape his fierce stare and hopefully find a robe to combat the frigid temperature. Yet, being the pest I knew him to be, the Serpent King's dark chuckle chased after me.

"To what do I owe you the pleasure of you being a royal pain in my ass this early in the morning?" I glared at him through the golden framed mirror.

"First off, it's nearly noon." He lifted a pompous finger at me, then raised another. "And second off, weren't you the one pestering me to take you to the library to learn more about the gods?"

I sighed with exasperation at the fact he was right, though I'd never admit it.

Instead, I spotted a velvet emerald robe hanging on the

back of the bathing room door and reached for it. The moment my body was wrapped in its warm embrace, I felt myself relax.

"There is a matching pair of slippers too," the king drawled, giving a pointed look at the ground.

Sure enough, he was right . . . again. I grumbled as I slipped my feet into the matching pair of deep green slippers.

Why wouldn't Adalina be a thoughtful host, considering since she was perfect from head to toe?

My mood soured upon thinking of the god who claimed the title of the Serpent Queen, and I moved toward the sink in hopes to wash away my anger. Scalding hot water streamed from the gold-plated chrome sink as I splashed my face and proceeded to scrub my skin.

When I looked into the mirror while patting my face dry with, of course, an emerald green towel, my eyes snagged on my chest—right where my serpent tattoo peeked out from my robe drifting open. Bits of my lacy black nightdress became exposed while I was bent over the skin, along with the head of the serpent marking—its maw wide open, fangs flashing as if ready to inject its venom into our enemies.

Quiet footsteps fell against the gold and white tiles, then the king was towering behind me, his eyes dipping to the bit of cleavage on display.

"Beautiful," he whispered softly, granting him one of my questioning glares through the mirror. As if remembering himself, his lips curved into a lazy smile. "I mean, it's beautiful seeing my mark permanently sealed into your skin." He dragged a finger along my shoulder, and I was thankful the robe was thick enough to prevent me from feeling his unwanted contact. Even though he didn't touch my skin directly, I still snatched his finger between my fist and spun to face him.

"What did I say about touching me unsolicited, Serpent

King?" I hissed through clenched teeth, all the while gripping his finger harder.

His nose pinched while his eyes slightly crinkled, the only sign I was causing him any pain.

Good, because I owed him decades worth of agony as payback for how he made me feel the night of our bargain.

"Apologies, my Queen," he forced out.

I gave his finger one more sharp twist, finally drawing a beautiful yelp out of the menace. I savored the sound, his pain, and the feeling of hurting someone for the first time in what felt like a century . . . even though I kicked his ass just the other night.

"The next time you touch me against my will, there will be no time for apologies. I will snap your fingers off and not even your immortal status will be able to properly heal them," I seethed, clutching him for another moment.

Something like amused surprise flared in his eyes, but it was gone as soon as it came. I released the Serpent King's finger, shoving his chest hard before proceeding out of my bathing chambers. Hesitant footsteps followed me back into my personal quarters as I shouted for my lady-in-waiting.

"Reena is enjoying breakfast with my mother, so I'm afraid you are stuck with me to help dress you." I glanced back at the annoying gnat I couldn't get rid of, noticing his smile was more forced than usual.

He tried to portray his usual arrogance, but it seemed like a shell of what it usually was.

Maybe my display of power in the bathing chamber truly ruffled his feathers.

Splendid.

I ignored the king as I made my way behind the gold and emerald stained-glass dressing screen. I shucked off my robe and nightdress, reaching for the gown that was already hanging atop the screen. The forest green velvet felt cool against my skin as I shimmied it up my body. I was grateful to find a side zipper on the dress, no sign of strings or boning within the garment, so I could dress myself with ease.

The dress clung to all my curves, but it flared out along my thighs, with a modest slit running up my left leg. With it only exposing half of my thigh, it was far more reserved than the gowns I wore in my queendom. A velvet train pooled behind me, but not long enough to be a bother. In fact, it helped make me look like the queen I was.

The dress was stunning, but I'd like it far better if it was red or black.

Right as I was glancing along the white and gold tiled floors for a pair of heels, the Serpent King's pale hand popped over the divider. He dangled a pair of shiny gold heels before my face, and after I didn't reach for them, he vehemently shook them.

A small smile danced along my lips as I finally reached for the shoes, and I was grateful he couldn't see the delight his silly action made me feel. Although I only lived in Morotis for a few weeks many decades ago, it seemed the king was paying closer attention to the things I liked than I thought.

Upon examining the heels closer, I noticed the subtle snakeskin design within the gold band crossing over my toes and along the straps I worked to criss-cross up the entirety of my calves. Once I was done putting on my heels, I straightened, smoothing my gown as I examined myself in the gold floor length mirror beside me.

I kicked my leg straight up, nodding with satisfaction that I could move with ease in this dress. Considering I was in a foreign realm that was full of potential enemies, I needed the ability to move freely, should I have to show Adalina who the real Serpent Queen was.

Feeling satisfied with my attire, I strolled out from behind the partition and to the vanity along one of the walls covered in golden, floral wallpaper. I grimaced at all the shades of gold and green in the room, at the sickening floral patterns surrounding me.

Gods, this room felt like my own personal form of torture.

Snatching a tube of lipstick from the vanity, I popped the cap open, only to be greeted with a horrendous champagne color with flakes of gold shimmering within it.

"Where is my red lipstick?" I snapped the cap onto the lipstick harder than necessary, already scanning the table for other options.

The king came into the reflection of the mirror as he moved closer behind me.

"About that, I felt your style could use a little revamping while visiting the Emerald Glades. Your whole Serpent Queen look," he said, gesturing at my face while frowning. "Well, to put it bluntly, it doesn't suit you."

I whirled toward him. "You have no right to tell me what does or doesn't suit me. How dare you try to dress me like your own personal doll." I jabbed a sharp nail into his bare chest, courtesy of him leaving a few buttons undone like he infuriatingly always did.

He glanced down at my finger spearing into his skin, then softly wrapped his hand around it.

"I see you for what you truly are, Seera. All I want is for you to stop pretending to be something you are not." His gaze slowly drifted up to mine, and my mouth parted from the sincerity shining within his clear green eyes.

I quickly remembered myself, clenching my jaw shut and slamming my face into a cold mask of hate.

"Let me remind you for a final time, you know nothing of who I am anymore. Whoever you once knew died the day we made our bargain, and you would know that if you ever cared to contact me in the past seventy-five years." I knew my last words were a mistake the moment they flew from my mouth, but it was too late, for the Serpent King's mouth parted with surprise.

I sniffed the air when a deep wrinkle formed between his brows, only to start coughing from the overwhelming cloud of smoke wafting off him.

So much *regret* clung to the king.

He released my finger, grinding his teeth as he realized his mistake of not hiding his emotions from me. He shook his head, like the motion could clear any of his unwanted feelings. Then, he turned to flee for the door.

"Reena will bring you breakfast. I expect you to meet me in the Emerald Library in thirty minutes." He barely barked his last command before slamming the door behind him.

I was left alone, desperately trying to piece together all that just occurred between the king and I.

He reeked of regret, but why?

He was the one that shoved me from his lands the moment our bargain was complete, his parting words so cold they still haunted my nightmares.

Warmth bloomed from my hand, pulling me from my thoughts.

I glanced to see I was tightening my hand into a fist so intensely that my sharp nails tore open the flesh of my palm. Blood coated underneath my nails, small beads of it slowly staining the white and gold tiled floors crimson.

A gentle hiss wrapped around me, then Ember was there curling along my shoulders. She gently nudged her head against my cheek in an attempt to soothe my vexed mood. I softly stroked the top of her head. When I was rewarded with a happy hiss, warmth curled into the void in my chest. I looked at my gorgeous scarlet snake, her black eyes squeezing shut as I pet her.

What did I do to deserve such a creature to stand by my side through the darkness?

As I continued to stroke her, a thought drifted in my head upon seeing the small bead of blood still at the tip of my finger. A devious smile spread across my face as I turned toward the mirror, then swiped the drop of blood across my lips. Although it was nowhere as deep of a color like the one I typically wore, the sheer red tint now painted across my lips was better than the champagne lipstick that horrid man wanted me to wear.

The Serpent King may think he can change me, even try to make me into some sick version of his own living doll. Since he was raised by a god, I couldn't say I was surprised by his vile actions. If there was one thing I was certain of, it was that the gods didn't care about anyone beyond themselves.

Yet, the king was an utter fool for doubting the force of the true Serpent Queen, but I'd happily remind him of his mistake when I faced all the gods one by one as soon as our mission was over.

After all, the Serpent King should know best that I was strong enough to shake the world when coming into power, and I wouldn't hesitate to do it again.

CHAPTER 32

THE SPARK

The Serpent King said to meet him in the library in thirty minutes. So, naturally, I met him there in forty.

As I strutted through the emerald stained-glass double doors, the king was leaning against a stack of books, his arms crossed across his chest.

"You are late."

"A queen is never late. You are simply early." I tossed him a dazzling smile before strolling past him and down the first row of literature.

The stacks of leather-bound books soared high above me, making them at least twenty feet tall. I breathed in the fresh smell of old books, relishing a scent that once was the only thing that comforted me late at night. My fingers trailed over the spines as I drifted through the row, books bound in various colors surrounding me.

I was grateful for once in my life to see more shades of color. Anything was better than the perpetual green and gold hues that stained the Emerald Palace.

"Where is your plaything?" The king walked beside me, making his shoulder lightly brush against mine.

Although the aisles might be big enough for one person to stroll through comfortably, they were hardly large enough to fit me and the behemoth insisting on walking by my side.

Browsing the shelves, I decided to ignore the king's not-so-subtle jab at my bodyguard.

He would not get the sick satisfaction of riling me up.

"I sent word I'd be preoccupied for a while, so I advised Landon to spend his free time training. We all need to be prepared to defeat this god."

He grunted his agreement, his eyes glancing over the various titles that we passed.

"It seems your mother has taken a liking to Reena . . . and Landon." I muttered the last bit under my breath, but the king's dark chuckle suggested he heard me.

"Sounds like someone is jealous," he crooned.

I scoffed, the sound jarring in the otherwise quiet library.

"Why would *I* be jealous? Landon is solely my bodyguard."

"Sure he is." He whistled casually as we neared the end of one of the stacks.

I stopped walking, instead rotating to face the man who loved to somehow always work his way under my skin. The king followed my lead, slowly turning toward me with a wicked smile already plastered upon his face.

"Maybe your mother should stop feasting her eyes on my bodyguard and spare some of her lust for her husband."

The king's smile dropped, his eyes frosting over with a layer of impenetrable ice. "That would be hard to do, considering dear old father is six feet under the ground." He tried to sound casual, but the anger simmering in his eyes suggested otherwise.

Without another word, he sharply spun on his heel, fleeing down the stacks to leave me behind.

Fuck, how was I supposed to know his father was dead?

I watched the king storm off, allowing him a moment to gather himself. I was never good at comforting others, and, quite frankly, I had work to do. So, I forced myself to forget about my insensitive remark and that I was the reason the king's dazzling smile faded.

Horror sliced through me, making my fingers still on a spine as I realized how troubling it was that I was suddenly worried about how I affected another person. After all, this was the man who broke my heart and rudely shoved me out of his lands.

So why should I care about the Serpent King's misery?

Shaking my head in hopes to clear the empathy infecting my brain, I focused on the books staring me down. Since I couldn't control the venom constantly coating the tip of my tongue, I figured I'd control the one thing I came to the Emerald Glades for in the first place: knowledge of the gods.

I itched to touch every single tome in this library, my old passion for the written word swiftly drifting back to me. My fingers grazed the books while I moved deeper into the stacks, but I stilled on a gold leather-bound book titled *The Magic of the Gods*.

Snatching it from the shelf, I traveled further into the stacks while acquiring a few other titles that drew my interest. I was overcome with the overwhelming feeling to grab each and every book I passed. A small smile slipped onto my lips as I felt my insatiable desire to learn coming back to me with every tome I acquired.

Glancing down at my growing pile, I knew I had more than enough material to dive into. I began searching for a spot to devour all my newfound books, but the moment I rounded the corner I came to a crashing halt.

Stewing in a dark alcove in the corner of the library, the Serpent King sat slouched in a deep forest green wingback chair.

I gnawed on my bottom lip, trying to decide if I should turn around to find a different spot to study my tomes. Yet, I couldn't stop my feet from inching closer to him—maybe it was the darkness that drew me closer to the king, or the smell of fresh rain emanating off him that piqued my curiosity. I was never drawn to the smell of one's sorrow, but there was something about the king's sadness that intrigued me. There was a hint of burnt leather hidden within the depths of his sadness, and the familiar scent soothed me.

After all, the emotion associated with charred leather was one I was very familiar with every time I gazed into a mirror.

Pure hatred.

As I entered the dim alcove with stacks of books jutting up on all three sides surrounding us, I brushed my knee against the king's legs to alert him to my presence. He looked so lost in his thoughts, in his despair, that he startled at my contact.

He looked up at me, sadness burning bright in his eyes.

Gods, I truly was a monster.

"I'm sorry about your father. I was out of line with my comment back there."

He continued to stare at me, allowing me to see every ounce of his emotions.

Why did he not shove them down? It would be easier if we continued to hide our feelings from one another. Seeing him like this, so raw and vulnerable, made me feel things I typically ran from. Usually, I didn't care when I hurt other people, because their pain fueled me, it gave me substance—something to numb the emptiness gnawing within me.

Perhaps, it was because we had history together or because my soul was slowly coming back to me, but I wanted to try to ease the agony I caused him. So, I shared something I've never shared with another soul.

"I never knew my father. My mother didn't deign to tell me one single thing about him." I wished I sounded unbothered by this fact, but my soft voice held a twinge of its own melancholy.

I always wondered what my father was like, if my life would have turned out differently with him in it. Was he a kind man? Was he a father that would've showered me with love instead of leaving me in complete isolation?

"Seems like we have more in common than we realized." The king's voice beckoned me back to the shadowy alcove, where I still towered over him.

I must have subconsciously taken another step toward him, because I was now practically between his legs. His hand flexed atop his thigh, almost as if he wanted to reach for me, to close any remaining space lingering between us.

A pang of disappointment shot through me when he opted to squeeze his hand into a tight fist instead, prompting me to quickly step back.

"May I?" I eyed the open chair across from him, still not sure if he wanted to be around me after my heartless comment.

However, he surprised me when he gestured to the other chair in a silent offer to join him.

I crossed the short distance to the seat and plopped down, dropping the books onto a golden circular table.

"Find anything good?" He perked up as he scooted his chair closer to the table. His pale hand reached for the book at the top of my stack, the one titled *How to Fully Tap into Your Magic.*

"I sure hope so. I grabbed what I thought would be useful

for our mission. I'd like to learn every weakness I can about the gods—I mean, the Ice Goddess."

I inwardly cursed myself for my small slip-up and prayed the Serpent King didn't catch it.

I glanced at him through lowered lashes, only to find him staring at me with narrowed eyes.

Fuck, he definitely heard me.

Time to swiftly change the subject.

"What did you say her name was again?"

After studying me for another moment, his lips turned down, almost like he didn't want to speak the Ice Goddess' true name. "Isolde."

A soft hum vibrated through my chest while I flipped through the pages of the book titled *The Origins of the Gods*, searching for any mentions of the mysterious goddess.

After browsing nearly the entirety of the tome, I was about to give up until I turned to one of the last pages and saw a female I've never seen before.

"Is this her?" I turned the book so the king could see more clearly, causing a deeper scowl to adorn his face at the sight of the photo.

"Yes, that is Isolde." A shiver coursed through him, making his shoulders quake.

Curiosity stirred in me, and I discreetly sniffed the air to detect the emotion coursing through the king. I was greeted with that bitter taste I'd grown to crave.

The Serpent King *feared* the Ice Goddess.

Glancing at her picture again, I noticed how pale the goddess's skin was. It was nearly translucent, her icy blue veins practically glowing beneath her skin. Then, there were her frosty eyes, which were so pale blue they appeared more white than anything.

"Why do you fear her?" I tore my eyes from Isolde's picture to glance back at the king.

He remained silent as he stared at the image, at her frost-covered lips tipping up into a chilling smile. I was about to resume my reading when he didn't reply, but the softness in his next words had me perking up with curiosity.

"I stole something from her long ago."

"What did you steal?"

A somberness fell over the Serpent King's face. "Someone she loved."

I did not expect him to say that, so all I could force out after hearing this intimate piece of information was a breathy "*Oh.*"

He shook his head, clearing whatever tender memories flashed behind that pretty face of his.

"It was pointless, since we both lost her in the end."

Silence stretched between us—I was totally out of my depth here. This conversation took an unexpected turn toward being far too deep and vulnerable for my liking.

I swallowed the discomfort churning in my mouth, distracting myself by flipping through the pages of *The Origins of the Gods.*

A particularly interesting section had my back stiffening and attention roaming once again to the king who was staring off into the distance, still looking lost in his memories.

"Why does it say the gods were created? Are they not born like the rest of us?"

His focus snapped to me, a charming smile quickly dancing along his lips.

"Maybe if you kept reading, you would find the answers to the questions you insistently ask."

There was the Serpent King I loved to hate.

I blew out a puff of air, my lips trilling to fill the unnerving silence of the library.

Fine. If he didn't want to help me, I'd do it myself . . . I have been my entire life, anyways.

I read on and found my answer after flipping through a few more pages.

"The gods were created by a higher being referred to as the Goddess of Life. This goddess was responsible for creating life and granting slivers of her various powers to different gods."

As I turned the page, I devoured every gorgeous inch of the Goddess of Life's portrait. Her glowing eyes matched her radiating golden skin. White hair cascaded in soft waves down her slender figure, ending just past the dips of her hips. I traced her smile with my finger, marveling at how bright and warm it was. There was nothing hidden behind it, not like when Adalina flashed her brilliant smile or when I wore a fake one every day. It felt like the goddess of the Emerald Glades was forcing herself to be kind, while, on the other hand, the Goddess of Life radiated true benevolence. Although I never met this god, there was a nagging feeling inside me that she was different from all the rest.

Suddenly, I felt bad for saying I'd destroy all the gods when my eyes took in the small inscription written below her photo.

The Dawn of Creation—The Dark Day.

There was no further explanation of what that statement could mean, so I pushed the book across the small table to sit before the king. He glanced at it, then turned his attention to me with a raised brow.

"Since I can't simply 'read on' to find this answer, explain." I crossed my arms over my chest, making the king's eyes dip to track the way the movement pushed my breasts tightly together.

Quickly averting his gaze, he cleared his throat and studied the line of text.

"Those are the dates of her life." He pushed the book back at me.

I opened my mouth, but nothing came out on my first attempt as I was still wrapping my mind around what the king was insinuating. I took a moment to compose myself, then tried again.

"Are you saying the Goddess of Life, the god who created the very existence of everything surrounding us, is dead?"

"That's right." He reached across the table, flipping the page to reveal another picture of a starkly different god. "All thanks to her."

My mouth was still slightly agape as I glanced away from him and took in the portrait of the god who supposedly slayed the deity that breathed life into everything around us.

Eyes as black as the night sky glared back at me, the god's onyx hair streaming around her moonlight-pale face. Naturally, her lips were also painted black and tipped into a smile far crueler than the Ice Goddess's. The picture was titled *The Goddess of Death* and written beneath in similar slanted writing were the following words: *01-The Dark Day.*

"The Goddess of Death is dead as well? How do the realms continue on without the very beings who control life and death?" I shot him an incredulous look.

"Just because they cease to exist doesn't mean everything else does. The only thing it affects is that no more gods can be created, plus no one really knows where souls go when they pass on. That was the Goddess of Death's role, to help souls easily transition into the afterlife, up until she—well, let's just say she got greedy and didn't want to help souls pass on anymore . . ." The king tried, yet failed, to hide the wince that flashed across his face.

In an attempt to change the subject, he reached for a new book from my stack.

"Why did you grab this one?" He tossed the thick tome between his hands, as if it were as light as a feather.

I glanced at the spine, noting he picked up the book titled *How to Tap into Your Magical Powers.*

"I was hoping to learn more about how the gods control their magic." I brushed back the sheet of black hair that was falling into my face from being hunched over the texts.

I straightened, looking down my nose at the king. "Considering *someone* didn't teach me anything about how to use my own magic, maybe there is a thing or two I could learn between these pages." I snatched the book from his hands, throwing a withering glare at him as I compiled all the tomes into a neat stack.

"Seera . . ." The tenderness in that one word stilled my fingers and made my gaze snap back to his.

Something flickered in his mesmerizing eyes, prompting me to discreetly inhale to decipher what the king was feeling. The most pungent burst of smoke barreled into me, causing me to flinch and press myself hard into the chair. I braced my hands against the velvet armrests as I took a few sharp breaths to clear the smoke out of my lungs, but it was no use.

The Serpent King's regret was so strong I was choking on it.

A cough escaped me, and I quickly pushed my chair back to flee. The stacks behind me rattled, and I winced at my rash reaction resulting in the disturbance of such precious tomes.

Luckily, none tumbled to the floor, so I raced to gather my materials. Unluckily, the king also shot to his feet, a look of concern blanketing his perfect features.

I couldn't bite back the coughs racking through my chest, the smoke of his regret still lingering in the air and suffocating my lungs.

"Seera, are you okay?" He reached for me as I cradled the books to my chest, but I sidestepped out of his reach and hurried out of the library.

I refused to let the Serpent King confuse me with his overwhelming feelings of repentance. I had far more important matters to focus on, like destroying the gods and finally ensuring my people bowed at my feet.

Footsteps pounded behind me, and I did my best to quicken my steps in order to put more distance between the king and I. But, my plan horribly failed as my heel snatched on the train of my gown, causing me to stumble backward.

The world flipped upside down, and I protectively gripped the precious books cradled against my chest as I fell. However, before my head could collide with the plush green carpets, strong hands gripped underneath my arms.

Then, *he* was there.

Suspended in the air, I stared into the piercing green eyes that haunted my dreams.

"We really need to work on your coordination skills," The Serpent King said all the while smirking down at me.

"My coordination is perfectly fine. I wouldn't have tripped if you weren't stalking my every move."

He chuckled, but it was nothing like his typical dark timber. Instead, his laugh was light and airy, almost high-pitched. I marveled at the sight of him so freely laughing, which only prompted him to swallow the beautiful sound upon seeing my dumbfounded expression.

The ground righted below my feet once more as the king gently lifted me up. The motion brought us far too close, considering his chest was now snuggly pressed against my back.

Then, his warm breath caressed my ear, sending small shivers to pass along my spine.

"I can't make up for the wrongs I've done in the past, Seera, but I'd like to try. Train with me today?" he whispered, his hands dropping from underneath my arms to lightly press against the curve of my waist.

I sucked in a sharp breath, confused that I didn't feel the urge to kick him in the groin when his hands wrapped around my body. Instead, warmth fluttered low in my core as I remembered a very similar moment when our bodies were pressed together like this many decades ago.

"Where do you want to train?" My voice was far too breathy, far too vulnerable.

I didn't need to smell the air to sense the Serpent King's surprise, because his fingers dug deeper into the velvet of my gown. I hated that the warmth budding between my thighs now sparked into a blazing fire from the glorious pressure of his fingers against my waist.

Suddenly, I couldn't stand how thick the material of my dress was.

"Meet me in the front grounds in an hour." His voice was husky, and I swore I felt more than his hard chest pressing into my backside.

So fucking dangerous, Seera.

"Fine. See you in one hour," I said, forcing myself to break away from his intoxicating grip.

I sped straight for the exit and back to my rooms.

My heels furiously clicked against the white and gold marble floors of the halls, walking so fast I nearly felt as if I was floating.

How could I be so stupid letting him that close to me, letting him hold me like that?

I swore to make the Serpent King's life a living hell before coming on this journey, just as he did to my life the moment he uttered such a brutal parting after our bargain. Instead, I shared something I'd never told to a single soul, and I even let him reveal one of his own secrets to me.

Then, there was the fact he saved me from falling—again. And the feeling of his fingers digging into my waist, his breath caressing against my ear, the hardness of his . . .

"*For Serpent's Sake.*" I hissed.

As I rounded the corner leading back to my chambers, I forced myself to forget the king and the moment we had in the library.

But as I entered my rooms, I couldn't deny the floral scent permeating through the space.

The one emotion I hated more than anything radiated from deep within my core . . .

Hope.

CHAPTER 33
THE SCREAM

I stood before the floor-length mirror as I unzipped my dress, my fingers stilling on the spot where the king's searing touch lingered.

I imagined it was his fingers slowly grazing over my skin as I shrugged my shoulders, letting the velvet material fall off my curves and pool around my heels.

The tightness coiling between my legs didn't relent ever since I fled from the king's bruising grip, and there was no way I could train in such a state.

Since I had to release the ever-growing tension within me before our training session, I did what I knew how to do best: please myself.

Kicking my dress to the side, I stood before the mirror and hooked my thumbs into the band of my lacy undergarments, making quick work of discarding those, as well as my bra.

I stood before the floor-length mirror, in nothing but my beloved heels, as I dipped my fingers into the wetness already gathered between my thighs.

There were two guaranteed ways to expel any tension within my core—violence or sex.

Considering I had to be on top of my game when I trained with the king, I convinced myself I was doing this out of sheer necessity.

Not because I liked the way his fingers felt digging into my waist.

I circled my clit, applying a glorious amount of pressure.

I was most definitely *not* doing this because I enjoyed the feel of his hardness pressing into my backside.

Dragging my finger down myself, I slipped it inside me. I bit back the moan crawling up my throat as I leaned forward, gripping the mirror as I closed my eyes.

However, doing so was a fatal mistake when flashes of those piercing green eyes raced through my mind.

I *should* open my eyes—I *should* stop thinking about the king—but instead, I slipped a second finger into me, reveling at the stretch it provided. I worked myself with a feverish intensity, but it didn't feel satisfying like it used to.

I craved *more*.

If the feeling of what was pressing into my back in the library was accurate, then I knew the king was *very* well endowed. I never had the opportunity to fully explore him all those years ago, and I now deeply regretted being such a prude when I was mortal.

As I touched myself, I wondered how big he was, if he liked it rough and painful like I did, if he moaned when he came.

Shoving a third finger in me, I rode my hand all the while I imagined it was his.

Fuck, now we were getting somewhere.

Slipping out of myself, I worked my clit while chasing after my release. With my other hand, I rolled my nipple between my fingers, hissing from the intoxicating sensation of pain spearing through my nerves. I opened my eyes, so I could watch how my breasts bounced from the jolt of agony.

That's it, almost there.

Dragging my fingers back down my center, I pushed them deep inside me one final time.

I knew what I was doing was wrong, but as I closed my eyes, my back arched when I visualized the Serpent King burying himself deep within me. My other hand reached around to grab my ass all the while pretending it was *his*.

As my orgasm shot through me, I couldn't stop myself from screaming out the name I've avoided saying for nearly eighty years.

I didn't shout for the Serpent King. The words 'the king' didn't tumble from my sinful lips.

No, I yelled for the man who utterly and completely destroyed me, and who was on the proper pathway to doing so once more.

As I came with a shattering intensity, I screamed out for *Alaric*.

CHAPTER 34
TENSIONS RISE

I arrived at the outdoor training grounds with only ten minutes to spare. I hoped to arrive a bit earlier to burn off any lingering nerves before my first ever training session with the Serpent King, but my personal detour kept me delayed.

A ghost of a smile tugged on my lips upon hearing metal scraping together, signaling my bodyguard was still here, the familiar sound of his frustrated grunts sounding from the training grounds. Such noises used to also excite me in the bedroom, but, after what I just did in my own chambers—and with another man in the forefront of my mind—they didn't entice me as much as they once did . . .

My smile slipped at this revelation, then completely dissolved the moment a flash of blonde hair reflected against the strong sunlight overhead.

The goddess of the Emerald Glades was sparring with my bodyguard.

Inhale. Exhale.

It is not time to kill her, Seera.

Rolling my shoulders back, I donned a fake smile as I approached the vast rectangular training grounds. However, my balance faltered the moment I stepped into the closed off ring, my shoes sinking into a spongy material.

This was less than ideal, since I forwent my shorter training heels for a golden stiletto that must have been at least five inches. Alas, I'd survive whatever happened today, for this wasn't my first—nor would it be my last—time training in my beloved heels.

As a matter of fact, whenever my horrid soul expired and drifted off to the Land of the Wicked, I hoped Reena would be kind enough to bury me in my favorite pair of heels: my black leather sky-high pumps with those beautifully wicked golden spikes ascending the length of the skinny heel.

My grin felt less forced from such a steadying thought as I took in the scene playing out before me. Landon and Adalina were locked in an intense match, their swords cutting through the air with splitting precision as they dealt brutal blow after blow at each other.

Much to my surprise, and possible demise, Adalina was decent with a sword.

Fuck, who was I kidding—she was more than decent.

If she could force Landon to retreat multiple times against her sturdy strikes, she must train regularly.

An annoyed huff fell from my lips, making my bodyguard's gaze cut to where I lingered. Our eyes locked for a split second, but that was all the time Adalina needed to inflict a shallow cut across Landon's chest. He swore, his fingers dipping over the cut and shining a bright red when he pulled them back.

"You were doing so well, until you allowed yourself to get distracted. A deadly mistake, Landon." Adalina sang my bodyguard's name like it was her favorite melody.

For the second time within seconds, my smile turned into a

scowl as I watched *my* bodyguard cast a bashful smile at the god—one he used to grant me when I first took him into my guard.

"You fight well yourself, almost like a warrior," Landon said, his chest heaving from exertion.

My jaw worked. He never was out of breath when we trained together.

Adalina let out a subtle laugh. "I fight like a warrior, because I *am* a warrior."

I perked up upon hearing her confession, irritation rippling through me at the fact that this god was a skilled fighter.

This would only make her that much harder to defeat one day—hopefully, some day *very* soon.

Landon reached for the hem of his navy blue shirt, lifting it to wipe away the sweat gathering along his brows. The motion left most of his abdomen exposed, simultaneously providing a significant amount of chiseled muscles for my eyes to feast on.

A small gasp rang through the warm air, and it appeared his small show not only distracted me, but the god standing before him. Adalina's gaze dipped to devour every inch of his exposed skin, and when her tongue darted out to wet her lips, I nearly closed the space between us to cut off the fake Serpent Queen's head.

Balling my hands into tight fists at my side, I swallowed my anger and sealed it away for another day.

The day I'd shake the world once more, and finally bring the rule of the gods to an end.

Adalina's bottom lip pouted the moment Landon dropped the hem of his shirt, hiding his muscles from the god's prying eyes. Something foreign built inside of me, right in the void where my soul used to be. I rubbed my thumb against the spot, curiosity stirring in me at what I was feeling as I watched

Adalina stare at Landon like he was something she wanted to devour.

Was that . . . no.

No, it couldn't be.

Yet, as a prickle of annoyance speared through my chest, I questioned if the Serpent King was right yet again when he taunted me about being jealous.

I scrubbed a hand down my face, a small groan slipping out as I fought the conflicting emotions rattling through my body.

Gods, I hated feeling.

Landon extended a hand toward Adalina, a silent offer to re-rack her weapon. She handed the hilt of her sword to him with a grateful smile, and Landon started off toward the weapon rack at the edge of the training ring.

"Don't put that away," I commanded, halting my bodyguard in his tracks.

He looked over his shoulder, cocking a curious brow at me.

"Do you have one more match in you?" I arched my brow right back at him, which made my bodyguard flash me one of his most devastating smiles.

"Always for you, my Queen."

The smug grin I cast back at Landon wasn't just for him, since I could feel the god's eyes burning into me from the sidelines.

And because I was feeling extra petty after her ogling my bodyguard, I turned to make eye contact with Adalina. The moment my gaze found hers, she was already staring at me like I anticipated. Although she tried to smile warmly back at me, I saw a crack in her facade. Her smile didn't fully meet her eyes, instead a darkness stirred in the pits of them.

With a small huff of satisfaction, I accepted the sword Landon thrust at me, but I frowned when I saw what weapon he offered up. I leaned forward, dropping my voice to a mere whisper for only him to hear.

"Did you give me a light sword on purpose?" I smiled through gritted teeth, not daring to let my mask of smugness fall before the god who was still watching me like a serpent about to devour a measly rodent.

My bodyguard also leaned in, a mischievous smile fell onto his lips as if he was about to reveal a secret.

"Once I see you can wield a weapon properly *and* win a match against me, then I will consider offering you a heavier sword." He grinned as he turned his back on me, already moving on to ready himself for our match.

I forced out a laugh to cover my anger at Landon's condescending words, but it came out far more high-pitched and awkward than intended.

How the fuck did Adalina make her laugh sound like the birds delicately chirping within the forests when I sounded like a dying animal?

My lips pressed into a tight line as I readied myself into a fighting stance and lifted my sword in front of me. I made sure to keep my back heel slightly propped up, just as Landon advised years ago, so I could move around my opponent swiftly.

"Begin!" My bodyguard shouted, signaling the start of our match.

He didn't wait for me to attack, instead his sword barreled straight for my heart. I quickly stepped to the left, already raising my weapon to deflect his next brutal strike. We continued to dance around the ring as Landon swung his sword against mine with a series of devastating blows. He left me with no chance to go on the offense, and I felt my irritation flare with each of his strikes.

My overthinking was holding me back, and it was making

me appear weak before the prying eyes of a god. The best I could do in this moment was defend against his strong jabs, but I had to do something else, anything to give me the upper hand.

An idea spurred to life in the darkest corners of my mind . . . I had to let Landon cut me, but I had to make it look real. If my bodyguard felt bad for landing a strike and simultaneously slicing me open, my plan could work. No, it *would* work because it had before—when we trained together earlier this week.

I was Landon's weakness, and I was ready to unleash the vicious queen dwelling inside me, who'd been begging for release since stepping into the Emerald Glades.

I was not above using other people's weaknesses against them, even if it was someone close to me.

When my bodyguard struck again, I jumped backward, faking a stumble courtesy of the spongy mat we sparred on. For a split second, my balance faltered and my sword clumsily bobbed in my hand, giving Landon the perfect opening to slash me across the ribs. I had no time to block his strike, and I was certain his sword rang true based on the stinging licking across my ribs.

I gripped my side in faked agony, pulling my falsely shaking hand back and examining the sticky liquid coating my fingertips—blood began to trickle from my gushing wound and onto the golden mat. To drive home my performance, I gasped and let my sword slip from my hand, so I could keel over and clutch my already healing wound.

"Oh, gods. Seera! I didn't mean to—" A pained look passed over my bodyguard's face as he lowered his sword, letting it also drop onto the mat.

He moved toward me, undoubtedly to coddle me like I was an infant.

He was such a fool for falling for this move twice.

I waited until he was a mere step away from me, reading myself to strike like the serpent I was. Then, like a tightly coiled snake finally making its move, I quickly slapped him across his face.

His head whipped to the side, a surprised gasp flying from his lips. I wasted no time curling the same fingers that just slapped him as I tore them back across his face in a raking motion. My sharp nails left bright red marks behind on his otherwise perfect complexion, and a pang of guilt stabbed through my gut.

Landon's face was the one spot where those *fuckers* didn't mar his skin with lash marks.

Now, I was the reason he had angry red lines rising on his light brown skin.

Focus, Seera. Be who you were always meant to be. Be the Serpent Queen.

My hand shot out, wrapping around Landon's throat as I moved to his side and readied myself to do a side kick straight to the back of his knee. Executing the maneuver perfectly, I released his neck as his knees crashed into the mat and dug my stiletto into the soft flesh behind his knee.

My bodyguard's anguished yelp fueled me as I planted my foot, spinning on the ball of it as I landed a sharp crescent kick straight across his face.

Time for the grand finale.

I landed behind Landon, who was still in shock as his head whipped to the side from the force of my kick. I leaned down, wrapping my right arm around his neck, essentially putting him in a chokehold. Bending him backward on my knee so I could see his eyes, I unsheathed the dagger strapped around my left thigh and pressed it against his throat.

"Do you concede?" I glanced down my nose at him.

My bodyguard's gaze flicked to my weapon, then slowly rose to meet my eyes.

I bit back my surprise at the look he cast me, right as a waft of cinnamon tickled my nose.

Landon's anger shone brightly in his eyes, but this was the first time he ever looked at me with such . . . *disdain*.

After what felt like an eternity, he spoke through gritted teeth. "I concede."

I waited another second before releasing my dagger from his throat. I shoved him forward to collapse onto his hands and knees before sheathing it back into the holster around my thigh. A booming clap split through the stifling air, making me whip my head to find the source of such a jarring sound.

The Serpent King stood next to his mother near the edge of the training ring, still loudly bringing his hands together all the while tossing me a conspiring grin. My attention split between the two of them, not missing how Adalina was watching me with an intensity that made the hairs on my neck rise. She dipped her head in acknowledgment of my victory, but I didn't miss the way her jaw ticked.

She was not happy I triumphed in the match.

So, I did what I naturally would do when anyone dared underestimate me. I gave her a grand smile and a petty little wave, my fingers gently fluttering in her direction.

The last thing I saw was her lips tightening so hard they turned white, before the king blocked my line of sight.

He gave me a smile so charming that I had to remind myself I was supposed to hate the man who broke my heart, not feel . . . whatever was stirring within my core at the way his elongated canines flashed a blinding white against the sun.

"I now see why your people view you as such a brutal queen."

A few days ago, I'd marvel at such a glowing compliment;

yet, today, the king's words felt more like an insult—like something I should not be proud of.

How odd.

My brows pinched at the revolting thoughts penetrating my mind, but I couldn't think deeper on it since Landon flanked my right side, bringing with him another waft of cinnamon.

He gained his composure enough to stand tall while glaring daggers at the Serpent King. The king cocked his head at Landon, looking at my bodyguard like was merely a small mouse he was about to enjoy devouring.

"Since you got your ass handed to you by your *queen*," he said the last word tauntingly. "I'm sure you wouldn't mind if I stole her for the rest of the afternoon? Should give you plenty of time to rest up and ice your ego." He slapped a hand against Landon's shoulder, a gesture that friends would do to one another, but this was far too rough to be considered a friendly gesture.

My bodyguard's jaw ticked, his knuckles turning bone white with how tightly he fisted them around the hilt of his sword, which was now sheathed at his hip as usual.

"She is all yours." Landon cast me another look of contempt, but, this time, there was also something else shining in the depths of his blue eyes.

I quickly sniffed the air, and, sure enough, two scents danced around my bodyguard. I easily detected the smell of cinnamon, signifying his anger, but I was surprised to gather a strong whiff of jasmine permeating off him.

Landon's hurt lingered in my lungs as he stormed away.

I've bested him in other matches, so why did this particular fight bother him so much?

I was still gazing after my bodyguard when the king spun

to stand at my side. He followed my gaze, and I could tell he was grinning without even blinking in his direction.

"Trouble in paradise?" he lazily drawled, clearly enjoying annoying me as much as I enjoyed pestering him.

I didn't take his bait, the only indication of my foul mood was my pinched brows and deep frown as I watched Adalina trail beside Landon back into the palace. Right before they passed through the archway, I watched her delicately brush her hand against his cheek—the cheek I cut during our fight.

She was doting on him like one of those desperate prostitutes in the Hook District of my Queendom. Actually, better yet, I bet the prostitutes there acted more discreet than this frivolous god.

"You really need to learn how to manage that temper of yours." The king's deep voice made me flinch, as I nearly forgot he was lingering nearby.

"What?" I turned my attention toward him.

His eyebrows rose as he nodded to my side, and my gaze trailed down to see what he was referring to. My hand was trembling against my side, slapping against my thigh with how furiously it shook. I balled it into a fist, willing the anger storming within me to dissipate with the soft wind that was whipping loose strands of hair around my face.

"Are you going to continue to stand here and give me unsolicited life advice, or are you going to finally train me like you said?" I crossed my arms over my chest, in an attempt to hide my trembling hands from the pest.

"This is actually a great segue into today's lesson. The first step to tapping into your full magical abilities is facing your emotions head on." The king crossed his arms, causing his black short sleeve button-up to tighten around his chest and biceps. I quickly forced my gaze away from his defined muscles, from the way they made me think of earlier when I had my fingers between my thighs.

"Wait, what did you just say?" I glared at him as his words finally sunk in.

Doubt flickered in his eyes, but it quickly shifted back into a wicked glint. "Your emotions control your powers."

I took a menacing step toward him. "Then why the fuck did you take away my emotions during our bargain?"

The king's lips parted, his confident facade slipping once more. "Seera, I can explain."

"I suggest you do so quickly, before I break your nose for a third time." My fist trembled with a flurry of anger as I raised it in front of me.

His eyes shot down to my tightly curled fingers, then rose to meet my eyes. Smoke rolled off the king in such intense waves I nearly fell into another coughing fit, but I swallowed his regret.

He would not fool me with false emotions. He would not weaken me again.

"Seera, I wanted to spare you from certain feelings, from the ones you begged me to rid you of. I had to take them away. You wanted me to do so in exchange for my power, remember?" His eyes were silently pleading for me to understand.

"I remember, yet what I don't recall is you telling me I'd not be able to access the well of power inside me after rendering my emotions to you."

The king winced. "It's complicated. You—you felt *so* much. I thought I was doing you a favor by taking those emotions away, but I did leave you with some feelings so you could access your power."

I was so furious at the Serpent King for keeping this from me, but I had one burning question I constantly wondered about for decades . . .

"Why—" I cleared my throat and the emotions that perpetually loved to knot at the back of my throat. "Why did you leave me with one emotion? Why not take it all away? Why did you leave me so fucking angry, all the damn time?" I hated how my voice shook on my last words.

His eyes dipped to my balled fists, to the way they quaked with fury, and he looked utterly devastated when he glanced back at me.

"Isn't it better to feel anger, than nothing at all?" he whispered, the wind stirring around us swiftly swallowing his words.

I wished it swallowed them before I could hear them, for I didn't like the fact he thought he was doing me a favor by letting me retain the emotion of anger.

"You had no right to make that decision for me. You tricked me!"

My words hit their intended mark as I watched the fight flee from the king's once bright eyes.

"Seera . . ." He said my name like he had a dagger buried in his chest, like it was his last dying plea. "I was trying to save you. You were drowning in your feelings. Please, you have to understand that I only wanted to ease your pain."

I held my hand up, stopping his pitiful advance toward me.

I couldn't stand it. I couldn't *stand* the way he was looking at me.

I swore to never allow him back in, yet here he was confessing his sins to me. He was begging for forgiveness in his own indirect, fucked up way.

I had to rebuild the wall between us, the one we so carefully crafted over the years, before it completely crumbled.

"That's enough. Are you going to hold true to your word of training me, or are all your promises shallow, petty lies?"

He stepped back, his chest rising with each hateful word I

289

shot at him. Slowly, he closed his eyes, taking a steadying breath.

"You aren't going to like this." His eyes opened, immediately locking onto mine.

"Try me." I closed the remaining sliver of space separating us with one stride, making my breasts slightly graze against his chest.

This was familiar, this tension between us safe. As long as we didn't step into uncharted territory of sharing secret truths, we might make it out of this mission unscathed.

Perhaps, I'd survive the Serpent King's charm this go around.

He bit his bottom lip when my body grazed against his, his eyes devouring the sight of my body pressed against his. When he looked at me through heavy lashes, I noticed how dark his eyes were, and they were *not* darkened by desire.

No, this was a darkness unlike anything I'd encountered before.

The king's eyes faded into a shade as dark as the stone mountain he resided in. His pupils flashed from black to gold, stretching from a round shape to thin vertical slits.

"I suggest you start running."

Those were his last words before the ground beneath me quaked and a burst of golden light flashed, temporarily blinding me.

A deep hiss split through the air, giving me all the fuel I needed to spin on my heel and run.

CHAPTER 35
TIDAL WAVE

I f I knew I would be running for my life today, I wouldn't have worn such high heels.

Granted I've fought in higher ones, but I was not a big fan of running in stilettos—especially when there was a wild beast chasing me through the lush green grounds of the Emerald Palace.

The creature was close enough that I could feel its warm breath licking up the back of my neck. I pumped my legs harder, shreds of grass itching my ankles as I sprinted across the lawn and for the safety of the palace. Maybe if I slammed the door on the beast hunting me it would magically disappear. Even though I was a skilled fighter, I'd never taken on a creature that could quite literally make the ground beneath my feet shake.

The emerald archway glimmered from the sunlight streaming through the stained glass windows, giving it an ethereal effect. I sighed in relief, pushing myself closer to safety.

The Serpent Queen would live to see another day, I just needed to make it a few more paces.

Running from your problems won't solve them, Seera.

A deep voice hissed in the corners of my mind, making my steps falter. The words cut deep, because, although I hated to admit it, they were true.

I had a tendency to run away from my problems.

When things got hard, I ran.

I ran away on my twenty-fifth birthday from the tower my mother locked me away in, instead of facing her.

I ran away from my people and my queendom when I felt threatened by the rebels, when I felt my control over my reign slipping between my fingers.

I ran from hearing the Serpent King's true feelings mere moments ago.

Now, I ran from whatever beast was chasing after me, rather than trying to defeat it with my magic, with the depths of my power that have been slumbering all these years, simply waiting for me to unlock it.

I must have stopped running, for, when I forced my gaze to lift from the white and gold tiled floors, I was standing on the threshold of the archway leading into the palace.

The beast should have caught me and been munching on my bones by now, so why was I still standing unhurt?

Slowly, I glanced over my shoulder to finally assess the creature that lurked closely behind.

Not even two feet away stood a serpent as tall as the tower I used to live in. My palms grew slick at the sheer size of the beast, fear trickling down my spine like droplets of water as it threatened to overtake my every instinct.

Instead, I swallowed the emotion and examined the beast, starting with its softly whipping tail. It was adorned with at least fifty rattles, and they made a beautiful sound as they swished, almost like the roar of rain pelting against a window. Next, my gaze roamed over its thick emerald green body, with golden scales interwoven throughout in a cyclone pattern all the way up its back and along the entirety of its neck. They glowed, almost as if they were pulsing with magic.

As my gaze soared high above to take in its face, a gasp tore from my lips.

Piercing green eyes stared down at me, and I immediately recognized the amused gleam shining through them.

"Alaric," I whispered.

The snake blinked slowly, as if that one word triggered a landslide of emotions.

After what felt like an eternity of staring at one another, that captivating voice slithered into my mind once again.

You haven't called me that since our last day together.

A deep sadness laced his words, making me realize my mistake.

I finally called the Serpent King by his given name amidst all my shock.

I opened my mouth to dismiss my slip, to say anything to break the tension brewing between us from one simple word—a word that felt far too intimate for what we were today.

We were not the people we were seventy-five years ago—the ones who stole intimate moments in the darkness of the caves of Morotis, whispering secrets late into the night.

The Serpent King and I were nothing anymore.

"Is this the part of our lesson where you tell me I can transform into a massive snake as well?" I bit my lip, suddenly feeling self-conscious over my poor crack at a joke.

Much to my surprise, a high pitched chuckle rasped through my head, once again sounding nothing like his usually deep bravado.

I liked it so much better, because it felt so much more like
...*him.*

Like the man I used to know and lo—

*I'm afraid you most likely do not have an animal form, but I feel
a well of untapped magic within you, Seera. We just need to find a
way for it to burst wide open.*

"And how do you suggest we do that?" I glared up at the
snake with a raised brow.

*A good place to start would be facing everything you've run
away from.*

His tone carried a startling softness to it, but that didn't
stop me from crossing my arms over my chest to stare the
serpent down and replying with one simple word.

"No."

There were some things I refused to face, especially before
the Serpent King.

Coward.

My low growl vibrated the back of my throat, and I instinc-
tively took a step toward the snake, readying for a fight. My
fingers twitched, itching to snatch the dagger strapped at my
thigh and point it straight at the king's thick throat.

As if he could read my thoughts, the snake lowered its head
to my level, granting me a better angle to sink my dagger into
its scales.

*Did you know you scrunch up your face when you're angry? It's
rather cute.*

The king's chuckle returned to his normal taunting timbre.

This time when I had the urge to reach for my dagger, I
heeded to it and unsheathed the blade with one quick flick of
my wrist.

"I am no coward," I said, pointing my weapon directly at
the serpent.

Its response was to dip its head further, forcing my blade to nick its flesh.

Point as many of your daggers at me as you'd like. I don't scare easily, Serpent Queen, and I'd happily be on the receiving end of your blade any day.

My brows knitted with confusion upon hearing the king's words—why would he say such a thing?

But pointing a dagger at me won't unleash your powers, Seera. You need to feel. You need to stop hiding behind that mask of yours. That beautiful mask of the Serpent Queen.

"You stole my feelings from me, what do you expect me to do?!" I exploded. "I am a shell of who I once was. There is no escaping the darkness that drowns me every single day of my miserable existence. And even if I could feel, I don't *want* to." The raw words flew from my lips before I could get a firm grasp on my loose tongue.

My confession hung in the limited air between us, almost like my own personal noose ready to wrap tight around my neck and finally end it all.

I couldn't handle the sorrow racing through the king's eyes, so I dropped my gaze to my heels.

How did he always find a way to crawl into the rawest crevices of my heart?

The emotions I constantly swallowed threatened to burst from the tightly-sealed well I shoved them into for the past week.

I'd fought rebels, executed countless traitors, broken the Serpent King's nose a couple of times, yet I couldn't face the fact my soul was truly returning to me. I couldn't handle who I was underneath the mask I wore everyday as the Serpent Queen, because I was too afraid to see what was left of the mortal girl from the tower.

I'd utterly and completely lost myself with each soulless passing day, and there was no coming back from the acts I committed over the past seventy-five years.

I accepted there was no salvation for the wicked long ago, so what good would it do now to face my feelings and sinful deeds?

I refused to accept that underneath all the gorgeous dresses, all the blood-red lipstick, and all the cruel smiles, was the girl I used to be.

The girl who prayed for friendship, for a relationship with her mother, for her absent father, for her suffocating feelings to go away . . . the girl who prayed to be *loved*.

No, I wouldn't survive if my soul returned—the weight of my emotions were far too heavy for anyone to withstand.

Perhaps, I was too harsh on the king earlier . . . maybe he was trying to save me from myself.

My vision blurred as I stared at the tiles, my dagger now dangling weakly at my side. Warmth kissed my cheeks, and I sighed as I tried to blink away the tears that slipped free.

For Serpent's Sake, crying in front of the Serpent King was not on my to-do list today.

As I used the back of my hand to swipe away my tears, a soft hissing soothed me. It almost felt like what I imagined it would be like to receive a warm embrace from a loved one.

Ember descended my right arm, her black eyes finding mine. She looked worried about my emotional state.

A rougher hiss joined hers, alerting me to Dante's presence as he wound around my left arm. When Dante nudged his head against my cheek to wipe away my lingering tears, I nearly fell into another fit.

Ember was my snake with the softer side, while Dante prided himself on the title of sassiest snake alive. Thus, the fact he was also concerned about me was too much to take.

Something snapped within me at the meaningful gesture from my snakes, at the fact they didn't leave me to suffer alone during dark times.

As I looked at them and saw adoration shining within their eyes, I completely unravelled.

It was as if a dam burst open, and my emotions flooded straight into the void in my chest.

I could no longer bite back my feelings with my serpents looking at me with a devotion I didn't deserve. An agonizing emotion speared into my heart like an arrow, momentarily stealing my breath away. I doubled over in pain as another wave of the feeling crashed over me.

I was so undeserving of any form of love, especially from the creatures I forced to be monsters alongside me.

Wave after wave, the weight of my past drowned me.

Finally, after nearly eighty years, I felt the emotion of *guilt.*

Guilt over executing thousands of my people, most of them for petty crimes.

Guilt over the fact I reveled in their pain, in their screams, in torturing falsely accused traitors.

At what point did I truly lose myself to the bloodshed, to the torture, to not feeling?

The thought of hurting others for my own sick, twisted pleasure now made me sick to my stomach.

Then, there was the heartbreak I worked so hard to forget.

Although the Serpent King stole my emotions, never allowing me to feel the true excruciating depths of my shattered heart, I was not so lucky today.

In this moment, it was as if someone took an axe and smashed it straight into my heart, cracking it wide open.

I felt *everything.*

The way my heart broke into a million pieces upon hearing Alaric's final parting words on the night of our bargain.

The countless nights I dreamed of him, only to wake up gripping the cold, empty sheets where he should have been.

My knees buckled underneath the weight of my feelings, under the agony of my past.

The weight of my loneliness throughout all these years as queen pressed down on my chest, intermingling with the years I spent locked away in the tower—with no one but the characters in my books to call my friends.

My hands started to quake as panic surged through my veins.

These feelings were the reason I bargained away my soul in the first place.

I couldn't bear this. I wasn't strong enough.

My breaths became shallow as I searched for a way out of these feelings, but there was no one coming to save me from all I've done, from all I've become.

I just wanted it to stop.

I wanted it to end.

Before I could think about how foolish I was acting, my grip strengthened on the hilt of my dagger and I moved with lighting speed.

With a flick of my wrist, I spun the tip of my dagger to press against my own throat.

I wouldn't take another life, nor deal with these feelings.

I'd do what I was best at to end all of this.

I'd run away. One. Last. Time.

I'd take one more life in order to end the nightmare I had wrought upon the world, upon myself.

Hot tears streamed down my face as I forced my hands to stop shaking so I could get a better grip for what I planned to do next, but it was no use. The tremors wracking through my body were past the point of control.

Before I could spill my own blood and end it all, a golden flash blinded me.

Then, *he* was there.

"Put that down." Alaric's tone was threatening, but I caught the concern hidden within it.

My hand quaked, but I kept the blade trained against my skin, hard enough I felt a bead of warm blood trickle down the column of my throat.

"I—I can't do this . . ." My voice broke, the blade bobbing against my throat harder as I swallowed the sobs that were begging to be released.

"You are capable of so much more than you think, Seera." Alaric held his hands up, almost like he was trying to approach a wild animal.

"No, you're mistaken. I can't do this. Don't try to stop me from finally committing a selfless act. It is better for all of the realms if I go through with this. Let me conduct an execution I should have completed long ago."

Anger flashed in his eyes, along with an emotion I couldn't easily detect.

But I didn't care enough to sniff the air; I didn't care to do anything anymore but fade into the darkness that constantly plagued my mind.

"I refuse to live in a world where you don't exist, Seera." Before I could stop him, the king whipped out a dagger from behind his back—one he must keep hidden in his waistband. "If you really want to end your life, then you might as well end mine too." He shoved his dagger at me, his lips pressed into a thin line, almost like he was holding himself back from exploding with rage.

"I won't end your life, Alaric. You have people who care about you. I have nothing but my horrible feelings to go home to if we fail on this mission. I have no one." I felt more blood drip down my throat, surely leaving a crimson streak along my chest as my blade dug deeper into my skin.

"I know you won't believe me, but I won't allow that to happen. If you let me back in, I won't do what I did to you before. I swear it, Seera. I won't let you go through life alone anymore."

Alaric mirrored my position, flipping his blade on himself and pointing the sharp tip against his throat. "Please, Seera, let me help you. Let me be the anchor I should have been for you for the past seventy-five years."

He was saying everything I once wanted to hear, but it was too late. What was even worse was I wanted to believe him, but I couldn't—not after everything he put me through.

"Why do you keep playing games with me?" I croaked around the sobs finally escaping from the depths I buried them in, like a prisoner breaking free after spending decades locked away.

"I'm not playing any games, Seera." His voice held a twinge of sorrow upon uttering his next words. "You aren't the only one who believes they are unworthy of love." His blade pressed deeper into his throat, finally nicking his flawless skin and pulling a beautiful, crimson bead of blood from the Serpent King.

I watched the blood drip down his pale chest, replaying his last words—ones I'd only dared to think. A kernel of curiosity rooted inside me as I watched a variety of emotions gleam in his eyes.

So softly, I found the will to want to sniff the air again, but I was confused when cherries and rose petals tickled the tip of my nose as it wafted into my lungs. Usually, I'd hate such a soft and sweet smell, but I found myself wanting to bask in this emotion.

Warmth flooded the void in my chest, and a sense of belonging raced through me.

I didn't know what Alaric was feeling in this moment as he stared at me, but whatever it was made my grip slacken on my blade.

I wanted to surrender to this feeling—to the warmth now floating through me.

Metal clanking against marble rang through the air the moment I let my dagger slip from my fingers, shortly followed by the sound of Alaric dropping his blade not even a second after I did.

We stared at each other for what felt like an eternity, the weight of all that just transpired hanging heavy between us.

Slowly, I took a hesitant step toward him.

He mirrored my actions once again, taking a small step of his own to close the remaining distance separating us.

We were so close I could smell his scent, and I choked on a sob at the familiarity of the amber notes mixed with a splash of cinnamon and a hint of smoke. *This* was the scent I craved when I went to bed alone every night for nearly eight decades, every night when this man's emerald eyes would haunt my dreams.

As soft as the warm wind floating about, Alaric lifted his hand to my cheek and wiped away a tear that slipped loose. He trailed his fingers up my cheek, delicately tucking a strand of hair behind my ear. He didn't drop his hand like I expected, instead he curled his fingers against my scalp and crushed me against his solid chest.

He was so cold, but I didn't care.

I preferred the cold anyways, so I nuzzled into him, letting his strong arms snake around my waist to hold me as I completely fell apart.

Aftershocks of guilt racked through me for what felt like

hours, but Alaric held me through every sob, every broken wail, every moment I wanted to give up.

As I cried against his chest and tried to break free from my endless guilt, a horrifying thought washed over me as I realized what just occurred.

If I could feel this deeply, then that meant we were almost out of time.

The Ice Goddess was close to breaking the bargain.

PART THREE: OUROBOROS

CHAPTER 36

FORMALITIES

A sharp knock startled me awake.

Blinking slowly, I braced myself for the bothersome harsh sunlight that streamed directly through the emerald glass-paned windows into my rooms, but when my eyes drifted open and I leaned to look out the windows, I was greeted with darkness.

It was nighttime? How did I get back to my rooms?

The last thing I remembered was . . .

Alaric.

I tugged the silk sheets up to my face while memories of being wrapped in strong arms floated back to me. But then, I groaned when I remembered my complete and utter breakdown before the Serpent King. Flopping back onto the fluffy pillows, I covered my hands with my face, as if that could shield me from the reality of what transpired with the man who broke my heart all those years ago.

Stupid girl.

"Your Majesty?" Reena's muffled voice sounded from the other side of the door.

"Enter," I moaned beneath my hands.

Perhaps if I hid in my room all night, Alaric would forget all I confessed.

For one last time, I could run from my problems.

A sharp inhale had me peep through my fingers, only to find Reena's wide eyes roaming over my sprawling figure.

"You've looked better." She pressed her lips tightly together, doing her best to stifle a laugh.

"Thanks for that," I groaned, my head pounding from all the tears I shed earlier.

I rolled onto my stomach, throwing one of the golden silk pillows over my head. Not even a moment later, my lady-in-waiting wrenched the pillow from my grasp.

She tugged on my arm. "I'm afraid you must get in the bath right away, my Queen, or you will be very late for tonight's festivities."

After a few more futile pulls, I relented and turned to face her.

"What festivities?" A twinge of curiosity crept into my voice.

"First get in the bath, then I will tell you." She smiled sweetly at me, which earned her a glare as I rolled out of bed and into my plush slippers.

Reena hummed with satisfaction as she buzzed into the bathing chambers and I followed her, stopping and gasping when I caught sight of my reflection in the floor-length mirror.

Holy gods, I looked like shit.

Black kohl was smudged underneath my eyes, and my skin appeared unusually puffy. Another reason I hated crying was what it did to my face—I looked years older with these bags under my eyes. I dragged a hand down my cheek as I continued to examine the bloodshot tint to them.

Seeing myself like this was revolting. Not once in all my

years ruling as the Serpent Queen had I ever looked so dejected, so miserable.

The feelings I tried to shove deep down had finally reared their ugly head, and it made me want to work that much harder to defeat the Ice Goddess.

My emotions were like an invisible disease, and I desperately wanted to find the end-all cure.

With a heavy sigh, I padded into the bathing chambers and watched the tendrils of steam rise from the bath. Lavender salts splashed into the water as Reena threw a handful into the gold tub, making the water swirl with a light purple hue.

Even though a moment of absolute solitude sounded amazing, I couldn't stand the thought of an ice bath. On top of that, a pang of sadness pinched my chest realizing I ever took such horrid baths to escape my snakes' presence.

They were the closest thing to family I've ever had.

"Your Majesty, are you quite alright?" Reena stepped toward me, lifting her hand, almost like she was about to rest it atop my shoulder to comfort me.

Instead, she thought better of it, stopping short and quickly moving on to wringing her hands within the folds of her gown. Her question was long forgotten the moment my gaze roamed over the complexity of her deep green dress.

"Is this new?" I reached for the fabric, crumpling the luxurious velvet between the pads of my fingertips.

"Uh—yes, Your Majesty. It was a gift." Reena's fingers fidgeted, giving away her nerves.

Slowly, I lifted my gaze to hers as my fingers stayed latched onto her dress.

"A gift?" The words rolled off my tongue, leaving a bad taste in their wake.

"Yes, from Adalina." Her throat bobbed.

She was deliberately avoiding making eye contact with me.

I hummed, letting my lady-in-waiting squirm for another moment before releasing her gown.

"It seems you two have gotten rather close." My words came out far more bitter than I'd intended.

Reena gaped. "She's been teaching me how to cook!" The pathetic excuse flew out of her mouth in a rush.

That was the best she could come up with for lacking in her duties? It was precisely her job to be at my side at all times, yet she'd practically abandoned me since we set foot in this new realm. And to make matters worse, she left me for a *god* we barely know.

"Since when do you like to cook?" I challenged, shoving my hurt down into the ever-growing well of emotions I've spent my life running from.

"Well, since . . ." A distant look passed through her eyes, her brow furrowing with confusion. "I suppose I don't."

My brows rose toward the golden chrome ceiling. "Are *you* quite alright, Reena?"

She shook her head, clearing the glassy look from her eyes.

"Yes, thank you. I'm simply enjoying my time in the Emerald Glades. There are so many different things to see and learn, and I do enjoy all the colors here." She nervously glanced at me before skittering over to the tub. Then, she gestured to the water. "Come, now. I'd hate for your bath to run cold before you even got in."

As I shrugged out of my nightgown and let the golden silk pool around my feet, I decided to let this conversation die out . . . for now. But this was far from over. Over my dead body would Adalina undermine my trust in the two people I brought with me on this journey.

Considering the gods abandoned the mortals, this was

undoubtedly another part of their schemes. Adalina wanted to create a divide between me and the only two individuals who were unwaveringly loyal to me.

Carefully, I stepped into the tub and sank beneath the scalding water. A small hiss slipped from my lips, but the scorching temperature felt great on my muscles after an afternoon of training and running. My head lolled back to rest against the cool metal rim of the basin, pulling a sigh out of me as I closed my eyes and relaxed for what felt like the first time in—well, in forever.

A splash sounded, breaking my short-lived moment of peace. I cracked an eye open to see Reena towering above me, a washcloth now floating in the water.

"Apologies, but we must move swiftly. You need to be ready in thirty minutes."

"Thirty minutes?!" I squeaked in disbelief.

Reena winced. "Adalina has invited us out tonight to experience all the Emerald Glades has to offer. She said it was to act as a proper send off before continuing on to the Ice Goddess's realm."

I scoffed. "Did she now?"

Reena gave me a nervous look, then dashed to the gold and white marble countertops and began to polish a small spot.

"And who is included in this *us*?" I pondered as I quickly worked the washcloth against my skin, scrubbing it hard enough to turn my complexion a furious shade of red.

"Just the Serpent King and you, of course," she said quietly as she cleaned the sink, but her next words were muffled to where even I couldn't hear them.

"Speak up, Reena," I commanded.

"I—apologies. I will be accompanying you . . . and Landon will be joining us as well."

"Why in all the lands was that so hard for you to spit out?" I laughed softly at Reena's odd behavior.

Of course my lady-in-waiting and bodyguard would accompany me to tonight's festivities. We were in a foreign realm full of potential enemies, after all.

So why was Reena acting like she wanted to be anywhere but here?

She scrubbed the sink with frenzied strokes, doing her best to keep her face turned away from me, but I could see her reflection in the mirror.

"The thing is, Your Majesty, Landon is essentially going tonight as Adalina's, uh," Reena's breaths were short, her chest rising and falling rapidly as she stumbled over her words.

"Reena, what is it?" I barked, doing my best to control my breathing as well.

"Adalina asked Landon to formally accompany her to tonight's activities." Reena's eyes pinched closed, and she looked a mere moment away from puking in the sink she just scrubbed to sparkling perfection.

I schooled my face into the mask of cool indifference I wore everyday as the Serpent Queen, not letting a crack of fury slip free.

"Ah, I see." I gave her my signature smile, the one I wore every day to indicate I was in charge—to show that everything was fine. "Reena, I can finish my bath on my own. Wait for me in my rooms. I'll be out momentarily."

She turned toward me like she was about to protest, but thought better of it and dipped her head, offering me a small, timid curtsy.

My lips turned down at the gesture, my eyes trailing after her as she scurried from the bathing chamber, so quickly you'd think her feet caught on fire.

Did she just fucking curtsy to me?

What in all the realms was going on today?

First, my lady-in-waiting was acting completely out of sorts and now Landon—*my* Landon—was going to be a god's date tonight and not accompany me as my bodyguard . . .

I sank below the cooling water, opened my mouth, and screamed.

CHAPTER 37
A PEACE OFFERING

The sconces lining the walls cast a warm glow over the golden silk evening gown clinging to my body. I stood before the floor length mirror in the corner of my rooms, admiring the way the thick silk material was spun with flecks of gold, making the dress sparkle with every swish of my voluptuous hips.

Golden fabric bunched in a swirling pattern at my waist, creating a beautiful waterfall effect down the length of the rest of the garment. The gown had only one strap, leaving my left shoulder completely bare, besides the thin gold chain that Reena slipped up my left arm to wrap around my bicep. A few diamonds hung from the golden band, clinking against each other as I spun side to side while admiring my reflection.

My ensemble was enchanting, magnetic—absolutely breathtaking.

I never thought I'd feel so beautiful in a dress that wasn't a shade of red or black.

But here I was, feeling like the most stunning woman in all the realms.

My lady-in-waiting styled my hair differently, which involved a magical heating tool called a 'curling wand' in these lands. Soft black waves cascaded all the way down past my waist, yet most of my hair was swept to the side, leaving my bare shoulder on full display. A generous slit ran up my left leg, stopping scandalously high on my upper thigh. Golden diamonds dripped down my neck—a gift left in my room from Adalina. I considered chucking the god's present out the vast window, but the necklace was simply too stunning for me to do so.

My lips were not painted my usual blood-red shade, for I felt it clashed too much with my dazzling golden look. So, I begrudgingly opted for the champagne colored lipstick the Serpent King offered me the other day. As much as I hated to admit it, it wasn't a *totally* terrible color. I actually liked the neutrality of it and the way the small flakes of glitter appeared to be dancing across my lips every time I smiled.

A glimmer of red caught my eye in the mirror, dropping my gaze to my hand.

When Reena presented me with the jewelry she brought from my kingdom, I was stunned that she included the ring Alaric presented to me seventy-five years ago.

As I placed it on my fourth finger, I tried to convince myself I wore it solely to have a splash of crimson adorning my otherwise golden attire.

My look was nearly perfect, but it felt like I was still missing that extra *something*. Letting my gaze drift over my reflection, my attention snagged on my hair.

A thump sounded at my door, and not even a second later, the Serpent King poked his head into my chambers.

"Are you decent?" He covered his eyes with his hand, pretending to give me a sense of privacy.

A half-scoff, half-laugh tumbled out of me. "Considering

you already opened the door, what does it matter now? Please, do come in."

He stepped inside, dropping his hand from his face. The moment his magnetic eyes landed on me, they widened as he sucked in a sharp breath. He braced a hand on the door handle, pressing his back against the white wooden door as he continued to drink in the sight of me in my evening gown.

"You . . . you shine brighter than the stars, Seera." His piercing gaze dragged up my body, all the way to my eyes.

There was awe sparkling in his magnetic gaze, which suddenly made a foreign emotion race through my chest.

Alaric made me feel *shy*.

The startling feeling had me averting my attention at the same moment I felt my cheeks warm. I didn't want him to see the way his words affected me, even after all these years separated from one another.

I turned back to the mirror, brushing my hands over my dress to avoid his scorching gaze. Yet, of course, Alaric crept closer, stopping near enough I could smell his intoxicating cologne and feel his warm breath caress my ear.

"As stunning as you look, your ensemble is missing one important detail."

Before I could inquire what, he reached behind his back and presented a sparkling golden crown, lifting it above my head.

"Another gift from Adalina?" My brows shot up at how exquisite the headdress was.

His smile was devoid of its usual wickedness, instead it felt rather bashful. "No, this one is from me. Consider it a peace offering."

I watched in the mirror's reflection as he situated it atop my head, securing the crown with a startling gentleness around my ears.

It was exquisite and thankfully not too heavy, the ends securing perfectly around the curve of my ears. It was almost like a tiara with the way it rested atop my head, but with all the grandness of a crown fit for a queen. No sharp metal dug into my scalp, and I wondered what magical material made the accessory so pleasant to wear.

All thoughts of comfort flew from my head as my attention latched onto all the diamonds glittering within the gold metal frame. A large emerald stone laid at the center of the crown, with a row of crystal clear diamonds fanning out on either side of the viridian stone. My eyebrows shot toward the golden ceiling as the diamonds reflected the light into a spectrum of colors. The left row suddenly became a beautiful blood-red, while the right row of gems looked like black opals. It was stunning—and absolutely magical.

"They change colors?" I asked in awe, still swiveling my head back and forth to watch the jewels dance with the flickers of light.

Alaric smiled at me, his hand dropping from the crown and onto my bare shoulder. Although he was naturally cold in temperature, it wasn't that fact that made a small shiver run down my spine. He glanced at my shoulder, noticing how my body reacted to his touch.

Yesterday, I wanted to break his nose if he so much as touched me against my will, yet today—today I felt entirely different.

With him behind me, thoughts of when I was in nothing but my heels before this mirror penetrated my mind . . .

Ever so gently, he gripped my shoulders to turn me to face him. Slowly, I glanced up and into his enchanting green eyes, only to find them already locked onto mine.

"I was wrong the other day when I tried to change you, Seera. If you like to wear red lipstick or black gowns, who am I to try to alter such essential parts of yourself? For that, I am sorry."

My brows were about to hit him square in his chiseled jaw with how far they rose at the fact the Serpent King was uttering an apology to *me*, of all people.

"Since when do you apologize?" A smug smile tugged at the corners of my lips.

He shook his head, making his hair dance between black and dark green—I always loved when it did that.

"Since an infuriating queen walked back into my life and flipped my world upside down." He brushed away a stray piece of hair that fell into my face, his hand lingering on my bare shoulder once more.

Then, his fingers dipped, faintly tracing along the diamond necklace dripping between my breasts. I sucked in a sharp breath when his finger tenderly dragged down the longest diamond, the one that ran along my serpent tattoo only to disappear within my cleavage. He stopped his slow descent, right at the peak of where my breasts pressed snuggly together.

When his eyes lifted to mine, they were no longer shining bright. Now, his pupils were stretched into slits, and it looked like he was holding himself back from letting the darkness completely devour the green in his eyes. His elongated canines gleamed as he bit down on his bottom lip and closed his eyes, his finger starting to quiver against my chest.

"Alaric," I breathed, softly grabbing ahold of his shaking finger.

His eyes shot open, revealing his pupils were no longer in the form of slits. Once again, they took on a clear emerald appearance.

"I never thought you'd say my name again after . . ." A pained look flashed across his face.

His throat bobbed, like emotion also had a tendency to gather at the back of his throat, but he swallowed it and pushed on. "After my parting words to you the night of our bargain."

The words I tried, yet failed, to forget, flashed into my head . . .

Our time together meant nothing to me, just a bit of fun in the span of my endless, immortal life. Since our bargain is complete and I got what I wanted from you, you can see yourself out of my realm.

A small whimper escaped from my lips, and I was horrified that his words still bothered me to this day. Alaric's eyes crinkled with despair upon hearing my whine, and I bit my lip to hold myself back from making any further incriminating noises.

His gaze shot to my lips, and then his thumb was pressing against my lip, prompting me to stop gnawing on it. I relented and released my lip from my teeth's sharp grip, yet Alaric's hand remained atop my flesh. His fingers moved from my lips to wrap around my neck, forcing me to look up at him.

"You have no idea how much I've hated myself everyday for saying such horrendous things to you, Seera. I will never forgive myself for the way I treated you after our bargain, but I was—" His lips pinched together, almost like he was trying to swallow his next words, but they bubbled out of him in a rush anyway. "It fucking terrified me what occured when we sealed our bargain. That kiss . . ." He blew out a breath, running his free hand through his black locks, messing up the gel that slicked them back in the first place. "That kiss didn't only shake the ground beneath us, it shook *me*."

I balked at the sheer honesty pouring out of the Serpent King, as I bit my tongue out of fear he would fall back into his awful habit of shutting me out. So, I simply looked at him, shock plastered clearly upon my face. There was no point in hiding my emotions from him anymore, for I was certain he could smell the zesty scent of lemons permeating off me.

He tugged on my neck, bringing me within an inch of his stunning face. Tenderly, he reached for one of my hands and I allowed him to hold it as he pressed our clasped hands against his chest.

"I should have come to see you sooner, but I—when I met you it had only been a few years since I lost . . ." It looked like someone slashed a dagger across his face, for so much pain stretched across his features. "Isa."

Why was I suddenly so nervous to ask the question burning inside me?

I forced myself to find a scrap of courage, even though I could barely think with Alaric this near to me. "Is that who you loved? The woman you mentioned in the library?"

His head dipped, bringing our lips that much closer. "So maybe you can understand why I was such a fucking menace when we met."

My laughter wrapped around us as he called himself the nickname I constantly cursed him as in my mind. Alaric gaped at me, the unfamiliar sound tumbling out of my lips surprising us both.

Yet, he gathered himself quickly, pressing on. "I felt undeserving of the way you looked at me when you lived in Morotis —you looked at me like I was worthy of someone as *pure* as you. Like I was deserving of . . . of being loved again."

Was I fucking dreaming?

All I could do was blink while I stared at Alaric gently stroking my hand with his thumb, the one still cradled against his chest.

"Seera." The way he said my name had my eyes rising to meet his.

He spoke my name like he was praying to the gods for forgiveness, but I was the only god who could offer him such salvation.

"I'm sorry for being such a bastard to you all those years ago. I don't deserve your forgiveness, but I need you to know what I said was never true. Our time together meant so much more to me than you'll ever know. Words cannot describe the way you made me feel when I was so broken, so consumed by darkness, prior to you walking into my life."

My lips parted as I was readying myself to say something, but words were utterly failing me.

"You don't have to say anything right now, if not ever, but I —I couldn't live with myself any longer pretending you meant nothing to me. And after what happened this afternoon when we were training . . ."

I dropped my gaze to the floor at the reminder of my breakdown, a bothersome feeling of embarrassment washing over me.

As gentle as a summer breeze, Alaric hooked a finger underneath my chin and lifted my gaze back to his. "I understand what it feels like when the weight of all your decisions come crashing down on you—how it feels too unthinkable to withstand. I get it more than you think, Seera, and it is nothing to be ashamed of. I recognize the darkness looming within you, because its claws are sunk into every fiber of my being as well. So please, know that you are not alone in this. For I am standing here before you in this moment, letting you know *I* am here. I will sit with you when the darkness wants to consume you, if you'd honor me with such a privilege."

I was *definitely* dreaming.

Discreetly, I pinched my thigh with my free hand, desperately trying to tear me out of this dream. It was too painful to hear everything I ever wished for. I needed to wake up, to rid myself of such false promises.

After pinching myself so hard I was sure to have broken skin, Alaric still remained before me, offering a sad smile. We stared at each other as I felt the walls we built so high between us over the course of nearly eight decades, topple over, lying completely ruined at our feet.

"So, my Serpent Queen, what do you say? Can we start over?" He took a small step back, releasing my hand.

Suddenly, I missed his touch, but he quickly offered his hand to me once more.

"Allow me to reintroduce myself. I go by the Serpent King, but people I'm close to call me Alaric. I have a bad tendency of forcing good manners on others, and I love to get underneath the skin of the most beautiful queen in all the realms." He flashed a dazzling smile at me, putting his elongated canines on full display and making something flutter in my belly as they gleamed.

The memory of those sharp teeth sinking into my flesh to seal our bargain flashed through my head—right after our world-shattering kiss.

I stood there dumbfounded, staring at his maddeningly, gorgeous face. His eyebrows tugged together with worry, and I realized his hand was still dangling between us, waiting to see if I'd accept his offer to start over.

I had two options: I could refuse him after he poured his heart out to me, leaving him feeling dumb and heartbroken like he did to me once upon a time . . . or, I could give a second chance to the man that made me feel things I thought shriveled up and died inside me long ago.

If we were going to enter a mysterious realm together to try to kill a god, it would be beneficial to have a real ally. Perhaps, a

TIFFANY ROSEWOOD

clean slate was exactly what I needed after spending years shrouded in a perpetual cloud of darkness.

Thus, I extended my arm to the Serpent King and grasped his waiting hand. The moment we touched, a volt of electricity tingled up my arm, almost like a spark of magic passed between our embrace.

Alaric looked at our hands, almost like he felt the strange current as well. In fact, it looked like he stopped breathing as he stared at our joined hands.

"You still have it." A mixture of awe and shock graced his sharp features.

I followed his gaze, all the way to the ruby jewel sparkling atop my finger.

"I—I wanted to wear something red."

Oh, for Serpent's Sake. That's the best I could come up with?

Internally groaning, I glanced back at Alaric, only to find him watching me, agonized.

We stared at each other, all the while softly shaking the other's hand.

"One last thing," he drawled, a newfound spark of mirth crinkling the corners of his eyes.

"What more could you possibly have to say?" I tried to sound nonchalant, yet a nervous laugh escaped me.

He offered me a sincere smile, a hint of red staining his pale cheeks.

"Will you do me the honor of accompanying me this evening?"

I hummed as I took my time, glancing at the ceiling while I contemplated how long I wanted to torture the king for.

His foot tapped with anticipation, making a smug smile slip onto my face.

Instead of answering him with words, I strengthened my grip on his hand and tugged him to my side. Moving my hand up and into the crook of his arm, I glanced sideways at him. Alaric wore a baffled expression, his eyebrows raised as he looked down at me.

The scent that permeated off him during my breakdown wrapped around us. I inhaled the sweet notes of cherries and roses, letting whatever heightened emotion Alaric was feeling to intoxicate my lungs.

"Is that a yes?" There was a hint of uncertainty lacing his words, so I decided to finally put the Serpent King out of his misery by granting him a solid answer.

"Yes, Alaric, I will be your date for the night. Now, if you are done pouring your heart out to me," I teased, smiling at him mischievously. "Lead the way and show me all the Emerald Glades has to offer."

CHAPTER 38
A NIGHT ON THE TOWN

I was thankful I opted for a golden pair of closed toe heels for tonight's festivities, since the pathway Alaric and I currently strolled along consisted of soft soil and loose twigs.

"You didn't tell me there'd be dirt pathways." I glanced at him, watching a playful smile spread across his lips.

"The Emerald Glades prides itself on staying close to its roots. The jungle is the heart of these lands, so we do our best to leave it undisturbed. So, yes, you will be trudging along dirt pathways for the remainder of the night. Unless . . . you'd like me to carry you the rest of the way, my Queen?" He flashed a winning smile, and the warm glow from the orbs floating around us revealed a hint of mischief glinting in his eyes.

"That won't be necessary." My eyes drifted up to the towering, lush green trees surrounding us.

Surprise sparked through my chest at the fact I didn't mind being engulfed in nature. I loved the structured, stone walls of my palace, but there was something so *freeing* about having no walls confining me anymore—just the jungle for me to get lost in.

Although it was nighttime, birds chirped high above, creating a tranquil melody as we continued to stroll arm-in-arm down the path.

"Fuck, sorry," Alaric muttered underneath his breath, dragging my attention back to him.

"What's wrong?"

He rubbed the back of his neck with his free hand, worry etched between his tightly knitted brows.

"It's just—I know how much you despise me calling you *my* Queen. I won't do it again—"

I placed my hand against his chest, cutting him off. He stopped walking, his eyes widening as he took in the way I softly pressed my hand against him.

"Alaric, it's fine. It doesn't bother me as much as it used to." Heat flooded my cheeks when his gaze found mine, his eyes sparkling with wonder.

"You truly mean that?" He looked like he was holding his breath while awaiting my answer.

"It's fine, really. I kind of—" I chewed on my lip, stopping myself from making a confession I wasn't sure I was ready to admit.

But of course, Alaric didn't let it go.

"You kind of what?" he drawled, a lazy smile tugging at the corners of his lips. A loose strand of hair fell into his eyes as he lowered his face closer to mine.

"Oh, *For Serpent's Sake*," I muttered. "I kind of don't hate it." I huffed, not liking how vulnerable I felt after my weak admission.

I tried to turn away from the king, but he snatched my hand that was pressing against his chest before I could. His touch anchored me in place, and my eyes roamed up to find his.

"Just so you know, *I* don't hate it one bit. I like calling you *my* Queen—I always have." He stared at me with such a nerve-wracking intensity, I had to press my lips together in hopes it would hide my rapid breathing.

Alaric spared me from having to answer him by patting my hand, allowing it to fall to my side as he latched onto my other hand wrapped around his arm. We walked for a few moments in content silence, only the sounds of the animals stirring through the jungle filling the warm night air.

Jovial music sounded as we neared a bend in the pathway, and the dark forest started to lighten around the curve ahead. As we rounded it, a small gasp escaped me.

Alaric leaned closer, his breath caressing my ear as he whispered, "Ready to experience all the Emerald Glades has to offer, my Queen?" He waved his hand grandly to the spectacle playing before us.

Hundreds of glowing orbs floated in the open space, in varying hues, creating almost an iridescent fairy-like feel to the forest.

Wait, those aren't orbs.

"Are those . . ." I searched my brain for the right term as I watched the colorful insects fly in the sky.

"Fireflies." Alaric finished my thought, and I offered him a small smile in thanks.

His grin widened when I smiled at him, making my cheeks heat. Swiftly, I glanced back at the insects. Flashes of soft greens, pinks, golds, and blues made it feel like we were at a party, and the cheery music was unlike any tune I'd ever heard. Typically, the music in my kingdom was somber, even eerie.

Alaric led me further into the town, which consisted mainly of a variety of wooden carts hosting different novelties for revelers to purchase or engage in. One wagon in particular was selling something that smelt so delectable it made my stomach rumble like a ferocious beast dwelled in its depths.

Alaric halted, glancing sideways at me with an arched brow. "Hungry, are we?" He bit his lip, looking like he was seconds away from chuckling.

"Considering I slept through most of the day, I haven't eaten since this morning. So, what do you think?" I shot him one of my best glares.

He was unable to contain his laughter after my traitorous belly grumbled again, tipping his head back and letting out a sound that took me right back to the moment I started to fall for this menace seventy-five years ago—the same night I puked all over his shoes.

His laugh was devoid of the normal deep timbre it usually carried. Instead, it was light and airy, and there was a slight wheezy hiss that escaped him between spurts of laughter. In this moment, Alaric looked like a normal man enjoying himself on a night out, nothing like the cold Serpent King he made himself out to be.

His jovial mood died out, his expression quickly turning serious. "What's wrong?"

"Hm?"

"You were looking at me like, like you—"

Oh gods, he caught me ogling him again.

I yanked on his arm, tugging him toward the delicious smelling cart to distract him from finishing his thought.

Dozens of fluffy, buttery pastries filled the display case atop the cart, and my eyes grew wide as I scanned every possible option to feast on.

"You're drooling," Alaric teased, reaching for the corner of my lip to swipe away said imaginary drool.

I swatted at him, yet my eyes never left the delightful sight of the croissants. Some were filled with cream, others with berries and chocolate, and my heart warmed at how all the pastries were in different serpent-shaped designs.

"Leandro, we will take one of everything." Alaric passed something over to the vendor, a currency of sorts that looked different from any I'd seen, but I was too filled with shock over his request to examine it closer.

"One of everything?!" I questioned, stunned, right as my stomach rumbled with an intensity strong enough to quake the ground beneath us.

He scoffed as he glanced at my belly, swiftly returning his attention back to the short gentleman.

The vendor looked kind, sporting a cap and smiling from ear to ear as he prepared multiple bags of fresh baked goods.

"Here you are, Alaric." The man surprised me when he addressed the king by his given name.

Leandro thrust some change back at Alaric, but he simply waved him off as he accepted the armful of bags.

"Keep the change and buy your girls those crossbows they've been begging for." He winked at the vendor before turning back toward me, yet his smile faltered when he caught my befuddled expression. "What?"

"You—you addressed each other so informally."

Alaric's lips tugged into a half smile as he nodded for us to continue onward through the market.

"As you may have caught on from my mother, we forgo our formal titles for the most part. The people of the Emerald Glades address us as they would their neighbors, family, or friends." He shrugged, like he wasn't saying the most absurd thing ever.

"Why?"

He shot me a sideways glance. "Why do we let them call us by our given names?"

I bit my lip, suddenly feeling unsure of myself.

"Seera, let me put it this way. Being in a position of power is a privilege and an honor not many people ever get to experience. It does me no good to act above the very residents who support my family every day. It is far better to have our people on our side rather than against us."

Shame raked through me at the Serpent King's profound words.

The moment I received an ounce of power, I used it for my own personal gain. But who could blame me? I was tired of being sheltered, hidden away, and isolated from the world.

I wanted to leave a name for myself when my body perished, a legacy of sorts. But now, I was questioning if it was all worth it, if all my brutal decisions that led me to being the Serpent Queen mattered in the end.

Was this truly the legacy I wanted to leave behind when my soul was fully claimed by the Land of the Wicked? To be remembered as the queen who didn't value her people? Who killed them for simply not worshiping at her feet? Who made public shows out of their executions?

Guilt roiled through my stomach, curbing any hunger I felt mere moments ago.

"Seera?" Alaric's voice drifted to me from far away, making me realize I stopped walking.

I was standing about ten paces back from him, in the middle of the market, lost in my self-loathing thoughts.

He walked back to me the moment he realized I wasn't beside him, his hands still full with bags of pastries.

"What just happened?" His brows were pinched as he moved closer.

Notes of his cologne filled the space between us and I breathed deeply, letting the hints of amber and smoke ground me.

"I'm a terrible queen." I whispered the words I ran away from decade after decade. "You probably think the worst things about me after what you just said. I'm nothing like that. I'm everything wrong with the people who hold power." My gaze dropped to the ground, kicking a small pebble as I avoided the disappointment I was sure I'd see in Alaric's eyes.

A crinkling noise sounded right before I saw all the paper bags topple onto the ground before me. I was so stunned that I forgot I was avoiding making eye contact with Alaric and glanced up at him.

"The pastries!" I gasped.

"Fuck the pastries, Seera." He stepped over the bags, closing the sliver of space remaining between us.

"Are you insane?!" I screeched, my eyes still locked on the brown bags holding my delicious smelling desserts.

Alaric braced both of his hands against my cheeks, pulling my attention back to him.

"I want you to listen to me very carefully. Can you listen for once in your life?" he challenged, arching a brow at me.

I pouted at him. "Since you bought me pastries, I suppose."

He rolled his eyes but gave me a soft smile. "You are the strongest woman I know, but I am not going to sugar coat the truth to you, Seera. You *have* made terrible decisions as the Serpent Queen, but every person in power has at one point or another."

"Have you?" I challenged.

He scoffed, shaking his head at me. "Remember when I told you I lost Isa before meeting you?"

A twinge of something stirred in my gut at the reminder of the girl Alaric loved—

No. It couldn't be.

I most definitely was not feeling *jealousy* right now.

I nodded, not trusting myself to say something incriminating, demonstrating exactly how jealous I really was in this moment. Alaric took a moment before sharing whatever was at the tip of his tongue, his hands dropping from my cheeks to drag down the length of my arms until they softly latched onto my hands.

"When Isa died, I became a king people feared. I hunted down every single person that was at the battle on the night that claimed her life, even if they never touched a hair on her head. I told myself I was searching for answers about what truly happened to her that night, but really, I wanted to destroy all the realms for taking the one person from me that made me feel *something*. The one person that was an example of everything that was right in the realms. It made no sense *she* was the one cruelly ripped from this existence."

His fingers started to tremble in mine, so I gave them a reassuring squeeze. The gesture must have grounded him, for he stopped shaking and pressed on.

"I tortured countless people in the depths of my caves, wishing with each slice of their skin that it would bring her back to me. That it would make me feel something, *anything*, besides the roiling despair I lived in every day since she was killed."

His chest was heaving by the time he was done recounting his dark past, and I wasn't sure if I was even breathing after hearing this part of the Serpent King's story for the first time.

"Alaric, I—I had no idea. I'm so sorry." The words felt pathetic, like they were not enough after all he shared, but they held a lot more meaning than he knew.

Before last week, I'd never once said sorry during my time as the Serpent Queen.

He raised our clasped hands to rest against his chest, dipping his head to bring our gazes leveled.

"You have nothing to apologize for. I'm sharing this part

of my life to help you see that you are not the only one who has made decisions they deeply regret. When I finally sliced open the throat of the last person alive from the night of that battle, I was left with nothing but my guilt and despair to wrestle with for decades. All of the bloodshed . . . it didn't bring her back." His voice broke, and he squeezed his eyes shut.

I allowed him as much time as he needed to process the horrors of his past.

After a few moments, his eyes fluttered open. "Your reign does not have to be one of terror, and your past does not define you, Seera. What matters in the end is how you right your wrongs, and the fact you care to consider doing so says a great deal about you." He squeezed my hands. "It is not your fault you revel in torture, in the pain of it all. If you want someone to blame, then blame me."

I was so lost in his words that I was only now realizing the noises from the night market had faded, sounding muffled as if I was underwater. All I could hear was Alaric's pleading.

"Blame me, Seera, for I am the one who demanded your soul. I know damn well you wouldn't have done half of the things you've done as the Serpent Queen if you had your soul. So, condemn me. Let me shoulder the burdens I've placed upon you," he begged, something peculiar stirring in his eyes.

I sniffed the air, nearly choking when a plume of smoke raced down my throat and into my lungs.

"You regret taking my soul?"

His eyes turned as sharp as a steel blade. "Every. Single. Day. Without a break in my miserable existence."

I had no idea Alaric felt this way, because he seemed delighted the night of our bargain as he claimed my soul, like it would be his most treasured possession.

Rendered utterly speechless, all I could do was break free of his crushing grip and dip behind him to snatch one of the pastry bags.

I plunged my hand into the sack, grabbing a chocolate chip croissant to offer to the male staring at me quizzically. His eyes dropped to the pastry, hesitantly grabbing it as he glanced back at me.

"A peace offering," I said, a gentle smile gracing my lips.

He laughed, his soft wheezy hiss wrapping around us like the delicate whip of the wind.

"A peace offering I paid for." He snatched the croissant, nonetheless.

"Semantics." I shrugged, latching his arm back in mine as I dipped to grab more of the bags.

We continued on through the market, and, much to my surprise, no one was looking at us—even after our intimate discussion.

"I enveloped us in my magic," he said, doing that peculiar thing again where it felt as if he was reading my thoughts.

"So they didn't hear a word of our conversation?"

"Nope." He ripped the flaky pastry between his teeth, taking a rather large bite. "Nor did they see us," he said with his mouth full.

I gasped. "My, oh my, Serpent King—where are your manners?"

He finished off the rest of the dessert, sucking his fingers to catch any remaining crumbs lingering on the tips. I tracked the way his tongue swirled across the pads of his slender fingers, each flick stirring a kindling of heat low in my belly.

"Tonight, fuck having manners. It's fun being bad, wouldn't you agree, my Queen?" he said, right before sucking his thumb clean all the while looking at me through lowered lashes.

Damn the gods.

I was in trouble.

CHAPTER 39
THE FIRST DANCE

"Seera!" a cheery feminine voice shouted through the chattering market, pulling my attention from the king who was still wickedly smiling at me after licking his fingers clean. I turned, hoping he didn't see the flush of pink staining my cheeks.

My lady-in-waiting was weaving through the thick crowd, all while waving her hands frantically in the air.

"There you are! Come along, you must see this." She tugged on my hands, leading me haphazardly through the crowd.

However, not one person bumped into us—instead, it felt like the crowd parted around us. Pride swelled through my chest, making me lift my chin. These people recognized a queen when one graced them with her presence.

As I continued to examine the faces flashing past, I noticed they weren't looking at me like I originally thought. Their eyes were trailing to something behind me, their heads slowly dipping. As Reena pulled me onward, I glanced over my shoulder to see what commanded the crowd's attention.

The Serpent King trailed behind us, giving warm smiles and nods of acknowledgment to his people.

I puckered my lips as I realized their respect wasn't being given to me, though my envy quickly dissipated as I took in the way they all looked at Alaric with warmth, regard, and . . . astonishment—like he was a walking god.

Thinking back on one of our previous conversations, it made sense. He did say he technically could be a god one day. My mind reeled, thinking of what the Serpent King meant by those words, but I had no time to ask him, as Reena abruptly halted in front of a wooden cart decorated with string lights twinkling in a rainbow of colors.

A bald man with a lanky, tall figure and kind brown eyes smiled at our group.

"Back for more?" he chuckled, his attention lingering on my lady-in-waiting.

She giggled, covering her mouth bashfully, making my eyebrows shoot skyward at her behavior.

Who was this man that made my lady-in-waiting act like a teenage girl experiencing her first crush?

"Your Majesty, this is Leighton. He makes the most marvelous cocktails! You must try one." She giggled again, picking up a tiny pink paper umbrella to twirl between her fingers.

"Pleased to meet you, Serpent Queen." Leighton extended his hand, and, after a moment, I accepted it.

"Likewise. Now, please enlighten me on which cocktail of yours I must try?"

Before the vendor could reply, a dominating, familiar voice cut through the air.

"We will have two Serpent Sunsets." Alaric held up two fingers at the man as he leaned onto the cart. My gaze hungrily roamed over the way the muscles in his forearms tightened with the movement, causing that damn spark right between my thighs to flare to life once more.

"Right away, my king." Leighton quickly jumped into action, tossing a variety of colorful ingredients into a metal shaker.

Something about Alaric ordering for me was *incredibly* arousing. And to top it off, he tossed me a wink that nearly made my knees buckle while he grabbed one of the small paper umbrellas.

I had to grip onto the wooden cart as the spark between my legs turned into a fucking blazing inferno.

When the king reached over, my breath caught when he gently placed a gold umbrella behind my ear.

"For my golden queen." His fingers trailed down my ear and along the length of my hair, grazing the tops of my breasts in the process.

My heart pounded in my chest, and I felt my control waning.

So. Fucking. Dangerous.

Grasping for the last shred of my control, I blinked at him while I tried to remember the last thing Leighton said.

"He called you his king?" I arched a brow and watched as Alaric bit his lip.

He shrugged his shoulders, looking more like a nervous boy than a king.

"About that . . . I'm sort of the king of this realm as well."

My jaw dropped with shock, but I quickly closed it as Alaric's reminder of deadly flying bugs flickered into my mind.

"You are the king of not one but two realms? How is that possible when your mother is queen?" I gasped, horror slicing through my veins. "Oh gods, are you two like—?"

Alaric straightened to his full height, shaking his head in disgust.

"No, absolutely not. That isn't how things work here, Seera." A shiver raked through him. "My mother is the ruling god of this realm, and I succeeded the throne beside her when my father died on the Dark Day." His lips thinned at the mention of his father.

A pang of guilt rattling through my bones at the fact I once again reminded him of a horrid memory.

"Oh, I—I'm sorry for assuming you and your mother were a thing—" I couldn't even finish the rest of my sentence as I watched Alaric squirm, clearly disturbed and disgusted by my insinuation.

I pursed my lips, doing my best to hold back the laughter wanting to bubble out of me, but it was no use. I exploded into a fit of giggles, gripping my stomach after a solid minute of my abdomen getting a good workout. Alaric glared at me, but I did catch his lips twitching upward a few times as he watched me laugh.

"What are you two talking about over here?" Reena came between us, draping her arms over both of our shoulders rather awkwardly, considering we were both taller than her.

"Two Serpent Sunsets, for the Serpent King and Serpent Queen!" Leighton exclaimed, and I sighed in relief that I didn't have to rehash what we were laughing about to my lady-in-waiting.

She released us from her clumsy embrace, squealing while she shoved between us to lean over the bar cart.

"Oh, isn't this the cutest thing you've ever seen, Seera?!" She picked up my drink, spinning it to show it off.

The beverage was in a decadent crystal clear goblet, allowing the colorful cocktail to shine through. Three layers gently intertwined together: the top layer a deep pink, the middle a burning orange, and the bottom layer a warm yellow —all swirling together to mimic a glorious sunset.

I let out a breathy gasp full of wonder as I was greeted by a miniature orange serpent slithering along the side of my drink, which moved toward the rim of the glass to plop a pink umbrella into my beverage.

"Reena, you aren't scared of the snake?" I grabbed the cocktail, worried she would drop the stunning glass upon seeing the reptile.

She surprised me by smiling down at the little creature. "At first, I was nervous when I saw the miniature snakes assisting Leighton, but I've grown fond of them in the last hour. They're *soooo* cute," she slurred, completely amazing me when she gently stroked her pinky along the top of the snake's head.

I chuckled in disbelief as I watched the serpent happily accept her affection, then slither down her arm to return to the cart.

"Reena, how many drinks have you had?" I brought the glass to my lips, staring at her from behind the rim.

Notes of strawberry and orange zest tickled my nose, making my mouth water from the delicious smelling concoction.

"Not that many . . . only like four." She casually raised four fingers, but a hiccup escaped her not even a moment later.

I laughed around the rim, finally taking a small sip. An explosion of flavors danced along my tongue—hints of strawberry, orange, and pineapple swirling together to offer the most refreshing beverage I'd ever tasted.

"Is it up to your standards, my Queen?" Alaric asked, bringing my gaze to rise to his.

Although Reena still lingered between us, I caught a hint of softness lingering in the Serpent King's eyes as he stared down at me.

I swallowed one more sip, bobbing my head in approval.

"It's quite delicious. Thank you, Leighton." I threw the man a small, shy smile, feeling self-conscious at showing any hint of gratitude to others.

I pondered if I did it correctly, but, judging by the way he beamed back at me, I suppose I wasn't half bad at showing kindness to others . . .

"My pleasure, Your Majesty," he said, while a small pink serpent dragged a tiny washcloth along the wagon, cleaning up any spills from all the cocktail mixing.

"And who is this hard-working lady?" I gawked at the mini snake as she batted her surprisingly long eyelashes at me.

"This is Valentina." Leighton softly chuckled, picking up the snake and giving her a gentle stroke of affection.

Twin hisses stirred through the mellow night market, both being too deep and powerful to belong to little Valentina. I glanced at my arms as warmth spread across them. Ember and Dante coiled around me, their eyes trained on the bar cart. Yet, my attention remained on my snakes, and an impressed gasp tore from me, causing them to finally tear their curious gazes from the small serpents and back to their queen.

Per usual, Dante turned his head in an air of annoyance, with a glittering red bow tie snugly around his thick neck. Ember looked at me with a warmer gaze, her black shimmering bow tie adorned with a gorgeous gold trim around its edges. I stroked her neck as she brought her face closer to mine, swiveling her head side to side as if to show off her newest accessory.

"You look stunning, my dear," I cooed while softly embracing the back of her head.

Ember hissed her thanks, even going as far to lick my cheek to show her gratitude for earning such high praise from her queen. I giggled as her tongue kissed my skin, tickling me in the process.

An irritated rattling ruined our lovely moment, making me

glance sideways to see Dante examining us. His midnight black body was nearly green with how envious he looked over me cooing at his sister.

"You also look dashing, Dante. I like your bow tie." I offered a finger toward him, not daring to touch him without his consent.

Much to my surprise, he jutted his chin toward my offer, the motion dripping with his signature attitude. He rolled his eyes to the side as I brushed his chin, all the while pretending not to enjoy my affection, but I noticed the way his tail stopped rattling the moment I gave him my attention.

An enchanting melody interrupted our wholesome moment, and we all turned toward the beautiful music. A quartet was set up in the middle of a clearing and all the carts were now pushed back to line the perimeter of the jungle's edge. The configuration created a makeshift dance floor around the band, prompting couples to start swaying around the quartet to the gentle strings of the violins.

"Reena, would you mind if I whisk away your queen for a dance?" Alaric warmly smiled at her.

"Not at all, whisk away!" She shoved me into the king's arms, and I tossed a glare over my shoulder at my beaming lady-in-waiting.

Alaric's strong arms wrapped around me surprisingly gracefully, so as not to crush my snakes, but still with enough strength to catch me from smacking into his chest.

Slowly, I raised my eyes to his, catching a wicked gleam shining in them.

"Dance with me, my Queen?" He tucked a loose piece of hair behind my ear, making the paper umbrella he gifted me earlier rustle. His touch was so tender that goosebumps prickled along my skin.

Alaric's eyes dipped to my lips, watching the way I sucked

my lip between my teeth. Something flashed in his eyes, but it dissipated too swiftly for me to sniff the air and detect.

"I—I've never danced before," I whispered.

"What?" He scoffed, looking at me incredulously.

"I've never really thrown parties as queen, only executions." Heat crept up my neck from my embarrassing admission.

He gave me a sad smile. "Well, we shall remedy that right this instant. My queen, will you do me the honor of being your first dance ever?" Alaric grandly bowed as he offered me his hand.

"You're ridiculous," I said, but I laughed and placed my hand in his.

"Only for you," he admitted while sweeping me onto the dance floor.

My heart fluttered from his remark, because I felt like I was the sole person in all the realms who could bring out this quirky side of the Serpent King.

The quartet fell into a softer, enchanting tune, prompting couples to slow their jovial dancing and sway side to side rather closely.

Was I expected to dance that intimately with Alaric?

I glanced at my snakes for some comfort, but of course the little heathens abandoned me in my time of need. I sighed, not knowing what to do with my feet.

"I can practically hear you overthinking," he whispered into my ear as he pulled me tightly against him.

My breasts were fully pressed against his chest, and he extended our joined hands out to one side while sweeping his other behind to brace my lower back.

"You're too tense, relax." The pressure of his fingertips against my back increased, pulling a sharp breath from my lips at how cold his touch was, even through the silk of my dress.

I began to glance toward my feet to see where I was stepping, but Alaric's commanding voice stopped me dead in my tracks.

"Eyes on me."

My brows rose at the command, but my gaze did return to his. In the past, if someone dared demand the Serpent Queen to do anything, they'd find themselves executed shortly after.

So, why did a slight thrill shoot through me at the way the Serpent King commanded me?

Suddenly, I felt very hot, my tongue darting out to wet my parched lips. Alaric's eyes tracked my motion as they dipped to watch my tongue swirl across my lips, making his once bright green eyes now dark with a spark of . . .

I sniffed the air, noting the way it smelt like vanilla and musk.

Fuck.

The Serpent King *desired* me.

I knew he had a possessive claim over me for some unfathomable reason, but this—this felt different.

"Alaric," I breathed as our bodies swayed around the dance floor.

His eyes shot to mine, a ravenous hunger scorching within them. His hand moved up my back, all the way to rest at the nape of my neck. He gripped me hard, like it was the only tether holding him back from doing something extremely careless. Yet, as his gaze continuously dropped to my lips, I realized he was indeed foolish, because he was going to kiss me.

My traitorous heart fluttered with excitement, but the logical side of my brain blared with alarm bells. The last time we kissed the whole world shook, and the human lands were never the same. The destruction I caused for my realm, for my people . . . I couldn't do that again, especially to such a beautiful place like the Emerald Glades.

Right as he dipped his lips toward mine, I planted my hand against his chest.

"We can't." My attempt to stop him only brought our faces closer, close enough I could feel the heat of his breath dancing across my skin.

"Tell me you don't want me, Seera," he breathed against my lips.

The sway of our hips pressed against each other was hypnotic, alluring, and *so* sensual. I felt his hardness press against me, causing heat to flare between the apex of my thighs.

"Better yet, let me tell *you* how I'd let all the realms crumble to ash if it meant I got one more taste of those perfect, pouty lips." His voice was husky, sheer lust coating every word falling from his beautifully wicked mouth.

For Serpent's Sake. This man was good.

I chewed on said perfect lip, wanting more than anything to tell Alaric that I didn't want him, but I was losing the battle within me with every shared breath between us—with every swish of our hips, with every touch of his fingertips along the nape of my neck . . .

My resolve completely crumbled, the fight in me dissolving like a dream upon waking.

I wanted him.

I wanted the Serpent King.

I wanted *Alaric.*

Damn the consequences.

Right as I was readying myself to close the sliver of space between our lips, a beautiful laugh split through the air.

A laugh I hated I recognized so easily.

Our romantic moment was ruined when I leaned away from Alaric to glance over my shoulder. I turned just in time to see Adalina being swept across the dance floor by a familiar set of defined arms.

Landon was casting an award-winning smile down at the god as he pulled her closer to him. They danced around the space like they were the only two people in all the realms.

A pang of sadness and surprise rattled through me at the emotion rearing its vicious head as I stared after them.

Jealousy.

I was jealous that Landon looked at a female he's known for only a fraction of our time together like *that*.

The drink I consumed earlier turned sour in my stomach, making bile quickly burn up my throat. I tried to swallow my feelings, like I always did, but I couldn't this time as they manifested in a very tangible way.

I only had enough time to rip myself from the Serpent King's arms as I vomited all over his shiny, black dress shoes.

CHAPTER 40
REPLACED

"Dear gods!" Alaric stepped away as I continued to wretch the entirety of the delicious pastries and beverages I had consumed. After another horrifying minute, my fit ended, leaving me gasping with my hands on my knees.

When I glanced up, Alaric was gone.

Of course he fled—I just threw up all over his fashionable shoes. He probably sprinted away in disgust and was buying a new pair right this instant.

My head drooped as humiliation finally burned brightly inside my chest.

"Here." I jumped upon hearing the king's resonant voice beside me.

He was extending a black handkerchief to me, and I accepted it, swiping my lips with the soft cotton material. My gaze dipped to my puke still lingering on his footwear.

"You didn't leave?" Disbelief laced my three simple words.

His brows tugged inward as he placed a hand to my back,

drawing soft circles upon it with the pads of his fingertips. "Why would I leave you?"

"Because I threw up all over your shoes. I thought you went to clean yourself off and get a new pair."

He shook his head at me like I said an amusing joke. "Seera, this isn't your first time puking all over my nicest shoes, and I doubt it will be the last."

I laughed into the handkerchief, startled by the king's kindness.

Giving him a sideways glance, I balled the tissue into my hand. "I'm going to hold onto this, just in case."

He pursed his lips, the corners twitching into a smile. "Good idea."

The romantic music ceased, signaling the quartet was taking a break.

"Ah, there you are!" a feminine voice sang, and I didn't need to turn to see who the annoyingly sweet voice belonged to.

I hated I had no mirror to ensure I cleaned all the puke from my face or to hastily reapply my smudged lipstick.

"May I?" Alaric asked, as he watched me fiddle with my hair and fuss over myself.

Feeling oddly timid, I dipped my chin, allowing him to step closer to assist me. Gently, he swiped his thumb along the bottom of my lip. He was cleaning me up exactly how I would, and surprise warmed my chest at the tender way his fingers brushed over my skin.

"Perfect," he whispered, his thumb lingering on my lip.

My lips parted as I stared at him, his eyes holding the same tenderness his touch did.

He was giving me *that* look again, but this time his gaze made me feel like I was the most precious thing in all the realms.

"What have you two been up to?" Adalina squawked in an obnoxiously loud tone as she finally drifted to our sides.

Alaric's fingers dropped from my lips, disappointment passing through me at how I instantly missed his touch.

"I was showing Seera around the night market. We had a lovely dance together." The king smiled at me, our dirty little secret still hanging in the air.

It was rather charming how he left out the small detail of me puking all over his shoes, which somehow looked sparkling clean as I glanced at the king's footwear.

"Hmm, I see. How did you like the night market, Serpent Queen? Is everything to your standards?" Adalina's eyes sliced to mine, her tone changing when she addressed me. A hint of frost laced her words, and I once more detected something deeper behind her lighthearted facade.

"It's breathtaking." I didn't have to force out a lie as my gaze drifted over the colorful fireflies flying above.

I was stunned to hear Alaric reply, not Adalina. "It is, isn't it?"

When I looked at him, I thought he would be marveling at the night market around us like I was . . . I did not anticipate his gaze to be locked onto me.

My cheeks burned from his intense attention, from his comment, from all the ways he made me feel incredibly special tonight.

Yet, for the second time this evening, Adalina's hum shattered our moment. I glanced toward her, only to see the god examining Alaric and I through darkened eyes.

Someone cleared their throat, and then my bodyguard came into view as he shuffled out from behind Adalina.

"Landon." My voice was a mixture between delight and sorrow.

"Seera." He stepped beside Adalina, barely granting me a small nod.

Music streamed around us once again, letting us know the quartet resumed their playing. The tempo wasn't as slow and sensual as their prior song, but it wasn't a very upbeat tune either—even the music matched my conflicted feelings.

"Care for a dance?" Landon offered me his hand.

I'm not sure why my initial reaction to his question was to glance at Alaric. It wasn't like I needed his permission to dance with my bodyguard, so why was I suddenly seeking his reassurance that he wouldn't be upset by me accepting Landon's hand?

What the fuck was wrong with me?

Alaric dipped his chin, encouraging me to go enjoy myself. He extended his hand to Adalina at the same time I planted mine in Landon's, and we all swept back onto the dance floor.

"Are you having a nice evening?" my bodyguard asked, placing his hand on my upper back, notably at a much more respectable spot than how Alaric handled me earlier.

"Surprisingly, I am. Are you?" I glanced up and into his icy eyes.

"I am enjoying the Emerald Glades, far more than I expected to." His gaze trailed away from mine, and I followed his line of sight as it pierced into the goddess swaying in Alaric's arms.

I shook my head, not quite believing how much could change in the matter of only a few days. It felt like an eternity since we sparred in the Emerald Glades training yard, yet it was only earlier this afternoon.

"Is there a particular aspect about this realm that you are so fond of?" My words came out sharper than I intended, which made his gaze snap to mine.

His brows knitted while he stepped away and spun me

around. When we moved back together, he was staring down at me in disbelief.

"Are you truly upset that I've grown fond of someone besides you?"

Ouch.

I gaped at him against my better judgement. "How can you grow that fond of someone you've only known for a day?" I bitterly whispered.

"The same way you can easily replace me within the same amount of time," he huffed, his shoulders growing tenser by the seconds.

"Replace you? What are you prattling on about now, Landon?"

"The Serpent King." He cocked his head to the left toward the male in question. "I see the way you look at him, Seera, and you never *once* looked at me like that in all the years I've served you." He spat the words, like they were coated in venom, and it felt that way as they sunk straight into my heart.

I couldn't make sense of Landon's irrational behavior, so I discreetly sniffed the air. An overly sweet, fruity smell danced along my tastebuds, and my nose crinkled at how potent my bodyguard's jealousy tasted.

"Is this all just a game then? Are you trying to get underneath my skin by chasing after a god, the very beings I banned worship of in our realm?" My grip on his hand tightened, my anger slowly awakening from its short lived slumber.

"It's not a game, Seera. Adalina appreciates me for who I am, and she doesn't try to turn me into something I'm not. She doesn't try to turn me into a monster." The look he tossed me was so full of disdain that it prevented my feet from poorly shuffling to the music any longer.

I stepped away from my bodyguard in a complete state of shock, looking at him like I would at a total stranger. The man who was always by my side, who was ever-loyal and there when I needed him, couldn't feel further away from me at this moment.

It was almost like we were standing on a frozen lake and a huge fissure burst through the ice, completely separating us.

Landon thought I was trying to turn him into a monster . . . and he was right.

After all, I did make him do terrible things.

Who was I kidding trying to pretend to be anything other than what I was?

I was a monster.

The demons of my past pressed on my chest, a heavy weight forcing my feet to drag backward.

"Seera, wait." A glassy look passed over my bodyguard's eyes, making me wonder if his inebriation was the reason he finally had the courage to speak his truth.

I held my hand up, and he paused his advance toward me.

"No, you've said enough." I backed away, curling my quaking hand into the silk material of my gown.

I had to get out of here before I completely broke down before the entire crowd, and worse, in front of Adalina.

I bunched my dress in my hand, and did what I always did best—I ran from my problems, sprinting down the pathway Alaric and I joyously walked along before everything went to ruin.

Who was I kidding?

This life of enjoyment, of dancing, of desire, of *hope* was not for the likes of me.

The likes of someone who was a *monster*.

"Seera!" someone shouted, but I didn't stop.

Hot tears streamed down my face as I raced into the jungle.

I sprinted into the darkness, running straight into the sanctuary of my oldest friend's arms.

CHAPTER 41
LOST

I ran with a wild intensity through the dark forest, not daring to stop even as my lungs burned.

My feet ached from my heels, and I cursed through my gritted teeth as I finally felt the excruciating pain of blisters forming behind the straps with each movement forward. Although my immortal healing sealed them quickly, they tore back open only seconds later. Now that I could feel proper emotions, it was quite painful. But nothing was more agonizing than the feeling shooting through the void in my chest—

Could I even call it a void anymore?

It felt like my entire soul flooded back into my body the moment Landon spat such volatile words at me.

I wanted to hate him, but I couldn't.

He only dared to speak the truth.

I was a monster.

I was a monster.

I was a monster.

That last word echoed through my head, but I tried to let the sounds of the forest drown out my hateful thoughts.

Birds sang, snakes hissed, and the leaves rustled from the monkeys swinging from branch to branch high above me.

Monster.

Monster.

Monster.

I squeezed my hands against my ears, willing the agony in my chest and head to cease.

What was I thinking, that I could handle this mission?

Now that my soul was returning, I was not as strong as I pretended to be. I couldn't handle this, no matter what Alaric said about me being the strongest woman he knew, because *I* didn't believe him.

I was not strong.

I was weak, and I was rapidly losing the never-ending internal battle I fought every day with each pump of my legs.

Even after years of ruling as the Serpent Queen, I so easily crumbled into the girl I had tried incredibly hard to run from.

Sobs wracked through my chest, but I didn't try to muffle the anguished cries rattling out of my mouth, for they quickly got swallowed in the solitude of the darkness surrounding me. I had no idea where I was running to, growing lost a while back when a fork in the pathway had appeared.

So, I kept sprinting as my one true friend—the darkness—wrapped around me in a comforting hug.

I was about to round another shadowy curve of trees, when my heel snagged onto something and my world flipped upside down. I yelped as I tumbled, quickly rolling to the side so as not to smack my face straight into the dirt ground. A pop sounded, followed by blaring pain shooting through my shoulder right as I hit the ground. I groaned, rolling onto my back, still breathing hard from all my running.

After gulping down mouthfuls of air, I slightly leaned up to see what I tripped over—a gnarled tree root stared back at me, and I moaned again while collapsing against the cold dirt.

Of course a fucking tree attempted to kill me, what's new?

I laid there, gazing up at the lush canopy and feeling a glimmer of satisfaction that I could see through the sheet of darkness. It was like a light shining down a dim tunnel as I watched the creatures of the forest happily moving about in the treetops, plus a few stars winked at me through the holes between the dense leaves.

I was ending my time in the Emerald Glades exactly as it started.

On the damp, dirt ground with a tree root digging into my ass.

With the jungle as my only witness, I barked a rough fit of laughter into the night. I laughed until my ribs hurt—it was either that or I would cry. Although both emotions were foreign for me, I'd much prefer the former right now. I most definitely needed a good laugh more than anything, so I cackled at absolutely nothing and everything.

My life was a complete and utter mess, and I had no idea how to fix it.

My laughter ceased the moment the hair on the back of my neck rose, a feeling of unease creeping over me. I glanced sideways, only to see a tree root writhing toward me.

So, I *wasn't* imagining things when I landed in this realm.

The root slithered like a serpent, and I watched with a mixture of horror and awe as it went behind me to press underneath my back.

Oh, For Serpent's Sake, was I about to be strangled to death by a fucking tree root?!

I was pleasantly surprised, however, when its sharp edge

poked into my back instead of wrapping around my neck, and it gently lifted me forward into a seated position.

It was helping me up . . . but *why*?

Maybe this was a lesson—that the first step to finding my will to live again was getting back up, no matter how many times I fell flat on my face.

I planted my feet firmly on the ground, doing my best to rise on shaky legs.

After what felt like an astronomical amount of effort, I stood all on my own.

The tree root rose with me, almost like it was looking at me.

"Thank you for the push," I whispered.

Its response was to wrap its gnarled self around my shoulders, almost like its version of an embrace, before slithering back to its home at the base of a nearby tree.

A sliver of hope burst through my chest . . . maybe I *could* do this. Maybe I could change my life for the better.

As I took a step forward, a step toward a new life not full of tortured screams and executions, a snap tore through the air—and then I was free falling.

This time, my face crashed straight into the ground, agony swiftly slicing through my already injured shoulder as I slowly rolled onto my side.

"What the fuck," I groaned, glancing down to see that my heel snapped.

My beloved choice of footwear decided to fail me during my time of need—if this wasn't a sign to completely give up on any prospect of living a worthy life, I didn't know what was.

"Seera!" someone shouted from far away.

On instinct, I opened my mouth to alert whoever it was to my presence, but then I let my jaw close as all hope died in my chest like a fire being doused with a bucket of water.

I didn't care to do anything—I didn't care to be saved, so I laid on the forest floor alone in not only physical agony, but emotional turmoil as well.

But then, *he* was here.

Alaric was with me.

He jogged into sight, stopping right before my feet. The king wasn't panting for breath like I was mere moments ago—in fact, I don't think he even broke a sweat.

Curse this perfect near-god behemoth of a man.

"*For Serpent's Sake,*" Alaric muttered as he looked down at me. "Are you alright? What happened?"

"A fucking tree branch is what happened," I moaned, right as a shooting pain went through my shoulder.

Alaric regarded me, his lips tugging into a frown. "You're hurt."

He moved with a swift grace, dropping onto a knee to examine my shoulder. I knew I was in trouble when a grimace flickered over his features. "This is going to hurt, and for that I apologize."

"What is going to—" I gasped, pain tearing through my ever fiber, making me arch upward and howl like a wolf into the night sky.

It felt as if my shoulder was lit on fire as a loud *pop* rattled through my bones. I panted through the pain, but whatever Alaric did helped ease the agony within moments.

"Ah, that's better. Thank you," I sighed, melting further into the ground.

"I don't know if I will ever get used to you acquiring such proper manners." Alaric tossed me a cheeky smile as he lowered himself onto his back to lay beside me.

"You're insufferable," I muttered.

He chuckled, and we laid there together, letting the

melodies of the jungle do any further talking for us. It could have been minutes, or hours, where we just laid in silence, enjoying the stars shining high above us.

When I was with Alaric, everything felt better, like he was a breath of fresh air right after a rainstorm. He cleansed my worries from my head, more so than any useless prayers ever did.

He simply allowed me to just *be*.

I didn't feel the need to wear the mask I wore as the Serpent Queen around him.

"This is nice," I whispered into the darkness.

"It is," he softly said back, his pinky latching onto mine.

I sucked in a sharp breath at his cold touch, but I returned the motion, wrapping my pinky around his.

"Seera, you are not a monster."

I glanced sideways at the king, his words taking me by surprise. "You talked to Landon?"

"Something like that." His tone was sharp, annoyance creeping between his features.

I scoffed while I imagined the Serpent King roughing up my bodyguard—it was inevitable—and it quickly turned into a full on laugh as I pictured the scene in my mind. As tough as my bodyguard was, I bet he nearly wet himself from the behemoth beside me interrogating him.

Alaric glanced at me with amusement lighting his bright eyes. "What is so funny over there?"

"I'm imagining you giving Landon a proper shakedown," I said through spurts of laughter.

He joined in, a few of his own wheezy, hissing chuckles bubbling from his lips. "He fucking deserved more than a shakedown."

His words made me fall into another fit of hilarity, and I

shook my head as I swiped at my eyes, tears of joy lining the corners of them. But when I glanced down at the liquid coating my fingertips, my mood flipped like a switch, Landon's parting words echoing through my head.

She doesn't try to turn me into a monster.

I watched the stars burning high above while my world collapsed around me yet again. Warmth flooded my cheeks, but I had no energy left to care that I was crying for what felt like the billionth time.

"Hey," Alaric breathed, releasing my pinky to drag his thumb across my cheek.

He rolled to the side, propping himself onto an elbow while swiping away my tears with a surprising gentleness. And just like that, I was transported back to the night under the stars with Landon, when he kissed away my tears. A fresh wave of sadness washed over me—that fragile moment with my bodyguard feeling like a lifetime ago, even though it was less than a week prior. I feared our relationship was forever changed, if not completely irreparable. We would never be the same . . . we would never go back to the people we were before this journey.

So, I cried, mourning my rather unconventional and complicated relationship with my bodyguard.

Alaric didn't press me about what prompted the shift in my mood, instead he leaned over me and continued to handle my tears like they were remarkable jewels.

He sat with me as the darkness weighed on my chest, as he promised he would. Fresh, warm tears spilt from my eyes at the fact the man whisking them away kept his promise . . .

I won't let you go through life alone anymore.

The Serpent King was a good man, one I didn't feel deserving of.

"Alaric," my voice broke, and it looked like I stabbed him in the gut with how his face crumpled when I cried out his name.

"I'm here, sweetheart." He brushed my hair off my face, softly tucking it behind my ear.

That name stole my breath.

Sweetheart.

It was my undoing seventy-five years ago, and it would be again in this fragile moment.

"I'm scared," I squeaked so softly, not wanting even the birds to hear my humiliating admission.

"So am I." He smiled down at me.

"Why are you scared?" I sniffled.

He glanced to the golden sky. "I'm scared of a lot of things, Seera."

"Like what?"

He paused, his brows tugging downward. "For example, losing my powers terrifies me."

"I can relate," I sighed, the worry of our impending mission stirring around us like the gentle breeze.

He continued to stare at the stars for guidance. "I'm scared of who I've become."

I reached up, tenderly touching his cheek. "You are not alone in that notion."

His eyes cut to mine the moment I touched him, intensely searching them.

"Above all, I'm scared of being a complete and utter fool for a second time. I'm petrified at the thought of losing the woman who made me *feel* again."

I couldn't stop my bottom lip from trembling as I dared to put myself out there again after nearly eighty long, terrible years.

"Alaric, you have no idea how much I fear that as well."

I stroked my thumb against his soft, freshly shaved cheek, and he leaned into my embrace like Ember reveled into the crook of my hand as I pet her. His eyes fluttered closed, a heavy sigh releasing from his lips, almost like he was breathing after being underwater for an eternity.

"I never deserved you, and I still don't," he whispered.

The world as I knew it shattered as I watched a silver tear fall from the Serpent King's closed eyes.

It was my turn to wipe away his surprisingly warm tears.

"Alaric, now I'm truly scared." He cracked his eyes open at my slightly amused tone.

"Why's that?"

"Isn't it alarming how similar we are? Sometimes I feel like when you shared your magic with me it somehow fused us into the same person. I feel like—*gods*," I chewed on my lip, completely beside myself that I was about to be *this* sappy, but fuck it. "I feel like our souls are intertwined. When I'm with you, it's equivalent to the experience of coming home after a long day and curling up next to a roaring fire with a beloved book."

Alaric's laugh roared through the jungle, a rather jarring sound for how silent it was besides us sharing secrets in the darkness.

"That is the most Seera thing you could say." He looked at me with pure and unfiltered adoration, like I was the most precious thing he'd ever have the glory to lay his eyes on.

The way he looked at me momentarily stole my breath, and we simply stared at each other, letting our vulnerable words hang between us like the stars hanging in the sky.

"I have to admit," he drawled. "This is all rather surprising for me."

I arched a brow, silently questioning him to continue.

"I truly thought you hated me after everything I did." His eyes crinkled as a small wince flashed across his face.

"I did hate you," I admitted.

I covered my mouth to stifle a laugh at his dramatically wounded expression.

"I hated you so much that I made Reena make a rather poor sketch of your face, one where your nose was indeed broken from all the times my fist cracked it. Then, I'd proceed to throw daggers at it as target practice. Every. Single. Night." I raised my head slightly off the ground as best as I could, bringing my face closer to his.

He assisted my pursuit by bracing a strong hand around my neck and lowering his head the rest of the way. For the second time that night, our lips were just a breath apart.

"Does it, too, make me a monster for finding great pleasure in the thought of you brutally throwing a knife at my face?" he growled, and I could almost feel the vibrations from his lips against mine.

A shiver coursed through me when he fully leaned his entire body over me, allowing me to feel *exactly* how much the image of me throwing daggers at him pleased the Serpent King.

A soft laugh floated out of me, and he greedily sucked the air puffing from my lips.

"Out of everything you admitted tonight, that is the one thing that surprises me the least." My voice dipped, growing husky with each word. "After all, wasn't it you that reminded me how much pleasure and pain are a beautiful combination?"

His eyes flickered with delight. "I knew you'd like that remark."

My hips hitched up, grinding against his hardness. "I enjoyed it more than you know."

"Is that so?" He chewed on his bottom lip, his beautiful canines gleaming from the moonlight.

"It's a shame we can't kiss," I whispered, running my hands down the length of his hard chest.

His eyes closed as a shudder racked through him. Once it passed, his eyes snapped open, their once bright and clear quality now dimmed to complete darkness as his pupils stretched into golden slits.

"There are other places I can kiss you."

CHAPTER 42
WILD

Alaric's lips slowly pressed against the column of my neck, testing the waters to make sure the whole realm wouldn't turn to ash.

He raised his lips barely an inch from my skin while we waited for the ground to quake, for the trees to snap, for the world to end . . . but nothing happened.

"Seems like we found a loophole to our no kissing problem."

"It appears so."

A soft moan slipped from my lips as Alaric kissed the side of my neck again, dragging his sharp canines over a particularly sensitive spot.

"Alaric," I squirmed beneath him, wrapping one of my legs around his waist.

"Mhm, I love when you moan my name. I'm going to make you do it a lot more tonight, but only if you're a good girl for your king." He applied more pressure with his pointy canines, this time hard enough to slightly tear my skin.

"*Fuuuck,*" I moaned into the quiet jungle.

Alaric dragged his hand up my leg wrapped around him, trailing a blazing path up my bare skin, thanks to the generous slit in my dress.

In this position, my gold lacy undergarments were on full display, and the Serpent King roamed his fingers all the way up to the apex of my thighs. Through the lace, he pressed his thumb with a sensational pressure against my center, making me tip my head against the damp forest floor as ecstasy coursed through my veins.

I felt the weight from his body lessen, prompting me to look down at him only to find his eyes locked onto where he teased my clit with his thumb.

"So perfect and wet for me, such a good girl." His tongue darted out to wet his lips, as if he was looking at the next meal he was about to ravage and feast upon.

Fuck me.

His dark laugh had my flesh pebbling, and I must have said that last thought aloud since he responded. "Oh, I have every intention of doing exactly that. But first, I'm going to sear every inch of your skin with my mouth. I'm going to make every part of you so clearly mine, you won't be able to scrub away the imprint of my lips from your skin, no matter how hard you try."

"Please," I whimpered, needing him pressed against me in every way I ever imagined.

"Mm, there are the manners I love to hear." He licked up my body, all the way to my neck as his fingers still worked me.

It was a beautiful pairing of pleasure and pain with the pressure he pressed against my center, accompanied by the gentle way he began to kiss the side of my neck.

"I've always loved this birthmark," he mumbled against my skin. "It's the most delicate thing about you—it almost looks like a teardrop."

I was momentarily stunned by the way he viewed my mark so differently than I did, for I always looked at it like a drop of permanent blood staining my pale skin.

I hid my surprise by grabbing ahold of his lush locks and pulling him back to look me in the eye. "Less talking, more kissing." I pushed him back to my neck, earning me a devious chuckle that made his lips vibrate against my skin.

I couldn't help but think about how those lips would feel against *my* lips . . .

I grabbed onto his hair, yanking him back once more. "Alaric, I want your lips on mine."

He tilted his head at me while scrunching his brows, like I should know we couldn't properly kiss by now.

"Not those lips." I glanced down to where his hand still worked strong strokes against my core.

He dragged his tongue along his top teeth as he followed my gaze. "Oh, I want that as well, my Queen." His eyes slowly roamed up my body, stopping square on my chest. "But not before I have those beautiful breasts in my mouth."

Well, I suppose I could wait when he put it like that.

"This dress is so tight, you will have to help me out of it." I motioned for him to get up so I could start to strip it from my flushed body.

"Oh, I have every intention of getting you out of this dress." His hand stopped working my clit to drag along my abdomen and up to the spot where the tops of my breasts peeked out of the golden silk material.

"But I don't need you to get up to do so." Before I could question what he meant, the sound of splitting fabric streamed through the jungle.

The cold air kissed my naked skin as my torn gown fell to my sides. Alaric dragged his fingers over my matching golden lacy brassiere—if one could even call it that, more like a scrap of lace barely covering my ample breasts. My nipples were already perked and peeking through the garment, ready for his lips to wrap around them.

"Gods, you have no idea how long I've dreamt of this moment." He cupped one of my breasts while grinding his hips, and I writhed at the feeling of his deliciously hard length pressing against me.

He dipped his head, not even bothering to remove my brassiere before wrapping his lips around my nipple. He sucked it, and when he bit down I hissed in delight as pain shot through me.

"Again," I groaned.

"Such an impatient thing," he teased.

But he heeded my command, wrapping his lips around my nipple and biting harder this time.

"Yes," I hissed, losing myself in the bliss that was Alaric's lips and sharp teeth.

He continued to cup my breasts, licking and sucking them into his mouth through my lacy garment, until he grew impatient with the thing and tore that off as well. My breasts sprung free, bouncing from his forceful action. Alaric didn't seem to mind as he watched them move like he was in a trance he never wanted to break free from.

"Fucking gods, Seera. You are the most stunning creation in all the godsdamn realms." He bit his lip before dropping his face between both of my breasts, pressing them together to smother his face between.

He buried his face in my chest, shaking his head slightly back and forth. I couldn't stop myself from laughing at the rather boyish gesture, and also at the way it tickled my skin. Alaric stopped, quickly moving his hand to wrap around my neck, applying enough pressure around it to cease my laughter.

"What is so funny?" He glanced at me through lowered lashes, looking like the most fearsome god.

He loosened his grip only slightly for me to reply. "That tickled."

His hand tightened around my neck again. "Apologies, my Queen. I know you wanted pleasure and pain, not tickles."

Abruptly, he cupped me. Then, using only one hand, he quickly tore off the scrap separating us. I cried out as he slipped a finger through my slick center and brutally into me, all the while choking me with a delightful pressure.

"Is that more of what you enjoy, sweetheart?" He stroked me, and I'd never felt anything as wonderful as I did when his finger worked inside of me.

All I could muster with his hand around my throat was a whimper and a bob of my head to encourage him to continue.

"Good girl." He lowered his lips back to my breasts, continuing his teasing exploration while he slipped a second finger in me.

He did exactly as he said he would earlier, marking every single inch of my skin with his mouth. A third finger shoved into me, and I reveled at the way he stretched me while trailing kisses down the length of the serpent tattoo wrapping around my abdomen. His lips burned into my skin, all the way to the rattling tail flicking along the curve of my ass. When he was done showering me in possessive kisses, he pulled his fingers from me, using them to trace the length of his mark along my body and all the way back up to my lips.

"It drives me to insanity seeing my mark on you." His eyes were glued to the way my tongue darted out to lick my lips.

"Let me taste." I glanced at the slick digits that were just inside me, then back to his eyes.

A wildfire of desire blazed in them as he pushed his fingers between my lips. "Whatever my Queen wants, she gets."

I sucked them, letting my hands drop to his belt, working it off while maintaining eye contact and tasting my pleasure from his fingertips. Once his belt was off, he used his free hand to help work his pants to past his knees. I palmed him through his undergarments, moaning at the way he pumped his fingers into my mouth harder and at the generous length between my own fingertips.

"Godsdamn, I was wrong," Alaric breathed, mesmerized by the way my lips wrapped around him. "You are a very, very bad girl." He shoved his fingers to the back of my throat, and I swallowed the gag that threatened to escape me.

My eyes watered, but I loved the pain sparking through every fiber of my being. I bit down to stifle my moans, making him hiss from my sharp bite.

"There's my vicious serpent," Alaric darkly chuckled, removing his fingers from my mouth and moving his lips back to my neck, my breasts, my abdomen, and all the way to between my thighs.

"Wait, it's only fair you remove your top too." I glanced down at him.

"Apologies, my Queen . . . you make me forget all my manners." He smirked, obliging me as he tore his shirt over his head with one hand.

My mouth watered when I took in the sight of Alaric's bare chest. Wispy dark ink covered his flesh and spread across the chiseled muscles trailing all the way down his abdomen. My gaze lingered on the v-shaped cord of muscles that dipped beneath his waist band, prompting heat to spark between my legs.

A flash of subtle movement caught my attention, tearing my eyes from his hips.

I watched in awe as his tattoos *moved.*

They swirled along his pale skin, shifting into an identical match to the marking etched upon my own skin.

"Beautiful," I whispered, dragging my fingers over his mark.

He glanced at me, a flicker of surprise gracing his eyes. Before I could say more, he dropped himself to hover before my clit, his warm breath arousing me as he admired the view.

"You're tickling me again," I giggled, making his eyes spear into mine with an unsatisfied gleam.

"Well, that won't do." He wasted no time lowering his lips to my clit, firmly sucking and releasing it with a popping sound.

"Better?" He smirked up at me with my wetness painted across his lips.

"Much." I barely got the words out before his lips were on mine again—sucking, licking, and exploring with a feverish intensity.

It was as if I was his last supper, and he wanted to lap up every single crumb before being walked to his execution.

When his tongue drove into me, my back arched off the floor, needing his lips pressed harder against mine. He met me stroke for stroke, pulling every ounce of pleasure and pain from me with a beautiful melody of moans coursing from the very lips he couldn't kiss.

My world as I knew it entirely shattered with every orgasm he pulled from me with each languid flick of his tongue.

"Alaric, I need you. *Now*." I looked at him, commanding my king to do as I said.

He glanced up at me, but he didn't remove his mouth from my center. Instead, he sucked my clit harder, making my hips buck from the startling spurt of pain shooting between my legs.

"Alaric!" I screamed, not really sure if I wanted him to stop, but I felt like I'd implode if I didn't have him inside of me right this instant.

After another beautifully tortuous moment, he tore his lips from mine, his arms wrapping around my thick thighs as he pressed gentle kisses into my stretch marks painted along the inner sides of them.

He continued to brand my body with his lips as they worked a blazing path up my body, all the while perfectly lining up his cock. I gasped at the feel of the tip of him against my wetness, my clit already so sensitive from all the attention he showered me in.

"Did you like that?" he purred against my neck.

"Immensely," I answered impatiently. "Now, *please* fuck me."

"Well, since you asked so nicely." With one brutal thrust, he shoved into me, pushing every inch of his impressive length deep inside me.

Both of our mouths parted as we got used to the feel of each other, and he slowly began to work his hips against me.

"Seera," he moaned my name up to the sky, as if he was worshipping one of the gods.

His hands wrapped under my waist, lifting me slightly off the hard ground as he moved to his knees and kneaded my ass in his palms all the while still pounding into me. He lifted my legs over his shoulders, his feather soft kisses against my calves so different from his relentless thrusts.

Rocks dug into my neck and shoulders, but I didn't care. All I could focus on was the way Alaric spread my legs further apart and fucked me senseless, my breasts furiously bouncing with each thrust of his hips. Alaric watched them move, and I didn't think it was possible for him to move deeper into me, but he found a way as he got lost in the hypnotic motion of my breasts bouncing from our carnal act.

In this moment, we were as wild and free as the jungle surrounding us. It was almost like the two monsters living in the confines of our minds were sick of all the constraints the world placed on them. Now, they tore free from their cages, unrestrained and thirsty to experience all the joys life had to offer.

After all, couldn't monsters feel pleasure too?

"Alaric, I'm going to—" I panted, not able to finish my sentence.

"That's it, come for me. Look how fucking perfect you are, look at how perfectly you take me." He gripped my chin, forcing me to watch where we were joined.

That one line along with watching us fused together was my undoing. I screamed out as my orgasm crashed over me like a bolt of lightning striking true. Pleasure was still racing through my veins as Alaric planted his feet and lifted us both in one swift motion. I squealed with a mix of surprise and delight at how effortlessly he scooped me up. He quickly moved my back against a thick tree beside us. Its rough bark tore my skin open, making me hiss from the pain, but I loved every scratch against my back from the way the king handled me. He remained inside me the entire time, already rolling his hips again as he stood and I tightened my legs around his waist.

Alaric's thrusts were strong, but felt gentle at the same time. Almost like . . . no, there was no way we were making love in any capacity. Although I never participated in such an act, this was far better than whatever that was like.

This was otherworldly, the way our bodies worked together to draw our pleasure from one another. It was electric, like our souls were fusing into one.

Alaric fisted my hair in his hand, cradling my head from banging against the tree as he picked up the pace. His teeth brushed against my neck, and the animalistic urge to feel them sink into my skin crashed through me, just like they did right above my lip when we sealed our bargain.

"Bite me," I whispered into his ear.

His hips slowed, nearly stilling. He pulled back, bringing his eyes to mine and searching them to see if I was serious.

"I want it. It's okay." I cupped his cheek, extending my neck like a sacrificial offer.

His fingers trailed over my birthmark as he started to move inside me again, but this time agonizingly slow.

"Anything for you, my Queen." He dropped his lips to my neck, then sunk his teeth into my flesh.

I cried out, intertwining my fingers into his hair as a pain unlike anything I'd experienced before ricocheted through my veins—almost as if two things which should never mix came together, like fire and ice. Such an act felt forbidden, but we never had a knack for following the rules of life anyway.

The tree quaked behind me from the intensity of Alaric's thrusts, and I matched him as I worked my hips to the tantalizing rhythm of his.

When it came to Serpent King and Queen, there were no rules we wouldn't break. I was sure if we kept playing with fire, we would end up crashing our lips together, ending every single realm in the process.

But for now, I forced myself to stop overthinking, to be in this moment with him. The pain faded to pleasure as he shoved harder into me, digging his canines into my skin.

I breathed through the pain, because I'd happily take this feeling over the misery that weighed on me everyday as the Serpent Queen. This pain made me feel so much closer to Alaric—the feeling that raced through me when he bit me was . . . *euphoric.*

Slowly, he retracted his teeth from my flesh, lapping at the blood that trickled down the column of my neck.

"Your blood is as sweet as that pretty little cunt of yours," he growled against the shell of my ear, losing himself inside me with each agonizing roll of his hips.

The combination of his wicked mouth and the way he fucked me with a renewed energy, like my blood rejuvenated him, was my final undoing.

Underneath the moonlit sky dancing with golden stars, Alaric and I created a new memory. We came together so intensely it felt like the stars fell and burned straight through us.

This time when I climaxed, I didn't bite back his name.

I didn't lie to myself, nor run from the fact *Alaric*'s name tore from my lips as my climax devoured every last bit of my self-control.

Our arms tightened around each other as we free-fell into the darkness.

I didn't know what the future held, but I felt better going into the next stage of this mission with the man currently buried deep inside of me.

If we could make up like this after decades of being estranged, we could do anything together.

How hard could it be to kill a god when I had the man of my dreams by my side?

CHAPTER 43
THE DANCE OF THE QUEENS

For the first time in decades, I didn't dream.

Perhaps, it was because I lived out all my dreams last night with the Serpent King.

"What are you thinking of that has you smiling like *that*?" My lady-in-waiting nudged me in the ribs, causing my small grin to slip off my face.

"Nothing." I threw my best glare at Reena hoping it would silence her, but alas, it seemed my lady-in-waiting had grown far less fearful of me in the course of only a few days.

"You are *so* thinking about *him*, aren't you?! What did you two get up to last night after you ran off?" Her grey eyes were wide, full of curiosity.

"None of your business, Reena. Now, enough with the questions. I'm running late for my fitting as it is."

We came to two hallways, the white and gold marble tiles sparkling down both directions.

"Which way to Adalina's chambers?" I asked, wishing anyone but her was hosting my appointment today.

Earlier this morning, I received a letter to meet the god in her chambers for a private fitting to dress me in proper winter attire. Although I knew the realm the Ice Goddess lived in was known for its frost and crystals, my mood instantly soured when I saw Adalina personally signed the invitation.

It was almost as if any moment of happiness I grasped was bound to flee with Alaric's mother looming nearby.

"Right this way, my Queen." Reena headed toward the pathway on the right, picking up her pace to match my long strides.

We didn't pass a single servant in the halls, which only served as a reminder of how odd the ruling god of the Emerald Glades truly was.

She liked to do her own cooking, cleaning, and tailoring— what was next? Was she going to let her people have a say in ruling her realm as well?

I shook my head in disbelief as we approached the most massive door I'd ever seen. It was made of pure, solid gold . . . the gods definitely didn't lack riches, that much was for certain.

Reena pulled open the door, allowing me to enter the god's chambers first. I wore my best smile as I entered, forcing my usual air of confidence to wash over my face, but my smile quickly dissolved when I was greeted by an unsettling sight.

Landon was sitting next to Adalina on a settee that was far too small for the both of them. A fire roared close by, and Adalina's laughter intermingled with the crackling of the logs. My bodyguard smiled back at her like she was the sun that brightened his entire existence.

It was all rather romantic, and, although I was exploring something new of my own with Alaric, a pang of jealousy speared my chest.

She doesn't try to turn me into a monster.

Reena gasped behind me and addressed the god. "Apologies, Your Majesty. We should have knocked."

Adalina tore her gaze away from my bodyguard, smirking as she saw my smile fall.

"Nonsense. You are right on time. I was just finishing up Landon's fitting," she said, blatantly placing her hand atop his thigh as she rose.

I caught Landon's eye for a brief moment, a subtle devastation drenching those clear blue eyes with sorrow. His smile swiftly crumpled as he stood and took a small step my way.

"Seera," his voice was timid, the short steps he took while approaching mimicked his tone. "Can we talk?"

I steeled my expression into my usual mask of indifference, shoving down all the horrible feelings Landon brought to the surface last night.

"No, we can't. I have a fitting to get to." I brushed past my bodyguard, feeling the divide between us cement into something so permanent it would be nearly impossible to go back to what we were once this mission was over.

Yet, after what transpired in the jungle after our fight, I didn't want to go back to the way things were before Alaric and I reconnected.

Everything was different now, and, while change absolutely terrified me, I felt a strange kernel of an emotion I used to detest stir in my gut . . .

Hope.

"Step right here." Adalina sang while she gestured to a circular marble platform in the adjoining chamber.

I followed her into the separate room, leaving my lady-in-waiting to deal with Landon's moodiness. I had a bigger problem to face, one with all-seeing green eyes glaring right at me.

"Where is the servant that will assist you with my fitting?" I glanced around the quaint room as I stepped up onto the platform.

The god's laughter rang through the otherwise quiet room, a smaller fire popping in the corner of her work space. Fabrics of all sorts were draped over emerald, plush chairs.

Even the god's space was deceiving, depicting a rather inviting and cozy den for such a venomous viper.

"I will be doing your fitting, and, Seera, please do not forget that we do not call them servants," she said, pouting her lip at me like I was a child she had to scold.

My hands curled into fists, and I relished in the spark of pain that burst through me as my sharp nails tore into the flesh of my palms. This was my only avenue of releasing my anger, since killing the god before me wasn't an option...*yet*.

Adalina stepped up to join me, quickly gripping my wrist with a rather surprising force as she sweetly smiled at me.

"Put your arms out straight, and let us begin."

I bit the inside of my cheek against every instinct within me shouting to jam my elbow into her when I felt her touch upon my skin. Swallowing my violent urge, I did as she said and raised my arms out to my sides.

"Have you ever been to a winter climate before?" she asked, dragging the tailor's tape across my wingspan.

"In my kingdom, it only ever rains. We have never experienced anything else." I kept my response short and clipped, dreading every brush of her fingers skittering across my skin.

Adalina chuckled, tutting to herself as she moved behind me. "Oh, you are in for a rude awakening when you go to Rime. The weather there isn't the only thing that is chilling."

If I was going to be stuck in a room with such an exasperating god, I might as well gain some useful intel from her for my mission.

"I take it that you and the Ice Goddess don't get along?"

"Oh, you could say that, alright." Adalina sighed. "Isolde doesn't give anyone a reason *to* like her. She has totally isolated herself in her realm. In fact, no one has seen her in decades."

She rounded in front of me, tapping the outside of my thigh.

"Spread your legs." The smile she cast at me held a rather crass element to it.

I resisted the urge to curl my lip in disgust as I did as she said. She crouched, running the tape along my inseam.

"Has anyone tried to visit Rime to see the Ice Goddess?" I glanced at the god below me.

"They have, but they have always failed." She looked up at me, a wicked gleam shining in her eyes.

"Excuse me?"

This was information I should've been privy to before agreeing to go on this mission, and a hint of alarm rang through me at the fact the Serpent King omitted telling me this.

"Isolde chooses who is allowed to enter her domain—she has a magical barrier around all the entry points in Rime. Considering all who have attempted to visit have been unsuccessful, it appears she doesn't deem any of us worthy enough to enter."

Adalina popped up and started to wrap the tape measure around my bust, but I didn't miss the tightness lining her jaw. This tidbit about no one being able to enter Rime to see the Ice Goddess bothered Adalina . . . *but why?*

"What makes you think Alaric and I will be successful at entering her realm if no one has done so before?" I narrowed my eyes at the god, trying to assess her every move for any tells of nefarious motives.

"It's a gamble if she will allow you both in, but it is one we must take. My son is in jeopardy of losing everything important to him, and I refuse to let that happen. Alaric must keep his powers intact, so there is no room for error. It is of the utmost necessity that this mission is successful, do you understand?" She leveled an intense glare at me, all the while pulling the tape around my chest tighter than necessary.

It was easy to detect the warning lacing Adalina's words, for I used the same tone many times as the Serpent Queen.

"I don't respond kindly to threats, regardless if they're coming from a god or not." I didn't back down, instead I brought my face closer to hers.

Her eyes darkened with delight, and her lips curved into a sinister smile. "I like that about you."

After another tense moment, she released the tape from my bust, allowing me the opportunity to discreetly sniff and detect what feeling filtered through the god.

Adalina reeked like a bushel of mint, a smell I rarely encountered. I racked my brain for what the scent meant, but the god's grating voice interrupted my train of thought as she stepped off the platform and went to her gilded white marble work desk.

"We are finished. I'll make sure to have your clothes done in time for your departure tomorrow morning." She didn't spare me another glance, already moving on to grab a deep green fabric behind her.

Typically, her blatant dismissal would bother me, but I was more than happy to put distance between us. I stepped off the dressing podium and headed toward her main chambers, but her singsong voice halted me on the threshold.

"And Seera, it is not very fitting for a queen to have such markings upon her skin for all prying eyes to see." I glanced over my shoulder, my brows knitting with confusion.

Adalina extended her neck, brushing a slender finger

across the side of her throat. My hand floated up to the exact spot on myself, right where Alaric bit me last night in the midst of our passionate sex.

I scoffed at the god's audacity to try to embarrass me. She really didn't know me if she thought I'd shrivel at such a remark.

I suppose it was time to remind her who she was talking to ... and what it meant to truly be *the* Serpent Queen.

Rolling my shoulders and raising to my full height, I slowly turned to face her.

"On the contrary, I think there is nothing more regal than having the best sex in my life and having a souvenir to show for it." My smile grew into a thing of nightmares as I watched the god's smirk melt off her face.

Adalina's jaw was practically on the floor when I spun on my heel and strode out of her work chambers.

Reena was curled up on the settee, a book cradled between her hands as she fiercely read the novel. However, when I strutted straight past, her footsteps swiftly trailed behind me as I pushed open the door with a victorious smile painted across my lips.

Adalina thought she could intimidate me by sharing how no one has been successful at entering Rime. Then, she threatened me to ensure this mission is successful. Finally, she tried to seal the final nail in my coffin by attempting to embarrass me about the markings adorning my neck.

What a fucking fool.

If there was one thing I loved more than executions, it was proving people wrong.

Now, I was more determined than ever to make this mission a success, simply so I could return and face Adalina once more.

When we met again, I wouldn't swallow my anger.

I'd let myself truly burn, and I'd make sure there was only one Serpent Queen still standing after I was done leaving a trail of ash in my wake.

CHAPTER 44
INTO THE FLAMES

The Goddess of Death's cruel eyes gazed back at me from the book I skimmed over: *The Feud of the Gods*. I read on with curiosity as the text began to dive into a devastating battle between the gods.

The Dark Day commemorates the all night bloody duel to the death between the Goddess of Death and the Goddess of Life. Their feud stemmed from the Goddess of Death's greediness. Lilith grew bored of helping souls pass on to the afterlife; instead, she began to dabble in dark magic. She consumed their souls for her own selfish gain. Some say the souls she devoured corrupted her and every time she claimed one, she drifted further from who she once was.

It is believed this blasphemous act transformed Lilith from a god and into an otherworldly being—some called her the dark witch, while others gravitated toward the onyx demon. In the end, neither side truly won the battle, as both gods perished in the dead of the night, along with the Goddess of Life's only daughter and two hundred additional casualties.

A knock pounded against my door, making me jump. With a quick glance at the clock, I cursed as I noted it was nearly midnight, which meant I lost track of time and failed to join the others for dinner in the main hall. At such a late hour, it could only be Reena bringing me leftovers from the evening's meal.

"Enter," I called, dropping my gaze back to the tome.

The door creaked open, bringing with it the savory smell of rosemary and thyme. I started to sniff the air like an animal on the hunt—food was a sure way to tear my gaze from any task consuming me.

"You can set it on the table—" My words shriveled upon my tongue as soon as I wasn't greeted with Reena's chestnut brown hair. Instead, I caught sight of slicked, black locks as Alaric entered my chambers holding a mouth-watering tray of food.

With his hands completely full, he kicked the door closed. I was scanning the contents of the meal when my attention snagged on a splash of crimson. In the center of the tray, there was a singular blood red rose propped up in a golden vase. The vase was beautiful, appearing to be modeled after two intertwining serpents . . . it reminded me of Ember and Dante.

I dragged my gaze back to Alaric, reveling in the way his freshly pressed pair of black trousers hung from his muscular legs in such a tasteful fashion. The way he styled himself made a spark of desire tear through my core. I fucking loved how his garments were never skin-tight, like how most men preferred to show off their strong physiques.

No, the Serpent King had style and class.

Although his clothes fit loosely on his tall frame, one could still see he was made of solid muscle underneath all that finery.

I mean, I *knew* he was most definitely made of solid, pure muscle after our activities in the jungle last night . . .

"If you keep looking at me like that, we shall skip dinner and go straight to enjoying dessert." He dropped the tray of food on the table by the fire, his eyes never leaving mine.

"Oh? What's on the menu?" I challenged.

"You." His eyes grew a shade darker, hunger flaring through them while his pupils flickered between black and gold.

As I watched the Serpent King come undone before me, my lip began to sting. I swiped a finger over it only to watch a bead of blood coat my fingertips.

For Serpent's Sake, I was about to gnaw off my own lip from gawking at Alaric.

But little did he know, I was happy to skip dinner and get straight to letting him devour me.

He strolled over with his hands tucked in his pockets, his signature wicked smirk making heat creep along my chest as he neared the bed.

Alaric was what I dreamed of nearly every night for seventy-five years, yet I was also terrified that my dreams were becoming my waking reality. Even though he stared at me like I was the only woman in all the realms, a part of me couldn't be foolish enough to forget we have been here before—and he still broke my heart in the end.

If he hurt me for a second time, I wouldn't survive it.

Alaric dragged his finger along the emerald comforter as he took his time sauntering over.

"What has my Queen been doing all day holed up in this room by herself?"

"What *you* should have been doing as well—research for our mission." I gave him a pointed look, then went back to flipping through the pages of the tome.

However, Alaric had something different in mind as a demanding pressure wrapped around my ankle hanging off the bed. Somehow, my attention always seemed drawn back to the behemoth now towering over me. His hand was clasped around me, and before I could tell him to let go, he tugged hard, making me slide onto my ass and between his legs. I squealed as I scrambled to sit upright, yet Alaric pressed his legs on either side of my outer thighs, pinning me in place. A wave of chills spread along my bare legs.

I glanced down at my lounging dress, now bunched shorter, which nearly looked like an elevated silk nightgown. And when I brought my gaze back to the king of my dreams, he, too, was transfixed by the little scrap of fabric clinging to my curves. His eyes flared as they shot to the skinny strap falling off my shoulder, then his gaze dipped to my ample cleavage.

As he held himself over me, his hardness pressed against my stomach, alerting me that another part of his body also flared to life at the sight of my considerable assets.

"You need to tame him if we are to get any research done tonight." I arched a brow while glancing at the Serpent King's package, then swiftly looking back to his eyes.

His high-pitched laughter wrapped around us, the combination of wheezy hisses mixing with the pops of the firewood warming something in my chest. The space around me suddenly felt much more comforting with the Serpent King in it. It almost felt like *home*—a new version of a home I'd actually want to return to at the end of a long day of being queen.

Alaric bent closer to my face as his fingertips skimmed down the length of my hair. They stilled at the swells of my breasts, spinning my locks around his finger all the while creating a light friction right over where my nipples peeked through the thin material of my gown.

"Don't get me wrong, you looked stunning last night, Seera. But right now, with you in this simple dress, your hair slightly tangled, and your lipstick smudged, you look like my fucking salvation."

His words stunned me, taking me back to the very first moment I met the Serpent King. They were so similar to one of his first statements to me.

Have you been sent here as my reckoning or my salvation?

"You remember?" I balked at him.

He lifted one of his legs, forcing it between mine to press against my center. I gasped as my back arched against the soft duvet, but he continued to plant his hands on either side of my head, hovering within inches of my lips.

"Of course I remember the day we met. I'll never forget the day a stunning little mortal uprooted my entire miserable existence." He dragged his thumb over my jaw and down my neck, all the way to the head of my serpent tattoo right between my breasts.

"Although, it's still up in the air if you will be my reckoning or salvation—with that rage of yours, I'm betting on the former." His lips tipped into a charming smile.

"You haven't seen me truly angry yet." I fisted my hand into the silk of his shirt, my scoff filling the small sliver of air we shared.

"You mean the night we had dinner and you broke my nose twice wasn't you being truly angry?" His brows shot toward the ceiling.

Now it was my turn to tip my lips into a coy smile. "Oh please, that was me on a pleasant day."

We both laughed, the sounds of joy bouncing off the walls were slowly growing less foreign to me.

I used to relish in the anguish of agonized screams, but this melody emitting from Alaric shifted something fundamental inside me. I greedily wanted to devour his unique laugh as much as I could. Violence didn't consume me as much as it once did, and I didn't know if it was thanks to my soul returning to me, or courtesy of the gorgeous man looking down at me like I was as dazzling as a fallen star from the night sky.

As our laughter faded, our eyes searched each other's. Gently, Alaric brushed back my hair and dropped his lips to my neck, leaving imprints of his claiming kisses against my skin. I turned my head to the side, giving him more access, which had him humming with approval. The vibrations from his lips sent shivers racing down my spine.

"Alaric," his name was like a prayer falling from my lips.

"What did I tell you about saying my name like that, sweetheart?" His hand roamed up my bare thigh and underneath my gown, gripping my ass with a ferocious intensity.

A surprised gasp slipped from me, causing his eyes to darken with desire.

"If you keep making those noises, we won't get any research done." His grip was bruising as he held me and rolled us, reversing our positions on the bed.

While I settled atop Alaric, a wicked smile graced his lips as his hand harshly smacked against my ass.

There was no stopping the way my hips rolled against his hardness, all the while I moaned his name again from the electricity of pain shooting through my body.

"*Fuck*," Alaric groaned, burying his face in my neck. "I despise myself for what I am about to say next, but I need you to get off me unless you are fine with the only thing getting done tonight being *you*. If you remain straddling me while moaning my name like that, I will have no choice but to claim you again." He dragged his teeth up my neck, whispering his next words in my ear. "I will fuck you so hard, sweetheart, you will be transported into another realm."

"Is that a promise?" I whispered back.

"Seera," he growled, his fingers tightening on my bare hips. "You truly enjoy other people's misery, don't you?"

"Guilty . . ." I trailed my sharp nails down his partially-bare chest, courtesy of the buttons that were already left undone. "Are you going to punish me for enjoying your misery, my King?"

All thoughts of research flew from my mind. When Alaric touched me, there was nothing else I could do but fall victim to my foolish desires.

"Your punishment starts right now." His voice dripped with a mixture of darkness and desire as he wrapped my hair around his hand and tugged *hard*.

Pain flared along my scalp when he dragged my head back, forcing me to meet his scorching gaze. "Are you ready to take commands for once in your life, my Queen?"

I tried to dip my chin, but his grip tightened with dissatisfaction.

"No. I need to hear you say it, sweetheart. Will you follow your king's demands like a good girl?"

My breasts grew heavy with need as pain laced through my veins, and I jolted atop him. Alaric's eyes dipped to my chest, hungrily devouring the way my breasts bounced from the movement.

"I will follow your demands, my king," I forced out through gritted teeth.

"Good girl. Now, I'm going to release you, but only for a moment so you can get on your knees for me."

I nodded, but he yanked my hair, making me remember to find my words. "Yes."

He gave my locks another tug. "Yes, *my* King."

"Yes, my King," I echoed through breathy pants, earning me the reward to finally be released from his punishing grip.

Now that I could glance at him without his fingers laced throughout my hair, I watched as his eyes turned nearly entirely black, filling with an endless well of want.

Slowly, I shifted my hips off his, backing down his legs while never breaking our eye contact.

For the first time in my entire existence as the Serpent Queen, my knees crashed onto the floor.

If I was to bow before any man, I was pleased it was for the godlike man glaring down at me.

"Such a good girl," he purred, leaning onto his forearms. Then, his eyes dipped to the bulge in his pants. "Take them off."

Wetness pooled between my thighs at his command. Slowly, I reached up to undo his belt buckle. I was never on the submissive side of the power dynamic games I played with Landon, and a thrill shot through me as the roles reversed and I unbuttoned his trousers.

Maybe I did enjoy being dominated, but only by the right person.

Alaric lifted his hips, allowing me to lower his pants and undergarments past his knees. Yet, my eyes never strayed from the mesmerizing sight of his cock springing free.

For Serpent's Sake, the Serpent King was *very* well endowed.

The dinner he brought was utterly forgotten as I set my sights on the only meal I wanted to devour tonight.

He tracked my ravenous stare. "I know how bad you want to suck me, my Queen, but this is a punishment, remember?"

I glared at the menace while awaiting my next command.

"You will wrap those pouty, infuriating lips around my

cock, then I am going to fuck your mouth until I cum—and you will swallow. Every. Last. Ounce. Of. Me."

I licked my lips as a hunger I've never experienced gnawed at the back of my throat.

"Answer me." The Serpent King's demanding voice pulled my attention back to his eyes and away from what I craved. "Do you understand?"

"Yes, my king. I will be a good girl and wrap my lips around your cock. I will let you fuck my mouth however you like, for as long as you like. Then, you can reward me. I will *happily* swallow every drip you pour down my throat." I couldn't stop the way my lips curved into a mischievous smile, and, by the way the king's cock twitched, I don't think he minded my small act of defiance.

"Before we begin your punishment—" His gaze dipped to my cleavage as he leaned forward. "Strip."

"May I stand?" I looked at him through lowered lashes.

"Please do." He happily smirked, propping a pillow under his head as he prepared to enjoy the show.

Slowly, I stood, beginning to slide the small straps of my gown down my shoulders. The material was loose enough to where it quickly fell off my body, pooling around my feet and leaving me completely bare before the king, since I forwent undergarments.

Alaric gripped his cock in his fist, his eyes savagely devouring every inch of my skin. He worked himself as he stood, spreading his legs slightly.

"Are you hungry, my Queen?"

My gaze flicked to his cock, then I dropped onto my knees as I stared at the way he touched himself. I desperately wanted to replace his hand with mine, pumping him until he came all over my chest.

"I'm starving," I rasped so closely to where he touched

himself, my warm breath making the king shiver with anticipation.

"Let me satiate your hunger, sweetheart," he said as he guided his cock into my already open and ready mouth.

I moaned as he hit the back of my throat, allowing me only a moment to adjust to the sheer size of him before he began my punishment.

He fucked my mouth with the intensity of a raging storm, thrusting into me like rain pounding against a window pane. My eyes watered at how feverish his movements were, at the way his cock continuously slammed to the back of my throat, at the way he wrapped his hand around my hair.

"*Fuck*, I didn't think it was possible for you to feel better than you did last night, but that mouth is positively wicked, sweetheart." He slammed into me again. "You take me like the queen you are." He tugged on my hair with his next thrust, making tears slip from the corners of my eyes. "Such a good fucking girl."

I moaned around the vast size of the Serpent King, the taste of him starting to coat my tongue.

Being with Alaric was like a drug, something I'd crave every day after experiencing how incredible it was.

I'd spend an eternity on my knees if it meant I got the privilege to consume every inch of the Serpent King as often as I pleased.

"Touch yourself." His command tore me from my thoughts, making my eyes raise to find his already locked onto me.

Tantalizingly slow, I watched as the Serpent King devoured the show I put on for him. I skimmed my fingers over my breasts, circling my nipples then squeezing one with a fierce pinch.

I moaned around his cock, making him squeeze my hair tighter around his fist.

Down and down, I let my fingers dance over my flushed skin until they were dipping between my thighs. I ran two through my slick center as I stared up at the king, then circled back to tease my clit.

"Oh, fuck," Alaric groaned, rolling his hips and making another glorious inch of him slip down my throat. "Fuck your hand, sweetheart. Envision it's my fingers pulling your sweet pleasure from you."

He watched as I slipped into myself, riding my hand while taking him like the sinful queen I was.

"Seera," he moaned, and I glanced up at him with tears streaking down my face. "Come with me."

Our eyes locked, and I moaned around him in response. I fucked myself harder as we both raced closer toward the cataclysmic edge. Alaric's eyes remained locked on the way my breasts bounced as I chased my own release.

He growled my name when he came, the delectable taste of him dripping down my throat. I swallowed it as it continued to spill into me, not daring to break our eye contact while I fulfilled his final command.

After devouring every last drop the king spilt into my mouth, I waited for him to slip from my warm embrace.

He collapsed onto the bed, patting the emerald silk beside him. "Come here."

I rose, my knees slightly stinging from the friction of the rug and what just transpired between us. Alaric rolled onto his side, extending his arm out for me to cuddle into his chest. I happily accepted, fitting into the crook of his arm like it was made for me.

Though we never got to experience most sexual acts when we were together for the first time, I still craved his touch. Some of my favorite moments were crawling into his arms—he held me for as long as I needed as I wept over the traumas of my past.

"What are you thinking about?" Alaric gently hooked a finger under my chin, raising my eyes to meet his.

Déjà vu roiled through me at his question—the memory of Landon and I laying in bed after one of our *meetings* coming back to me. When my bodyguard asked me this question, I avoided the truth. I ran from my feelings.

Maybe, it was time to try a new approach.

Maybe, it was time to test out speaking the truth rather than a lie.

"I'm thinking about . . . about a similar moment like this one when we first met." I trailed my fingers along his back as we embraced.

His lips tightened into a sad grimace. He released his finger from underneath my chin to brush back my hair. "I want to make a promise to you, Seera." He softly gripped the back of my head as I curiously gazed back at him. "I know this promise will mean nothing without action behind it, but I want to tell you anyway."

He paused, and I chewed on my lip as a knot formed in my gut.

This conversation felt like it was tipping toward dangerous territory, like my heart was rapidly being led to its own execution.

"I swear I will never treat you like I once did. I promise, when we complete this mission, I will return your soul to you with no qualms. If you want it back after all of this, it's yours."

My mouth parted as I processed he was offering me something I've never been granted the pleasure of receiving before: a choice in my own destiny.

This changed *everything*.

My trust rekindled a smidge from his promise. "Alaric, I—"

That nagging feeling returned in my gut, making my thoughts churn. "Wait, if you return my soul to me, I'd lose my powers . . ." I glanced at him, my newfound trust in the man staring at me with lowered brows quickly waning.

"Is this all just a game to you?" I whispered, suddenly feeling stripped bare, not only in the flesh but down to my very core. "If you think for one second I'd give up my powers just so I could feel again, you're a bigger fool than I thought." I slammed my fist against his chest, trying to break out of his embrace.

His fingers dug into my back, holding me in place as hurt flashed across his face.

"I told you once, and I'll tell you everyday if I must, I'm not playing games with you, Seera." His fingers dragged down my skin to soothe the anger festering inside me like a deadly disease. "We can make a new bargain."

Slowly, my fists uncurled against his skin as a seed of hope rooted inside my chest. "A new bargain?"

"If you stopped jumping to conclusions, then I would have been able to properly finish my thought." He arched a scolding brow at me. "As I was *trying* to say, we can make any bargain you want. After I return your soul to you, yes, our original one will sever and you will lose your powers."

My hands balled against his chest once more, dividing his attention between them and my eyes.

"Easy, my vicious serpent. Let me finish." His demanding tone irked me, yet my traitorous legs twitched from his command.

"I will offer you my magic in exchange for anything you'd like to offer me. It can be as frivolous as your favorite pair of heels, or, my personal preference would be another round of fucking your mouth senseless."

"Alaric!" I slapped his chest at the wicked words spilling

out of his lips, but it only made him tip his head back and laugh.

However, the mirth kissing the corners of his eyes dissolved as he reached between us to grasp my hands in his.

"I'm serious, Seera. Whatever you want, you can have it. I'm going to prove to you that you can trust me again. Until the day I take my last breath, I won't stop trying to be a better man for you. I just want to correct my biggest mistake." He released one of my hands to caress my face, nestling our still-joined ones between our chests.

"You always deserved a better life than what the gods dealt you. If I can help remedy that in any way, it would be my greatest honor."

His thumb trailed down to swipe over my bottom lip, and his eyes grew with worry as he watched it begin to tremble.

Oh, for Serpent's Sake, not again.

"Hey, it's okay, sweetheart." He crushed me against him, and my tears found a new home in the crook of Alaric's neck.

He held me for what felt like ages, gently stroking my hair as I fell apart in his arms.

With one final sniffle, I pulled myself together as best as I could and croaked, "Don't you ever call my beloved heels frivolous, you behemoth."

His hissing laughter still felt like the sun kissing my skin after being trapped in my mother's tower for twenty-five long years.

"If you are up for some further *research* tonight, I have an idea," he whispered against my hair.

I pulled back, taking in the way his eyes gleamed with mischief. I could practically see those evil little gears in his wicked brain turning.

"What did you have in mind?"

"I want to take you somewhere in order to help aid our

mission, but we have to be careful not to get caught." He offered me a roguish smile. "Are you up for playing with fire, my Queen?"

I ran my free hand through his hair, giving his locks a sharp tug as I leaned in and whispered against his lips.

"Lead the way, and I'll follow you into the flames, my King."

CHAPTER 45
FAMILY

I t took us another ten minutes before we crept through the halls, because my stomach insisted I scarf down something beyond Alaric's cock.

So, we sat across from each other and quickly ate our steaks and rosemary potatoes, with a generous side of red wine. The crimson alcohol was necessary after the king told me what his slightly dangerous plan was.

We were going to sneak into Adalina's personal rooms.

"I didn't know you had it in you to be so bad, breaking into mommy's quarters and all," I whispered, playfully shoving him with my shoulder.

He grinned, shaking his head at me like it was second nature at this point. His hair was slightly mussed from our *research*, a thick piece drifting into his eyes. Perhaps, I did what I did next because of the wine coursing through me or maybe it was because I felt *free* when I was around Alaric.

I planted my hand on his bicep, and Alaric halted our pursuit down the quiet halls. He turned his head slightly to look at me, and I took the opportunity to brush his beautiful locks out of his eyes.

Alaric's breath hitched, his piercing green eyes fluttering closed as I raked my fingers through his hair. When I was done fussing over him, I let my fingers trail down his cheek as I admired the Serpent King.

"Perfect," I whispered, bringing my fingers further down his neck to trail over the bare exposed bits of his chest. I reveled when my gentle touch made Alaric shiver.

With a small smile, I looped my arm through his. "Can't have my king looking a mess on our secret little mission."

I resumed our trek through the halls, but I caught Alaric smiling at me when he didn't think I was looking. My heart nearly leapt out of my chest at the adoration clearly shining on his face as he looked at me.

I walked on the balls of my feet, forgoing my heels for once in my life. Considering it was past midnight and Adalina made it a point to have few servants, we didn't run into a single soul as we padded down the long halls. When we passed a familiar painting, I knew we were drawing close to the god's chambers, for it drew my attention now as it did earlier today.

It was an abstract painting, leaving the interpretation up to the eye of the beholder. The painting was within a rectangular, golden frame, and there was a clear divide on either end of the canvas.

The top corner was pitch black, while the diagonal corner was stark white, almost like no paint was truly on the canvas. Towards the middle, the two colors bled together, creating a murky grey. In this area, there were flecks of various shades, so that it took on a translucent quality. Gold, green, and blue hues were splattered around the canvas, along with a particularly eye-catching splash of crimson red. If given a cursory glance, it looked like a completely random blob of colorful, smeared dots. However, I noticed something within the chaos—what looked like a pair of half-black, half-white wings.

"Seera?" Alaric's voice called me back to the moment, making me realize I had stopped walking to admire the work of art.

He followed my gaze. "I never understood why my mother kept this piece so front and center. It's rather dull, compared to the other pieces in her collection."

I tilted my head, leaning to look at it closer. "This piece feels special. It's different, in a good way. It makes me think and . . . it makes me feel." I chewed on my bottom lip. "Not much makes me feel."

A spark of cold brushed against my fingers, pulling my gaze toward the ground. Alaric's fingers wrapped around mine as he claimed my hand in his.

"That was the past, Seera. You can feel things now, and I hope *I* make you feel something at the very least." An uncertain smile tipped the edges of his lips.

While it was sweet of Alaric to try to comfort me, a pang of despair pierced my chest. We both knew if we were successful in our mission tomorrow, I'd have no soul once again.

It was everything I signed up for, and I only cared to hold onto my power, no matter the circumstances.

So, why did I suddenly feel so empty thinking about not having my soul?

I'd never get to feel everything I felt over the course of the past few days—I'd never get to fall deeply and madly in love with Alaric. I'd never get to experience all the jovial and frivolous things madly-in-love couples did.

Even though Alaric gave me an out, an opportunity to reclaim my soul . . . was it worth the risk? Could I really trust the man who brutally broke my heart?

Nonetheless, these were tomorrow's problems, so I gave

him the best smile I could muster and let him know how I felt while I still could.

"You make me feel more alive than I've ever felt in my entire existence, Alaric."

His lips slightly parted, but he quickly remedied his look of awe by replacing it with a radiating smile of his own while squeezing my hand.

"Come on, we have a room to break into." He pulled me into his chest and snuggly wrapped his arm around my waist while we walked in a comfortable silence the rest of the way to Adalina's chambers.

The god's gaudy, solid gold door came into view as we neared the end of the hall, and excitement whirled in my chest because Alaric and I were about to do something risky together.

This was the closest I'd ever come to having a true partner in crime.

My elation deflated, swiftly replaced with panic when I saw Alaric reach for the door handle, ready to barge straight in.

"What are you doing?" I furiously whispered, yanking him away from the door. "I thought we were breaking into her room through a secret portal or something, not fucking walking right in!"

He tried to act nonchalant as he glanced at me, but the way his jaw ticked signaled he was anxious deep down.

"It's fine. My mother is probably still in her side room working late into the night on our clothing for Rime. If we are quiet, I'm sure she won't hear us." He turned back to the door, but I slammed my hand against his chest.

The Serpent King tossed an irked sideways glare at me, but I didn't budge.

"What are you not telling me?" I asked, narrowing my eyes at the menace.

He sighed, rolling his neck side to side. "I didn't want to worry you, but I can't portal us into her rooms."

"Why not?"

He could barely look at me, a wince flashing across that beautiful face of his. "Because I can't transport us . . . my portal magic is gone."

"*For Serpent's Sake*," I breathed, my knees growing weak. "Does this mean Isolde—"

"I don't think she has completely severed our bargain, for I believe we would feel *something* the moment it broke." He rubbed his chin, looking deep in thought. Then, his attention snapped to me as he scanned my face. "Wait, is *your* magic still intact?"

His question made a swarm of nerves buzz through my gut. If I didn't have my magic anymore . . . dread roiled inside me, making me nearly puke for a third time on the Serpent King's shoes.

Nothing terrified me more than being powerless.

With my eyes squeezed shut and panic frying my nerves, I attempted to summon my snakes in the nicest way possible, if only to spare me from Dante's endless attitude for waking him at such an hour.

My darlings, if you wouldn't mind waking up. It's important.

No warmth spread along my arms, and I didn't feel my serpents comforting weight fall upon my shoulders.

No—this couldn't be happening.

I uttered a word I never used down the bond, desperate to feel my snakes slithering along my body.

Please.

Silence greeted me as dark thoughts pelted my mind. My snakes had to come back to me—I needed them. I sent one final plea through our mental channel.

Please, don't leave me.

I had to smother the sob that wracked through my chest when they didn't appear, when my arms were left cold with only a wake of goosebumps prickling my flesh.

My world as I knew it for the last seventy-five years completely shattered.

My snakes were *gone.*

My companions, who laid with me during my darkest hours, had been unfairly torn from my grip, from my mind. Even though Dante had an attitude that rivaled my own, he was *mine.*

He was my *family.*

And my sweet, Ember, who savored my compliments like they were precious rays of sunshine. Tears stung the corner of my eyes, eventually slipping free, and I desperately missed the way Ember licked away my tears when I was sad . . .

I couldn't stand another moment of living in such agonizing despair—living in a world where my snakes no longer existed—and so, I gave up and let my knees buckle underneath the crushing weight slamming down on my chest.

Alaric's strong arms caught me before I could fully collapse onto the tiled floor.

"Breathe, sweetheart. I've got you," he whispered against my ear, my limp body hanging in his arms. "I promise we will get them back," he reassured me, making a promise I was uncertain he could uphold.

If we didn't kill the Ice Goddess, I'd never get to see my snakes again . . . but if we did kill her, I could lose my soul—my ability to feel joy, happiness, and above all, *love.*

In this moment, I was reminded once again how incredibly unfair life could be.

Although Alaric presented a rather appealing option of making a new bargain if we survived our mission, it was all just words.

If he betrayed me again . . .

I allowed myself a few moments to collect myself within his strong embrace, before I let the endless pit of anger lying within me awaken. My blood boiled with an all-consuming fire, and the time was approaching for me to finally burn this entire beautiful palace to ashes.

Leaning out of his arms, my eyes speared into his. "Isolde will pay for this, but to do so, we need to find something to destroy her."

Alaric nodded, looking like he would willingly follow me down the pathway of destruction I was craving to create.

If there was anything that could destroy a god, what better place to hide it than in one's personal quarters? Determination had me standing strongly on my own two feet.

I would not lose my snakes.

I would not lose my power.

I would not lose who I was.

I was the Serpent Queen, and I was ready to let myself bite back like the monster I was.

"Let's fucking break into your mother's chambers."

His lips tugged up into a proud smile as he placed a finger under my chin.

"There's my vicious serpent."

CHAPTER 46
SECRETS

For once, I was thankful Adalina's door was made of solid gold and not wood, for it didn't creak once as we snuck into her quarters.

As Alaric expected, she had not yet retired for the evening. Her rooms were massive and rather dim, but a sliver of warm light streamed through a small crack at the opposite side of the room. The god must still be working on our attire.

I would never admit it aloud, but Alaric was right . . . *for once.*

I glanced at the king, then gave a pointed look toward the other room, signaling where his mother was. He held a finger to his lips while grabbing ahold of my hand as he led me to a nearby door I failed to notice.

Luckily, it was already open, but, unluckily, that meant we couldn't close it behind us. Should Adalina come out of her work chambers, she would notice the door was no longer open and grow suspicious. So, we crept through the dark corridor like two extremely well-dressed bandits.

The passage felt endless, and my feet quickly grew cold

with each step across the smooth marble tiles. I tightened my lips as the want to speak to Alaric burned on the tip of my tongue. I wondered how much further until we got to wherever he was leading me, but I swallowed my irritation and continued to follow along before he completely disappeared into the dark shadows.

After a few agonizing moments in silence, I grew tired of staring at the darkness. I glanced sideways, trying to make out any indication of where we were.

An *oof* sounded as I ran into something solid. My gaze drew forward again, only to be scolded by bright green eyes cutting through the darkness and piercing straight into my own.

Well, at least our exceptional immortal eyesight was still intact, for I didn't miss the way the behemoth rolled his eyes with a severe annoyance as I shrugged and mouthed 'sorry.'

Alaric turned and proceeded sharply to the right, shoving his way through swaths of fabric. Sequins, satin, velvet, and silk materials danced around his broad shoulders as he pushed them to the sides. In that moment, understanding dawned on me that we were in Adalina's closet.

My lips turned down as I extended my neck to glance down either side of the long passageway. I could barely see the light from the god's main chambers anymore with how far we'd traveled through the darkness.

Adalina's wardrobe was *huge*.

Jealousy slithered over my skin as I examined the swaths of fabric still swaying from Alaric roughly brushing past them. I made a mental note to demand someone make me a closet even grander than this one upon returning to my queendom.

I swiftly lost myself within the garments, in the pieces of fabric that had become my own personal armor throughout the years of being the Serpent Queen.

I skimmed my fingers over the various fabrics, even going

as far as to yank a gorgeous silk robe off its solid gold hanger. My eyes rolled so far back in my head at the fact Adalina was pretentious enough to have even her hangers made of gold, but my mood shifted as soon as the soft emerald material caressed my skin.

It was a rather stunning robe, completely spun from a butter-soft silk. A large serpent design, made of golden sequins, extended up the entirety of the back of the garment. Its head crept over my left shoulder and stopped right atop my heart. With its tongue sticking out, it reminded me too much of Dante. I nearly fell into another round of sobs, but, instead, I gripped tighter onto the reins of my anger for the Ice Goddess.

Crying made me feel weak and hopeless, but anger—anger made me feel like I could conquer kingdoms, destroy palaces, and even go as far as to kill a god.

I was tying the deep green sash around my waist when I heard a small clicking noise. My attention swung to where Alaric pressed his palm against a dark stone wall. The wall was hidden behind layers of Adalina's clothes, and he glanced over his shoulder to look at me, a devious smile spreading onto his lips.

His hushed voice drifted through the shadows. "I discovered this secret passage when I was a kid, but I haven't returned here since . . ."

I sniffed the air to see what emotion Alaric was feeling as he looked back to the wall, but I was met with nothing but the musty scent of the stuffy wardrobe around us. Rage pulsed through my veins like a caged animal rattling its bars at the reminder my powers were gone, but the king's voice brought me back to the present.

"If we have any chance at finding a relic to defeat a god, I could think of no better place to hide it than in there." He gestured to the passage shrouded in a foreboding darkness.

I prowled toward the opening, only to be greeted by the soft sound of water dripping in the distance. I glanced into the seemingly endless dimness, seeing nothing but steep stone steps that descended further beneath the Emerald Palace.

I was peeking into what I believed to be Adalina's lair, and there were no gilded walls hiding down here—only the dark sense of a looming evil that matched what I always saw buried deep within the god.

I smirked at the Serpent King, prepared to finally claim my vengeance. "Ready to follow me into the darkness?"

He leaned closer, placing his hands against the wall and caging me in. When he tucked a loose strand of hair behind my ear, I let my eyes flutter closed. The intimate act was slowly becoming a habit of his, but I didn't mind . . . it steadied me, while also making me feel taken care of for once in my life.

"Wherever you go, I'll follow, even if it is into the depths of where the wicked rest." He gestured toward the stairs. "Lead the way, my Queen."

CHAPTER 47
INTO THE DARKNESS

It was charming when Alaric offered to follow me into the darkness. It wasn't charming, however, to navigate myself down the treacherous steps.

The stairwell curved into a spiral configuration, almost like a tightly coiled serpent readying itself to strike. The king definitely should have taken the lead down this stairway to what felt like my very own Pit in my queendom.

The further we descended, the greater the sound of dripping water grew until it became like a steady stream. A sense of dread rolled over me like an eerie fog, and the stones grew slick beneath my bare feet.

"I appreciate you being chivalrous and all, but I have no fucking idea where I am going," I tossed over my shoulder, but the words were quickly swallowed by the roar of the nearby water.

Alaric's chuckle rumbled off the black stone walls that felt as if they were closing in on us.

"Just keep moving forward and watch where you're going.

I'd hate for you to miss a stair and lose a few of those pretty teeth of yours."

The Serpent King's laughter grew wheezy as he undoubtedly imagined me smiling at him with a few missing teeth, probably both of my front ones, knowing the menace he was.

Our talking ceased as I focused on making it down safely, growing even more grateful I opted for no shoes during such a dangerous trek. If it wasn't for some of my immortal abilities remaining intact, I'd lose a toe or two from how cold the stones were beneath my feet.

A shiver trickled down my spine as I realized how confined I was in this moment. The stairwell wasn't vast, in fact it was only large enough for us to go down one at a time. The stones felt like they were growing cooler the further we traveled down, but I let the frigid temperatures shock my body into remaining alert.

Yet, the battle of not getting lost within the darkness of my mind was slipping from my grasp as the jet black stone walls closed in on me—they looked too similar to where my mother kept me confined.

Once again, I was back in the tower that stripped me of a normal existence, of friendship, of sunlight and fresh air . . . of *love*.

Panic settled against my chest as the space around me shrunk, and I braced for the darkness to crush me once and for all.

But before it could consume me, a roaring gush of water broke my spell of terror.

The tight space looked like it would expand after only a few more steps, so I picked up my pace as fast as I could manage without slipping on the wet ground. As I rounded the final curve, I gasped at what laid before me.

My feet hesitantly shuffled across sharp, onyx stone, toward where a raging waterfall laid on my left. It flowed down the side of the cliff I was standing on, the water crashing into a pool shaped like a giant serpent slithering through grass. Instead of the typical blue hue though, the river was a deep green. If it wasn't for the streams of glittering emerald water falling into the pool, I'd think it was black with how dark it appeared.

"Alaric, now would be a great time to explain what the fuck this place is."

I skimmed over the cavernous space, noting the torches sparsely lining the walls. The flicker of light illuminated another set of steps leading to what looked like a hidden grotto covered in tendrils of ivy.

It was a beautiful sight, one that should make me feel wonder and enchantment, but I couldn't shake the dread tightly coiling around me.

What was Alaric's mother hiding down here?

We both glanced over the cliff, watching the glittering viridian water sparkle as it crashed and flowed into the river.

"When I was younger, I followed my mother to her rooms. She was crying, and I was worried about her since my father recently—" He cleared his throat. "My father just passed, and I was worried about my mother. I'd always been quiet on my feet, so she didn't hear me as she sobbed and ran into her closet. I didn't want to bother her, but I wanted to make sure she knew I was there if she needed someone to talk to . . ."

"So, I followed her, quietly clinging to the shadows of her wardrobe. When she pressed her hand against a random wall and it sprung open, I nearly blew my cover with how in awe I was. Granted, I was ten-years-old, so a secret passageway was incredibly fucking cool, and I had every right to react that way to the revelation of one existing in my home this entire time."

My lips tugged into a soft smile as I imagined Alaric as a

kid, with uncombed and shaggy black hair flopping into his face, green eyes wide with wonder while he smothered a gasp with a small hand.

My heart physically hurt thinking of the younger version of him—it hurt to reminisce when life made us both lose our precious innocence long ago.

He waved his hand at the cavern. "So, that's how I discovered this place. Every time my mother grew sad, mostly after my father's death, she disappeared down here for hours. I don't know what she came here for, but I started to frequently come here after Isa died . . ." He stared off into the shimmering waters, swiftly growing lost in his memories.

I couldn't stand the pain that tugged his brows together and made his lips quirk into a frown. As much as it would hurt to know these details, I was learning it wasn't always about what I wanted.

Maybe, Alaric needed to remember Isa, to talk about her with someone.

"What was she like?"

His eyes snapped to mine, his sadness quickly turning to shock. "I—do you truly want to know about the woman I used to love?"

A pang of jealousy pinched my heart, but I nodded nonetheless.

He continued to stare at me with a bewildered expression, but he took a steadying breath then told me about the most intimate part of his past.

"She was . . . she was enchanting. Her laugh was contagious, and she was fierce, yet soft. She forced me to train her, to make her a better fighter." A smile full of sorrow spread across his face as he glanced at me. "She, too, hated swordplay."

I scoffed, but remained silent to allow him a safe space to honor Isa.

"She was always doing things she shouldn't, and I often shouldered the blame when she was undoubtedly caught in the end." The sorrow on his face melted, turning into a more peaceful expression. "Above all, she never balked. She never hid. She was resilient, but she never lost her kindness . . . she was—she was my best friend."

A silver tear clung to the corner of the Serpent King's eye, prompting me to reach for him.

"She sounds wonderful." I laced my fingers through his, the gesture stealing his attention from the flowing water and back to me.

My heart shattered when I saw the utter devastation painted across his face.

"You don't have to suffer alone anymore, Alaric. I'm here for you, just as you promised to be for me. If you want to talk about Isa, I will always listen."

The tear finally slipped free, leaving a streak of silver to stream down his pale face. Softly, I brushed it away. His eyes fluttered closed while he grasped my hand, rooting it against his cold face.

I held him as long as he needed, as he sat in the confinement of the grief he carried alone for decades. His tears splashed against my hand, and, for the first time, I marveled at the beauty of the small, silver droplets coating my fingertips.

It was an honor to see the Serpent King unravel before me.

Thus, I stood there, holding his hand while I stroked my thumb across his cheek and swiped away his abnormally beautiful silver tears. Maybe it was a magical ability only gods possessed—to shed colored tears—and Alaric did mention how he could technically be a god one day . . .

Finally, he gently blinked, revealing glassy, bright green eyes, which locked onto mine.

"Thank you," he whispered against my hand, tenderly planting a soft kiss against my palm.

I released our conjoined hands that remained by our sides, moving to wrap my hand around the nape of his neck and rub soothing circles against his skin. He shuddered from my soft touch, and I leaned on the balls of my feet. Alaric braced his hand against my lower back, anchoring me firmly against him as I brought our faces closer together.

"I want you to listen to me very carefully. Can you listen for once in your life?" I mimicked the words he said to me at the night market.

Warmth spread through my chest when Alaric's frown tipped into a smile.

He dipped his chin in response, then I grabbed his hair gently and forced our eyes to meet.

"I know what it feels like to live with guilt, Alaric, and I know what it's like to live with the fact you lost someone you once deeply cared for, maybe even loved."

His lips thinned as he processed my words, putting the pieces together of who I could be talking about.

"Wait, did you just say, lo—" I pressed a finger against his mouth, stopping him from saying the four-lettered word I was terrified of.

For Serpent's Sake, I was trying to relate to him, yet I exposed myself at the same time. I spoke in a rush, quickly trying to cover my vulnerable slip-up.

"My point is, eventually, we need to let go of our guilt. The same applies for me. If I keep allowing my guilt and sorrow to fester, I fear there will be nothing left of me. As it was, before you came back into my life, I was a husk of who I used to be." I tightened my grasp around his neck. "Alaric, you might have lost someone incredibly special to you, but you have people who will accompany you through the darkness. As you offered to me, I will gladly sit with *you* while you cry, yell, or rage through whatever emotions that trouble you."

Another silver tear spilled down his cheek, absorbing into my hand that was still lingering against his face.

Smiling up at the man of my dreams, it was easy for the first time in my life to confess my feelings. "As long as you don't push me away again Alaric, I'd love to learn how to work through my own demons instead of running from them, with you by my side. No one should go through life alone, especially during the hard bits."

He smiled at me with tears lining his eyes. "I'm so proud of you, Seera."

Godsdamn it, now I felt warm liquid pooling in my eyes.

"I've said it before, and I'll say it again—I don't deserve you, but it would be my greatest honor to work through all that we've been through, together. With you by my side, life has felt less heavy. Seera, being with you feels like breathing for the first time in years after drowning in my own self-induced hatred. And for that, I'll forever be indebted to you."

Tears quickly gathered at the corner of my eyes, and Alaric leaned in, claiming the physical embodiment of my emotions with his lips. His mouth swallowed every ounce of water that leaked from me, showering my cheeks with agonizingly soft kisses. His lips drew dangerously close to mine, and my heart leapt in my chest.

"Alaric," my voice was breathy, and I did my best not to move since he was within an inch of my lips.

"Seera, you know I can't control myself when you say my name like that," he growled against my skin, sending a wave of vibrations racing for my lips.

I savored the feeling of his lips pressing against me in any capacity, an intense yearning warming my chest. With the wine muddling the clarity of my mind, I let myself drift to the one and only memory of when our lips crashed together.

"Are you ready?" Alaric searched my eyes for any shadow of doubt. This was my last chance to back out of our bargain, to not sell my soul to him.

But what choice did I have?

It was either return to my homelands and risk my mother capturing me again, only to lock me away for good in her tower, or I could sell my soul to the handsome king who stole my heart over the course of the past three weeks.

I wasn't ready to let Alaric go, and if I had to sell my soul to keep him near me, I would do it.

"I'm ready," I said with a newfound confidence that I gained during my time in Morotis.

He smiled down at me, but it held none of the softness I'd grown to adore. I thought he'd be ecstatic to finally have our lips meet, so why was he looking at me with such a cold and calculating glare?

A million thoughts raced through my head as our lips collided. I was prepared for a soft kiss, but this was far from a lover's kiss.

This was a carnal act, one used to claim all of me—my lips, my body, my soul.

This was not an act of passion.

This was a display of possession.

Alaric kissed my cheek again, making the memory dissolve into the mist spraying us from the nearby waterfall.

"Seera," he whispered against my skin. "Where did you drift off to?"

"I—I was thinking about when we first kissed, and I was wondering if it would feel differently this time . . ."

His cool lips lifted from my flushed skin, his eyes searching mine. "How so?"

"Our first kiss was fine, but it was not full of the passion and desire I thought it would be brimming with. It felt more like an act of possession—it was my first kiss, Alaric."

"Truly?" He leaned back, shock tugging his lips down.

"Who else would I have kissed locked away in a tower?" I arched a brow in challenge.

His soft laugh filled the small bit of space lingering between us. "Good point." He cocked his head, his gaze drifting to my lips. "I regret making your first experience lack all the things a proper kiss should entail. If I could do it again . . . if I could make it right—" His hand snaked up my spine, all the way to the base of my head.

There was no escaping from the king's claiming grip, and I wasn't sure I even wanted to.

"Alaric . . ." That one word was charged with seventy-five years of need, of longing.

His agonized groan crawled over my skin, and I watched with alarm as his eyes darkened. Panic gnawed inside me at the tell-tale sign the Serpent King was on the edge of losing control.

"Alaric—" He cut me off, planting a finger firmly against my lips.

"I told you there would be consequences for saying my name like that, sweetheart." The green in his eyes dissipated into complete and utter darkness.

I tried to mumble against his finger, but he moved quicker than lightning, claiming my lips with his.

Fucking gods, Alaric was kissing me . . .

And it was nothing like our first kiss.

His lips softly pressed against mine, allowing me a moment to adjust to the contour of his full mouth.

Since it was too late to stop the foolish act of the king, I explored this forbidden territory.

If our theory was right about the world ending when we kissed, then I had every intention of making my last kiss the best one yet.

Hesitantly, I moved my lips against his, but I swiftly lost myself in the taste of Alaric. He tasted like cherries, and I wanted to devour the sweetness seeping from his lips.

My tongue darted out, and he granted me the pleasure of exploring further by parting his lips for me. Our tongues tangled in a wicked dance, and I grasped onto his locks, tugging him into me to deepen our kiss.

His hand roamed down my back, while the other tightened against my throat. A shock of pain jolted through me when I felt his canines nip at my bottom lip, and a wildfire blazed low in my belly.

There was no better feeling in the world than kissing Alaric. I could happily die in his arms, doing exactly this.

A loud whipping sound split through the air, forcing us to come up for air.

Then, the quaking began.

I felt the stone below us shift, and I watched in horror as a fissure began to tear the platform into two. The cave trembled with the ferocity of a wild beast awakening from an eternal slumber, and shards of stone fractured from the ceiling, raining down on us like sharp daggers.

The crack was nearly about to separate Alaric and I, but before it could, he scooped me into his arms and jumped backward. We watched as the gaping crevice quickly devoured the cliff we were standing on.

Why was this the reaction our kiss always provoked?

I buried my face into Alaric's chest, and he placed his hand atop my head to cover it from the falling rubble.

"Whatever happens, don't let me go!" I shouted into his shirt, the booming growing louder with every passing second.

"Not even the gods could tear you from my arms, Seera," he whispered into my ear while stroking my hair softly.

Even with the world crumbling around us, he tried to keep me in a state of tranquility.

The ground trembled ferociously, but it was as if time stopped when Alaric hooked his finger underneath my chin, forcing me to look up at him.

Stone rained around him, and strands of his black hair hung into his eyes. They were no longer as dark as the depths of my mind—instead, they were the brightest green I'd ever seen.

At this moment, Alaric looked like my own devastatingly beautiful reckoning.

"Fuck it." His eyes dipped to my lips, stroking his thumb against my bottom lip. "If the world is going to end, I'd rather die with the taste of your lips lingering on mine."

Alaric dipped his head, planting a kiss against my lips that felt like it sucked all the air out of the lair collapsing around us.

I faintly heard a loud snap cleaving the air while our lips intertwined in their own destructive dance, but I was too distracted by the taste of cherries and rose petals between the languid flicks of our tongues.

While I kissed the man who fulfilled all of my dreams, I *finally* realized what these notes represented . . .

Long ago, there was one thing I craved more than power. One thing that consumed my every waking thought, a feeling that now slammed into me as our lips fused into one—*love*.

A furious crack that felt summoned by the gods had us begrudgingly breaking apart, then the ground below Alaric's feet completely disintegrated into rubble. His arms tightened around me right as the sensation of floating washed over me.

The Serpent King held true to his promise, never once

letting me go. Frigid air whipped my hair around our faces, and I knew we were free falling toward our untimely deaths.

Yet, I was not surprised this was occurring, for every time I was around Alaric it felt like we were living on borrowed time, our impending demise was on the horizon whenever we came together.

So, I locked my hands around his neck and smashed my lips against his one final time, desperately craving the taste of sweet cherries to be the last thing I consumed before meeting whatever awaited us in the Land of the Wicked.

CHAPTER 48
OBLIVION

Someone I once considered insignificant said their life flashed before their eyes, right before I executed them. Yet what they didn't say was the things you never got the chance to experience during your lifetime stared straight into your soul when death reached for you with its bloody claws.

Alaric's lips tasted like cherries the entire time we fell to our end, not even us hitting the water and sinking into the abyss could break our world-shattering kiss.

The water was so cold it felt like a million knives stabbing into my skin. The shock of the frigid temperature nearly had my iron-clad grip slipping from Alaric's neck, but the moment our bodies sank beneath the water he pulled me tighter against him.

Under the dark river where no light reached, we remained tangled in each other's arms, lips sealed together like we were each other's salvation from the havoc we brought upon the realms. My hair floated around us, and if I wasn't moments away from passing out from a lack of oxygen, I'd feel like I was in a real-life fairytale.

But this was no ordinary story.

Instead of me landing the prince, my fairy-tale ended with the most devastatingly handsome villain to ever exist.

Unlike the fairytales I grew up reading and loving, I knew our story didn't end with a happily-ever-after.

Monsters didn't get to ride off into the sunset on a white horse.

No, we drowned in the depths of our despair, or in this case, in the darkness of Adalina's maleficent river.

It seemed impossible that drowning would be the end of two feared immortals, but these waters felt *haunted*—like they wanted to claim me, like they wanted to devour my skin and bones.

I couldn't breathe.

I couldn't breathe.

I couldn't *breathe.*

The Serpent Queen's vicious existence was nearly reaching its end.

Right when I was about to break our kiss, allowing water to fill my lungs until the darkness finally claimed me, Alaric surprised me by parting his lips and pushing air into my mouth.

Even when he desperately needed the last of his oxygen, he gave what remained in his lungs to buy me more time.

To save *me.*

Alaric was wrong when he said he didn't deserve me, for I was the undeserving one.

If anyone should have the right to live, it was him.

Out of the two of us, *he* was the good one.

With another wave of air flooding my lungs, I let my eyes open underneath the murky water as his lips stayed pressed against mine. However, the pressure of our kiss quickly lessened, and Alaric didn't open his eyes, even after he must have felt my lashes fluttering against his skin.

In fact, I didn't feel his heart beating against me in our embrace.

No.

I gripped onto his arms as I finally severed the realm's longest kiss, so I could look at him better. With his eyes shut and his hair floating around him, he looked like he was simply in a peaceful slumber, in a beautiful state of oblivion.

But I knew better.

Alaric wasn't sleeping.

Everything I once loved flashed before my eyes . . .

Alaric would never again smile at me like I was the most precious being in all the realms, or hold me when the darkness tugged me into a fit of sorrow.

He would never again kiss my skin like he was worshipping the gods.

We would never build a life uniquely perfect for us, nor would we sit with each other through the misery eternally looming around us.

No, I'd never get to do all the things people did when they were in love, because Alaric's body sank against me, completely lifeless in my arms.

CHAPTER 49

ASCENDING

I kicked and clawed until my lungs burned.

But it was no use.

The water wouldn't let us go.

With each flutter of my feet, I dragged a limp Alaric in my arms and prayed to the gods who abandoned me. Perhaps, there was one who would take pity on my soul and answer my plea to save the man I loved.

Yet, it felt like no matter how hard I tried, I was no closer to breaking the surface. It was almost as if the water was sucking us deeper down into despair instead of up toward salvation. Maybe it was my lack of oxygen or because my vision was quickly blurring, but I swore when I glanced down I saw phantom hands wrapped around my ankles, tugging me further into the inky depths.

I fought whatever was trying to drown me as I kept kicking, but, when a particularly sharp pain sparked up my calf, I looked down to whatever forces were trying to destroy me.

And that's when I saw *it*.

A spark of gold, shining a few feet below where we were

floating at a standstill. We were closer to the bottom of the river than I thought . . . could the phantom hands be trying to gather my attention, not for nefarious reasons, but because they wanted me to see what laid in the shadows of Adalina's river?

An intense tug shot through my chest, directing me toward the sunken object.

There had to be a reason I was being pulled in the opposite direction of safety, so I followed the sensation connecting me to this item, dragging Alaric with me all the way down into the darkness.

My vision was nearly black by the time I reached the bottom of the river, but I felt a force of power pulsing from the object that lay slightly covered by a layer of black sand. I brushed off the debris, a wave of confusion crashing over me at what I saw—a dagger made of pure gold with its hilt fashioned after a serpent with emerald jeweled eyes.

Could this be the answer to slaying a god?

As I wrapped my hand around the hilt, a kernel of hope seeped into my chest.

It felt as if the gods were finally answering my prayers when my fingers clenched around the surprisingly warm metal.

With the taste of cherries lingering on my lips, I glanced at the man who made me feel love for the first time in my entire miserable existence.

Even in death, he was devastatingly beautiful.

My vision completely darkened . . .

If I was truly about to meet the Land of the Wicked, I wouldn't change anything about my last moments, besides being able to see his enchanting eyes one more time.

A beautiful woman with white hair streaming past her slender hips smiled at me with a brightness that rivaled the desert sun.

She seemed so familiar, almost like I knew her in a past life. Her eyes stunned me, glowing like molten gold, but there was a quiet sadness held within the pits of them. I had the feeling this woman used to glow brighter, for her skin had a faint golden sheen to it, like it was struggling to not completely wink out of existence.

"I wish we were meeting under better circumstances, but I would be lying if I didn't say I was happy to see you again." She stroked my face with delicate fingers, almost like she would shatter me if she touched me too intensely.

My head was resting in the golden woman's lap, and I couldn't remember how I got here.

"Do I know you?" My words felt sluggish, like I mouthed them underwater.

Her smile faltered. "You did, once upon a time, before a dark force separated us. My final act before we were torn from one another was one of protection, to keep you safe from the same darkness that claimed me."

I glanced around, noting shimmering pieces of golden flakes floating around us. Besides that, I couldn't see much else beyond the blackness and the golden woman before me.

"Protect me? How?" I turned back to her, my brows knitting with confusion.

Her hand dropped from my cheek and to the side of my neck as she softly touched where my birthmark was.

"This was my last act of rebellion. My final act of my unwavering love. Please forgive me, for I had to alter your memories to make the enchantment hold. It was the only way to disguise you, to hide you from Lilith."

"Enchantment?" I mimicked, not feeling connected to my body the more we spoke.

I searched the woman's blazing eyes for more answers, and I watched as a molten golden tear spilt down her cheek.

My vision blurred, and I felt the Land of the Wicked summoning me.

After decades of terror and destruction, I felt ready to answer its call.

As my eyes shut for the last time, the most beautiful vision welcomed me.

Emerald eyes crinkled with happiness in another life, one where I got to tell Alaric I loved him—all of him, even the dark bits.

"Please, save him," I whispered with my eyes closed, readying myself to leave behind one wicked life, only to enter another eternal one.

The woman softly stroked my hair and whispered back through the darkness. "Isa, only you can save him, my beautiful golden daughter."

EPILOGUE
LANDON

I'd rather be whipped to the brink of death like on the day Seera saved me, than feel the perpetual numbness crushing my chest with each passing moment.

Every time I opened my mouth to cry out for help, something terrible sputtered from my lips instead, just like the night I danced with my Queen.

If I could feel guilt, I'd drown in it. But I barely felt anything beyond the poison seeping into my soul. A sense of wrongness washed over me, but I was helpless at fighting it off.

Maybe this was what I deserved—maybe my past was finally catching up to me.

The god with beautiful blonde hair and piercing green eyes strutted into my chambers, where I sat on the edge of the bed with my head cradled between my hands.

"Landon, how are you feeling today?" She smiled, a twinkle of something wicked gleaming in her eyes.

I opened my mouth to say I felt terrible, like I was losing vital pieces of myself every day, like I wanted to crawl out of my skin and die.

Instead, a lie flew from my lips. "I feel fine."

She hummed with delight. "Fabulous, because our fun together has just begun." Her smile widened, growing into something made of nightmares. "It's so nice to have a companion again, especially one who falls in line so easily." She curled a slender finger, beckoning me like she had since the day I arrived in the Emerald Glades. "Come along, we have souls to corrupt."

Darkness stirred in my chest, raptured at what the goddess offered me. But the small sliver of my soul that remained in my chest—that begged to be saved—pleaded to any god listening.

I begged for someone, *anyone*, to save me from the demon I followed out of my chambers and into a realm of destruction.

TO BE CONTINUED . . .

ACKNOWLEDGMENTS

A lot of the time, I say too much. I feel too much. I *am* too much . . . according to society.

Well, I am here to say f*ck that—f*ck society's view on me, on us.

I worked incredibly hard on THE SERPENT QUEEN, with plenty of people waiting on the sidelines for me to fail. But this part of my story isn't for them. This part of my story is for YOU. For the people who stuck by my side through this crazy self-publishing, debut author journey. I see each and every one of you, and I wish I could thank you all individually by name. However, I *can* thank a few special people who helped shape THE SERPENT QUEEN into all she is today.

First, I want to say thank you to my mother. Without her, I quite literally would not be here today. On top of that, I wouldn't have an ounce of kindness infused in my bones without that saint of a lady. She always taught me to see the good in others, regardless of me b*tching about how they did me dirty. I love my mother so much, and she has always been my number one supporter. So, Sue, this is for you. I'm sorry in advance you have to read about snakes, considering you're the reason I grew up afraid of them. Every summer, we would come across at least one snake in our yard, and I knew immediately what was happening because Sue would be howling like a wolf at a full moon. I hope my book helps you get over your fear of snakes just a smidge mom, and I hope I can repay you one day for all the kindness and support you've shown me throughout the entirety of my life.

Secondly, I'd like to thank my alpha reader, Nerina Rayne. Nerina, you have been such a breath of fresh air while I figured out what the heck was going on during my initial drafts. I'm eternally thankful I could voice note you all my unhinged ideas and plot holes dilemmas and that you would also be lying on your floor voice noting me back. You made me believe in genuine friends again, who truly just want to help someone out of the kindness of their hearts. You are such a talented writer, and I can't wait to read your published works one day. You are an inspiration, girl! The Serpent Queen is forever grateful you loved her story, and she will spare you another day because of that. Also, Evander is still waiting for you to write his fan-fic! :D

Next, I'd like to thank my beta readers. Jenn, Aurora, and Haley—you girls mean so much to me. Thank you so much for taking a chance on reading my book baby and for being so kind with all the feedback and guidance you gave me. All of your advice really helped shape THE SERPENT QUEEN into what she is today, and I will forever be grateful to have found such wonderful friends like you three.

And where would an author be without her editors? This section is dedicated to my two editors: Julia Greenshaw and Jenn Trocine.

First, thank you to Julia for helping edit and format TSQ! Thank you for explaining to me countless times when I should capitalize Queen (I swear, I still question this sometimes ngl.) Above all, thank you for never losing your patience with me and helping me with any silly questions I had. It was so fun working with you while you were also in the thick of self-publishing your own debut book. Congrats girl! WE did it!

Secondly, thank you to Jenn for helping edit TSQ! You truly

put up with so much of my over-thinking/spiraling—you deserve a year-long break from me. On top of managing me, you polished THE SERPENT QUEEN to perfection! I am blown away by how hard you work, even though life loves to throw curveballs at you. You are seriously one of the strongest women I have the pleasure of knowing. You may be an incredible editor, but above all, you are an amazing friend. I love you girl. Also, the Serpent Queen thanks you from the bottom of her cold heart for making her story "grammatically correct." <3

Now, this section is for ALL of the artists I worked with on my debut book. Thank you SO much for working with me as I figured out how to properly speak to an artist. Thank you to those who showed me patience, kindness, and empathy. Thank you for bringing my characters, my CHILDREN, to life! The artists I worked with are truly some of the most talented individuals ever. I am in awe of every single one of you and your artistic styles! A special shout-out to Malarie Weber (@abookshelfofmagic) for creating THE SERPENT QUEEN's commandments artwork. Thank you also to Elaine (@elainem.art) for creating that stunning portrait of our queen featured in my book. You have been an absolute delight to work with.

Can we take a moment for the beautiful hand-drawn map in TSQ?! Monika (@monsmaps.books) thank you SO much for working with me on this! I can't believe you drew all of that by hand. You are talented beyond measure, my girl. It was an honor working with someone so fun and professional as you. It feels like I've known you for years, even though we just met this year! I hope I can come meet you one day in Croatia. Also, keep your pencils sharpened—we have more work to do together!! <3

To my Street Team: Aleira, Bradie, Heather, Brenda, Sam, Tiff, Holly, Carsen, Hailey, and Riley. Thank you for all your support and love before even reading one line of my book. The fact you believed in ME, first and foremost, will forever mean more to me than you ever will know. I love you girls. Thank you again for supporting me. And a HUGE shout out to Holly for helping create the most incredible graphics for TSQ. Your patience is unmatched when dealing with an indecisive queen like me. Thank you so much!

Even though I know they will never see this, I need to say thank you to Sleep Token for fueling my creativity/drafting phase. THE SERPENT QUEEN wouldn't be possible without their genius lyrics and music. Seeing them live during their EIA tour was everything, and I can't wait to worship with them again one day. Thank you ST for saving me during my darkest hours.

Of course I need to thank Sensei Sarina for helping choreo-graph Seera's takedown of Landon in Part Two, along with teaching me all the techniques I wrote in TSQ. Also, thank you to my friends in karate that helped me along the way in my self-defense/martial arts journey!

Thank you to Jellybean, my beautiful and sassy Boston Terrier. You aren't particularly a dog who likes to sleep at my feet in my office while I write, but you are a dog who reminds me to take breaks (specifically, so I could throw the ball for you.) Regardless of your attitude or all your deadly gas, I love you my little bean. My life would be dull in comparison without you. Lowkey, you kind of remind me of Dante a little though, with all that side-eye attitude . . .

FINALLY!!! Thank you to YOU! To my friends, my readers, my PEOPLE! I never had many friends growing up—hell I still don't. So, I am eternally thankful you are here reading some-thing that is quite literally a sliver of my soul. Thank you for all your support and love. Thank you to everyone who has commented, liked, shared, or talked about THE SERPENT

QUEEN. Thank you if you've ever sent me kind words via DM. Above all, thank you if you loved my characters and my story. This is my soul story and means everything to me.

There is one last person I must thank, and her name is Tiffany.

Tiffany, thank you for never giving up on yourself, on this crazy dream of ours. Thank you for pushing through the darkness seven years ago when it almost claimed us for good. You are so brave, so strong, and so resilient. I am proud of you. Look at all we've created together with time, patience, dedication, and a shit ton of strength. I know you are particularly hard on yourself, but I want you to remember this line our queen so wisely said when the darkness presses in on you during those moments . . . *After all, couldn't monsters feel pleasure too?*

You deserve all the happiness, love, and joy coming your way, Tiff. I hope you allow yourself to enjoy every bit of it, every step of the way.

We did what we once thought was impossible.

Congratulations, beautiful. <3

ABOUT THE AUTHOR

Tiffany is from Southern California, where she enjoys going on sunset strolls with her Boston Terrier, Jellybean. She started out as an avid romantasy reader within the Bookstagram community. When her own fictional characters aren't plaguing her every waking thought, you can find her reading, content creating, singing/crying along to Sleep Token, or watching The Vampire Diaries. She is a passionate mental health advocate after fighting her own life-threatening battle with depression in 2019. She survived, and she wants everyone out there who also struggles to know they can too. Please keep going, please never give up, and please always fight. You are not alone. If you are struggling and need assistance in the U.S., please call 988.